He didn't consciously plan to take her in his arms. He didn't even know she was crying until she was against him and he heard the catch of her breath and felt the moisture of her tears. She pressed her face into the collar of his uniform and clutched at his back, making no sound other than the soft gasps of her weeping.

Once, perhaps, he'd known what love was. But he'd chosen to let the ability die out of him. It was too much work, too confining, too demanding of what he was not strong or wise or good enough to give.

Jesse lifted her head. "I'm sorry," she said, scrubbing at her face with her knuckles. "I don't usually do this."

No. She wouldn't. An unbearable tenderness washed through David. "Do you think I begrudge you, Jesse?"

He bent his head and kissed the high curve of her cheekbone, catching the salt of a tear on the tip of his tongue. He found another tear trapped in the lashes of her left eye, two at the edge of her jaw and one more nestled in the corner of her lips.

One by one he disposed of her tears, entranced by the velvet texture of her skin and the scent of her hair and the subtle alteration in her breathing from distress to excitement.

This closeness was what they both wanted. Mutual solace, a forgetting of sadness and pain. Would it be so ~~ible~~ to surrender? Would he be risking too much?

~~He~~ touched his mouth to hers. Her fingers dug into the ~~back~~ of his jacket, and her lips parted.

Also by Susan Krinard

TWICE A HERO

PRINCE OF SHADOWS

PRINCE OF WOLVES

PRINCE OF DREAMS

STAR-CROSSED

BODY AND SOUL

SUSAN KRINARD

BANTAM BOOKS

NEW YORK TORONTO LONDON
SYDNEY AUCKLAND

BODY AND SOUL

A Bantam Book / August 1998

ISBN 0-553-56919-8

Published simultaneously in the United States and Canada

Bantam Books are published by Bantam Books, a division
of Bantam Doubleday Dell Publishing Group, Inc. Its
trademark, consisting of the words "Bantam Books" and the
portrayal of a rooster, is Registered in U.S. Patent
and Trademark Office and in other countries. Marca
Registrada. Bantam Books, 1540 Broadway, New York,
New York 10036.

PRINTED IN THE UNITED STATES OF AMERICA

OPM   10 9 8 7 6 5 4 3 2 1

BODY AND SOUL

CHAPTER ONE

I T WAS TOO beautiful to be real.

Jesse Copeland knew that, knew it even as she dreamed, felt a joy so deep that she had no name for it.

And no name for the place in which she found herself. The garden was filled with roses, lush and not quite tame, as if the hand that pruned and cared for them gave them the freedom to test the limits of their captivity. Birds sang in green trees. A fountain played the melody of running water, and the sky was as blue as an artist's vision of heaven.

But that was not the truest beauty of the dream. The miracle of it lay in the child cradled in Jesse's arms—a child with blue eyes and dark hair, laughing up at her from the security of boundless love.

Love that filled the garden, overflowed Jesse's heart. She sang to the child, this child of her own body, born of pain become happiness. The pain had been worth it. The fear, the separation, all was behind them now.

A gate creaked, and Jesse looked up. Her heart, already so full, made room for another. He walked into the garden and smiled at her—smiled as he'd smiled that day when they'd lain in the long grass and made this child.

Oh, how she loved him. She had known he would come back because of the child, and now she had everything she'd ever wanted. He was husband, father, master of the estate. And she was his lady.

Jesse handed his daughter to him, watching the wonder in his eyes. Yes, surely this would be enough. He would never want to go away again. He would be hers forever. He would never leave her. Never.

He met her gaze. She yearned for him with everything inside her, imprinting him on her heart, memorizing his soul.

"You will not leave me," she said. He only continued to smile, unanswering, and it wasn't for several heartbeats that she saw the sadness in his eyes.

Sadness she could not bear. She shaped her lips to speak his name. Her mind refused to give it up. She could not remember, no matter how hard she tried. And without his name . . .

All about Jesse the garden began to dissolve. She reached for her love, and her hands passed through his body. He was leaving her. Leaving her alone, abandoned, as he always did. . . .

In a flash the scene changed, and she was on the edge of a cliff, with the river raging below. The cliff where someone else had died, fallen among the vicious rocks and seething water. And her love was hanging there on the narrow ledge below, little more than a wraith, reaching up to her. Begging her to save him.

Her love. His fate lay in her hands. She hesitated. She had failed before. Another had died here, only a boy, and she was afraid. But she gathered her courage and extended her hand, straining until it seemed her arm would stretch no farther. His fingers brushed hers. They touched for an instant. And then he slipped free, and was falling . . . falling endlessly, into the river, to dash among the rocks in absolute darkness.

He was dead, gone forever, lost. She was alone. She railed against that fearful solitude, beating at the darkness with her fists.

The darkness gave way and Jesse woke with a start to the bright light of morning.

She rolled to face the digital clock on her bedside table, grateful to dismiss the dream with something so mundane as the time. She stared at the numbers until the minute changed, until she remembered.

Bobby Moran's funeral was two hours away.

⚬ ⚬

ONLY A SMALL number of the residents of Manzanita turned out for the service. Jesse stood with a cluster of search and rescue volunteers, men and women from the team that had tried to save Bobby from the river.

It had been Tri-Mountain Search and Rescue's first failure in a long time. Jesse's as well. She hadn't known Bobby except by reputation. But as she listened to the minister's solemn words, she remembered her dream of joy and sorrow and utter aloneness. Bobby Moran hadn't been in the dream, but the nameless man she'd tried to help had died in the very same way.

She hadn't been able to save him. Just like Bobby.

Bobby's mother was at the graveside, her eyes hidden behind dark lenses, her hand clutching the fingers of Bobby's younger brother. Bobby's friends—the "bad boys" of Manzanita, whom Jesse had seen shivering and pale and anything but tough—formed their own tense knot off to the side. There were a few others who might have had genuine regrets at the untimely end of a druggy kid the gossips had always said would come to no good.

The gossips had been right.

Snatches of conversation reached Jesse, muffled behind

hands as if the bereaved mother wouldn't notice. The consensus was obvious.

"I hear they found so many drugs in his bloodstream afterwards that he probably would have died of an overdose anyway," Mrs. Sandoval said to Mrs. Van de Castle, pulling a long face of spurious sympathy. "Dale Braden told me that he virtually jumped right off that ledge—he was that far gone."

Jesse shivered and held her body rigid against the inner chill. She still saw it in her mind—oh, so vividly: the darkness before dawn and Bobby perched on the edge of the narrow ledge along the river, giggling at his own cleverness as he swayed over the chasm. He'd seemed unaware of whatever injuries he'd sustained in the initial fall from the cliff above, where his stone-sober friends huddled and watched the rescue.

Jesse had been the one chosen to go down after him. She was small enough to fit with Bobby on the ledge, unthreatening enough to talk him into cooperation. She was as fit and expert as any member of the Tri-Mountain Search and Rescue team. She'd worked a whole year to prove herself worthy.

But she'd failed.

"He wasn't much use to anyone around here anyway," Mrs. Sandoval continued, edging past Jesse with a narrow-eyed glance. "His poor mother will probably be better off—"

"What did you ever do to help him?" Jesse interrupted.

Mrs. Sandoval and Mrs. Van de Castle stopped and stared. Mrs. Van de Castle turned very red. She made an abortive gesture toward Jesse, let her hand fall to her side. "Everyone knows you tried," she stammered. "It wasn't—"

"No one could have helped him," Mrs. Sandoval said. Her lips narrowed to a thin line. "Some kids are bad from the day they're born, and nothing will ever change that."

Jesse's fists ached at her sides. "Maybe the problem

was that no one believed in him," she said evenly. "Maybe that's all he ever needed."

With a snort Mrs. Sandoval grabbed Mrs. Van de Castle's arm and dragged her away. "Bad blood," she said. "It always tells." Jesse could hear her begin a new story for her captive audience as the two women left the false serenity of the cemetery—a story about another woman, long dead, and her crazy daughter.

Bad blood. Jesse looked across the neatly tended green lawn, beyond the aspens clustered above weathered headstones. Joan Copeland was there, resting beneath a simple marker. The flowers Jesse had left on Saturday were withering, but no one else would care.

No one in Manzanita remembered Jesse's mother as anything but an unstable drunk who'd drowned herself in the river seventeen years ago, leaving her orphaned daughter behind. They probably hadn't even thought of Joan until the prodigal daughter had come home.

Jesse deliberately unclenched her hands. She'd returned to Manzanita a year and a half ago to make peace with herself, with her past, with the unnamed fears that hovered at the very edge of her consciousness. She'd thrown herself into the search and rescue team, honed her body into a tool that wouldn't let her down. She taught the city folk who came to the Trinity Alps how to respect the wilderness and meet it on its own terms.

As she met her fears on her own terms. She'd led countless hiking and kayaking tours, joined in difficult rescue operations that saved lives nearly taken by the mountains and the chill waters of the river.

Bobby Moran was the exception. And that one exception was a hard, cold knot in Jesse's heart.

Mrs. Moran was the last to leave the graveside, and Jesse walked across the lawn to meet her. The words of condolence she intended seemed grossly inadequate in the face of so much pain. But she had to try, to let Mrs. Moran know she wasn't alone. . . .

"Mrs. Moran?"

The woman looked up, her sunglasses an anonymous

mask, her body drawing back as if from something fearful.

"Mrs. Moran, I wanted to say—"

Bobby's mother thrust out her hand, palm out and
fingers spread. Her son shrank behind her. "Leave us
alone," she cried hoarsely. "Please go away."

The command was biting with panic and anger, and
Jesse withdrew immediately. Mrs. Moran almost ran
across the lawn toward the road, ignoring those few people who tried to offer sympathy. Jesse stared after her,
the knot in her heart more bitter than before.

"Jesse?"

Kim Mayhew, the Tri-Mountain Search and Rescue
Ops leader, looked at Jesse with concern in her eyes. "I
can see what you're going through," she said. "Everyone
on the team knows how it is."

It was the truth, of course. Kim had been in local
search and rescue for ten years, and she'd seen her share
of deaths. Maybe if she'd gone down to the ledge, Bobby
wouldn't have died.

"I'm all right," Jesse said with careful neutrality.
"Don't worry about me."

"We all did our best," Kim said, "but the one thing we
can't control is human nature."

"I know," Jesse said. "We all did our best."

"But you don't believe it yet. I know it's something
you have to work through." She set a hand on Jesse's
shoulder. "Maybe you should take it easy. Bow out for a
bit—"

"No." Jesse held Kim's gaze steadily. "I'll be fine. I'll
be ready when the next call comes."

She prepared herself for Kim's answer, for her to say
Jesse wasn't good enough, strong enough, skilled
enough, that she had screwed up too badly to remain on
the team. But Kim only sighed and dropped her hand.

"Just remember that you only have to give the word,
and everyone will understand."

Jesse nodded, waited for Kim to leave so she wouldn't
have to hold on so tight; but the other woman lingered,

gazing across the cemetery. Toward the grave of Joan Copeland.

The crowd was scattered now, everyone gone back to his or her daily routine. But there was someone standing over Joan's plot, someone kneeling to lay fresh roses on top of Jesse's wilted daisies.

A man. Tall and well built, dressed in a sober gray suit. A man who didn't belong in Manzanita, bringing flowers to a woman no one remembered except with pity and disdain.

An icy sense of recognition seized Jesse even before the man looked up. Vaguely she heard Kim ask her a question, but the roaring in her ears blocked the words. Roaring, racing, like the turbulent waters of the river sweeping her under and sucking her down.

The man at the grave stood up, brushing off the knees of his trousers, and turned. Slowly, deliberately, he raised his head and stared directly at her.

And Jesse knew him. No conscious thought put a name to his face. She knew him so utterly, so completely, that she felt it like a fist in her stomach.

"Jesse?" Kim reached for her again, but this time Jesse jerked away. Her perception narrowed, excluding Kim, excluding the rest of the world.

She remembered. A blank spot she hadn't even known was in her mind began to fill with visions too intense to be anything but genuine.

The man didn't move. He didn't take a single step toward her, but Jesse felt a terror so blinding that for a moment she lost even herself. Lost herself in the memories. . . .

Another funeral. Another beautiful, sunny day seventeen years ago, and she was eleven years old, watching the earth hit the casket as the minister intoned words of peace and hope. She was looking at Gary Emerson—so charismatic, so handsome, so well liked by everyone in town. Gary Emerson, who'd tried to redeem Joan Copeland and failed, who'd been like a father to her rebellious daughter.

So everyone said. But Jesse knew the truth. Gary was bad. Evil. He was a murderer. . . .

They buried her mother in the ground, and something broke inside Jesse. As the few mourners began to pray, she screamed. She went at Gary with her hands, with her feet, with her whole small body, as if some much vaster and more powerful soul had possessed her own. And she heard herself accusing him, crying out in a voice she'd never heard before: "You killed her! You killed her! You let her die!"

Then the others caught her and pulled her back, and she saw Gary's startled face, bleeding from the rake of her small nails—hated, hated face. Like a savage, she fought the ones who held her, and nothing would calm her, not until Doc pricked her arm with a needle. And she heard voices murmuring shocked words like "crazy" and "poor child," saw Gary bending over her with pity in his eyes.

Poor, bereaved, crazy Jesse Copeland. She wasn't right after that. They had to send her to a hospital, and when she got out no one else wanted her. When she got out she'd erased from consciousness what had happened that day at the funeral. . . .

Some muted sound pulled Jesse out of the past, and she found herself trembling with realization.

She'd forgotten. She'd packed those memories away just as those who'd sent her to the hospital had boxed up her mother's things and set aside her childish belongings.

After all these years Gary had come back to Manzanita, and the images raced through her like a flash flood, tearing at the moorings of her reason.

The fear. The hatred. The rage and grief that possessed the mind until nothing else was left. They were coming awake within her, spinning her down into chaos. . . .

"You're white as a ghost," Kim's voice said beside her. "You'd better sit down—"

Sit down. Sit down and wait for Gary to come to her, with his easy smile and smooth voice. Wait for the memories to drown her as the river had drowned her mother.

But Gary wasn't coming. He only stood and watched her fall apart.

She clamped down on her panic and glanced at Kim. The older woman was concerned, yes, but Jesse hadn't revealed too much. Not yet.

"Who is that guy you're staring at, Jesse?"

It was possible to answer Kim as if nothing were wrong. "You wouldn't know him. He lived here . . . a long time ago."

Kim shaded her eyes and whistled softly. "Good-looking—not that Eric would appreciate my saying so. Sure doesn't look like a townie." She cocked a brow at Jesse. "You knew him, huh?"

There wasn't any point in hiding it. Kim would hear soon enough, once people started talking. And remembering.

"When I was a child," Jesse said. "He . . . knew my mother."

There would be more questions. From Kim, and from others with personal experience of that funeral seventeen years ago.

Why had Gary Emerson returned?

She looked at Kim and through her, floating above the fear. "I have to go. Don't worry about me—I'll be okay."

"All right. Take it easy now, you hear?"

Jesse nodded, turned and walked away. She felt Gary Emerson's stare, but she walked instead of ran; that much she could command. She walked, her legs nearly steady, down the narrow potholed lane, over the bridge at Gooseberry Creek and across the empty cement lot behind Manzanita Hardware. She moved automatically, chasing the same thought over and over until she was too numb to feel the terror or the irrational rage.

Gary had come back, and with him the ghost of the child she'd been. The child who had hated so powerfully, who had forgotten herself when they put her mother in the earth. Jesse had left that child behind long ago, because the alternative meant a journey into shadowy places she did not intend to revisit.

Survival had been all that mattered after the hospital, climbing out of the darkness and staying out for good. Years in foster homes, working her way through college, proving her strength and self-reliance. Proving she didn't need anyone. Not needing made her free—free to meet every challenge she set herself and to teach others to do the same.

She hadn't failed in that. She hadn't failed when she'd returned to Manzanita and made a place for herself here.

But Gary had come back, and the foundations of independence and discipline she'd built began to crumble like ancient ruins.

Jesse found herself halfway across town with no recollection of the journey. Behind her was Marie Hudson's new restaurant, with stylish café-style chairs and tables lined up along the outdoor porch. The library was directly across the highway; not so strange she'd wind up here, where Al was working.

Al Aguilar, her best friend, who'd sold her the land on which she'd built her cabin, just across the field from his own modest house. The one man she knew she could trust. He was a librarian now, but once he'd been a psychologist. A doctor who worked with the mind.

There wouldn't be many people in the library at this hour. It was never crowded at the best of times. But Jesse hesitated. What could she tell Al? That she was afraid she was being sucked back into the distorted memories of a grieving child?

Or that after seventeen years—despite all the evidence, all the incontrovertible facts—she still felt in the deepest part of her soul that Gary Emerson was responsible for Joan Copeland's death?

She turned to face the short strip of buildings that held the restaurant and post office. Someone was standing in front of the tiny, vacant storefront at the end that had been up for lease well over a year. The gray-haired man was hammering a poster just above the grimy window.

Gary Emerson, the poster said in bold red and blue letters. *Gary Emerson for State Assembly.* The man stepped away from his handiwork and called to someone inside the building. The sounds of hammering and sawing drifted out the open door.

Jesse stared at the poster. In the hospital she hadn't thought about Gary, or wondered what had become of him when he left Manzanita. His part in her life had become the biggest blank in her memory. Only after her last stint in the Peace Corps had she determined to come home, visit her mother's grave and face the sadness that had kept her away so long.

But Gary had remained an unreal phantom, a shape her mind rebuffed whenever she got too close.

Until today. Strange how clearly Jesse could remember certain things now: how Gary had been liked by nearly everyone in town, how he'd had Manzanita eating out of his hand. Before Joan died there'd been talk of his running for mayor, other modest ambitions that meant a great deal in a small town.

State assembly was something else. In seventeen years Gary had outgrown the meager rewards a place like Manzanita could provide. He had power; power and prestige and respect.

All Jesse had struggled to make of her life was here in Manzanita. She believed in her work for search and rescue, in spite of the doubts that had come with Bobby's death. She enjoyed her job at the Lodge. But Gary's return had unleashed the turbulent and unreliable fantasies of a troubled child. If there was the slightest chance that those fantasies had a basis in fact . . .

Yes. Jesse squeezed her eyes shut. Damn it, yes. She'd overcome that childhood breakdown. What she felt and remembered wasn't some symptom of mental illness. There had to be a reason for what had happened—today, and at that funeral so long ago.

She only had to find it.

"Lookin' for something to do, young lady?"

The man who'd put up the Emerson sign was standing in front of Jesse, smiling amiably as he swung his hammer. "We could sure use a bit of help settin' up the new campaign office. Let me tell you, Gary Emerson's goin' to be the best thing that ever happened to Manzanita." He squinted at her, rubbing the bridge of his nose. "You are from around here, ain't you?"

The bizarre incongruity of his question almost startled a laugh from Jesse. She didn't have time to form an answer. A second man emerged from the shop and took the elder by the elbow. Wayne Albright, who knew her well enough. He'd been at Joan's funeral.

"Come on, Fred," he muttered. "Don't go bothering people. I need your help inside." But the glance he cast at Jesse was wary, as if he expected her to march after them and pull down the signs with the same fury she'd once attacked Gary Emerson.

He remembered.

Jesse turned around and walked in the opposite direction. Toward the library, and Al. There was little enough traffic to dodge on the highway; even in the summer season Manzanita was a quiet town.

The library was quietest of all. It was deserted except for a retiree reading a magazine in one of the chairs clustered by the window.

Al was seated at the reference desk in the far corner, buried in a pile of books. "May I help you?" he said without looking up.

"What can you tell me about memories?"

He closed the heavy volume he'd been reading. "Jesse. Sit down."

He didn't show any surprise that she'd come. He was like that, Al Aguilar—placid, calm, steady. He reminded Jesse of a Buddha statue she'd seen once in Asia, perched high above the turmoil of human existence. When she was a child, he'd been like a deeply rooted stone in the middle of a raging river, someone who would listen to her without judgment.

"Memories?" he prompted, pushing the books aside.

"I saw Gary Emerson at the Moran funeral," she said. "It was . . . unexpected."

Al snorted—his version of an obscenity—and settled in

his chair, salt-and-pepper hair grazing his collar. His dark eyes held a flicker of emotion that didn't disturb the tranquillity of his features. "I saw the signs across the street. State Assembly. He's come back the big man he always wanted to be."

Al's scorn was no less cutting for its mildness. He had been one of the few people in Manzanita who'd held out against Gary's easy charm and broad smile. Along with a lonely eleven-year-old child.

"Yes," she said, grateful for the evenness of her voice. "When I saw him today, I . . . remembered. Al, I had flashes of things that happened at my mother's funeral. Things I'd completely pushed out of my mind."

"Such as?"

She ran her finger along the edge of Al's desk, letting the repetitive motion work a calming rhythm as if she were sanding furniture in her workshop. "You were there. You know."

He nodded. "Memories don't always work the way we expect them to."

Jesse breathed out slowly. She wouldn't have to explain. "I didn't ask for them," she said. "I can hardly remember the hospital anymore, except that I was there."

But she remembered the feelings. How much she hated that place, hated being crazy—though no one ever used that word. The reasons for her breakdown hadn't mattered after she'd begun to get well. All she could think of was escape.

"There was no purpose in dwelling on the past, Jesse," Al said. "It wouldn't have made any difference."

So deftly he avoided the embarrassing questions, the too personal observations. He didn't care what she'd done back then, or how disturbed she'd been. They'd never demanded anything of each other, she and Al, and that was why she could ask for his help.

"It makes a difference now," she said, meeting his gaze. "I hadn't thought of Gary in years, but when I saw him today, something happened to me. I was eleven years old again. And I hated him. I hated him so much that I thought I might be losing my mind."

The very calmness of her words must have convinced Al of her urgency. He leaned forward, resting his weight on his good arm, and studied her face. "Irrational feelings don't necessarily equate with mental illness. In this case, it's understandable—"

"There's more to it than that. Everyone in town knew I didn't like Gary when he was with us. But when my mother died—" She swallowed. "When she died, I was convinced Gary killed her."

The library was very quiet for several heartbeats. Al's brows drew together in the faintest of frowns. "You know that's not possible, Jesse. He wasn't in the area at the time of Joan's death. He was never even a suspect."

No. Not upright, much-admired Gary Emerson. He'd been innocuously distant from the tragedy.

Just like Jesse. She'd been somewhere out in the hills when Joan drank herself into a stupor and plunged into a current too swift, too strong. . . .

"They ruled her death an accident," Jesse said tightly. "I wasn't in a state to question that when I was in the hospital. Maybe if Gary hadn't come back to Manzanita, I never would have."

"But you are now."

"I have to. If he had nothing to do with her death, if there's no reason I should hate him, then maybe I am losing it. And I refuse to believe that." She braced her hands on the desk and tried to make Al understand. "I know there's something wrong about Emerson. Something dark. I think I always knew it. Either my instincts are right, or I won't be able to trust them again."

Al looked out the window toward the new campaign office. "You can't bring back the dead."

"But I can bring back the rest of my memories. The childhood I lost so much of in the hospital. All I get are fragments, and if I could just remember the time with Gary, when he was with my mother . . . I know the answer is locked somewhere in my mind."

"And if the answer isn't what you want to see?"

"It can't be worse than not knowing." She shook her head. "You're a psychologist. There must be some way you can help me."

Al pushed his chair away from the desk and stood, grabbing his cane. He paced toward the window, the cane beating out an uneven rhythm that revealed what his voice and face did not. "I'm not in practice. I haven't been in years."

"But you didn't leave it because you weren't good, Al. You have the knowledge and the education. There's no one else I can trust."

His sigh was almost inaudible. "Did you have some specific therapy in mind?"

"I've heard that hypnosis can help with the recovery of memories. Can you do that, Al?"

"I've had some training—" He hesitated and stared out the window for several seconds before he turned back to her. "It's a controversial therapy, particularly with regard to so-called repressed memories. If you want my opinion as a psychologist, I don't think you should rush into this. You have a stable life, Jesse, and Emerson will soon be gone."

A stable life, where the only dangers were from the elements and nature, not to her mind and heart. That was what she'd fight to keep.

She got up and joined Al by the window. "I respect your opinion. But this is something I have to do." She wondered how to explain so illogical a feeling to Al, who had such firm control over his emotions.

She'd thought her own control was securely intact. How wrong she'd been. One crack, and it could shatter into a million pieces. If she let that disintegration begin, she might find herself back in the hospital.

Anything was better than that. Anything.

"I want you to think about it, Jesse," Al said. "Sleep on it, and if you still feel this way tomorrow morning, we'll discuss it further."

She nodded, but she knew her resolve wouldn't waver.

Gary Emerson could leave town in the next few minutes and it would make no difference.

She looked across the street. Wayne and his older friend were arguing over the placement of another Emerson sign, and a small group from the restaurant had gathered to watch and gesture over the new source of activity. Gary was already making waves in Manzanita.

Would she meet him again, today or tomorrow, at the post office or on the way to her job at Blue Rock Lodge? Would he do as he'd done this morning—merely stare at her, as if she were still the little girl who'd gone at him tooth and nail, screaming of betrayal?

Would she repeat the same performance, attack him like a deadly enemy? Hatred was better than fear—the devastating, paralyzing fear that made her turn tail and run. But she couldn't seem to master either emotion.

Somewhere in her memories she'd find the way to face what she didn't understand. Face and conquer Gary Emerson.

"I'd better get going," she said to Al. "I have a hiking group at the Lodge this afternoon." She didn't let Al see any hesitation as she walked out into the sunshine and crossed the highway.

People in the group observing the sign-hanging noticed her approach. Heads turned and leaned together in a buzz of conversation. Jesse walked past them to the post office, emptied her box, and headed for home.

Home was at the edge of town, hidden in a copse of trees near the back of Al's three-acre lot. The modest patch of ground with its tiny creek and woods had provided welcome solitude when she'd come back to Manzanita. A hill rose directly behind the cabin, and every morning Jesse could see the deer arrive to graze on the gentle slope.

The cabin was sanctuary; no one invaded her privacy here. This was a place she'd made for herself, and not even the malignant specter of Gary could enter uninvited.

She pushed open the door and went into her small kitchen, setting a kettle on for herbal tea. She thumbed through the junk mail and found the letter from her father's lawyer; monthly, regular as clockwork, and to be ignored like the others. She put it on the pile of like letters on top of the refrigerator. Even after his death, her father tried to atone for abandoning his wife and child.

Jesse had inherited the money he'd accumulated after he'd left them. The lawyer was constantly reminding her of that, sending her reports and financial statements. She could be wealthy. All she had to do was accept her inheritance.

Guilt money. She wanted nothing to do with it. She would have given the world when she was seven years old to know that her absent dad still loved her.

Now it was far too late.

She poured her tea and sat at the kitchen table. An hour to get herself together, and then it was off to Blue Rock for the hiking group. She couldn't turn up at the Lodge in less than top condition, mentally or physically.

She wouldn't let them down.

She finished the tea, put the kettle away, and changed into her oldest jeans. The smell of wood shavings in the workshop was soothing and safe. In the rhythm of sanding and polishing, she found the comfortable silence within herself that no one could touch. And if, in that silence, she remembered a dream of love and happiness, roses and a laughing child and a man with blue eyes, she didn't for a moment let herself believe it was real.

⌘ ⌘

THAT NIGHT THE dream was different.

Jesse had come home at eight, gratifyingly tired, and dropped into bed soon after. During the hike, herding her city folk over one of the easier mountain trails, she'd almost managed to put thoughts of Gary and the funeral behind her. Her drive home from the Lodge had turned up no sight of him, or of anything else that could trigger painful memories.

Maybe Al was right; the past was dead and buried.

Digging it up again was more dangerous than simply
waiting for Gary to leave. Surely this unwanted mental
turmoil would go away, sooner or later, and leave her in
peace.

She'd almost convinced herself when she went to bed,
focused only on the oblivion of sleep.

And then the first dream came, lancing through her
brain like an electric current.

She knew at once where she was. The cabin at the
resort she shared with her mother—plain, cozy, the furniture worn but serviceable. The best accessories were
saved for the guest rooms and lodge. But now, four years
after Dad's disappearance, even the guest rooms were
becoming run-down, the resort steadily losing money.

Angry voices crackled in the air as Jesse crouched just
outside the open living room window. Mom's voice—
and Gary's. Mom's words were slurred the way they
often were when she'd been drinking. Gary sounded
nasty and contemptuous and frightening.

"Do you think you can threaten me?" he asked with
dangerous softness. "Do you believe there's anything you
can do to hurt me, you bitch?"

A sob caught in Joan's throat. "I . . . took you in
. . . I can't pretend—"

Her words ended abruptly. Jesse grabbed the edge of
the windowsill and lifted herself with her arms, feet
braced against the wall.

Gary had Joan by the shoulders, a grip that must have
been painful. Only Jesse's terror kept her from crying
out.

Because she'd always hated Gary. Always feared him.
Even though he gave her smiles and easy banter meant to
be friendly—smiles that barely hid the same contempt he
showed her mother. In public he acted the perfect surro-
gate father.

In private they were enemies in an undeclared war. A
war Gary forever seemed to be winning.

"I'm warning you," Gary said, shaking Joan again.
"Now you know what I can do. You know what will

happen if you push me too far. There's something that matters more to you than the pathetic courage you've found in that bottle."

"No," Joan whispered. She shuddered violently. "You wouldn't. Please."

"You should have thought about that before," he said. "You'd better start thinking with whatever brain you've got left." He released her and she stumbled into the kitchen cabinet. "In a few days I'm going to Redding with Wayne and the boys. When I come back you'd better have forgotten all about this, Joan." He reached over to the counter and grabbed a bottle by the neck. "Here. Go find yourself some little hole in the wall and have a blast."

Joan clutched the bottle in both hands, her eyes dull with resignation. It was then that Jesse noticed there was water on the cabin floor. It began as a trickle that made its way across the braided living room rug and onto the kitchen linoleum, seemingly come out of the wall itself.

But then there were more trickles, rivulets that became streams, streams that became rivers. They joined together, and the floor was covered in an inch of water, two inches, rising to lap about Joan's ankles.

Gary watched, his face expressionless. He walked to the front door and paused there. The water didn't so much as dampen his feet, even as it rose higher and higher, to Joan's knees, her hips, her waist, tugged at her body with increasing force.

The river. The river had come into the cabin, and it was pulling Joan under. She held the bottle above the flood, then above her head, as if it were something precious she couldn't let go even to save her life. Her eyes were empty.

As if she were floating somewhere separate and apart, Jesse saw herself frozen against the window, unable to move. Shock was some great invisible force pressing her shoulders, locking her throat.

"Mom," she croaked.

But Joan didn't hear. She didn't even struggle as the

water reached her neck and then filled her mouth and covered her head. Her hair stirred at the eddying surface of the flood, and then that too was gone. The bottle, finally released, floated and bobbed in circles.

And Gary watched. With no remorse he saw her drown and did nothing.

A scream tore from Jesse's throat.

Immediately the river vanished, the water and cabin and resort along with it. Between one moment and the next, Jesse found herself in the cemetery. It was dark, terrifying, sinister with its gravestones and solemn attendants. The aspens leaned over Joan's grave, rustling leaves like bones rattling, whispering words no one dared say aloud.

Everyone knew Joan Copeland was a drunk. She'd gone down to the river and had a few too many, and she'd fallen in. Gary had arrived too late to save her.

Gary.

He looked at Jesse, smiling, wearing false sadness like a mask. False, fake, evil. Now, standing beside the minister, dry-eyed and numb, she felt the heat building up inside her. Heat, crackling and snapping like leaping flames along her nerves, searing her from within.

Flames. Fire. Panic and fear and rage. She felt herself begin to cough as black plumes of smoke wreathed around her, invisible fingers squeezing her lungs and robbing her of oxygen. No one saw her struggling to suck in air, no one came to help her.

But Gary kept watching. Watching and smiling, satisfaction in his eyes.

Hate. Hate moved Jesse then, propelled her across the burning grass though her feet singed and cracked with every flying step.

He would pay. By God, he would pay for what he'd done. He'd killed her. He'd killed her and the child as well, poor innocent, who might have been saved. . . .

She screamed. The words came out of her mouth as if another moved her lips. Her fingers curled to rake and tear at that loathed face.

A face that changed. Blond hair became dark, and brown eyes blue. Not Gary. Jesse stopped her headlong rush an instant before she struck him.

Sorrow. Sorrow in those eyes now, in an achingly handsome countenance she knew as she knew her own soul. He spoke her name without sound. He offered his hand, and she reached out to take it. Her own hand burst into flame, grew charred and black and began to crumble.

Her body was collapsing, disintegrating, and even her will couldn't keep her from falling into the fearful void. He left her, as he always did. She loved him, she hated him; with her last breath she shrieked his name.

"David!"

CHAPTER TWO

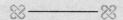

DAVID!"

The cry echoed in his mind as he crossed through the portals between life and death and found himself in the World again. Even before he became aware of the faint shape of his own body, of the unfamiliar room around him, he knew he was Back.

Back from the limbo where he'd heard that desperate appeal. The limbo that had been his home for uncounted years, where he knew the passage of time only from those souls who journeyed through his private perdition on their way to the next existence.

He knew it wasn't 1815, nor even the century into which he'd been born. He'd known it before his own name had summoned him to the earthly plane. But not one of his temporary visitors had made him feel how long he'd been gone, or how much he'd lost.

She did.

She no longer cried out but tossed on her narrow bed, throwing the sheets from her body. Her back was turned to him, sweetly curved, the bedclothes just brushing the swell of her hips. In the morning light he could see that her hair was nearly straight, falling a few inches below her shoulders, cut simply and left uncovered to tangle about her head as she slept. It was golden in color; guinea-gold, begging a man to touch the thick strands.

Her body, petite and compact, was clothed in something like a man's nightshirt. Fine-boned hands clutched at her pillow as if it were a lifeline.

He moved closer to the bed. He thought he could feel his booted feet connect with the paneled wooden floor, but it might have been imagination; imagination and longing for what he'd once taken for granted. The ordinary pleasure of walking on solid earth.

Or the pleasure of seeing a woman. After so long in limbo, he would have found her lovely had she been a crone of ninety years.

Her body was no crone's. She pushed the sheets down around her legs and kicked them loose. Her calves were bare. Bare and taut with the smooth muscle of one who did much walking. Her feet were small and strong, each toe flawless. David stared at her feet, reveling in the sensuous perfection of them. No mud, no blood, no cracked boots full of holes. Only feminine softness.

He might have thought he'd found his way to heaven at last. But heaven was not for David Ventris. Never for him.

Unless . . .

The key to his salvation rolled over with a sigh, her arm flung above her head on the pillow, and he saw her face.

He didn't know what he'd expected. If she'd looked like Sophie it would have been difficult. But this woman was nothing like. Her face held none of Sophie's delicate, petulant prettiness. It was stubborn and firm jawed, handsome rather than beautiful in its unadorned simplicity.

Yet in this body was the soul of the woman he'd betrayed.

The woman to whom he must atone. The woman who must grant him forgiveness and set him free.

David caught his breath—if breath it was. To win his freedom he'd do anything.

But it all rested on her.

He knelt beside the bed. Her lips were slightly parted, the lower fuller than the upper, revealing the hint of straight white teeth. Her skin had seen much of the sun, but it was youthful and smooth, or so he thought it would be should he dare to touch it.

Lashes darker than her hair shadowed her cheek. He began to wonder about the color of her eyes. Would they be brown as Sophie's, or blue as his own?

If she opened those eyes, would she see him?

He rocked back, wondering if he'd imagined the click of his boot heel on the floor. His hands, resting on the bed for support, seemed to feel the coolness of cloth where the woman's body hadn't warmed it.

He touched his chest. It felt solid. He could put his finger through the hole where the musket ball had pierced his jacket, though the wound was long since gone. He could see his fingers brush the braid at his sleeve, the saber at his hip.

Air seemed to enter his lungs. He heard the beat of his own heart. With every passing moment it seemed that his form grew more solid, more fully in this plane.

But he could still sense the cord that bound him to limbo, a chain he could not break. A chain he himself had forged. It tugged at him, unrelenting. Reminding him what he had to lose.

They had told him little and promised him nothing, his silent and invisible wardens. They didn't speak in words at all, but he understood the conditions that defined his presence here. He'd waited for this call, and they'd let him come. But they wouldn't help him. And if he failed . . .

I cannot fail, he told the woman. *I won't go back.*

She didn't wake. He tried to see Sophie in her, tried to remember when they'd been happy. She'd loved him once. And she'd died hating him.

He laughed, though the rough sound didn't make it past his throat. He was afraid. He knew himself for the coward of cowards, all his so-called heroism in battle a sham.

After countless years she'd called him, opened the door, and let him return. But she was no longer Sophie. The girl he'd known was long dead, six years before he himself had stopped a French ball at Waterloo. There was no certainty that this woman would remember anything of her former life, and a very good probability that her call had been a fluke, the mere shade of a memory that fixed on his name in the midst of a dream.

But if she *did* remember, she could hate him still. She could refuse to help him. She had the power. There was no running this time.

Except back to the anteroom of hell.

He heard birdsong outside the window, smelled green grass and a hint of pine, felt sunlight on his cheek. The world called to him, summoned him away to experience the joy of life again.

He had almost forgotten what joy was. Those last few years on the Peninsula had taught him to think of the world as sere brown hills, ceaseless dust, the stink of unwashed bodies and blood. In the very struggle for survival, he'd put the past away where it couldn't touch him, even as he sought the oblivion of death.

But death didn't bring peace. He had been trapped in a prison worse than any torment an earthly enemy could devise.

Endless nothingness. Endless loneliness, with only the memory of Sophie's fate to haunt him. Waiting for another chance at life that had finally been offered.

But without this woman's forgiveness there would be no life.

She murmured something in her sleep, some faint protest, and without thinking he reached for her. His fingers found her lips and connected with warmth and softness.

He snatched his hand away when he realized what he had done. He had *touched* her. He had *felt* her.

And then she opened her eyes.

They were hazel—browns and grays and greens all intermingled, shot with gold light that matched her hair. They didn't see him, didn't focus or throw off the tranquil void of sleep.

He looked for Sophie in those lovely eyes, for her sadness and desperation and that terrible need for him. A need he had not been able to fulfill.

I can't give you what you want, he told her silently. *But you can release us both.*

Her eyes were closed again, her breathing deep and regular. David rose and went to the window, pushing aside the thin curtains. Mountains rose up on every side of this narrow valley, mantled in green and brown, brilliant with color and energy. The scent and sound and feel of life was in his nostrils and ears and mouth and eyes.

God. He could get drunk on the world and forget everything else, no matter how short his stay here.

The irony left him breathless, and he laughed once more. He was not truly alive, had no right to walk this earth except by dispensation. The chain would always pull him back.

He'd thought to evade his guilt in death. Now he knew there was no escape. Not as long as Sophie held him.

"Sophie," he said, and went to stand over her again. She didn't hear him, didn't wake.

But he felt a more potent stirring of his newly recovered senses, the leap of desire in his veins. More bitter irony. Sophie or not, she moved him. He could not be immune to the sweet feminine shape of her body, the warmth that radiated from her like the essence of life itself. She was water to a man dying of thirst.

Thirst he could not assuage until he was allowed to pass on and live again. He could not, *would* not feel more than he must to achieve his goal. Everything he did must be to that one purpose.

He had learned discipline in the war. He knew how to lead men on the battlefield: how to inspire them, to lend them courage even when he was drowning in his own terror; how to treat their wounds, how to help them die.

This slip of a woman was a more daunting opponent than any he'd faced on the battlefields of the Peninsula.

Recklessly he sat down on the edge of the bed, feeling it give under his weight. "Well, my lady?" he whispered, his voice hoarse with long disuse. "We gamble for high stakes, you and I, and I don't know all the rules of the game." She'd called him; he knew she'd be able to see him, that he could speak to her and be heard. But how would she react to the presence of a ghost?

He skimmed his hand a hairsbreadth above her hip. "Who are you?" he asked. "Will you remember?"

But he willed her not to. Not until he found the way to make her believe in him, accept him, trust him as a benevolent visitor. A spirit, perhaps, come to help her in her earthly tribulations. He would learn what she most wanted to believe and use it to his advantage.

And then, when the time was right, he would tell her the truth—just enough to fulfill the conditions of his unearthly bargain. Enough to get what he wanted.

He smiled bitterly. "I give you fair warning, my lady," he said. "I haven't changed. I never change."

He hadn't meant her to hear him, but she did. And this time when she opened her eyes they centered directly on him.

He acted on instinct, willing himself to insubstantiality. He snapped to his feet and retreated across the room.

The woman blinked and sat up, body rigid with shock. Her gaze swept back and forth across the place where he stood, searching for what she could no longer see.

"Oh my God," she said. She put shaking hands to her mouth, then to her cheeks. She squeezed her eyes shut and massaged her temples fiercely.

"Dreams," she muttered. "That's all it is."

But her skin was very pale, and her fingers trembled as she fumbled for a smooth, narrow object on the table beside her bed.

David knew she'd seen him. She'd seen him and was afraid, as anyone would be afraid to find a ghost at her bedside.

Belatedly he moved toward her, hoping to ease her fear, but his second thoughts were overdue. Suddenly he felt his energy, his tentative life drain from him, sucked back into the chain that bound him to his immortal prison.

There was no way to fight it. He hadn't the strength, not yet. He'd bent the laws that governed life and death, and there was a price for that liberty.

But even as he lost his grasp on the earthly plane he knew it was but a temporary defeat. He would return.

The last he saw of the woman was her wild eyes as she spoke urgently into the object she held in her hand, begging for help. As she'd unwittingly called *him* with the power of his name.

He carried the image of her troubled face into limbo, knowing it would not leave him.

Until she set them both free.

⧗ ⧗

"IT CAN'T WAIT, Al. I need your help. Tonight."

Jesse gripped the receiver in a white-knuckled fist, staring at the wall where she'd seen him.

Him. There was no one, nothing there now but a zebra-stripe pattern of sunlight cast by the window blinds, and still her heart pounded as though she'd been running a marathon straight up a mountain.

"What happened?"

Al's voice was calm and blessedly sane, but it didn't quiet the shaking that ran in spasms through her body. "Nightmares," she said, forcing her gaze to the comforting solidity of her unremarkable table lamp.

"About Gary?"

"Yes." That was the truth. She *had* dreamed of Gary, but she wasn't about to mention the incongruous end of the dream—the bizarre hallucination that had brought her up out of sleep convinced someone had been standing beside her bed. Someone almost translucent, and yet utterly real. A vision of perfection who spoke to her in a rich, musical voice. Not Gary, but a man so authentic, so exquisitely detailed that for a moment she had believed he existed.

David. That was the name she'd called in her sleep. *His* name. She felt as if she'd spoken it a thousand times, and she had never seen the man before in her life.

The man for whom her body, her heart, her entire soul yearned. Whose touch still burned her skin. Who left her panting with need, wanting what she'd never wanted, defenseless and afraid.

She had called that name expecting an answer. She sat on the edge of her bed, wide awake and longing for a dream, certain that she had missed some vital message, that she'd given up a part of herself when he'd vanished into thin air before her deluded eyes.

She knew who to blame for the delusion. She'd never hallucinated like this, not even during her worst periods in the hospital.

Gary was the source of the maelstrom that drove her to the edge of the abyss, the catalyst that pushed her mind to create imaginary apparitions who answered her frantic, unconscious cries for help. This was her warning, and she wouldn't ignore it.

"Jesse?" Al's voice rumbled in the earphone.

"You told me to sleep on it, and I have. Will you help me?"

Al's hesitation was weighted with reluctance. "I don't know if I'm . . . the right one for this job, Jesse. Maybe you should—"

"Go somewhere else? The next nearest shrink is probably in Redding—and I trust you, Al." She spoke with every ounce of persuasion she could muster. "I want to try the hypnosis, as we discussed. I have to do this."

If she hadn't known Al Aguilar better, she'd have sworn he was uneasy. True, he'd left his career as a therapist, but Jesse had absolute faith in his competence. His composure wouldn't be shaken by anything she could throw at him. He wouldn't call her crazy.

But it was hard, so hard to ask for help. It was only possible because her need for Al didn't go beyond this, wouldn't consume her or make her weak and vulnerable. Not like the way she'd felt when she'd called out to the man of her dreams.

Impossible. Dangerous. Crazy.

"What do you know about hypnotherapy?" Al asked after a pause. "It's no magic cure, Jesse. It's only a deep form of relaxation. Guided imagery. There are no guarantees that—"

"I don't need guarantees." Jesse shifted the receiver to her left hand, flexing the cramped muscles of her right. "I'm beginning to remember more from my childhood, but it's not enough. I'll take whatever we can get."

"You may not be . . . comfortable with this kind of therapy. It requires giving up a certain amount of conscious control."

Oh, Al knew her. "I realize that," she said. "But I have to try."

A sigh reached her faintly over the line. "Okay. But we're going into this slow and easy, Jesse. If it doesn't feel right to either one of us, we stop. Agreed?"

"Agreed. What about tonight?"

Papers rustled. She heard the creak of Al's bedsprings as he got up. "I have to drive out to Redding to pick up my niece early this afternoon. I've mentioned her—the one from boarding school." He coughed. "Her grandmother—my brother's mother-in-law—died in March, and she's coming to live with me for the summer."

Jesse vaguely remembered Al's referring to an orphaned niece, but he hadn't hinted that she'd be coming to stay in Manzanita. Jesse could guess Al's feelings on that score; he valued his privacy and liked living alone.

He wouldn't know what to do with a little girl. Especially one who'd lost her family.

"Megan should be . . . settled in here by six," Al said. "Meet me in my study at seven. Wear comfortable clothes and . . ." He sighed again. "Try not to expect too much."

"Tonight, then," she said, and set the receiver in its cradle with hands that no longer shook. Now that she was taking action, the fear was passing. It always did. She looked at the wall—where *he* had been—and felt the full absurdity of her fleeting belief in a mirage.

"You weren't really there," she told the air, "and I don't need you."

But she wondered why she'd chosen those words to warn off a figment of her own imagination.

She got up and grabbed the terrycloth robe that hung over the bedpost. *Gary* was no phantom; in her dream she'd seen him arguing with her mother. But had the dream revealed the truth of the past, events she'd repressed over the years? What did the argument mean? And the imagery of Gary watching—watching as Joan died . . .

The only thing she was sure of was that Gary was guilty. Guilty of some terrible crime.

And that he must pay.

❈ ❈

"THAT'S THE BEST breakfast I've had in weeks," Gary said, patting his stomach for emphasis. He flashed a grin at his adoring audience and slid his chair from the table. "I think I can safely say your restaurant will be a rip-roaring success, Miss Hudson."

Marie Hudson smiled from her position of anxious vigilance beside the table, her gaze hooded as she murmured throaty thanks for the compliment. Bedroom eyes, that one had, and she'd been using them to good effect during the meal; she was pretty enough, and hot for a man from the looks of it. No reason not to take full advantage of what minimal pleasures this piddling backwater town had to offer.

Gary had moved beyond Manzanita and its petty concerns, but these devoted Emerson supporters wouldn't have the brains to recognize that. They saw him as a native-son-come-home—exactly what they wanted to see, though Gary had first arrived in Manzanita when he was twenty-six and left just two years later.

Two wasted years in the middle of nowhere. But he wasn't about to disoblige these innocents, who wanted so badly to help him. Their votes were worth as much as anyone else's. And he didn't have to expend any effort at all to win them over.

He made a grand gesture of pulling out his wallet. "The tab's on me, folks. You've all been good enough to help me with my campaign, and it's the very least I can do to show my appreciation."

Earnest applause rippled through the crowd. Gary automatically noted the ones who were most enthusiastic. There were always a few who could be counted on to go above the call of duty. Wayne Albright was one of them; he probably didn't have anything else to do but hang out in the bar and guzzle beer, just as he'd done seventeen years ago. Now he had a purpose, putting up signs and making himself feel important as a grassroots supporter of Gary Emerson's state assembly campaign.

Gary always knew which ones needed a purpose, which could be bought, which seduced.

Especially the latter. He managed to brush his arm across Marie's full breasts as he stepped sideways from the table, felt the hum of contact jolt through his body. Marie didn't move away, and when he glanced casually at her snug cashmere sweater, he saw the pucker of her nipples, bold and prominent.

He'd have something to do tonight, anyway. His business in town wouldn't take more than a day or two.

He frowned, quickly masking the expression from his observers. *Business.* Surely it wouldn't amount to anything.

Gary shrugged off the moment of unease and shook hands all around, nodding and laughing at jokes and comments he barely heard. Every one of his supporters felt that his attention was entirely for them; that he liked them, that he admired them, that he needed them. They were so easy to play. The politicos and seasoned campaigners in Sacramento were different, but even they had their weaknesses. And money could open all the right doors.

Money wasn't a problem now that he had Heather. She was waiting for him in Sacramento—with her nice, rich, influential daddy—but he wasn't letting her lead him around by the balls. After they were married, she'd learn to get good at waiting. And turning a blind eye to his pleasures.

Gary winked at Marie as he walked out the door. She simpered, tugging at her sweater for a better display. Yes, he'd definitely have some entertainment tonight—after he'd taken care of business.

One by one his admirers dispersed, reluctant to return to whatever dismal lives they led. Only Wayne and Fred Sykes lingered, Fred gibbering on about the signs he'd begun to put up around town.

"That's just great, my friend," Gary said, slapping the old man on the shoulder. "It's dedication from people like you that's going to win us this campaign. And I won't forget."

Fred grinned, nodding and pawing at Gary's sleeve. Gary detached the old man's hand and took it between his own. "You go on, now. I'm sure there's more that needs to be done to get our campaign office running. You're just the man to handle it."

He gave Fred a little push toward the office. The old man went readily enough, still nodding to himself.

"Needs a bit of fixing up," Albright said, jerking his chin toward the storefront. "But with all the folks interested in helping, I think we—"

"I hear Jesse Copeland came by."

Albright broke off, looking sideways at Gary. He

scratched his stubbled chin. "She did. Fred . . . he asked her if she wanted to help with the campaign. He wasn't here when it . . . when that stuff happened."

That stuff. There had been a time, just afterward, when Gary had actually dreamed about it. But in the dreams Jesse Copeland hadn't been a crazy little girl, pummeling at him with hands and feet that couldn't do any real damage. In the dreams she'd been an avenging demon, intent on dragging him to hell.

But in time the nightmares had stopped. He'd kept track of Jesse until she'd been in the hospital for several months, and then had put her out of his mind—her and her dead drunk of a mother and the incident he'd hidden so well from the stupid, gullible townies. The luck he'd always pursued had finally turned up when he left Manzanita.

He charmed his way into a job with the right connections and began the serious pursuit of delayed ambition, clawing his way up the ladder of politics—first local, building a name, then moving up into the state arena. Until he had almost everything he wanted: money, admirers, the promise of power. The man he'd been seventeen years ago no longer existed.

Then he'd come across the article about the Tri-Mountain Search and Rescue team and seen Jesse Copeland's name. She was back in Manzanita, hale and whole and all grown up, and suddenly his past wasn't so far away anymore. Not when the smallest indiscretions of youth could haunt a man in high office. And Gary intended to go much, much higher.

Jesse was the only link to a phase of his life he'd left behind. There was no good reason to believe she knew anything. She'd been a kid when Joan died. She'd gone nuts and then disappeared. In seventeen years there'd been no hint that she even remembered him.

But the article had nagged at him. He'd begun to see Jesse's face, hear her voice accusing him as she'd done at the funeral. And the dream had come back.

The dream had driven him here—that and the fear that

he might have made a mistake. No, not fear; caution. And Manzanita was in his district, a town he'd visit eventually, one more blip on the campaign trail. It would be a simple matter to make absolutely sure.

He sighed for Wayne's benefit and shook his head. "I've never forgotten the day of Joan's funeral. It was such a tragedy." He looked off above the buildings, toward the mountains that cupped like sheltering arms about the narrow valley. "It's . . . difficult."

"Yeah." Wayne stuffed his hands in his pockets and shrugged. "You know, she only came back a year and a half ago. Peace Corps or something like that, before. When she first showed up, no one knew what to expect. But she . . . well, she's different. Quiet. Joined search and rescue and works up at the Lodge. The new one, I mean—Blue Rock," he clarified, as if he didn't expect Gary to know that the Copeland place had been shut down after it was sold.

But Gary had made it his business to know.

"I'm glad she's found peace here," Gary said. "She went through so much, and there was a time when I thought she might not recover."

"It was bad," Wayne said with the enthusiasm of a man who'd made a life's work out of prying into other people's business. "She was in that hospital for months, and then under some kind of special care for a couple years after that. Medication, shrinks, the whole works."

"Poor child."

Wayne circled his finger in the air next to his temple. "Some folks still think she's a little strange. Keeps to herself. Can't figure what she's thinking." He glanced up at Gary. "People haven't forgotten how you tried to help her mama. Folks are watching to see what she'll do now that you're in town."

Good old Wayne. He was just as reliable a gossip as he'd been seventeen years ago, when he and Gary had shared a beer or two at the Manzanita Tavern. Wayne thought that old acquaintance made him a natural inti-

mate of the Gary Emerson who'd come so far up in the
world.

Gary let his delusion continue. "I hate to think that I
might make things worse for her."

"No one blames you." Wayne was as earnest as an
overgrown, overweight, balding puppy. "Seventeen
years, Gary. She's either over it or—"

He left the sentence unfinished, but his meaning was
clear. Jesse Copeland might have come home, but she
was on the fringe, not quite accepted, not yet one of the
citizens of Manzanita.

After a single day, Gary was sure of his own welcome.
The people in these small towns had long memories and
minds that hung on to old opinions like pit bulls. Joan
Copeland hadn't had a good reputation. Her daughter
had been mentally ill. Gary Emerson, however, was the
salt of the earth. You could trust him with your money or
your wife or your life itself.

"She's never mentioned me, then," he asked casually,
studying his manicured fingernails.

"Hell, no."

Of course not. If Jesse had ever expressed a suspicion,
he would have heard. And no one would have believed
her—just as they wouldn't have believed her mother.

If she'd been exactly like her mother, he'd have dismissed her as he'd done Joan's pathetic, drunken threats
to expose him. But when he'd seen Jesse across the cemetery yesterday morning . . .

He remembered the shock he'd felt, as if he'd expected
her to be exactly what she'd been when he'd known her.
But Jesse had grown up. She was no longer the knobby-
kneed brat with scraped hands and tangled hair. She was
striking, fit and tan and pretty. She didn't look remotely
crazy. And though they hadn't spoken, he'd seen her
face, watched it change as she recognized him.

Shock, like his. Loathing. And fear. Fear that might
have been the remnant of her old dislike of him, or because she blamed him for her illness.

Or it could be something more. It could be because

Joan had told Jesse before she died. Told her—or even passed on the evidence Joan claimed to have hidden.

Gary snorted. *If* there'd been any evidence, Joan had taken it into the grave with her. She'd never had the guts to use it, and she wouldn't have endangered her precious child. He'd searched the resort thoroughly before and after her very convenient death.

But he was here in Manzanita now, and this time he'd leave no stone unturned. For whatever reason, Jesse was afraid of him. He knew how to use fear to his advantage. If she had anything on him, if she even suspected, he'd find out.

No, it wouldn't take long at all.

"I have a few more people in town I need to talk to this afternoon," he told Wayne. "I'm dining with the mayor and his wife tonight. Maybe after that we can go grab a beer at the tavern—for old times' sake."

Wayne grinned. "You betcha. Just like old times."

Gary gave Wayne's shoulder an affectionate slap. "You just keep things going on this end, old buddy. See that those flyers get out to everyone in town. I'll see you to-night."

He left Wayne headed back for the office, such as it was, and dropped in at Marie's once more. A few words, some expert fondling behind the counter, and he'd set up his rendezvous with that nice little piece of T&A. By the end of this day he'd have more than earned his reward.

His rental car was parked at the Manzanita Inn, a motel made up of utilitarian rooms overlooking the high-way. He stopped to change his clothes—the innkeeper had insisted that he take the "Honeymoon Suite," the only room that actually boasted a couch and miniature refrigerator—and put his wire cutters and flashlight in the trunk.

There weren't any signs to the old resort; they'd long been torn down. Gary didn't need them. He drove up the last few feet of pitted driveway to the padlocked gate and parked. The current owners had put up a fence around the property and obviously hadn't touched it since. Maybe they thought the place was haunted.

Let them stay superstitious, the fine upstanding people of Manzanita.

Gary walked up to the gate, laced his fingers through the chain link, and rattled it to test the lock. It was rusted solid, but still intact. The heavy-duty wire cutters made short work of a small portion of the fence.

He scooted through the opening and strode down the lane and through the screen of trees toward the lodge. The office and lodge looked more weathered but otherwise unaltered; one cabin by the lake was partially collapsed. The surface of Wagon Wheel Lake was calm and still. Deserted.

This was a waste of time. He'd gone over the place seventeen years ago. If Joan's "evidence" hadn't turned up by now, it never would.

Four hours later Gary brushed the dirt and dust and pine needles from his jeans and checked his watch. He'd been over every building in the resort; all the guest cabins had been stripped, and only Joan's cabin remained as it had been the day he'd left. Hatch's hidden grave in the woods was untouched and invisible now, covered in years of branches and rotten leaves.

Gary was more convinced than ever that Joan had been bluffing. But if there was the remotest possibility that she'd passed something on to her daughter . . .

He started back for the car, whistling under his breath. He knew exactly who to call for a little break-in work. Jesse lived in a small cabin at the edge of town; it shouldn't be difficult to search. Just for insurance.

Just in case that look in Jesse's eyes had been more than an old childhood grudge.

He left the way he'd come, and pushed the cut portion of fence into place. A day or two more, and he'd be out of this town—and the Copelands would be consigned to that dark corner of his mind he carefully left alone.

There was no room for dark corners in the brilliant career of up-and-coming Assemblyman Gary Emerson.

There were no limits, and nothing—no one—would hold him back.

❊   ❊

JESSE WAS HER name.

It had come to David in limbo while he gathered the strength to return, illumined in radiance amid the bleak barrenness of his eternal prison.

Jesse. Unusual, yet it suited the woman who bound him to the world. As once she had called him from within her dreams, so now her name was a beacon guiding him to her. He found himself on a mountainside under a vast blue sky.

And she was there.

In the full sunlight her hair was true gold, her slender body clothed in snug blue trousers and loose shirt that reminded him how far he'd come from his former life on Earth. She wore a pack and sturdy boots, like an infantryman on campaign.

There the resemblance ended. Framed by the mountains around her, she was more beautiful than he remembered, as if she drew into herself the vibrancy of earth and sky. And when he looked beneath the surface of her lovely form, he could sense the very burning of her soul.

Sophie's soul reborn.

He stood just downslope from her, yet she didn't see him. And she wasn't alone. As he concentrated on keeping himself invisible, he took the time to study the others gathered around her.

They were a motley group, most of them dressed like Jesse—male and female, young and old alike. He caught snatches of Jesse's voice against the wind, speaking to her charges in the firm, persuasive tones of a good commander spurring his troops to greater effort after a long and weary march. He moved closer to listen.

"All right," she said, hazel eyes sweeping the assembly, passing over David with no glimmer of recognition. "We've got this one final slope, and then there's a nice

grove of pines where we can stop for lunch. You can see
it from here—right around that bend." She smiled at an
older couple standing closest to her. "This has been a
toughie, I know, but I think you'll find it worth the effort
when we get to the top. The view's spectacular."

"It's got to be better than my own feet," quipped the
gray-haired man of the couple. "Haven't had the energy
to look up for the past mile."

There was a chorus of sympathetic chuckles. The
man's wife leaned against him companionably and
grinned. "That's nothing to what I've had to look at. I've
been behind you all the way!"

Laughter rippled among the hikers once more, but
David noted the way Jesse gazed at the couple with a
shadow amid the shifting green and gray and brown of
her eyes. "I'm not worried about you two," she said.
"You're going to outlast us all."

"That's the nicest piece of malarkey I've heard in a
long time," the man said. He glanced at his wife. "Well,
Dee? Think we're too set in our ways to adopt this young
lady?"

Jesse made some appropriate jest in reply, but that sadness was still there in her eyes. She moved from one to
another of her charges, tightening a pack strap here and
sharing a quiet word of encouragement there.

At last the troop began to walk, moving up the hill in a
staggered line, Jesse lingering to help the elderly couple.
Then they too went ahead, and only David waited behind her.

The set of her shoulders betrayed her. She sensed him,
felt his presence as surely as he'd felt her sadness. But she
refused to turn, hitching up her pack and marching forward to join the others.

"Sophie," he whispered.

She came to a sudden halt. The people ahead of her
were just rounding the bend and entering the stand of
trees; as the last of them slipped out of sight she turned
slowly to face him.

He had yet to learn fine control of his spectral body, or

how much it could affect the world around him. He had thought to remain invisible to her in this place. But it was as if her searching eyes found the part of him in hiding, dragged him like some furtive night hunter into the inevitable light of day.

"You," she said. "Oh, God."

He might have offered up a prayer himself if he'd still believed that anyone listened. Instead he moved toward her—carefully—and smiled. He could see the mountain through the ethereal substance of his raised hands.

"Jesse," he said. "I mean you no harm."

Most society women he'd known would have swooned upon being presented with a ghost. Sophie certainly would have done so. Jesse only planted her feet more firmly on the brown earth and her hands on her hips, though her legs were shaking and her mouth trembled.

"Go away," she said. "I refuse to give in, so you might as well beat it right now."

"You do see me, Jesse," he said softly.

"You're not real," she insisted, clamping her jaw against any telltale quivering. "I don't know how I conjured you up, or why, but there's not a thing wrong with my sanity. So—" She drew in a deep breath and glanced over her shoulder at the copse of trees. "Go away."

He expected her to spin on her booted foot and start back up the hill. The need to escape was in every line of her supple body—God, how well he recognized that impulse. But she stood very still and glared as if she were waiting for him to defend his presence, explain himself, make her believe . . .

"I am here, Jesse," he said. "I'm real." He flexed his fingers, willing them to greater solidity. They stayed uncooperatively translucent. "I fear I've become a bit rusty at this sort of thing. I've been . . . too long away."

Away, her lips formed. She looked at his feet, up the length of his legs, past the belt at his waist and the braided jacket with its high, snug collar. Her gaze came to rest on his chin, and he lifted his hand to touch the stubble he was sure would be there. He couldn't recall the last time he'd shaved. One had no need for such mundane activities in limbo.

One never . . . *changed* at all.

"Why?" Jesse asked in a strained voice. "Who are you?"

"You called me," he said.

"A dream," she muttered. "Only a dream."

"You aren't asleep now, Jesse." He smiled crookedly. "I've botched it, haven't I? Do you remember my name?"

Once again her lips formed the word, unwilling to give it voice. *David.*

He snapped to attention. "David Ventris, Captain Lord Ashthorpe, late of His Majesty's Light Dragoons." *Very late,* he almost added, but doubted that she was in any case to appreciate his black humor.

"You—" She wet her lips. "You're some kind of soldier."

"Yes," he said. "I was a soldier. In a war that I suspect was very long ago." He looked up at the mountains, too rough and thick with trees to be the ones he'd known at the Lakes, yet so beautiful. "This is America, isn't it? and it's been—" He met her gaze again. "How long since Waterloo, Jesse?"

"Waterloo?" she repeated. "The battle with Napoleon? Why would I—" She caught herself, closing her eyes and sucking in great lungfuls of air. "I'm not. I can fight this. I'm not going back—"

Not going back. Oh, yes. He understood that vow.

"I know about madness," he said. He focused on a pebble near the toe of his boot, gauged the amount of effort it might take to kick that pebble. "You have no reason to fear for your sanity. Not that I blame you."

She laughed, a brief and broken sound of sheer disbelief. "You don't blame me. That's just great. I have nothing to worry about now, do I?"

But her bravado was all show. David had seen that kind of performance many times in war, when men were so terrified that they might commit the rashest of acts to assuage the fear.

A miscalculation now could send her over the edge. He crouched to lessen the threat of his presence and hung his arms over his knees. "Not from me, Jesse. Didn't you ever believe that there might be things in the world that can't be explained by mere logic?"

She looked at him—*at* him, not through him—with a fierce, suppressed panic. "You know what I think. I made you."

"Did you?" He couldn't laugh anymore, not past the knot in his throat. She thought she'd made him, and yet it was the other way round. If Sophie's soul hadn't come into this new life shaped by what he'd done, she couldn't have called him.

But if she didn't acknowledge his reality, he could go no further. He had to get through to her. When he saw how much she despised her own fear, he thought he knew the way.

"If you made me," he said, "then you must know why I'm here. Or are you afraid to find out?"

The challenge worked. He felt her stare as a shaft of radiance, blinding in its intensity, piercing all the way to his own restless soul as surely as he had looked into hers. There was a change in her expression, a stern and fixed concentration that made him wonder if he had risked too much.

If she saw too far, if she could read his heart and know everything he'd done—everything he must do—he was finished.

But she let him go, breaking free of any tentative binding between them. "No," she said coldly. "No. I won't let it happen."

There was no warning of her charge. She strode directly at him, fists clenched, and the impact of her touch stunned David into immobility. At first there was a resistance, as if the very air had taken on solidity. Then the barrier was breached, and for a heartbeat two bodies shared the same overlapping space.

It was ecstasy—beyond sexual, beyond anything physical. The essence of life itself poured from Jesse into him, a flow of warm light and glorious sensation. In that moment David held Jesse's heart in his cupped hands. Exaltation peaked and shuddered through him, shaking him apart.

And then it was over. Jesse stood behind him, her face white, her eyes glazed with shock.

David stumbled, fighting the weakness in legs that possessed all the frailty of human flesh and blood. The realness Jesse had given him.

"Jesse," he croaked, and stretched his hand out to her, as if somehow she could understand what he required and give it to him without pain, or struggle, or any need of the dark and terrible truth.

She flinched from his hand and started away, jogging up the hill. He rose to follow, cursing a body that wouldn't obey him.

Between one instant and the next it betrayed him completely. The brief union with Jesse had been too much, drained the energy from him as surely as a mortal wound had drained his life's blood into the earth.

"No," he shouted. "Curse you, *no.*"

But limbo tugged at him, the only enemy with the power to tear him away. His legs lost form, his hands became transparent, even the beating of his heart went still. His spirit had no anchor to the world, no bridge to reach her.

He thought he saw Jesse turn to him, but his vision was fading. The sunlight, too, was dim, the mountains replaced by the grim, infinite battlefield that was his personal Hell. They mocked him, the merciless wardens of that place, who remained mute and showed themselves only in the reflection of his despair.

"David?"

As her name had called him back, so his name on her lips almost held him, though she stood a hundred yards distant. She lifted her hand, slow and uncertain in her fear. But her hesitant offer wasn't enough; the winds of limbo swept him into their icy embrace, and his answer was as lost as his soul.

CHAPTER THREE

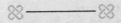

THERE WERE TIMES, when Al knew he'd detached just a little too much from the world, that he could look at Jesse Copeland and remember he was human.

Today was one of those times.

She'd swept into his study on a cool wind from the mountains, flushed with exercise, vibrating with energy. But there was a hectic color in her cheeks that signaled her distress. She moved with stiff restraint, as if she were holding herself together behind a brittle shell that might crack at the slightest provocation.

Al pointed her to the leather recliner and observed her with a faint frown. He couldn't erase her anxiety; he'd learned long ago the dubious value of mouthing platitudes and reassurances that everything would be all right.

Jesse would not have appreciated them. She had always been so self-reliant, so determined not to need anyone. But she, unlike Al, hadn't learned the peace of indifference, the inertia of resignation. For all her efforts to become unmoved by the world, she was far too much alive to adopt the dispassion Al had carefully cultivated for the past twenty years.

And now she asked for his help. As he watched her settle into the recliner, he remembered her as a child: so vulnerable, so confused, virtually abandoned by a mother who'd either been drinking or living to fulfill Gary Emerson's every whim. Gary had disliked Jesse, and the feeling had been mutual—even if most of Manzanita was convinced that Jesse was the one with the problem.

Gary Emerson was still Jesse's problem.

Al's fist clenched on the desk, and he was remotely interested to observe his own anger. He might damn Emerson to hell, but it wouldn't help Jesse. When all was said and done, she could only help herself.

"Make yourself comfortable," he told her. Awkwardly he maneuvered his desk chair closer to the side of the recliner. "This is our first session to explore your response to hypnotherapy. Are you clear about what we're going to do?"

She nodded against the padded headrest, but her jaw was set, her eyes squeezed shut too tightly. For Jesse to attempt this was a measure of how profoundly Gary's return had affected her. To need was to be afraid. To let go was to lose yourself. She wasn't one to give up control, or trust another person with her innermost thoughts.

Yet she trusted Al to guide her into the still, fathomless waters of her unconscious mind. He wondered if he trusted himself.

"Did you see Emerson today?" he asked.

Her head jerked to the side. "Not *him*," she said in a muffled voice.

Not him. But the emphasis on the second word had meaning. Al had known from the minute she'd walked into his house that something new had happened. Something that had frightened her badly.

"Do you want to talk about it, before we begin?" he prompted.

For a moment she seemed ready to say more, and then she clamped her lips together. "No. I'm ready."

Al rubbed his palm on his knee. Jesse was tense; a series of relaxation and breathing exercises seemed the best method of induction. Even that might not calm her enough.

It was a start. "Jesse, I'd like you to relax as much as you can. Listen to my voice and don't try to concentrate. Be aware of your body's responses, but don't fight them."

She nodded again, brows drawn. Al suppressed a sigh. Jesse was bound to demand too much of herself in this first session.

"I want you take three deep, slow breaths," he said. "Think of the air moving in and out of your lungs. Let go of your tension, let it flow out of you."

She obeyed with the earnest concentration of an Olympic athlete trying for a world record. He repeated the breathing exercises several times; each time she relaxed a little more, until the knotting of her muscles began to loosen. By the end of the fourth exercise, the crease between her brows was gone, and her lips parted gently.

He'd held no great hope that he would succeed this first attempt, and he'd been prepared to try other methods if necessary. But Jesse had surprised him.

"How do you feel, Jesse?" he asked.

"A little sleepy," she said, her words soft around the edges. "My arms are tingling."

"Good. Everything is just fine." He glanced at the clock on the wall. "When you feel ready to begin, to explore the past, I want you to lift your little finger."

Her finger twitched. Jesse had confounded all his expectations and was already in a medium trance. In theory it could happen this way; in fact such a rapid induction was rare.

Al felt a flash of excitement, a hunch that he was on the verge of something he hadn't anticipated. But he pulled himself back from the precipice with the ease of habit and well-honed discipline. There was nothing remotely mystical in what he and Jesse were doing. Solid ground lay in the objectivity of the mind. He was here to help Jesse find that solid ground.

"As you journey into your past," he told her, "you'll experience only as much as you feel comfortable with. At any time, you have the power to rise above your memories. You always have control. Your memories are unable to hurt you."

"Hurt," she murmured. "It . . . hurts."

Al stared at her hand, relaxed against the armrest. Her voice was still distant, untroubled. He had planned to guide her slowly, step by easy step, into her own childhood, but it seemed she had already gone ahead of him.

He could bring her out now. It wasn't too late. But Jesse wanted this badly, and he couldn't let her down.

"Can you tell me what hurts, Jesse?"

Her eyelids trembled. "Why did you leave me?"

She wasn't speaking to him. He thought quickly of who she might mean: her mother was the most logical contender, or her father, who'd left Joan and Jesse when she was only seven. He'd been unable or unwilling to deal with Joan's severe mood swings and drinking—

"I love you," Jesse said with sudden vehemence. "If you leave me, I'll die."

With an eerie, thoroughly irrational sense of foreboding, Al heard in her words not the cries of an abandoned child but something else entirely. "Jesse," he said. "Can you tell me who you're talking to? Who you love so much?"

Her throat worked. "He won't listen. He said he loved me. Our child—" She moaned. "Gone. I'm so alone."

The prickles along Al's spine redoubled. "Jesse, can you tell me where you are? What year it is?"

"David," she whispered. "Don't go back. Please." Her breath came rapidly now, in short pants. "I won't ever see you again. I know. I *know!*"

She didn't hear Al, was so engrossed in whatever memory or delusion she'd found that she couldn't or wouldn't answer his questions. He leaned over her, willing her to listen.

"Jesse, you are able to see yourself protected and separate from what you're experiencing now. You're safe. You can—"

"No!" She tossed her head. "I'm not safe! He hates me. I can feel it! When he comes into the room . . ." A long shudder racked her body. Her hand shot out to grasp at air. "David!"

"Who hates you, Jesse? Is it Gary you're afraid of?"

She lapsed into silence, as if she'd finally heard his instructions. Al let her rest, considering how best to bring her out of trance. This was too much, too intense. It wasn't her childhood she spoke of.

Another part of her life, perhaps. When she'd been on her own, in college or the Corps, before her return to Manzanita.

"There's nothing to live for," she said dully.

Al gripped the arm of his chair. "Where are you now, Jesse?"

"In my bed. I'm always in my bed. It hurts to get up. I don't care. The roses are all dying."

"The roses. Can you tell me about the roses?"

"In the garden. I don't go there anymore." Her lips stretched in a thin, bitter smile. "When he left I told the gardener to let them die."

"Why are you in bed, Jesse? Are you ill?"

Her hand lifted to touch her flat stomach. "He didn't believe me. Something is wrong. But when the doctor comes—" She broke off, and Al saw her eyes look sideways beneath her lids. "You," she gasped. "Go away. I don't want you here. Get out!"

"Who do you see, Jesse?"

But she grasped her stomach, pressing down and

wrapping her arms about herself as if to protect it from attack. "Send for the doctor. Please. It hurts." She whimpered, the cry broken by a cough. "There's something wrong with the air. I . . . can't breathe." She coughed again, a weak and strangled sound. "There's smoke. I can't get up. I know—I know he did this. *He* did this." Her face contracted in a grimace of rage. "They both did it. I hate them. *I hate them!*"

"Listen to me carefully, Jesse. I want you to prepare yourself to leave your memories now. I'm going to begin counting backward from five to one. With each number, you'll feel yourself coming a little closer to consciousness. At the count of one you'll find yourself fully aware, relaxed and able to—"

Jesse screamed.

Al kept his voice sure and calm. "You'll come back able to remember everything that happened, without fear and in complete control of your memories. Five . . . Four . . ."

Jesse opened her eyes. For a moment she blinked at the ceiling, mouth working, and then she looked at Al with complete awareness. She'd brought herself out of trance as swiftly as she'd gone in.

Al leaned forward. "Are you all right?"

"I think so." She sat up, massaging her forehead. "Yes. I'm all right now." She gave him a lopsided smile. "It wasn't exactly what I expected."

That was one hell of an understatement. Al stood up and pushed away from his chair. "It was a mistake to enter into this so quickly. If something had gone wrong—"

Her touch on his arm brought him to a halt. "It wasn't your fault. I talked you into it." She swayed, and Al steadied her as best he could when he was none too sure of his own balance.

He guided her to the chair and resumed his own. "You weren't able to describe much of what you experienced while you were under. Do you remember what happened?"

There was still a paleness to her face, a distance in her gaze. "It's fading quickly," she said, "like a dream after you wake up." She sighed. "No. Most of it is gone now. Except— At the end I saw fire. Fire and smoke. I felt as if I were dying."

"You screamed," he said. "Do you remember any such incident in your childhood? A memory you may have suppressed?"

She shook her head. "I was always . . . afraid of fire. I wouldn't go near the fireplace at home. But nothing like that ever happened." Her clear hazel eyes focused on him. "Nothing I felt—it wasn't what I needed to remember."

Not her childhood, or her past with Gary. "When you think of who you were in those memories—were you ever a little girl?"

"No. It was as if I were—" All at once the wariness was back, the same guarded disquiet she'd shown when she first arrived. "It wasn't home," she finished. "My mother wasn't there. And Gary—"

Al had seen her rage during the trance when she'd declared hatred to someone she couldn't describe. It flashed in her eyes now, and her fingers dug into the leather of the chair.

"Gary," she repeated. "I didn't see him. I don't remember. *I don't remember.*"

"The mind isn't easy to understand," he told her. "Maybe this was your personal symbolism. Roses, illness, fire . . . the pain you felt. Your answers may be there—if you still intend to pursue this."

"I'm not about to quit now. My dreams last night—" Leather protested at the grip of her hands. "I'm close. I can feel it."

No. Jesse Copeland would never give up, not even if it killed her. "There was a man you spoke to," he said. "David. Can you tell me anything about him?"

Her body stiffened. "I don't remember."

"You can tell me, Jesse. There's something important to you about that name."

I love you, she'd said. Al couldn't forget the sound of her voice when she'd spoken those words.

Or the look on her face—the silent anguish he saw now.

"Did you know him?" he asked. "Before you returned to Manzanita?"

She turned a wild glance on him. "I don't know who he is."

But she did. There was no doubt in Al's mind that the name meant more to Jesse than she'd ever admit. Love, and hate, and consuming need.

"You mentioned a child," he said.

"I . . . don't remember."

Al looked down, from his good hand to his pinned-up sleeve, feeling the gray walls of detachment close around him. "We'd better give it a rest, Jesse. More may come back to you. It can't be forced, and it shouldn't be."

"No," she said. The tension left her shoulders, as if he'd given her the permission to relax that she could not allow herself. "You're right. Thank you, Al. I appreciate what you've done."

And what have I done? he thought. But he walked her to the door of the study, watching her with a remote and clinical eye. Her walk was steady now, her expression self-contained. She was the competent Jesse Copeland most of the world witnessed every day.

The world hadn't been with her in his study tonight.

She walked down the hall and paused at a half-open door, the bedroom farthest from the study. Al didn't know how she'd guessed. He stood back as Jesse opened the door a fraction wider and looked in.

"Your niece," Jesse said. "She must have been very tired to sleep through this."

Through the scream, she meant. But the child was a motionless lump in her bed, bundled up in covers and apparently oblivious to their presence. Her small table lamp still burned on her nightstand.

"Megan," he said, by way of introduction. "She was

so tired when we got back from the airport that she asked to go straight to bed."

He heard the relief in his own voice and wondered if Jesse could sense how little he knew about meeting the needs of a child like Megan. A ten-year-old girl hadn't been part of his modest plans for a life with no complications.

"She's afraid of the dark," Jesse murmured.

It was a simple remark, but Jesse made it as if she'd experienced that fear herself.

"Not an unusual reaction," he said, "given her recent loss."

"Her grandmother," Jesse said. "Were they very close?"

Al tried to remember when he'd ever seen warmth in his late brother's mother-in-law. They hadn't met often over the years. "I doubt it," he said. "She spent a lot of time in boarding schools. Until recently she was with other relatives, but they couldn't keep her."

"Poor kid." Jesse leaned her head against the door-jamb. "I'm sorry."

Of course Jesse would understand. She'd been in foster homes, bounced from one place to another. She would know how Megan felt. She would know how to handle a little girl. How to make a kid feel welcome, and happy, as Al could not.

"I have a sitter coming in to look after her tomorrow, while I'm at the library," he said. "Megan is quite withdrawn. I haven't been able to reach her. I think she needs someone else to . . . talk to."

"You're her uncle," Jesse said. "Family."

He clutched his empty sleeve with his good hand. "That's not always enough."

"But you are a psychologist, Al. You could—"

"I know my limitations. A woman might do better with her."

She backed away from the bedroom, averting her face. "Maybe I can drop in tomorrow. If you think it'll do any good, considering . . ." She trailed off, but Al knew how she was judging herself, finding herself inadequate. Or worse.

"I have no doubts about your mental competence, Jesse," he said.

But she turned for the back door without another word, and as he watched her start across the open field to her cabin, he was bemused to find in himself an unanticipated insight that had very little to do with intellect and nothing at all to do with logic.

Something new had awakened in Jesse Copeland. He had witnessed a birth there in his study, when she'd spoken to people she saw only in her mind. Or in her memory. He had felt it in the shiver down his spine—a feeling he hadn't experienced since Vietnam.

Al relied on facts, on what he could see and touch and analyze. But what Jesse had discovered was not so easily bound within those walls of rationality. She was no longer as safe as she wanted to be.

Perhaps she'd never be "safe" again.

Al closed the door and stared at the smooth wood. For the first time in decades he envied those who knew the comfort of blind faith.

⊗ ⊗

SHE'D LIED TO AL. It was a strange thing, to lie—to deliberately withhold the truth from the one man she thought she trusted.

She'd lied to her hikers for the rest of their excursion earlier that afternoon—lied by behaving as if nothing had happened, as if she weren't desperately holding on until she could let herself react. None of her people guessed that she'd been shaken to the core. If she was a little quieter, a little more withdrawn, they hadn't noticed. She'd given them the spectacular views they wanted, and led them back to the Lodge without incident.

But *he* had been with her every step of the way. Even his disappearance hadn't brought relief.

She didn't whisper the name as she marched unseeing across the calf-high lawn, though that single word dominated her thoughts like a permanent lodger.

David.

Yes, she'd lied to Al. She knew that name. She had met its owner, a creature of myth and fairy tales, a soldier in an antique uniform who spoke as if he knew her, who began as misty illusion and crystallized into sudden, terrifying reality the moment she . . .

Touched him. No, that was too simple an expression for what had happened when she'd walked through the being who called himself David Ventris. There was no language to describe that moment of union, when she'd felt another . . . life, consciousness, spirit . . . join with her own.

And then the hypnosis, where she'd sought answers and found only more questions: disjointed impressions of yearning and pain and fear flooding through her, sweeping by too swiftly to grasp and hold. Most she could no longer recall, but she'd revealed only part of them to Al.

She hadn't told him that the person she'd been in those waking dreams wasn't herself. That she'd worn clothing and existed in a place that bore no resemblance to the world she knew.

And that, in some way she couldn't remember, David Ventris had been in those visions with her.

Jesse closed her eyes and stumbled over a buried tree stump halfway to her cabin. The jarring didn't knock sense into her brain. That sense was long, long gone.

If David had been sent as a test of her rationality, the results were inconclusive. A few seconds of sharing the same physical space with a ghost had almost convinced her that such supernatural entities actually existed, in spite of every logical assumption to the contrary. That David Ventris was as vital and alive in his way as she was in hers—a ghost possessing her dreams, her hypnotic memories, as if they'd shared something inexplicable but very real.

In her visions he'd been as familiar to her—to the person she'd been—as her own soul.

As if once . . . sometime, somewhere . . . she'd loved him.

Jesse shuddered and paused at her doorway. *"You called me,"* he had said. Called a man she'd hadn't "met" before a dream last night.

Did a ghost even qualify as a man?

She laughed weakly at her own absurdity and opened the door to her cabin. Sanctuary no longer, for he'd been there in her dreams, at her bedside.

As he was here now. Sitting at her table—sitting, solid as you please, holding yesterday's *Manzanita Herald* in his hands. Glancing up with a quizzical look, as if he had discovered an interesting item in the paper he was waiting to share with her.

He dropped the paper and rose, pushing back the chair. "Jesse," he said. "I've been waiting for you."

She didn't doubt it. There was something grotesquely appropriate in finding him here, invading her home once again as he had her body and her mind.

"Please forgive my informality," he continued, in the wake of her silence. "I didn't intend to leave you so abruptly before, but—" He gazed at her with eyes of a dazzling and vivid blue. "There are things we must discuss."

Jesse stood frozen in the doorway, her hand still on the knob and a frantic laugh stuck in her throat. She could run the other way, as she'd done on the hillside. She could make one final pitch for reason and sanity.

But the outrage at this further imposition bubbled over, and she slammed the door shut and strode recklessly toward him—stopping just short of any danger of accidental touch. She couldn't see through him now.

He was *real*.

"Tell me," she demanded, "can you just . . . pop up anywhere you like? Walk through walls, appear and disappear, with no regard for privacy? Or are there rules wherever you come from?"

"Then you do believe in me."

His question startled her anew. The way he said the words and his lopsided smile implied that her belief was very important to him. His grin was surprisingly engaging. It suggested goodwill and sincerity and a desire—a need—to be accepted.

Acceptance was too much to ask, but Jesse felt herself sucked into those eyes, seduced by that smile into an unwilling but undeniable belief. The fact that he was staggeringly handsome didn't help. Not Gary's slick good looks, but a devastating combination of boyish charm and seasoned maturity. His chin was firm, his brows thick and well shaped. His black hair was just a little too long, falling over his forehead. His face was darkly tanned, the eyes creased at the corners with sun wrinkles.

He wore the same uniform he'd had on this afternoon: short blue jacket with tarnished buttons and braid in horizontal stripes across the chest, a long and slightly curved sword that hung at his hip from a shoulder belt, snug light-colored trousers that hugged distinctly muscular legs, black spurred boots coated with dust. There were holes in the jacket and a patch on his trousers, but their raggedness made him seem more what he claimed to be.

A soldier. A soldier as Al had been, but from a war nearly two hundred years ago. In a faraway and different land.

"I don't know what to believe," she said slowly. "But after we—" No. She wouldn't talk about that mystical communion. She couldn't even think about it without shaking. If she treated this whole business as if it were the most ordinary thing in the world, she'd be more likely to get through it intact. "You seem to be able to . . . affect things. Doesn't that make you real?"

"Ah. The paper." He picked it up. It rustled in his hands. "I've been practicing. It's something of a skill to become solid. A chancy business, at best."

"Then you are a ghost."

"For lack of a better definition," he conceded with a wry twitch of his mouth.

She dared herself closer to the table. "You're here to haunt me. Is that it?"

He set the paper down and ruffled the pages. " 'Haunt' is such an unpleasant word."

"Unpleasant?" She laughed shortly. "What do you call this . . . barging into my life, invading my space, making me think I'm—" She stopped herself. *Calm.* "Don't ghosts haunt specific locations? I built this cabin myself. No one like you ever lived on this ground."

He refolded the paper and sat down again, his very tangible weight shifting the chair on the floor. "I've been reading about your village," he said, dodging her question. "It's rather discomposing to realize how much has changed since I was last . . . here. Of course, I didn't make it to the colonies."

"Before you . . . died."

"Another unpleasant word." He spread his hands flat on the table as if to test their substantiality. "But one with which I am somewhat familiar."

Jesse looked at his hands. Strong, long-fingered, scarred but elegant. His hands alone convinced her that he was no concoction of some personal psychosis.

"And where have you been all this time?" she asked, reluctantly fascinated.

His gaze met hers, its brilliance shadowed. "Ah, Jesse. There are places no mortal words can describe." One hand lifted to touch a hole in his blue coat. "Have you ever seen a battlefield?"

In the echo of his question she could have sworn she heard the staccato blasts of gunfire, the roar of cannon, the shrill whinny of a frightened horse, the screams of a dying man. She tasted dust in her mouth, felt the scorching heat of fire and a brutal sun on her skin.

She felt for the nearest chair. "I've seen death," she said. "I've seen places like battlefields, where the victims were innocent."

There was startlement in his eyes, as if he hadn't expected an answer. He didn't read minds, then. He didn't know of her past. He could walk through walls, in her dreams, through her body—but there were places even he couldn't go.

Yet the awkward intimacy between them felt remarkably potent, as if he were a long-lost lover turned up on her doorstep.

Jesse had no long-lost lovers.

"You said I called you here," she said.

He recovered his poise quickly enough. "You dreamed of me," he said softly.

There was no disputing that, no lying to him as she had to Al. "Yes. But until two nights ago, I'd never seen you even in my dreams. Why now?"

"You don't know . . . why you called my name," he said, watching her face.

She couldn't admit how little she did know. "*Are* you here to haunt me? What do you want?"

"There is much to explain, Jesse. Much even I don't understand—"

"You could start by telling me why the hell you've chosen the worst possible time to complicate my life. Why *me*, David Ventris?"

He looked toward the window and she saw the tension in his jaw, the telltale body language of someone hiding a vital truth. "If you would trust me—"

"Trust you?" She slammed her open hand on the table, inches from his. "Who *are* you? How does this work? Are you some distant ancestor I haven't even heard of? Or does everyone have their own personal ghost, and I'm the only one who can see mine?"

There was an answering flash of anger in his eyes. "I see that you won't accept what you can't immediately comprehend." He shook his head, just as suddenly contrite. "I'm not here to curse you. You have nothing to fear from me."

"Does that mean I have some control over this? Can I send you back to wherever you came from?"

"It isn't that simple."

"Are you telling me I need an exorcist or a . . . ghostbuster to get rid of you?"

"I've no doubt that you could send me back to perdition, Jesse." He trapped her with his eyes, holding her fast. "You wanted to know who I am? I'm a lost soul, and you are the key to my salvation." His voice, so properly British, held a false lightness that mocked his own words. "If you refuse me, I'm quite simply damned."

Of course. She'd envisioned a whole bizarre list of things a ghost might include in his conversation, melodramatic Dickensian statements that went hand in hand with popping in and out of thin air, perhaps accompanied by a good dose of chain rattling.

David wore no chains, but he hadn't disappointed her.

"Damned," she repeated. "But you didn't tell me where you go when you're not on Earth. Where you came from."

The planes of his handsome face took on a bleakness, a despair that transformed him from a man of confident ease to one whose gaze revealed long intimacy with pain. Jesse had seen that look too many times not to recognize it.

"I told you that there were no words," he said. "The place . . . is beyond your comprehension, Jesse. It is endless nothingless, eternal loneliness. I call it limbo, but it has no name. Or hope."

Before, when they'd touched on the hillside, she'd sensed David's very being. Now his portrayal came to life within her imagination, and she could *see* what he described. *Feel* what he felt in that place.

He had mentioned a battlefield, but this was far worse. Here there was no life or death, only unbearable isolation that went on forever.

So hopeless. So alone. No way out.

She could drown in those emotions as she drowned in his gaze. With a firm grasp on her will, she pulled herself out of his illusion.

"What did you do in your life," she said, "so terrible as to earn that kind of punishment?"

His gaze dropped to his clenched fists. "That is . . . the difficulty. I remember very little of my previous existence on Earth. I know only that when you called my name, I was able to return. I was given another chance."

"A chance . . . to do what?"

"My memory doesn't tell me." He looked at her again, as intently as before. "In . . . that other place, I lost myself. Now that I'm here, I am just beginning to regain what I was. And I am convinced that *you* have my answers, Jesse."

It seemed both bizarre and appropriate that she should be haunted by a ghost who claimed to have lost his memory, when she was in the process of rebuilding her own.

But he actually thought she could provide answers for him. A man who called himself damned.

"I don't have any answers," she said. "Not yours or anyone's. I don't know why this is happening, but I can't help you. I . . ."

Have enough troubles of my own, she finished silently. But he was staring at her, swallowing her up in that piercing blue.

"I don't believe that," he said. "There's generosity in your soul. Too much to refuse help to one who needs you." He held out his hand in a gesture of supplication, fingers cupped. "You won't turn your back on suffering. Not even mine."

"How do you know?" she asked with a touch of bitterness.

"I saw you on the hill with your troops," he said. "They followed you as men follow a leader they trust with their lives. One who cares for them, protects them."

She couldn't meet his gaze. "You don't remember your own life on Earth," she said, "but you're so sure of me."

"One must be sure of something, even when all else is gone. Isn't that true, Jesse?"

Oh, yes, he knew that need; he spoke as a man who had struggled against all hope to find something to put his faith in. As if suffering had been his lot far longer than human life could compass.

For years, working with the Corps, Jesse had tried to relieve what misery she could, in countries where such misery was as common as hunger and injustice. She'd been careful to keep a little of herself apart, because to do otherwise meant losing the detachment that let her function. As she'd lost it with Bobby Moran.

Now, if she allowed it, she could slide right into the all too personal pain of a man who wasn't even alive.

She closed her eyes. "Why me?"

"Because we have a connection, you and I." She heard the skidding thump of the chair as he stood. "I don't know what it is, but I feel it. As you do. You couldn't have called me otherwise. And what happened on the hillside . . ."

Oh, God. "It's crazy," she said. "Crazy—"

"No." He moved closer to her, boots clicking on the floor. She could feel the flesh-and-blood nearness of his presence, his face inches from hers. "No, Jesse. Don't."

Her heart pounded in her throat. *Don't,* he told her, but she didn't know what he commanded. With an effort she shut off her emotions and opened her eyes. He was very close: his eyes, his mouth, his formidable reality. She could hear his breathing, as rapid as her own.

"Don't deny it, Jesse," he said. "Don't deny *me*."

Before she could think to pull away, he seized her wrist. There was no sharing of space now, no arcane overlapping. His hand was warm and firm and strong. She felt the brush of scars and callused fingers.

Masculine. Intimate. His touch cut to the very quick of her, spiraled in a wild electric dance through every nerve of her body.

It had never happened to her before. Never. She'd long ago accepted that there was a part of herself no man could reach.

David reached it. He reached it and grasped it and claimed it for his own.

She snatched her hand free, but the tingles and pulses and sparks left her too dizzy to stand. She staggered, and

David skirted the table to catch her. She dodged him and found refuge against the wall.

God help her. She closed her eyes again, but the visions were waiting. And David was always there.

Yet suddenly another name took shape in her mind, a name she'd heard David speak on the mountainside but hadn't remembered until this moment. A name that meant something, that seemed to hold a hope of understanding.

"Who is Sophie?" she whispered.

CHAPTER FOUR

S O SHE HAD heard him.

He hadn't meant to speak that other name aloud. It had been carelessness to voice his thoughts when he'd realized, almost from the beginning, that she must not know the truth.

Perhaps he'd gone too far, and too swiftly. She'd broken away, rejecting his frontal attack, yet the vibrant force of her life itself still coursed through him from the simple touch they'd just shared. It pulsed in his heart and lungs and nerves and groin, as heady as an overabundance of whiskey or a dangerous escapade taken a step beyond recklessness. He felt the pull of it long after he turned to the window and hid his face from her searching gaze.

He'd nearly forgotten himself in that touch. Her pointed question was a warning that it was time for a strategic retreat.

"Sophie," he repeated, crafting the illusion of puzzled reflection. "It sounds . . . somewhat familiar to me."

Jesse's footsteps moved across the polished wooden floor behind him. "You called me that on the hillside, as if you thought I were someone else."

He had no intention of answering honestly. "Someone else," he said, staring out at the twilit darkness. "It's possible . . . the name is one piece of that memory I must find."

"Someone in your previous life," she said. "A woman. And I reminded you of her. The way you said it . . . She was important to you."

She spoke with a still, grave certainty. Was it her soul's memory, unacknowledged? Could she sense so much?

"You already guess far more than I do," he said, "but I believe you may be right." He turned halfway, offering a crooked smile. "You see? You can help me, Jesse."

"Help you to remember your life?" She laughed humorlessly. "Maybe you'll understand my skepticism when I tell you that there are parts of my own life I can barely remember. And I'm no ghost."

By God, no, she was not. Jesse *was* life. She was the symbol of what he'd lost and what he must regain. She was the plan and the battle and the victory all in one stubborn body and soul.

Life.

"I do understand," he said. He lowered his voice to a seductive murmur. "Another reason we've been drawn together. We have a great deal in common, and there's so much more to discover." He moved back to the table, noting the way she kept it between them to forestall any further risk of a touch.

Afraid, but not of him. And she hated being afraid as he hated the fetters that tied him to limbo.

"You have power you don't even know you possess," he said with perfect candor. "And it's not in you to run. Is it, Jesse?"

She jerked her head in denial, mouth set. "Whatever

I . . . imagined, whatever you may believe, I'm not in
the business of saving souls."

"Not even your own?"

Her flinch spoke volumes. It had been a shot in the
dark, a blind guess, but now he knew he was right. Jesse
was more than merely afraid. He'd been thrown on the
mercy of a woman deeply troubled—forced to win not
only her acceptance, but her goodwill and trust. And
there was no trust in her eyes.

Surely they were laughing at him, those grim guardians
of his prison. His punishment was far from over.

"Perhaps," he said, "we're meant to help each other."

For a moment, just a moment, he thought he saw a
softening in her gaze—as he'd seen on the hillside just
before he'd left her, or when he'd held her hand. The
fragile, trembling hope of a child offered unexpected
comfort, or a soldier given a second chance at survival
after a deadly skirmish.

But she shrugged, throwing off the fleeting vulnerability like an overladen pack. "What makes you think I
need help? I'm not the one who's damned." She strode
across the room, vanishing into the small, oddly
equipped kitchen. David heard the sound of running water and the click of a glass. When she returned, she was
firmly entrenched behind a shield of false nonchalance.

"Oh," she said, "I might find you useful if·I could send
you out to haunt someone on command. That's the only
practical function I can think of for a ghost."

"Indeed," he said, watching her with narrowed eyes.
"And who would you send me to haunt? Have you enemies, Jesse?"

He saw her answer in the stiffening of her shoulders
and the rise of her chin. But she wasn't going to admit
anything so personal to him. Not yet.

"An army of ghosts would have been useful in the
Peninsula," he said, easing around the table. "Boney's
soldiers were as superstitious as the next man. We'd have
won the war in half the time."

Jesse had fortified herself against a recessed shelf of

books that David had perused earlier. Her collection included volumes on carpentry and wilderness survival—odd choices for a woman.

But David already knew she was no ordinary woman. *What battle are you fighting, Jesse? How do I make you put it aside long enough to set me free?*

"Did you die in the war?" she asked. "Or don't you remember that?"

The suddenness of her question made him pause, just long enough for her to slip through the door into the next room. He followed, smelling the faint tang of sawdust and some spicier scent mingled with the ubiquitous evergreen and grass and fresh air. The main room of her cottage was as compact and unadorned as the rest, furnished with a small sofa, a rather plain armchair, more shelves and a few unfamiliar objects he had yet to name.

Jesse didn't pause in the room but walked through yet another door. This was the source of the sawdust scent: a workshop filled with furniture in various stages of completion, assorted pieces of wood and tools for cutting and shaping. Wide windows looked out over a cluster of trees, barely visible as silhouettes on a background of indigo sky and the first glimmer of stars.

"That is one event I can hardly forget," David said, stopping just inside the door. "You have heard of Waterloo?"

"I've heard of it." She was sorting and stacking small sheets of rough paper in rows along a worktable, compulsively precise in every movement. "Wasn't it the last engagement of your war?"

My war, he thought with dark irony. *If only it had ended there.* "I didn't know it then," he said. "It was a terrible battle. I learned only after my death that Wellington was victorious. A French musket ball made sure of that."

For the first time in many minutes she looked at him. "Did you . . . die a hero?"

He couldn't miss her tone of oddly innocent yearning. Was it a hero she was after? He was bound to disappoint her. But she didn't have to know how little heroism there'd been in throwing himself in the path of certain death.

To make it stop. To end the guilt and the meaninglessness of life, only to realize too late what he'd traded for in exchange.

"I served my country," he said. "I fought for many years. That I know."

She stared at him for several more heartbeats and then down at the worktable. He noticed that the nails on her small fingers were short, practical, more suited for labor than for the social rounds Sophie had once enjoyed. But Jesse wouldn't worry for hours about the drape of her gown or the arrangement of her hair or the perfect *bon mot*.

Sophie had wanted to please everyone with authority: the witches at Almacks, the leading bucks of the *ton*, the peers with more rank and power and money. She'd fawned on anyone who could give her approval.

Jesse didn't want his approval. He had to make her want it. Want to keep him with her as long as it took.

"I was good at leading men," he said, crouching to examine the legs of a sturdy, unpainted chair. "They trusted me. They knew I wouldn't take them anywhere I wouldn't go alone."

"So you remember your years as a soldier, but nothing before?"

Under the level tone of her question was the sharp thrust of a bayonet. He rose, dusting his trousers. He felt sawdust on his hands; he rubbed the texture of it between his fingers, savoring the very fact that he could.

"Not yet," he said. "But it will come." He met her gaze. "I can see from your window that the night is beautiful, Jesse. Come walk with me. I find I have a dislike for walls." With deliberate steps he approached her, passed her by as she stood very still, opened the workshop door and walked out.

She followed, as he'd known she would. Her footsteps skimmed the long grass with the hesitance of a doe's. He didn't look back but continued up the gentle slope of the hillside behind her cottage, toward the cluster of pines.

The evening breeze was cool, and there was enough moonlight to mark his path. David remembered nights like these with Sophie, when they'd both been foolish enough to believe in romance. On such a hillside he'd lain with her, had planted a seed in her body.

Elizabeth. Elizabeth who'd lived but one short year.

"What will happen when you recover your memory?"

Jesse had come up behind him, and he sat down beside a thorny flowered shrub, stretching his legs. He could see the lights of the village, scattered like embers and burning with the perpetual glow of some new science.

He plucked a serrated leaf from the shrub. "My answers will be there," he said. "Just as yours are in the memories you've lost."

She stood over him, unmoving. "You *can't* read my mind," she said at last. "You'd better understand right now that I didn't ask you to come here. You're the one who needs me."

The leaf tore under the pressure of his fingers. "And there's a price for your help."

"There are rules," she said. "And I want to get them very clear. You said you didn't intend to leave me so abruptly before. Does that mean you don't have control over your coming and going?"

"I only know that after a time I . . . lose my strength on this plane and must return to the place I came from," he said, plucking a second leaf. "There *are* rules, and I'm just beginning to learn them myself."

"Then how *do* you come here?"

He looked up. "You always bring me back."

Her profile was frosted in moonlight, and he felt rather than saw her tension. "And am I the only one who can see you? My hikers didn't notice you. Yet you're . . . almost solid."

"If I exert enough will, I can alter my form and give myself substance. I can do this"—he tore the leaf in half—"if I concentrate. But I suspect that it is my proximity to you that makes so much possible."

Her gaze dropped to his fingers on the leaf. "I don't want you showing yourself to anyone else. That has to be part of the deal."

The corner of his mouth twitched. "I'm your ghost, Jesse. I'd hazard a guess that no one else could see me, even if I willed it so."

Slowly she sank into a crouch, poised on that knife edge between acceptance and rejection, relaxation and flight. "Even if you can walk through walls, there is such a thing as common courtesy. And privacy." She stared at him, and he imagined a blush heating her tanned skin. "I want some warning before you barge in out of nowhere. And if you can make yourself invisible . . . if you have any sense of honor, you won't—"

She broke off, flustered, and he grinned to himself. *Ah, but I've seen much of you already,* he thought, remembering the way she'd looked in that nightshirt the first time, all curves and softness.

And he wanted to see more. His smile faded. She was wise to warn him, and a fool to call upon his honor.

"Shall I scratch on your door and beg admittance?" he asked.

"Knocking will be just fine. Or rattling your chains, or whatever it is ghosts do."

A joke? David searched her face, but the light was too dim to be sure. If she could unbend enough to make jests . . .

"The chains are invisible, Jesse," he said. "But you can break them."

She plunged her hands into the grass at her feet, curling her fingers against the earth. "Don't expect too much, Captain."

"David. You did call me that."

"A ghost by any other name," she murmured, and gave a short laugh. But her voice dropped very low when she spoke again. "David."

"It's been long since I've heard a woman speak my name," he said, equally hushed. "You do it well."

Her breath caught. "Don't push me. Don't . . . repeat what you did in the cabin."

Their touching, she meant. That moment of intimacy that couldn't be denied. It must have affected her strongly indeed to compel such a tacit admission.

Warnings. He walked a fine knife's edge himself.

"You're all I have, Jesse," he said.

She turned her face away. "Didn't you learn in your war that it's dangerous to rely too much on anyone? Or is that what got you killed?"

"And what taught you never to trust?"

Handfuls of grass came up as she pushed to her feet. "There's something else you'd better understand. If you did something so terrible that you deserved the punishment you're suffering, I won't be the one to absolve you of it. I believe that people pay for what they do. If there's any justice in the world—" She let the torn blades fall to the ground. "If there's any justice, evil is punished."

He rose with the speed of movement he'd learned in the war, still remembered by his ghostly form. "Look at me, Jesse. Do you believe I'm evil?"

Her glance brushed his face but refused to linger. He would have seized her had she run, despite her warnings, but she stood very still and waited for the reassurances that would convince her of his worth.

Yes, his gaolers were laughing. They'd assigned him a harsh judge indeed.

"Whatever sins I may have committed," he said, "is not nearly two centuries of prison punishment enough?"

"I don't know. How can I?"

Her anguish touched something within him, slipping through his own defenses, his own overwhelming need for what he must win from her. She suffered; he could offer comfort. It was in his power. Long after Sophie's death, when he had no distraction from memory, he'd tormented himself with thoughts of how he could have comforted her when she'd begged for it.

But Sophie's need had threatened to engulf him in a morass of despair. He'd spent his life staying one step ahead of that ravenous demon. There was no greater danger to him now than caring about this woman, becoming involved in her pain beyond what he must understand to liberate himself.

"I'm not wrong about you, Jesse," he said. *"They* weren't wrong when they sent me to you."

"Who?" Her fists tightened into knots at her sides. "Who sent you?"

"I never see them. They leave me alone in my punishment. Except this one time when they allowed me to return."

"Then it's not *my* forgiveness you require," she said. "I'll do . . . what I can. That's all I can promise."

"I ask no more."

"And if I choose to send you back—" She met his gaze with a fierce intensity. "For whatever reason, you have to go. Do you agree to my terms?"

So it was in war, whether fought with words and wits or muskets and swords. Terms and feints and retreats. Jesse sensed that they were adversaries, and yet she was willing to risk helping him when she had no incentive to do so.

Except for that connection between them she couldn't possibly understand. A connection David could not afford to forget but must never allow to weaken his resolve. And he had no doubt that if she commanded him to leave her, he would be forced to obey.

He must make sure she never gave that command.

"Very well," he said. "I accept. And in exchange . . ." He looked at the shrub whose branches he'd been slowly denuding of leaves. He'd barely noted the pale blossoms; now he recognized them for what they were.

Wild roses. The blossoms were simple, but they were roses nonetheless. Sophie had loved her roses.

Carefully David chose a slender flower stem and took it in his fingers. He felt the cool life of it, exerted his will and snapped it clean.

"In exchange," he repeated softly, "I offer you the only thing I have to give. My friendship."

And before Jesse could move away, he closed the space between them, offered the flower with a half bow and a warm look that belied that small formality.

Jesse stared at the rose. Her hand moved of its own accord, fingers twitching at the last minute to avoid touching his as she took the stem.

"Thank you," she said, with as much hesitation as if he'd asked her to lie with him in the long grass. The thought did not go unremarked by his not-so-spectral body, but the proof of his desire was hidden by the darkness.

"Roses," she said. "I dreamed . . ."

"A garden," he said. He picked a second rose for himself, raised it to his nose. "I remember roses in a garden. Not wild like this, but grown with care. And there was a fountain—"

Jesse gasped and dropped her blossom. She put her finger to her mouth. David was near enough to see the flick of her tongue, the white flash of her teeth.

"A thorn?" he asked. She shook her head, but he ignored the unspoken warning and came closer still, close enough to see the tiny dark bead on her fingertip.

"Forgive me my carelessness," he said. "Let me help you."

He took her stiff hand in his and turned it palm up. Her fingers curled away from him. But when he lifted her hand, she didn't resist, not even when he brought it to his mouth.

His tongue tasted blood. He knew blood so well. He'd seen his fill of it in war, envisioned Sophie's blood on his hands.

Jesse's was as exquisite as the finest claret.

"Don't," she whispered. "It's nothing."

The urge was powerful, irresistible: to take her in his arms, master her with passion so that she could deny him nothing. Reckless, hotheaded, irresponsible—all he'd been in life and could resume so easily.

He folded her fingers close to her palm and let her go. "One forgets that roses have thorns."

"It's a good thing to remember," she said. "Thank you for reminding me." She turned and started down the hill, crushing the fallen rose under her foot.

"Can there be beauty without risk?" he called after her.

"There is no risk if you know what you're doing."

"Then I'm in excellent hands."

She swung around, stepping out of his path. "I think we've talked enough for tonight. You'd better go and—recharge your batteries, or whatever it is you have to do."

She was right. He had to go back; already he could feel the toll of his extended physicality, a pulling from that other place. The fear rose in him: fear of that nothingness, knowing it would become more and more unbearable with every day spent on Earth.

"Then I'll return tomorrow," he said. "In the morning—"

"No. I have to work. I'll—call you when I'm ready."

He bowed. "As you say. But don't expect me to enjoy the separation. If only you knew—"

"Jesse? Is that you?"

The voice was not one David recognized, but at the sound of it Jesse threw him a look of panic and made a chopping gesture that couldn't be misinterpreted.

It was easier now for David to alter his form. He made himself fade, though he knew the woman coming up the hill would not be able to see him.

"Kim," Jesse said. She cleared her throat and stepped squarely in front of David. "This is a surprise."

"Sorry it's so late." Kim looked past Jesse up the hill, squinting against the darkness. She was taller than Jesse, bigger boned, attractive in an earthy way that reminded David of the women who'd followed the army in Spain and Portugal.

"I found your invitation to my engagement party buried under junk on my desk," Kim said, "and I wanted to make sure you got it." She held out an envelope. "It's tomorrow night, at Blue Rock. I hope you can come on such short notice."

Jesse took the envelope and held it in both hands. "To-morrow night? I'm not sure—"

"I know I screwed up, but it would mean a lot to me if you came." Kim grinned. "Eric has never met you, and he's such a great guy. I want to show him off. By this time you probably wonder if he even exists."

Jesse almost looked over her shoulder and stopped herself, tensing with the effort. "I'd like to meet him. I don't see why I can't come."

"Fantastic. I've reserved the pool deck and the main room at the Lodge for the evening; it should be fun." She cast another glance behind Jesse. "Seven o'clock. Let's hope no one calls for search and rescue in the middle of the celebration." Her pleasant mouth grew serious. "How are you doing with that, Jesse? Are you okay?"

"Yes. Fine."

"Good." She scuffed her foot on the grass. "Tell me if this is too personal, but are you seeing someone?"

Jesse grew very still. "Why do you ask?"

"I . . . thought I heard you talking to someone up here. I didn't mean to eavesdrop."

"No," Jesse said sharply. "There was no one."

"Sorry. I didn't mean—"

"It's nothing. I talk to myself sometimes." She smiled and waved vaguely toward the mountains. "You know how it is."

"Sure." Kim wrapped her arms around herself and shivered. "It's cold up here. You'd think I'd know enough to bring a jacket. Well, I'd better get going. See you tomorrow night."

"Later. And thanks for the invitation." Jesse watched Kim pick her way down the hillside, her own arms drawn across her chest. Only after Kim was safely out of sight did she turn.

"Are you still here?" she asked.

David had the sudden insight that he'd be wiser to

maintain his invisibility. There was no welcome for him now.

"They called me crazy once," Jesse said to the air. "Did you know that, David Ventris? It's not going to happen again."

And she marched the rest of the way down the hill, walked into her cottage, and shut the door.

⚛ ⚛

MARIE'S DAMNED LACY curtains let in the sunlight, but that wasn't what woke Gary up. His alarm was much more pleasant, and Marie's mouth surprisingly expert.

Gary stretched and closed his eyes. He was always hard and aching in the morning; it wouldn't be difficult to let this go to its inevitable conclusion. He liked the idea of filling Marie's pretty mouth with everything he could give her.

He opened one eye to glance at the clock beside the bed. Damn. Nearly ten o'clock. He could stay in bed and screw Marie all day as he'd done all night, but his business in town still wasn't finished.

With a low grunt he grabbed Marie's shoulders. "Sorry, baby. Much as I'd like to oblige your appetites, I have other things on the menu today."

Marie rocked back, straddling his thighs and giving him a very tempting view of what she had so enthusiastically offered last night. Her hand wrapped around him possessively. "You have somewhere important to go?"

"Duty calls." He sat up, giving Marie another moment or two. Her long peach nails were pale against the flush of his shaft. "Don't you have your restaurant to open up?"

"We're closed Wednesdays."

Gary almost reconsidered, but he hadn't gotten where he was by indulging himself every time he got the urge. Not for many years now.

"Why don't you be a good girl and make me some coffee," he said. "Seems I was up all night."

She shrugged, though the look in her eyes was sharp. "Your loss." She dismounted and slipped from the bed, casually retrieving her black lace negligee from the antique chair in the corner of the bedroom. Expensive tastes, Marie had; more Bloomingdale's than backwater country. And ambitions. Too bad she didn't have Heather's money.

Too bad he wasn't as generous as she probably thought he was.

He got up and pulled on his briefs and trousers. The scent of strong black coffee drifted in from Marie's kitchen. He sat down at the table and watched her move about, noting the exaggerated sway of her hips.

"You have any plans for tonight?" she asked.

"That depends." He sipped the coffee. Just right. Maybe he should consider making Marie a permanent addition to his entourage. It wouldn't be difficult to persuade her; her fancy restaurant wouldn't last a year in this hick town. Heather was frigid as hell and couldn't make a good cup of coffee to save her life. . . .

"I was just talking to my friend Kim," Marie said, draping herself across the opposite chair. "She's invited me to her engagement party tonight. I can bring a guest."

So Marie wanted to make her liaison with him public. Already she had expectations, even if they were only to draw attention to the restaurant and glean a little reflected glory at the side of Manzanita's new celebrity.

"Who's Kim?" he asked.

"We both came to Manzanita around the same time, about three years ago. She works up at the Lodge." Her lids dropped over her eyes. "You know, with Jesse Copeland."

"Oh?"

"I heard you were asking about Jesse," Marie said, matching his indifferent tone. "News spreads fast, and you're big news."

"And what have you heard about me and Miss Copeland?"

If she noticed the edge in his words, she didn't let on.

"That you have some kind of history together. She was a kid when you knew her. And you were with her mother. She committed suicide, didn't she?"

"You've been a busy little girl." Gary set down his cup and smiled at her. "It's no secret. I came to Manzanita when I was in my twenties, looking for work. Jesse's mother was kind enough to give me a job at her resort. We became friends, and then . . ." He sighed. "Joan was a drinker. Impulsive, emotional. She needed help, and I tried to help her. She didn't know how to manage the resort and it was losing money. I did what I could."

"And Jesse?"

"Strange, troubled kid. Her father abandoned them several years before. I'm afraid she never did like me. Or any man." He gazed into his empty mug. "I tried to show Joan how she was hurting herself and Jesse with her behavior, tried to help her make the resort profitable again. But she'd already chosen her path. One day she got bad news from the bank, and while I was away—"

"She killed herself." Marie shuddered.

"They called it an accidental death. She drowned in the river. Her blood was full of alcohol. It would have killed her if the river hadn't."

Marie got up and made some busy work at the counter. "I heard that something happened between you and Jesse at her mother's funeral."

"Her attack on me, you mean. I'm afraid the child was too grief-stricken to be quite sane at the time. I would have helped her, but whenever I came near her she had hysterics. I had to leave town, for her sake, but I've never forgotten."

"And that's why you're so interested in her now."

Interested. Gary coldly considered the word. No. He'd never been *interested* in Jesse Copeland. Or her mother, beyond what conveniences she could provide at a time when he needed a place to hole up.

Jesse had been a hostile, angry child—always watching him, condemning, as if she had the power to see through his pretense as no one else could.

To hell with that. The girl hadn't been psychic, only unbalanced. She meant nothing to him, except as an inconvenience to be dealt with.

And yet she remained lodged in his thoughts, bound to his inexplicably rekindled fear of exposure. As if a child he'd nearly forgotten, this woman he didn't know, had some claim on him, had the power to make him feel . . .

He shook his head sharply and turned his attention back to Marie. "I didn't know Jesse was here until I arrived," he lied with the ease of long practice. "I'd hoped to speak to her, but if she still hates me as she did then—"

"You'll get a chance to find out if you come to Kim's party," Marie said. She turned to lean back against the counter, her expression deceptively cool. "Then you can forget about her."

Gary pushed away from the table. "Don't you worry, little girl. One Copeland was enough for me." He strolled to Marie and caught her face between his hands, kissed her hard the way she liked it. After she was gasping for breath, he released her and went to the bedroom for his shirt and jacket.

She trailed after him. "I don't think Kim knows about you and Jesse, except that you knew each other once. But she did mention she was worried about how Jesse's acting lately, ever since the Moran kid's funeral."

"Did she?" Gary buttoned his shirt in front of Marie's ornate full-length mirror and smoothed a wrinkle in his sleeve. "And how is Jesse acting?"

"Kim told me she heard Jesse talking to herself last night, up on the hill behind her cabin. As if she was having a conversation with someone who wasn't there."

Gary closed his eyes. "Just like her mother."

"So why waste your time worrying about her? She's not your responsibility." Marie linked her arm through his, rubbing her breast against his ribs. "There's a lot better things you could be doing."

Jesus, yes. This party Marie mentioned—it would be the perfect opportunity to confront Jesse. Test her. Uncover anything she might be hiding. And then exorcise her from his thoughts forever.

"Oh, I'm not worried." He cupped Marie's breast in his hand and squeezed. She bit her lip with a wince, but he knew she liked it rough. Just like Joan Copeland.

He let her go and shrugged into his jacket. "I enjoyed our rendezvous, Marie. You're a very talented girl. I hate to see you waste yourself on this town."

"Maybe I won't have to."

"Anything's possible." He looked into her eyes, hinting at promises as potent as any aphrodisiac. "You get your beauty sleep, babe. We'll have a nice *private* dinner at your restaurant tonight, and we'll go to the party. But don't tell Kim I'm coming. Let's make it our surprise."

She followed him to the door and watched him walk to his car, was still waiting as he backed from the narrow gravel driveway. By the time he left the side street and pulled out onto the highway, he'd put her from his mind.

But Jesse was there in Marie's place, ready to haunt him again. Gary gripped the steering wheel until his fingers went numb.

How would she react tonight? What would she do when they stood face to face after seventeen years?

It was a calculated risk. He knew damned well that she hadn't seen more than a glimpse of Hatch when he'd turned up at the resort seventeen years ago, and certainly none of what happened afterward. But if she did know something and blurted it out tonight . . .

Why, everyone knew she was crazy.

CHAPTER FIVE

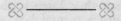

JESSE ARRIVED AT Al's study an hour before their seven o'clock appointment, another day's work behind her and a hundred unanswered questions seething in her mind.

She paused at the door to organize her thoughts and count her blessings. At least she hadn't run into Gary. Avoiding her, maybe, which could be good or bad news.

It could be proof that her gut feelings were right.

And David Ventris had been as good as his word. He had left her alone. Not that her solitude had been peaceful. When she wasn't keeping herself busy with the Lodge guests, her mind was constantly wandering back to her conversation with David. The way he looked. The rich timbre of his voice. The seductiveness of his touch, that had resonated through her body as no other man's touch had done.

He had too much effect on her, after only two meetings, when she'd barely come to accept that he was real.

She both dreaded and anticipated their next rendezvous, and her very ambivalence was troubling in itself. How could one be attracted to a ghost? She had to keep careful control over the situation, never let it get out of hand, remember the bargain they'd struck. She had to compartmentalize David into a mental box where he couldn't interfere with her other goals.

And tonight . . .

She'd insisted on this second hypnosis session in spite of Al's better judgment. This time she *had* to remember her childhood.

Focus. Focus on my past.

Nevertheless, she'd come early to spend an hour or so with Al's computer. He had access to the Internet. If there was any information to be found about a man named David Ventris, or his family, it might be somewhere in that vast and intimidating web of electronic data.

If she could figure out how to get to it. Jesse walked through the door and started for Al's vast desk.

The chair in front of it was already occupied. On the seat was a child—a ten-year-old girl with blunt-cut brown hair and glasses, legs folded beneath her, who stared into the bright screen of the computer with a concentration that admitted no intrusions.

Megan. Jesse stopped to observe the girl, reluctant to interrupt. Megan was small for her age, thin, barely level with the computer. She wore a loose T-shirt a size too large and baggy pants. Her fingers were nimble on the keyboard, an adult's sureness in their movements. The glow from the screen reflected on her glasses, obscuring her eyes.

A lump tightened Jesse's throat. For a moment she imagined herself as a child sitting in Megan's place, adrift in her own world, though she'd never owned a computer. She'd had the woods, the hills, a different kind of flight from loneliness.

So much had been taken from Megan, but her loneliness could be eased; Jesse could do something about it.

Maybe not much—maybe she wasn't wise enough to help a child in pain. Not strong enough, haunted as she was by her past and a very persistent ghost. But she'd been handed a chance, here and now.

And she'd promised to try.

"Megan?"

The girl went still, hands suspended above the keys. Jesse moved around behind her. There were graphics of animals on the screen: running wolves beneath explanatory boxes of text.

A flick of Megan's finger on the plastic mouse beside the keyboard and the image disappeared, replaced by a list of what Jesse recognized as Internet addresses. Slowly Megan swiveled around in the chair. Her eyes were dark gray, but the too cumbersome tortoiseshell glasses swallowed them up. Her small mouth was expressionless.

"Hello," Jesse said, squatting to Megan's level. "I'm Jesse. Maybe Al's mentioned me. I live—"

"I know who you are," Megan said. She looked Jesse over without a trace of curiosity or welcome. "Al's not here right now."

"I know." Jesse straightened and looked at the screen. "Actually, I came in here to try to use the computer. You seem to know how to do it pretty well."

Megan shrugged. "It's easy. What do you need it for?"

A trace of sharpness there, guarding her territory. Jesse knew that feeling too well. When you were abandoned, when you'd lost a little too much, you carved out your own space with ferocious determination and held it against all odds.

"I only wanted to borrow it to get some information," Jesse said. "About a person from the past. Is that possible?"

"You can do anything on the Internet."

"I wish I knew more about it, but I'm an amateur. How did you learn?"

"A little in class, and I did the rest on my own." Megan swung back to the screen. "I had to use the ones

at school. Grandma didn't have a computer. She thought
it was a waste of money."

Jesse almost asked Megan about her grandma. A child
who'd recently lost her caretaker of many years would
need to talk about that loss, and she doubted Al had
made much progress. He'd said he couldn't reach
Megan.

But something held Jesse back. It was too soon. She
had to let Megan get to know her first. And it seemed
very, very important that she make that connection—a
gut-level feeling, like the ones she'd had about David. Or
Gary.

The difference was that Megan was a child, and Jesse
could call the shots.

"You know, I think I'm going to need some help with
this," Jesse said. "I'm a little intimidated."

The look Megan cast her was dubious at best—testing
for condescension or an adult's hidden agenda. Incipient
rebuff was in Megan's stiff posture and pinched face. She
hesitated, biting her lower lip between slightly crooked
front teeth. "Do you . . . want me to show you?"

An opening. A hint of trust. Jesse nodded and came to
stand beside Megan. "Thanks. I'll watch you, and maybe
I'll learn something."

"Who do you want to look up?"

"A man named David Ventris. Lord . . . Ashthorpe, I
think. He lived in the early 1800s, in England. He was a
soldier who fought Napoleon, but I don't think he was
famous. Is that something I can find?"

"Maybe. It might take a lot of looking." Megan
frowned and clicked the mouse. The screen changed to a
page with bands of color, playful lettering, and the words
"Net Search" at the top.

"You can type in the subject here," Megan said. She
moved the mouse and positioned the blinking cursor in a
blank space. "The best kind of site might be genealogy,
since he lived a long time ago. Is he someone from your
family?"

"No. Just someone I was curious about."

Megan typed in the word "genealogy" and clicked the mouse. A few seconds later there was a new list of addresses. Megan scrolled to the bottom of the screen and typed "England" in another blank space.

"Eighty-eight entries on that subject you can check," Megan said, "but some of them are for specific names. There's a genealogy home page, here. Or you can e-mail one of these people." She indicated one of the addresses with a bitten fingernail. "People who do research on stuff like that."

Jesse considered the screen dubiously. Megan was right; it would probably take a lot of looking, something she'd have to do in her spare time.

And what would it prove in the end? That David Ventris was real? She'd already accepted that. She had no reason to doubt his stories of what little past he remembered.

"Thanks," she said. "At least now I know where to start." She crouched again, taking note of Megan's sneakers. They were hot pink—a tiny shout of defiance amid the drab anonymity of Megan's other clothing.

"How do you like Manzanita so far, Megan?"

Megan's shoulders rolled forward in a hunch, away from Jesse. "How should I know? Al won't let me out of the house."

Al. Not Uncle Al, or any indication of a feeling of closeness. Or family.

"He runs the library," Jesse said. "There wouldn't be one in this town without him. He probably thought you needed to rest after coming here."

"I know how busy he is," Megan said. "He doesn't want me."

The bluntness of the words chilled Jesse. "Why do you think that?"

"He likes to be alone. He doesn't want a kid around." Megan moved the cursor on the screen and clicked the mouse until the monitor went dark. "I didn't want to come. I didn't ask him to let me live here."

Jesse swallowed and kept her hands on her knees so

that she wouldn't reach out and hug Megan with all her strength. Too soon. She'd scare the girl off for certain.

"He's your uncle," she said as evenly as she could. "He cares about you. He just doesn't know how to show it. Maybe you both need some time to get used to each other."

"When the summer's over I can go back to school," Megan said. "Then we'll both be happy."

But there was no anticipation of happiness in Megan's eyes, only dull resignation. She didn't want to get to know Al, didn't want to open up only to be hurt again.

"Well," Jesse said, "since you'll be here for the summer anyway, I wonder if you'd be interested in seeing some of the area with me. How are you at hiking?"

Megan slid from the chair. "Where?"

"There are lots of good trails around here. I take groups at the Lodge up into the mountains, and I've found some really beautiful places. Some of them no one else knows about but me."

She didn't imagine that renewed spark in Megan's glance. "I can hike," Megan said. She walked across the room, studying Al's bookshelves with feigned concentration. "But I don't need anyone to go with me. I can take care of myself."

Oh, God. It was like looking in a mirror. Jesse saw the reflection of herself in Megan's bitter wariness.

"Maybe you can most places," she said, "but the thing about these mountains is that you need to take time to get to know them. Sort of like people you can't figure out right away. Even hikers with experience don't go alone." She moved cautiously around the desk. "Did Al tell you I work for a search and rescue team? We go out to help people when they get lost or into trouble."

Megan's jaw set. "I don't get lost. I went everywhere by myself at Grandma's. She didn't care."

And that was the problem, wasn't it? Grandma didn't care. How long had it been since anyone had cared about Megan?

"But I would care if something happened to you,"

Jesse said. Bobby Moran's pale, lifeless face flashed in her mind, and she pushed the image aside. Megan was not Bobby. "Sometimes when people out here get in trouble, they've just miscalculated how dangerous a situation is, or forgotten to take enough water, or didn't carry warm enough clothes. I could show you how to avoid those kinds of problems."

Megan stared at Jesse with that same calculating assessment, a balancing act between a child's needs and self-protection. "Why?" she asked.

Why do you care? she meant. How could Jesse answer that, when Megan was so suspicious of anyone's interest? "Because it helps to have friends when you come to a new place," Jesse said. "I had Al when I came back to Manzanita. Everyone needs someone."

"Oh," Megan said. Her face closed like a door firmly shut. "You're doing a favor for Al."

"That's not true, Megan. I—"

"What isn't true?"

Al walked into the room and stopped beside the desk, leaning heavily on his cane. "Hello, Jesse. I see you've found Megan. Have I interrupted a philosophical discussion?"

"Not at all. Megan was just showing me how to use the Internet."

"Good. Good." Al looked at Megan with the detachment Jesse had always admired but which seemed so inappropriate now. "I'm pleased to see you're keeping yourself occupied, Megan. Mrs. Plummer said you've been very quiet."

Megan folded her arms across her chest and hunched against the bookcase, unresponsive. Al cleared his throat. "I also thought it would be good for you and Jesse to get to know each other. Jesse lives so close, and since I'm at the library almost every day—"

"I don't need another baby-sitter," Megan said. She stared at the carpet between her pink tennis shoes. "I can do things by myself."

"But I can't allow you to go out on your own." He

glanced at Jesse. "I'm sure that Jesse would be happy to show you around town. There's a swimming pool at the Lodge, and probably other children to play with."

Megan's head swung up. "Playing is for little kids, and I don't like to swim. I have a book I want to read in my room. Can I go?"

She didn't wait for Al's permission but strode for the door, fixed on escape. Al made no attempt to stop her.

A door banged shut down the hall. Al raised his brows and closed the study door with exaggerated care.

"You see what I mean," he said. "Megan's defenses are very high." He gestured Jesse toward the recliner. "What were you two discussing?"

"I was suggesting that she come hiking with me." Jesse leaned back, hand over her eyes. "I'm afraid it didn't go too well."

"I had hoped . . ." Al sighed. "She won't come out of her room most of the time. She isn't eating. Mrs. Plummer expressed some worry, but all this could be a manifestation of grief. If there were a child psychologist closer than Redding—"

"I don't think it's psychology she needs," Jesse said. "You said you didn't know how close she was to her grandmother."

Al pulled the desk chair to the side of the recliner. "My brother's mother-in-law came from a wealthy family. She didn't approve of her daughter's choice of husband, but she took Megan in after Cesar and Helen were killed. I wasn't in close contact with any of them."

"I have a hunch that your brother's mother-in-law didn't approve of Megan, either," Jesse said. But she couldn't put into words any of the thoughts that crowded her mind, transform them into neat explanations that Al could understand. They weren't rational. What Jesse saw in Megan's pain hit too close to home.

"I still believe you may reach her where I can't," Al said. "Will you keep trying?"

Jesse closed her eyes. *Keep trying.* Al cared enough about Megan to want the best for her, and for some reason he thought Jesse could provide what Megan needed.

"You're doing a favor for Al," Megan had said, with a too adult cynicism. It might have started that way, but after their brief conversation Jesse knew it had become much more. More, even, than seeing herself in Megan.

A strange compulsion had awakened inside Jesse, every bit as inexplicable as the appearance of a ghost and the return of Gary Emerson. As if, somehow, events had come into some bizarre conjunction, and she was still too unenlightened to see the pattern they formed.

But that was fantasy, an effort to regain some control by seeing purpose where there was only coincidence. The simple fact was that she might be able to help Megan. If she'd made it her business to know Bobby Moran, to reach out before he'd become senseless with drugs and hopelessness, he might still be alive.

"I'll keep trying," she said. "But it may take time."

"She wants to return to boarding school in September."

"No." Jesse sat up, moved by the protest that came so instinctively. "That's the last thing she should do. We've got to convince her not to run."

Al cocked his head. "From what, Jesse?"

Without warning the image of David Ventris filled her, mind and body. It was as if he made a crack in her heart, unexpected as a fissure torn out of the earth by a sudden quake.

Such unstable ground made a poor foundation for reason. Jesse lay back, determined to clear her mind for Al's hypnotic suggestions. *Stay away, David Ventris. I don't want you here.*

"It'll make more sense when I've answered my own questions," she said. "If you're ready, I'd like to continue the hypnosis."

She heard skepticism in Al's silence, but he only settled more comfortably into his chair and rested his cane against the recliner.

"You remember how we began last time," he said.

"We'll do it the same way tonight, but we'll try to slow the process down, give you a greater sense of control over your memories. This can't be rushed, Jesse."

"I understand. Just one thing, Al—if I start to scream again, bring me out. I don't want to upset Megan."

"I don't intend to let it go that far. We'll take this very easy."

Al was as good as his word. He seemed to understand that Jesse needed time to unwind after her talk with Megan, and his voice took on a soothing cadence both distant and enfolding. Step by step he took her through the induction. The relaxation came on so gradually that Jesse wasn't aware of the precise moment when she crossed the threshold between full consciousness and that other state where her body was floating and her thoughts were nearly still.

"Jesse? Do you feel ready to go back into your past?"

She knew she answered, though she felt more than heard her reply. There was something strange about her own voice—not quite right, higher in pitch and oddly accented.

And the man who spoke to her seemed to be very far away, as if she were hearing him from the opposite end of a long, dark tunnel. She found herself in an open space outside the gaping entrance . . . in a garden with a cobbled path at her feet and growing things all around her. The tunnel seemed gloomy and forbidding, and she had no desire to reenter it.

The man in the tunnel began to talk about numbers, and counting off on a calendar. Jesse listened to it all with annoyed disinterest. He was keeping her from going where she wanted to go, and it was most vexing. She longed to explore the garden and find where the path might lead her.

Then he was asking her about her childhood. Her mother. He gave a name she didn't recognize. "Your mother, Joan," he said. And that was quite ridiculous. Mother's name had always been Letitia.

There were more suggestions about remembering

when she was eleven, but it was increasingly difficult to concentrate on the voice in the tunnel.

She wandered away from the dark and crumbling entrance, answering the voice only when she must to keep him appeased. She knew how to make people believe what she wanted them to believe, do what she wanted them to do.

The garden was lovely, filled with every manner of blossom and flowering shrub, but she soon reached the end of it. A path that began as cobblestones disintegrated into smaller and smaller pebbles until it turned to earth, a vague tracing through tall green grass. Cultivated roses quickly gave way to wild ones, tangled about the weathered white fence that tilted and finally disappeared into a wood. What had seemed a flat and protected space was a small valley, surrounded on all sides by hills.

She knew these hills. She loved them. They were green, bare along the tops but graced near the valleys with a skirt of trees. Often, when she couldn't bear the boredom and commonness and restrictions of home, the dull and unimaginative company of her shabby-genteel parents, she roamed these rocky peaks. And *he* would come. . . .

He was waiting for her now.

"Jesse? If you can hear me, raise your finger."

Her finger obeyed without any command from her mind. The voice went on with questions that made very little sense, asking her to remember. Asking how old she was, what she was seeing. And what she was seeing was . . . not right.

Not right. Why did she feel herself as two people? Yet it was true, and the half of her the voice spoke to was a stranger here.

No. Not a stranger. She touched herself, the pale long-sleeved walking dress and the white gloves and the bonnet on her brown hair. Familiar and yet unfamiliar. Frightening and ordinary. She stripped off a glove and looked at a hand that should be tanned from the sun rather than pale, strong and capable rather than soft and delicate.

"*Jesse*," the voice called, sharp with warning. It wouldn't leave her alone, unless . . .

She turned inward. Her other self *was* there, the one called Jesse, and she felt as though she might swoon with the overwhelming fear. She was divided as cruelly as a broken heart, and she didn't like what she saw from the corner of her inner sight. Pain, and loss, and things she didn't dare think about.

But only Jesse could make the voice leave them alone. Only Jesse could unshackle them to keep the rendezvous in the hills.

"I will show you," she coaxed her silent partner. "I'll take you, if you make him give us time."

Jesse didn't want to let go. Jesse was also afraid, and Jesse was searching for something that could not be found in this garden or among these hills. But at last the man's voice grew quieter and quieter, and she knew Jesse had done as she asked.

Free. With the freedom came a kind of forgetfulness, and as she started for the nearest hill she remembered the division in herself and the tunnel and voice as no more than a dream.

She knew where to go. She knew he would be waiting. He had asked her to come to their special place, to say his goodbyes.

Her walking boots slipped on rocky ground, propelling her with desperate haste. He was the one person she could not sway with her games and stratagems. She had begged him not to go to the war, but it was all he could speak of since his father died. That he was now viscount in his own right could not influence him; his mother's objections made no difference. No one's opinion mattered when set against his will to do as he pleased.

If she could only convince him to wait. If she could only make him see how much she needed him, how she could not live without him. But such talk made him laugh, and the laughter always came before he walked away.

"David," she said, breathless with her exertions. His

name was a charm, but it was as fleeting as a fairy's promise. She would give anything to bind him, keep him by her side forever.

Anything.

"Sophie. You've come."

He was there, perched on a rock beside a tiny brook and twirling a fern between his fingers. He dropped the fern as she approached, and she saw how he'd stripped the frond nearly bare.

"David," she repeated, and went into his arms. He was so handsome in his expensive coat and snug breeches and polished boots, the finest gentleman in the Lake District. His eyes were brilliant blue and his black hair fell over his eyes, resisting the taming touch of her fingers.

He made her feel so alive, so daring, so privileged. He let her dismiss her parents and their modest and mediocre ambitions. She wanted so much more. When she was with David, climbing the fells or racing in his phaeton, she escaped into another world of excitement and delight.

His mouth caught hers, firm and possessive. She submitted gladly. When he kissed her she was a fine lady, not just the squire's daughter, and she knew in her heart he would marry her and give her the luxury and security and high estate she had dreamed of.

But his kiss now had another effect. It emptied her mind of the arguments she'd planned to use to make him stay, sent her blood rushing like a waterfall. He had so much power over her. In his arms she forgot everything but how much she loved him.

David's nimble fingers made short work of the ribbons of her bonnet and sent it tumbling to the grass. "My lovely Sophie," he murmured into her hair. "Do you know how much I want you?"

The words had some significance that eluded Sophie as he bent his head to kiss her neck above the collar of her walking dress. All she heard was "want," and want meant that he valued her, that she was important. He was a warm and teasing wind that made her wish to lie down and loosen her clothing to let him nearer her heart.

He knew her thoughts. He found the fastenings of her gown and worked at them gently, never ceasing his kisses. Heat kindled within her. He had done this before, reached under her bodice to caress her skin, and his touches had given her delight.

But this time he didn't stop at her bodice. This time she could feel the afternoon breeze on bare skin at her shoulders, then at her back, with only David's skin as covering.

New sensations coursed through her body. She wanted . . . oh, she wanted to give herself to sensations and become lost in them. Abandon herself to pleasure. Papa said pleasure was a sin and David Ventris was a devil because he pursued it, that he was wild and useless and a bane to his family and his title. Always running from his duty, from all restraint.

Restraint was what she hated, all the things she couldn't have. She and David could run away together. . . .

"Lie with me, Sophie," he whispered. "Let me love you."

Somehow they were in the grass, side by side, David's coat her pillow. His hand had found its way to the tender, naked skin of her breast.

"Yes," he said. His mouth replaced his hand, a more daring kiss than she could have imagined. She gasped and arched into him. The hot place inside her was ready to burst with a need she couldn't name.

Yet in the midst of the urgency and the heat was something that kept itself apart, that could still question. And that something—that someone—pushed David's hands and mouth away and waited until his gaze lifted to her face.

"You'll leave me," she said. "I don't want you to go."

He cupped her face in his hands, kissed both her eyelids and smiled sweetly enough to woo the angels from heaven. "You know I'll be back. If you give me everything, Boney's best can't touch me. Your love will make me invulnerable." His eyes, his words were rich with emotion and sincerity. "Let me, Sophie. Let me inside you."

It had never been possible to refuse him whatever he asked. Surely this would bind him to her as nothing else could. She loved him, and her heart and body became his willing accomplices. Love was the center of existence, and as he touched her and caressed her and covered her with his body, they become one being.

Perfect. Endless. Never to be separated for all eternity.

Sophie crested on a wave that lifted her above the hills, so high that she pierced the very sky itself. And though the tunnel waited for her there, summoning her, she was too lost in ecstasy to be afraid.

Not even as she rushed into the dark entrance and the voice returned.

"Jesse?"

She opened her eyes slowly. At first the name meant nothing to her except as an abstract concept, unimportant to the being she was. She saw a ceiling rather than sky, but that, too, meant little in the dreamworld of happiness that wreathed her mind like a soft mist.

Her body hummed with pleasure; her lips were tender with his kisses. She touched her mouth in wonder.

Real. It had been real. Even as she felt the recliner under her back and breathed in the old-book scent of Al's study, she sensed that other place around her, that other self waiting. She clung to the joy, untroubled by implications that might have shattered her bliss.

Al asked her if she was all right, and she gave some vague answer. His face was unreadable, but with her heightened awareness she knew his concern as a grayness in a warm golden light.

"I couldn't reach you," he said. "Jesse, you weren't answering my questions. It wasn't your childhood, was it?"

She closed her eyes. "I need to be alone for a few minutes," she said. "I need . . ."

But Al didn't wait for her to complete her request. He got up and left the room, closing the door behind him.

The floating silence lasted no more than a minute before it was filled by a new presence. Jesse felt it come to her on that golden light, take shape and form that she recognized with a sense beyond the five she had always relied on.

"David," she murmured, and opened her eyes.

He stood beside the recliner, and his face was so dearly familiar that she thought she'd slipped back into the dream.

"You called me," he said. But he didn't hold out his arms, and his blue eyes, so vivid in the dream, were almost wary.

Jesse rose from the recliner, her hands awkward at her sides, her breath coming fast. He was different from the dream—older, with deeper lines around his mouth and eyes, and the worn uniform that imparted an even greater strength to his lithe body. Less laughter in his face, more experience. But Jesse was caught in the grip of desire she'd never encountered except in that vision of otherness.

Desire. A wanting so undeniable that she thought he must hear her mind begging him to lie down with her on the floor as they'd lain in the grass. Feel him moving inside her, his hard muscle against her thighs and belly and breast.

The veil of doubt lifted from his gaze. "Jesse," he said, his voice rough with hunger. He came for her at last, pulled her into his arms. She lifted her face, and his mouth, fierce and hot-blooded, met hers.

CHAPTER SIX

S HE WAS PLIANT and supple in David's arms, firm
muscle and tension and prickly pride yielding to passion.
The unspoken passion that invited him to take what only
last night she had so patently denied.

There was no denying this. He kissed her, but not as
he'd kissed Sophie. Not gently as he'd done before they
were so unprosperously wed, or under a cloud of fear or
anger or guilt as on those rare times when they came
together after Elizabeth's death.

For she was not Sophie, this woman who held him
with a fervency that matched his own. Matched, equaled,
met openly, with lips and tongue and body and heart.

He had no sense in this moment. Only sensation. He
lifted her higher, the stirring of his manhood pressed to
her belly.

"Jesse," he sighed into her open mouth. God, it would
be so easy to lay her down on the chaise longue behind

her. She'd give herself willingly, thanks to whatever strange miracle had put the desire and welcome in her eyes.

In all the days of the war he'd never resorted to taking a woman by force. There'd been willing women enough, camp followers in plenty. He hadn't even considered celibacy those long years away from Sophie.

He'd been celibate now for nearly two centuries—two hundred years of emptiness.

Simple desire he could have ignored. Any other woman he might have resisted. But he wanted to plant himself in Jesse's body, as deep as he could go, as soldiers did on the eve of battle or in the aftermath of destruction.

The way he wanted Jesse now was stronger than any lust he could remember, in life or death.

It was lust for life. He told himself that even as he deepened the kiss, felt Jesse blossom under him like a flower in the sun. Jesse *was* life. That was all she was to him.

Why not pleasure himself where and when he could? Why question Jesse's inexplicable change of heart? Hadn't he been punished enough?

His hand moved from Jesse's waist to find her breast, and he walked her one step back, and then another, until her legs bumped the chaise and he could ease her down. . . .

Firm hands lodged against his chest, halting his advance. After a beat of incomprehension he focused on Jesse's face.

Shock. Disbelief. Confusion. Jesse stared at him in panic, every trace of that impassioned invitation gone from her eyes.

"Let go of me," she said.

His shock was scarcely less than her own. He compelled his arms to release her by sheer force of will. She scrambled across the chaise, putting its bulk between them.

"You touched me," she said. "I told you—not to touch me."

At least she didn't claim he'd come back without permission. Unfulfilled desire pounded in David's veins. Yes, by God, his veins and his flesh and his manhood, his very substantial body that knew a very material frustration.

He smiled to rein in his anger. "You didn't want it, Jesse? That's not what your eyes were telling me."

Her hand moved to her face, as if she had to reassure herself that it hadn't altered. "What are you talking about? I was . . . dreaming. . . ."

"Were you?"

Between one heartbeat and the next her dazed expression gained an edge, panic and confusion replaced by grim resolve. "How did you know what I was dreaming?" she demanded.

He hadn't known. He'd heard her and returned and found her waiting. Wanting. "Was I in your dream, Jesse?"

"Yes. And you know it. Because—" She braced herself on the back of the chaise. "Because it wasn't a dream. The connection you were talking about. The way I've been seeing you—" She shook her head. "Either you've taken over my thoughts, or somewhere—sometime—you and I were—"

Words failed her, and she leaned more heavily on the chaise, fingers pressed into the soft brown leather. "There's nothing wrong with my mind. There must be an explanation."

Her monologue was low and urgent, bent on convincing herself. The panic was still very close to the surface. And he was the cause.

"Tell me what you're thinking, Jesse," he said. "However things may seem, I haven't done anything to your mind. I don't have that power. Help me understand what troubles you."

She looked up. "You *know*," she said. "You must know. Everything you did, what you've said, since you came to me—" Her mouth hardened. "You said you'd forgotten your life. But you knew we had a connection."

"And I said you felt it as well." He took a step closer. "What happened just now is proof of that."

"But you were lying to me, weren't you?" The chaise creaked with the force of her grip. "About why I was the one you came to. You *lied.*"

David remembered the shock when the French musket ball had ended his life. Jesse's accusation was like that ball, and with a sickening sense of foreboding he wondered if she had discovered it all.

What he'd done. What he was trying to do. How he was deceiving her.

But as he watched her, it came to him that she was bluffing. For once her expressive face was still, and her eyes observed him with the sharp concentration of a warrior facing his most cunning enemy, waiting for a fatal slip.

No, by Boney's rotting corpse. Whatever she'd experienced, it hadn't revealed the whole truth, or she couldn't have kissed him so wantonly. That kiss had been genuine.

It was time to call her bluff.

"I'm not lying," he said slowly, "when I tell you that once, long ago, we were lovers." He sighed, all heartfelt regret and remorse. "Yes, I knew. But I judged that it would be too much to tell you at first." He rested his hand on the chaise, inches from hers. "It was difficult to hide it. Difficult to be near you, and not . . . act."

Her cheeks surged with hot color under the tan. "Lovers," she echoed. Accepting, however reluctantly—for how could she ignore what had just passed between them? "It was in England. In a place with hills."

"You saw it, Jesse. How? What did you remember?"

"It was . . . so clear. You were younger than you are now. You hadn't become a soldier yet. And I was different." Her eyes narrowed. "But I'm telling you things you already know. Your memory—"

"—is a traitor. It gives me the barest glimpses and lets me be sure of only one thing." He dared to cover her hand with his. "We meant something to each other once. You were dear to me in life. That's why you have the power to save me."

She was silent and looked away, but it was not the silence of rejection. The air itself was taut with unspoken feelings. Jesse's feelings, which she wasn't ready to share. Or trust.

What she remembered, what she *felt* might just be enough.

"I know that we were happy together," he said. "Ah, Jesse. I can see those hills, where we used to walk. And the blue of the lakes below. I can see you in a white gown and bonnet, as fair as summer. Such fragments come back to me."

"Such as my name?" She pulled her hand from beneath his. "It was Sophie. Oh God. Sophie."

"I couldn't be sure of the name," he said quickly. "Not enough to trust what came to me when I saw you. But I should have trusted your good sense." He bent his head, willing her to hear his sincerity. "Forgive me."

She backed from the chaise. "No. You were right the first time. I'm not this Sophie. She isn't me, no matter what happened in that other place. I'm Jesse Copeland. Don't forget that, Captain Ventris."

How hard she fought—him, the unexplained circumstances that had allowed her to recall some fragment of their past together, her own unnamed fears. David admired her for that.

Admiration had been no part of his shallow love for Sophie. Only pity. And anger. And shame.

"I won't forget," he said. The promise emerged with unwonted harshness, and he fought to even his tone. He couldn't afford to be less than agreeable when he'd come so far with her. "This isn't England, and I'm no longer alive."

"Then you don't expect us to be—for things to be the

way they were," she said. Her skin was still flushed and she moved farther across the room, as if mere physical space could keep her safe. "What just happened was a mistake. I told you that I was searching for memories of my own. I was confused for a few minutes. That's all."

Confused, yes, but not in a way David could make use of without the greatest care. For all her passion, she'd resist him tooth and nail if he approached her again. If he'd given in to his desire and taken her, even in her brief acquiescence, she wouldn't have forgiven him. He would have lost the game before it began.

A dangerous game. Jesse's body was as neat a trap as any his otherwordly gaolers might set him. It could make him forget that he fought for his very existence. For eternity itself.

If and when he seduced her, it would be to further his cause. Or because she wanted him badly enough to ask.

"Perhaps we were both confused," he said.

"Then the rules I set still stand. Agreed?"

"If you agree to share what you remember," he said. "It's very plain to me now. Your memories will not only restore my own, but I am convinced I can help *you*, Jesse. If you'll let me."

Obviously that idea didn't appeal to her. She glanced at the study door. "Not now. My friend is waiting outside."

"Your friend?"

"Al. The man who—made it possible for me to remember."

A man. David noticed the sudden tension in his gut. "Your lover?"

She looked startled and then piqued. "No. He's the best friend I have in this town. I trust him completely—with everything but you."

David smiled wryly. "Then you wish me gone. Very well. But I'll return to claim what you promised."

Her flush suggested that she read his words in the way he intended. She didn't realize just how bold an invitation she'd issued. *She,* Jesse Copeland, and not Sophie Johnston.

"I have a party to attend tonight. After that—come to the hillside behind my cabin. We'll talk then."

He issued a brief military bow and then, on a whim, sidestepped the chaise and seized Jesse's hand. He lifted it to his lips and kissed the air a half inch above her warm flesh.

"Where the roses bloom, Jesse. Don't forget."

She didn't pull her hand away this time, though her fingers were still in his. "Not likely," she said. The dry hint of a smile played about her mouth, and David felt a surge of satisfaction. More than that—exaltation, as if he'd just led a victorious charge in battle.

By Wellington's bloody beak, she liked him. He'd make her like him so well that she'd grant him whatever he asked, no matter what the past.

He willed himself to fade before the magic did. Jesse strained to see him long after he was no longer visible. But he didn't leave. He made himself little more than spirit, the merest shadow in the corner of the room, and waited.

Jesse opened the study door and peered into a dim hallway. "It's okay, Al. Can we talk? I'd like to ask you a couple of questions about . . . what happened to me."

The man who entered was big—not quite thickset but by no means a lightweight, with dark graying hair and beard. He reminded David of certain Spaniards he'd met during the war, but lacking their high temper and pride. This man carried himself quietly, like a bear walking on eggshells.

It was then David noticed that he leaned on a cane, and the sleeve of one arm was empty from the elbow down. Wounds a man might come by in war. David studied him with greater interest.

Al looked about the room, his stolid face thoughtful. "Are you feeling better, Jesse?"

She cast her own final glance toward the ceiling and

sat down on the edge of the chaise. "I had a chance to think about what I experienced. It was more of what happened before, Al. Not my childhood, but something else."

"I told you that I couldn't reach you this time," Al said. "You were under very deep."

"I lost track of your voice after the beginning," she admitted. "I didn't—talk about what I was doing?"

"No. But it didn't seem to be a bad experience, so I decided to let it continue. Was I right?"

Jesse sagged in obvious relief and hugged herself. "Yes. The vision I had wasn't like the first one. It was all . . . good."

"But you don't look happy." Al sat down opposite Jesse, his manner that of a concerned physician. "What disturbed you about it?"

"It wasn't my life I was living in the vision. It wasn't even me. Not—who I am now."

"I see." He hesitated. "Have you heard of past life regression?"

She laughed hoarsely. "I've not only heard of it. That's exactly what I think happened. I was in some other life. In another country and another century."

Al's impassivity faltered. He began to rise, caught himself and settled down again. "Damn," he said, the word almost uninflected. "I didn't intend for this to happen. If I hadn't begun to suspect, I'd have discounted it as fantasy."

"Reincarnation, you mean." Jesse leaned forward and briefly touched Al's knee. "Don't worry. You're not the only one who's questioning everything you ever believed."

He stared at his knee where her hand had been. "There is no proof that reincarnation exists. Any number of other explanations might account for your perceptions."

"It's true that it isn't what I expected, but there are reasons this makes a weird kind of sense, happening now." She looked up, directly to the place where David watched, but her eyes revealed no suspicion of his presence. "Not because of Gary, but . . . other things I've . . ."

"You don't have to explain." Discomfort charged the silence between them before Al spoke again. "I don't think it's wise to continue, Jesse."

"Yes. I agree."

"And your hopes of revisiting your childhood?"

"I'll have to find another way. I'm not giving up on the business with Gary. Not ever."

Al gripped the head of his cane. Though he showed so little emotion, the force of his blunt fingers gave him away. "What are you planning to do?"

"I don't know. Maybe it's time for me to . . . talk to him."

David wondered who this Gary might be. It was evident how little Jesse relished that prospect of speaking to him.

Al leaned forward. His cane scraped against the hardwood floor, a muted sound of protest.

"Don't trust him," he said softly.

"You see?" She met his gaze. "Even you know there's something wrong about him."

"Only observation, Jesse. He's an ambitious man, and ambitious men can be . . . dangerous."

"I know." Jesse's jaw took on that set look, and she stood. "Thanks for your help." She unbent enough to smile, as if Al were the one in need of reassurance. "What we've done here . . . it hasn't been useless. Maybe someday I'll be able to explain."

"I'd like that, Jesse." He used the cane to lever himself to his feet. "About Megan—"

"I haven't forgotten. I promise I'll do what I can." The awkwardness remained as she went to the door. "Good night."

"Enjoy your party," Al said. But Jesse had already left. David lingered in the room; Al leaned on his desk with the look of a man newly defeated.

A man who'd been a soldier knew about defeat. Al had

lost much in whatever war he'd fought, though he'd kept his life. David had seen soldiers not quite so fortunate pass through limbo. Pass through and move on. If there were others like David, condemned to linger between life and death, they existed in their own private hells.

Al was a man who kept within walls of his own choosing. David was in no doubt that the man cared about Jesse much more than he revealed. But Al wasn't likely to interfere with David's plans for her. Her speech with Al, even her touches, had not been of the intimate kind.

Fortunate for Al. The mere thought that another man might hold Jesse's heart heated David's unearthly blood. A natural enough reaction, given the circumstances. At least he wouldn't be forced to test his ability to haunt anyone but Jesse.

As for this talk of one named Gary—it was evident that Jesse's problems had something to do with that name. And she'd mentioned her childhood in almost the same breath.

Jesse's childhood. David knew nothing of it, couldn't guess how it differed from Sophie's. Sophie had been anxious to escape her stifling, proper, and unambitious parents. But Sophie's only escape had been through marriage to David, and even that hadn't been enough.

Any assumptions about Jesse that David based on his knowledge of Sophie were of little use to him now. The only way to learn more was to stay at Jesse's side. A party might uncover another side of her. Like the kiss.

He needn't bother to reveal his presence. He'd promised to go when she asked, but there'd be no harm in his merely observing her public actions. And he found himself eager to know what troubled her.

As if he really could help her. As if he wanted to.

"Be careful, Jesse," Al muttered. David came out of his thoughts as the big man went to the door. David slipped out behind him.

Never fear, David silently told his fellow soldier. *I'll look after her. She means more to me than you can possibly imagine.*

❋ ❋

THE PARTY WAS already in full swing by the time Jesse arrived.

She had put on a pair of nice cotton pants less casual than her usual jeans, and a washed silk blouse and matching scarf she'd bought once in Redding on a whim. Her hair was up, and she'd applied a translucent dusting of blush and a touch of lipstick. The small, routine motions of getting ready had helped keep her most recent memories at bay, though her hands had trembled pinning her hair and she'd had to redo the lipstick twice. The face she met in the mirror was a stranger's.

Thinking was the danger. The more she thought about what had happened in Al's study, what she'd come to understand, the more impossible it seemed. And the more inevitable.

She and David Ventris had been lovers in a previous life. There lay the perfect explanation for her feelings, her desire, the hot rush of physical sensation when he touched her.

And kissed her. Good Lord, she had forgotten herself in that kiss. She'd wanted him to make love to her. She could claim that it was only an extension of the dream-vision, a memory of that previous life, but she'd be lying to herself. It was more than that.

She was not Sophie. She was Jesse Copeland, and there'd been enough of Jesse guiding her will to know exactly what she was doing before she'd recovered the good sense to break away. She was too damned attracted to him, drawn to him, pulled as much by her own emotions as any echo of a previous life.

She couldn't allow him to pierce her defenses that way again. It shouldn't be so difficult to manage, as long as she remembered he was a ghost. You couldn't date a ghost, desire a ghost, need a ghost. . . .

She quickened her stride and marched up the stairs and onto the recreation deck of Blue Rock Lodge. Distraction was what she needed. She'd never been one for parties, but there was a kind of comfort in the cheerful bustle of people celebrating a happy event. Paper lanterns had been strung along the posts and trees edging the platform, and the soft liquid tones of rhythm and blues played on the Lodge's piped stereo system.

Jesse recognized a few of the other Lodge employees, several current guests and a number of people from town. She scanned the group clustered along the freestanding bar that had been set up close to the central lodge. Gauthier, the kayak instructor, downed a beer as he laughed with John Whitehorse, who ran the hardware store in Manzanita. Mr. Meredith, co-owner of the Lodge, was dancing with a much younger female guest.

It was typical that Kim could throw such a large party together so quickly and without any fanfare. She was an extrovert and immensely popular with the guests at the Lodge, generous with her attention. She was also a damned good search and rescue leader.

Very likely Kim could even handle a reincarnated lover. Jesse caught herself on the edge of a lunatic laugh and walked the perimeter of the deck, taking note of every person she passed. It was several moments before she realized what she was doing, and why.

There was no reason Gary would be at Kim's party. Even if he were, Jesse'd be damned before she'd let him scare her away. Hadn't she told Al, in all her false bravado, that she intended to talk to him? But she didn't know what she would do when she saw him again, and the small hairs at the nape of her neck continued to prickle at every overheard fragment of small talk and laughter that floated across the pool.

Mr. and Mrs. Weber, the elderly couple Jesse had led on several hikes during the past week, beckoned her to join their small gathering. Jesse did so with silent gratitude. She smiled and took Mr. Weber's offered arm.

"Here's our girl. And don't you look lovely this evening." Mr. Weber said. He beamed at his wife and the middle-aged couple beside them. "Mabel and I offered to adopt this young lady, but I think she's holding out for a handsome young man instead. Someone who can keep up with her on a vertical climb." He patted Jesse's hand. "Kim is mighty nice to invite all of us to her party. Have you met the lucky groom?"

"Not yet," Jesse said. "I think he was a guest at the Lodge before I began working here."

"Well, I must say this place does romantic things to a body." Mr. Weber released Jesse's hand and looped an arm around his wife's waist. "Something in the mountain air. I'm surprised no one's snapped you up yet, Jesse."

"Don't listen to him," Mrs. Weber said, rolling her eyes. "Good men don't grow on trees or pop up out of thin air. Took work to grab this one." She winked. "You find someone like my Ossie, you do the snapping."

Mr. Weber snorted and pulled his wife close for a peck on the cheek. Jesse stared at the redwood deck at her feet.

Men popping out of thin air. No, they weren't common. And she didn't even know if David Ventris qualified as "good."

She glanced skyward. In less than an hour it would be dark, and when she went back to the cabin he'd be waiting for her. Waiting with that seductive half smile and reckless edge that made an unexpected and totally outrageous kiss seem natural.

And he said he wanted to help *her*.

"I don't know," Mr. Weber said. "Jesse has that look on her face, eh, Mabel? The look of a woman in love."

"Don't tease her so, Ossie. If you had any sense, you'd—"

"Who's in love?" Kim materialized beside them, her arm tucked through the elbow of a tall, athletic blond man who grinned at everyone with impartial goodwill. "Jesse! I'm glad you could make it." She acknowledged the older couples with a smile and turned back to Jesse. "I've been anxious to introduce you to Eric. Here he is. Isn't he to die for?"

Something in Kim's choice of words made Jesse's

stomach clench. She hid the reaction and offered her hand to Kim's fiancé.

"Good to meet you, Eric," she said. "I understand you met Kim before I came to work here."

"Hello, Jesse," he said. He cast a mock-wary glance at Kim. "Do me a favor and don't ask *how* we met."

"Ha," Kim said. "He was in my beginner's kayaking group. He knocked the kayak over first time we went out. Everyone was drenched." She laughed at Eric's grimace. "Love at first capsize."

The way she and Eric gazed at each other convinced Jesse it was love, sure enough. The same love that bound Mr. and Mrs. Weber together so strongly after so many years.

All at once it seemed as though Jesse saw couples everywhere. She'd never envied them before, or yearned for some elusive happiness beyond her hard-won independence and self-reliance.

There was no earthly reason to start now. "I'm happy for both of you," she said. "Will you be staying in Manzanita?"

"It looks as though we'll be moving south. Eric's law firm is in the Bay Area. Not that we don't plan to come up often. And I hope you'll be able to come to our wedding in San Francisco, Jesse." Kim actually blushed. "This time you'll get a real invitation. Eric won't let me forget."

General laughter followed, and Jesse joined in. It was good to see Kim happy. She deserved it. And Jesse realized she'd miss Kim's companionship at the Lodge and on rescue missions.

But Jesse was used to being alone. Alone was simple, and you could still help people without getting tangled up in sticky, painful emotions. . . .

"Well, we'd better make the rounds," Kim said. "Not everyone's met the lucky guy yet."

"Including me," a new feminine voice commented. "Where've you been keeping him?"

Marie Hudson sauntered up to the group, gorgeous

and overdressed in a black sheath that hugged her
model's figure. She smiled at Kim and turned the weight
of her attention on Eric. "You weren't kidding when you
said he was gorgeous. So how come we haven't seen him
until now?"

"He hasn't been up much since last year," Kim said.
"His job in San Francisco keeps him pretty busy—"

"Oh, San Francisco. I love that city." Marie rattled on
about various upscale boutiques and restaurants while
the other couples drifted away. Jesse found herself
watching Marie with a strange fascination.

She didn't know Marie well, and had never felt any
desire to further the acquaintance. Like Kim, Marie had
come to town as an adult, only a couple of years before
Jesse's return. Though she and Kim were friends, they
seemed to have little in common. Marie was the town
flirt, with tastes that seemed a bit too grand for Manzanita. Her clothes were big city. Even her restaurant was a
small oasis of trendiness, nouvelle California cuisine in
an ocean of burgers and steak.

Maybe Marie had been running from something. Or
maybe she thought she could remake Manzanita into a
colony for displaced yuppies. Jesse saw no indication
that Marie had the persistence or self-sacrifice necessary
to keep a restaurant in business. She wanted too much.

At the moment Marie was loading it on with Eric, but
Jesse was very much aware of the way the woman's gaze
flicked toward her again and again. She was the kind
who relished gossip, and Jesse knew people were talking
about Gary's return and his past with Jesse. Maybe Kim,
without understanding the significance of the incident,
had told Marie how Jesse had reacted when she'd seen
Gary at Bobby Moran's funeral.

Kim wouldn't spread that around, but Marie would.
She finally released Eric from her clutches and turned to
Jesse with a tight little smile.

"How are you, Jesse? Long time no see. I've heard so
much about you lately."

Out of the corner of her eye Jesse saw Kim and Eric

swept away on a new tide of well-wishers. She and Marie
were alone, and Marie's expression held more than a hint
of sly calculation.

"I've seen your new restaurant," Jesse said, refusing to
rise to Marie's unsubtle bait. "I haven't been able to drop
in yet. Is it going well?"

"Beautifully. I do hope you'll come and try our cuisine.
It's quite a change for this town. I'm sure you didn't get
much in the way of decent food in—what was it? Africa?
South America?"

"In some of those places, any food is good food."

Marie made a delicate face. "Oh, have I offended you?
I am sorry. We each have our sensitive areas, don't we?"

All it would take to burst Marie's bubble was an am-
biguously less-than-worshipful comment about her appearance, but Jesse wasn't about to sink that low. And
witty comebacks were not in her repertoire.

"Kim told me you're still feeling badly over that boy's
death last week," Marie said. Her scarlet mouth drooped
in spurious sympathy. "You really shouldn't take things
so seriously. It's best to know when to let things go, or
. . . sooner or later you pay the consequences."

There was an uncomfortably personal note in Marie's
tone, and Jesse'd had enough. "It's been nice talking to
you, Marie, but I see a friend over there I haven't had a
chance to visit with yet, and—"

"Speaking of friends," Marie said, taking her arm, "I
have one I'd really like you to meet."

"Maybe some other time."

"But I insist— Oh, here he is."

The shiver at the back of her neck told Jesse who had
arrived even before she turned to follow Marie's eager
gaze.

Gary. He glided to Marie's side with the smooth ease
of a venomous snake and looked directly into Jesse's
eyes.

"Jesse," he said softly. "I'd been hoping to find you.
To see how you were . . . after all these years."

Sickness blossomed in Jesse's stomach, and the once

solid deck bucked under her feet. She'd been anticipating this, knew it had to come sooner or later. She'd thought she was strong enough.

Don't lose it, she begged herself. *Not now.*

But though she kept her feet and met Gary's stare, she couldn't bring herself to speak. Her throat had closed up, choked with memories just beginning to resurface.

And hatred. The burning, virulent hatred was still within her, like some noxious black smoke, just as it'd been at Bobby's funeral.

"I know this is rather unexpected," Gary went on. "I saw you at the funeral the other day, but it didn't seem the right time . . ." He trailed off, assuming a mask of hopeful concern. "Jesse, I've never forgotten you. Or your mother."

Oh, God. Jesse felt dizzy and realized her lungs were void of air. She had to say something, find some response—

"I heard about your mother," Marie said. "What a sad way to lose someone. It must have been difficult for you to come back to town—after everything that happened."

Jesse swung on Marie. "Don't you talk about her," she snapped. "You don't know a damned thing."

Marie flinched and hung on Gary's arm. He detached himself with a sigh. "She's right, Marie. You don't know. I was there when they pulled poor Joan out of the river." He held Jesse's gaze. "Why don't you get yourself a drink, Marie. Jesse and I have some catching up to do."

Marie didn't want to go, that was clear. But she made a beeline for the bar, resentment in her stiff, high-heeled stride.

A faintly derisive smile lifted the corner of Gary's mouth. "Marie isn't as subtle as she likes to think she is, but she does have her assets." He looked Jesse over with a connoisseur's appraisal. "You've grown up to be quite lovely, Jesse. Very much like your mother."

His very mildness was filled with menace and contempt. In Gary's eyes was all the proof she sought, evidence of crimes buried like so many ancient bones. The metaphor was strikingly apt. Only one person in the world could dig up those bones. And, by God, she was going to do it.

"You never loved her," Jesse said hoarsely.

He gave a good approximation of wounded startlement. "What makes you believe that? You were too young to . . . completely understand what goes on between a man and a woman."

Innuendo shaded his words. A game, that was what it was to him. Scenes like the one in her recent dream flashed in Jesse's mind: episodes of nasty verbal sparring with her mother. And with her. Now it had a new overtone that made the gorge rise in her throat.

"You know," Gary said, "I often thought of returning to Manzanita . . . once you'd grown up and enough time had passed. I know about the hospital. It did my heart good to hear you'd come through just fine."

His heart. He spoke as if he actually had one. "You didn't care what happened to me."

"You're wrong. I cared very much. I made sure to keep track of everything that happened . . . after you left us."

She heard the threat in his voice. It wasn't her imagination. There was something he wanted from her; he had engineered this meeting for his own purposes. Why? Had he come to Manzanita for more than his political campaign?

Where was the clue she was missing?

She felt as if she walked in a dream far less real than her visions of happiness with David Ventris in some other country, some other age.

David. She tried to picture him with her now, watching over her like the guardian angel he definitely wasn't.

He'd offered once to haunt her enemies. He'd agreed to come when she called. But she was not a coward. Not a child. She didn't need David Ventris.

"You never knew me," she said. "Not then, and not now."

"And you underestimate me. I can see you're not so

different from Joan. She was very . . . sensitive." Gary shook his head. "She had a serious problem, Jesse. You suffered from it as much as she did."

How easily he turned things around. Her knuckles felt close to cracking with the strain of holding back. If only she could strike out and wipe that smug confidence from his handsome face . . .

"She never did have much time for you, did she?" he asked. "Poor, neglected child."

Now he was mocking Jesse outright. He'd taken all Joan's time once he'd come into her life. Demanded it. Controlled her as if she were a puppet.

"You ruined her life," Jesse said. "You tormented her, made her worse than she'd ever been."

He sighed. "Children do misinterpret what they don't understand."

"I understood enough. I heard you fighting—"

His mock-indolent demeanor vanished in a heartbeat. "What did you hear, Jesse?"

"Enough to know what you are." Recklessness took her, erasing the fear. She replayed the dream, piecing together the fragments of conversation. "She stood up to you, and you threatened her. She was afraid what you would do if—"

"If what?" Suddenly he was only inches away, his hands on her arms, his face too close. "What did she say about me? What dirty little lies did she tell you?"

His grip was like the bite of a rattlesnake, pumping poison into her blood. He had the grotesque stare of a madman whose mask of sanity had shattered.

"What did she say?" he snarled, teeth bared. He shook her, hard. "Answer me!"

He was afraid. Gary Emerson was afraid . . . of her, of something she'd said or implied. So afraid that he'd forgotten who and where he was.

Her instincts had been right. But his touch paralyzed her, and the accusations she wanted to shout were trapped in the unreasoning terror that reduced her to that eleven-year-old child, incapable of fighting back.

Only hatred made the fear go away. She gathered up the splinters of it and made it whole again. She imagined it as a hammer, breaking his hold, smashing his bones.

"Let go of me," she said.

An unnatural stillness surrounded them like an airless bubble. Curious faces were turned in their direction. Gary jerked and released her, as if her imaginary hammer had struck.

But it was no longer Gary who held her attention. The moment he let her go she felt the other presence, glimpsed the unmistakable vision of a second man beside her. A man in an antique uniform with a long curved sword in his hand, facing Gary as he would face a deadly enemy.

CHAPTER SEVEN

GHOSTS, DAVID THOUGHT, ought to be immune to shock. Surely there was no greater blow than death and realizing that one was condemned to perpetual limbo.

It was now very obvious to him how badly he'd underestimated the obstacles set in his path to salvation. One of those obstacles stood before him: alive with menace and devastatingly familiar to David's arcane and ghostly perception.

Avery. His brother. Avery was here, in a body older and taller—a shell that had disguised his true identity until this moment.

Avery, reborn. His eyes were the same. Eyes that fixed on Jesse in open threat as he released her and clenched his fists at his sides. His handsome face, twisted with violence, underwent a rapid transformation, becoming calm and cold and unmarked by his brief and brutal rage.

He smoothed his tie and smiled at her. "I see that we have a great deal to discuss," he said to Jesse, as if they'd been holding an ordinary conversation.

God. David tightened his grip on his saber before it fell from his hand. Like some grotesque farcical play endlessly repeating itself, they were all here together. Again.

Avery and not Avery. Sophie and not Sophie. He alone was the same.

"You may have heard that I'm running for state assembly," the man called Gary went on, his voice deeper than Avery's had been. "We've both come a long way, haven't we? It would be most unfortunate if trouble came of any . . . misunderstandings between us."

The threat was still there, indisputable. Jesse held his gaze, outwardly calm, but David felt her hidden turmoil—her rage, her dread—intermingled with his own, inseparable.

How could it be otherwise? His emotions were as tangled and piercing as a thicket of thorns. He had never found or confronted Avery in the years following Sophie's death. Sophie's *murder,* for that was what it had been. David had no doubts even before his own death at Waterloo. And after, in limbo, he had been as certain of Avery's crime as he'd been of Sophie's hatred in the last minutes of her life.

After Sophie's death Avery had disappeared. Nothing was resolved. Nothing finished.

And *this* was Jesse's enemy. She knew him as Gary, and she hated him as Gary—hated and feared him for reasons David did not yet recognize.

But it went so much further than the events of this life, this ugly contention to which David was covert witness. The pattern played out, inevitable as death itself.

Only this time David was with her, not on some distant battlefield facing the wrong foe.

The impact of Avery's presence was too overwhelming to absorb here and now. David was shaken to his jeopardized soul, as immobilized as the woman at his side. And he knew what Avery was capable of. He *knew.*

He had to get Jesse away. He hadn't let her see him, but he sensed that she felt his presence. To distract her with his earthly form would only prolong her agony.

But if he could reach her another way . . .

Jesse. He formed the word in his mind, projected it to hers. *Jesse. Listen to me. I'm with you.*

She started, though she kept her gaze on her enemy. *Don't be afraid,* he said. *Go, Jesse. Now.*

He saw the response in her body, an aborted motion trapped between defiance and the desire to obey. Her lips formed the shape of refusal, but she remembered to whom she would speak.

A ghost that her enemy could not see.

"Perhaps we should find a more private place to talk, Jesse," Gary said. "I've been by the old resort. A real pity no one ever did anything with it—but it may serve our purpose. I think that you and I need to come to an . . . understanding."

"I'm not going anywhere with you," Jesse said in a rasp. "Never."

"Maybe you'd prefer the river. I hear there's a nice ledge up where—what was the poor boy's name?—oh, yes, Bobby. The place where poor Bobby died."

A hot, cruel lance of pain arced out from Jesse, catching David like a blow. Without further thought he sheathed his sword and closed the space between himself and the man who'd been his brother.

He didn't know if what he planned would work. He hadn't tried to reach any other mortal on this plane. For all his talk of haunting, his limits remained untested.

"Do you hear me?" he hissed, his face inches from Gary's. "Do you feel me here, you blackguard?"

Jesse made an inarticulate sound. Gary blinked. "What did you say?" he demanded of Jesse.

"Leave her alone, Av—" David caught himself before he spoke his brother's name. Gary wouldn't recognize it, and Jesse would question later. "Bugger off, d'you understand? Leave the lady alone, or I'll make your life hell."

Gary blew out his breath in a startled puff and took a step backward. He waved his hand in front of his eyes. It passed through David with no effect.

David seized the lapels of Gary's coat in his fists. Without solidity he couldn't move Gary, but it wasn't necessary. He saw the sudden, wild confusion in Gary's brown eyes.

"How does it feel to be on the other end, you bastard?" he whispered in Gary's ear. "I'm here this time. My name is David Ventris, and I know who you are."

With an awkward lurch Gary broke free. He glanced around and wiped the back of his hand across his mouth.

"I'll . . . see you later," he said to Jesse. He turned to retreat, and David let him go. It was Jesse who needed his attention now.

She stared after Gary far too long. "I wasn't alone," she said.

"No," David said. "I know he is your enemy, Jesse. We must leave this place."

She surveyed the groups of merrymakers ranged about the wooden terrace. "Gary saw you."

"Not quite. Nor can anyone else. But we must go."

"Just . . . stay out of sight. Please." She started across the terrace, her walk a bit unsteady, and spoke with the dark-haired woman who'd come to her cottage the previous night. She made her farewells to a few others, constantly watching for the man who'd fled. David kept pace with her, silent and imperceptible. He knew that Gary had gone.

But not forever. That was the grand joke of it. There was no doubt in David's mind that Avery would return.

And David had to know why.

Jesse descended broad wooden steps to a cool path that wound its way among the trees and past several small log cottages to a quiet area some distance from the noise of the party.

"David?"

"I'm here." He materialized, holding himself midway between spectral and solid. "Are you well?"

"Yes." She blew a loose strand of blond hair from her forehead and closed her eyes. "I didn't . . . expect you to come. Thank you."

Her gratitude was stiff and grudging, but David felt a fierce pleasure in hearing the words. In knowing he'd been able to help her, when before . . .

"Who is he, Jesse?" he asked. "Why do you fear him?" *What is he to you in this life?*

She looked away. "We shouldn't stay here. Someone might hear me talking to thin air and decide I'm crazy again." With a quick glance right and left, she walked away from the stone-lined path and into the woods beyond the buildings. Here the sun's waning light barely penetrated, but Jesse was certain of her course.

As they moved deeper among the pines and undergrowth, David let himself become more substantial. The dusty smell of fallen pine needles and bark and earth filled his nostrils. A bird called sharply overhead.

Jesse came to a stop beside a stream. The clear water tumbled over rocks and fallen branches, dark green and brown with the reflection of trees above. Only the faintest hint of music reached them, weaving in and out of the stillness.

With a sigh Jesse sank to a crouch on the bank. She leaned forward to plunge her hands in the current, laving them as if to scrub something unclean from her skin.

"Are you going to say I called you again without meaning to?" she asked. "Is that why you came to my rescue?"

Her strained cynicism didn't deceive him. The confrontation with Avery had left her badly unsettled.

As it had David.

"I could hardly ignore a lady in distress," he said. "But I was with you all along. I confess to being very curious about your party."

"Then you didn't keep your word." But she spoke with oddly little heat. "What made you decide I needed help?"

He knelt beside her. "I have eyes . . . of a sort. He was threatening you, was he not?"

Her fingers glistened with drops of water as she withdrew them from the stream. "What did you do to scare him off? You said he didn't see you."

"But he felt me. It seems I have some ability to make my presence known even to those who can't see me. A ghost must be good for something." He tilted his head to better observe her face. "You didn't answer my question, Jesse. Who is he to you, and why is he your enemy?"

"It doesn't matter. I'm supposed to be helping *you,* remember?"

"And I offered my friendship. Is that so difficult to understand, when once we cared for each other?"

"I don't . . ." But she didn't finish the sentence, or raise a barricade of denials against his quiet siege.

"You did say I'd be useful if I could haunt someone upon your command," he said. "Have I not done so?"

A smile brushed the corner of her mouth. "The look on Gary's face—" She sobered again almost instantly. "No. You can't help me with this."

"Because I'm not a real man?" He leaned closer to her. "I can be real enough. Haven't I proven that to you, Jesse?"

The kiss they'd shared in Al's study came to life again, a breath of passion to warm the cool evening air. Jesse averted her face, but her lips parted on a soft gasp and her lashes hooded the acknowledgment in her eyes.

He badly wanted to turn her face to his, take her lips, hold her supple woman's body and feel the pulse of her desire. She would respond, in spite of her resistance. She couldn't help herself.

He could. He must control every moment of their time together, the relationship being woven between them like a fragile spider's web.

An apt comparison. But *he* was not the spider out to make Jesse his prey. Avery was the true villain. Wasn't his very presence here proof of that? Hadn't Avery's greed and jealousy led him to commit the evil that had somehow crossed into yet another lifetime?

That evil must be stopped, or all David's plans and hopes were at an end.

He looked into Jesse's eyes. "Confide in me, Jesse," he murmured. "Trust me."

Her head bowed low over the water, more strands of hair coming loose to veil her face from him. "I . . . told you I'd lost part of my memory," she said slowly. "Those memories involve Gary. Gary Emerson. I knew him when I was a child. He was my mother's—" She seemed to choke and covered her mouth with her hands. "My mother's lover. And I believe he had something to do with her death."

A bitter chill gripped David's throat like a strangler's garrote. "How?"

"Until very recently I barely remembered anything about him. But then he came back to Manzanita, and I—" She gathered her legs under her and rose. She went to the nearest tree and embraced the rough trunk— turned for solace to an inanimate object rather than the man at her side.

David wrapped his arms around his ribs. "Then this is what has troubled you. When did he arrive?"

"Two days ago. At a funeral for a . . . local boy."

Two days. And two days ago Jesse had called David's name as she slept. Called him and let him return to seek redemption.

"How long had it been since you last knew him, Jesse?" he asked.

"Seventeen years." She pressed her cheek to the wood. "I was only eleven when my mother died. She fell in the river. Gary wasn't anywhere near her at the time. He had the perfect alibi. But I know. I *know* that somehow he was responsible, even though I—" Again she broke off, swallowed, closed her eyes. "At my mother's funeral, I had a kind of breakdown. I attacked Gary. They had to sedate me, and I was in a hospital for months. That was when the memories got confused, until finally they weren't real anymore."

"But you remember now."

"I can feel it in here"—she drew back from the tree and thumped her fist over her heart—"that he did something terrible. But I have no way of proving it. I thought if I could make the memories come clear, I could find the proof. But no matter how hard I try, I can't find it. *I can't find it.*"

"He did something terrible." Had her memories of her past life intermingled with her troubles in this? David moved up behind her carefully, hands at his sides. "I understand your pain, Jesse. More than you can imagine."

"Not my pain. My mother's." Her fingers hooked into the ragged bark, tore off a loose chip, crushed it in a white-knuckled grip. "My mother drank," she said. "After my father left us, she drank. Often. She didn't have a good reputation in town. The resort wasn't doing very well when Gary came. He needed a place to stay. He said he'd help her fix up the resort." Her words became a disjointed recitation, flat and icy. "Everyone in town liked him. He always knew how to make people like him. They thought he was too good for my mother."

"But you didn't."

"No." She let the crumbling bark fall from her hand. "He treated her badly. The way he talked to her, his contempt—I hated him for that."

"And he mistreated you as well?"

"No. Not like Mom. He pretended to ignore me, most of the time. But I always knew he despised me, whatever he told other people."

So she had seen through him—as Sophie had seen through Avery. But David hadn't listened then. Hadn't believed.

"There was nothing I could do to make my mother see what he was," Jesse said. "She thought she loved him. She wouldn't listen. And then it was too late."

David threw caution to the winds and touched her

rigid back, laid his palm against her warmth and felt her breath shudder out in a long rush.

She could have evaded him with a sideways step. Instead her weight settled on his hand. Accepting. Needing his comfort.

"If you were a child," he said, "you couldn't be responsible for your mother's choices. You can't blame yourself."

She shook her head, and in that emphatic gesture David recognized his mistake. His argument wouldn't wash with Jesse Copeland. He'd known her only two days, and yet he had touched her soul.

If Jesse believed in anything, it was responsibility. She would assume it even when it wasn't her burden to bear.

So unlike David Ventris, who'd accepted no limits to his will, his pleasure, his freedom.

Perhaps Jesse could feel what he was through his very touch, as he felt her. But though his most powerful instincts demanded that he remove his hand, put distance between them again, he defied those instincts. For her sake.

He cleared his throat harshly. "What if you do learn he had a role in your mother's death?"

Her fist came down on the tree trunk. "All I know is that he has to be stopped before he hurts someone else."

What was it she'd said on the hillside last night? *"I believe that people pay for what they do. If there's any justice, evil is punished."*

If Avery had suffered punishment for his crimes, David had never learned. But Avery hadn't been condemned to limbo after death. He'd been reborn, granted a second chance that he'd squandered.

"He was warning you at the party," David said. "Threatening you in some way."

"Because he is guilty. He knows I can see it, even if no one else can. It was as if he were testing me."

David slid his hand to her shoulder. "But if you have no proof—"

"He's running for state assembly. Even a hint of scandal or wrongdoing could hurt his prospects."

State assembly. Some high political office, no doubt. This was America, where there were no kings or peerage. In such a world Avery would have sought power where he could find it. Sought and protected it by any means necessary.

"So he must stop you from making any accusations," David said.

She laughed. "Everyone knew I wasn't rational about Gary Emerson. I was even crazy once. Why should he think I could touch him now?"

Her despair was a terrible thing to witness. She feared a return to her childhood madness as much as she feared Gary Emerson.

But Sophie hadn't been mad when she'd written David about Avery's malicious behavior toward her. David had simply chosen to ignore her ramblings as more of his wife's irrational neediness and obsessive suspicion.

He could not ignore Jesse.

He curled his fingers around her shoulder, felt the tight-wound tension of muscle over delicate bone. He began to rub through the thin fabric of her blouse, working at the knots under her skin. Little by little her head lowered, came to rest against the tree trunk.

"I'm such a coward," she said. "I'm so weak—"

"You're no coward." He paused in his ministrations and gazed into the shadowed woods. "Believe that, if nothing else." *I know what cowardice truly is.*

She gave him no answer. The woods grew hushed with the transient serenity of dusk. Darkness closed in around them, creating an intimate space where scent and touch and subtle sounds defined the tiny world they inhabited.

It seemed only natural to move his hands yet again, slide them to her arms, press the length of his body to her back, rest his chin in the hollow of her shoulder. His touch became an enfolding, a sharing of warmth that needed no words.

"I'd haunt him for you, Jesse," he said, savoring the

fragrance of her skin, the silken tendrils of hair at her nape, the curves that fit him like a finely tailored glove. "I'd pursue him to the ends of the earth if you but give the command."

Even as he spoke he knew the rash statement was more than an empty promise designed to win her gratitude. Wasn't this the answer? Wasn't it the way to earn his peace—rid Jesse of Avery's incarnation in this life? He could break the pattern that had destroyed Sophie and drawn him to the woman who stood so quietly in his embrace.

Break the pattern, and with it his own eternal chains.

But it was Jesse who broke away, slid out of his arms and faced him with lifted chin and steady gaze. Some ambient light from the terrace, or the afterglow of dusk, reflected in her eyes.

"I appreciate the offer," she said. "But it's my problem. I'm not running from it. I'm not asking anyone else to solve it for me. I'm going to find the proof I need and expose Gary for what he is, no matter how long it takes or what I have to do."

The resolve in her voice didn't mask what David heard beneath: hatred. Hatred powerful enough to span two lifetimes, though Jesse didn't realize it. Hatred that would spur her to rash and reckless acts against a man who had once destroyed her.

David felt a violent desire to draw his saber and slash at the inoffensive undergrowth, thrust and hack until his arm was too weary to move. By God, Jesse Copeland was stubborn. He'd been able to manipulate Sophie, bend her to his will—but Jesse would resist more obstinately the harder he pushed. He had no power over her. None.

Reason, then. Calm reason.

"You'd do well to take a soldier's advice and proceed with caution," he said. "A frontal attack will fail, Jesse."

Her gaze was bleak. "Don't you think I know that? Gary holds all the cards."

"And if Emerson's threats become more direct?"

"What can he really do to me?" she said. But under the bravado was that thread of fear. David had no doubt that there were things Gary could do to her. A murderer could always kill again. . . .

Unless that murderer's own fears were great enough to stop him.

Yes. Resolution crystallized in David's mind. He'd been able to frighten Gary away from the party. Could he do more than that? Not pistols at dawn, however tempting the prospect might be—but there were other unique methods of confrontation a ghost might undertake. Especially with the man who'd been his own brother.

Stopping Gary was surely the key. If he learned the source of Avery's guilt in this life, so much the better. But that was a minor concern compared to keeping him from Jesse.

And keeping Jesse away from *him.*

He drew Jesse's attention back from her own dark thoughts. "There's nothing more you can accomplish tonight," he said. "You should go home and rest."

"I couldn't sleep." She hugged herself and looked in the direction of the party. "I left too early. I'll go back and help Kim celebrate."

Of course she would refuse to let fear dictate her actions. But she ought to be safe enough; Gary would very shortly be otherwise engaged.

He smiled with little humor. "It's an odd thing, but I don't remember that you were so blasted difficult to convince in our previous life together."

He'd had no intention of making more than a casual comment, but Jesse started and her gaze dropped to his mouth. Her voice took on a husky sensuality. "I thought we'd established that I'm not that woman."

Desire dealt David an unexpected punch well below the belt. He went to her and trapped her face between his hands.

"No," he said softly. "You're a woman of great courage. What need of armies with you in the vanguard? I suspect that you could have defeated Boney single-handed."

He bent his face to hers, drew out the moment just before their lips touched. Jesse closed her eyes. In spite of her fiery words, she wasn't fighting him now. She wanted him—

And he wanted her too much. He dropped a light kiss on her forehead, a chaste salute that did nothing to assuage his internal fire, and released her.

"I've outstayed my time here," he said. "As you once so aptly put it, I must 'recharge my batteries.'"

She would not look at him. "You have a pretty good handle on the modern world for a man who's been dead almost two hundred years."

"Yet all such knowledge is useless to me. Without life."

"I promised to help you."

"Then you must take care of yourself. Good night, Jesse."

She stared at him until he faded and she could see him no longer. He followed, invisible, while she made her way back to her party, and waited to see her securely ensconced among her friends.

Only then did he turn to his hunting. He drew on senses within himself he'd barely used, concentrating on the soul-spark he had once known as Avery.

Like a guttering candle, Gary's essence was a dim illumination that drew David to a long, two-story building at the edge of town. A lighted sign proclaimed the place an inn. David had no need to search further.

Gary stood outside one of the doors on the lower floor, bathed in the harsh glow of an overhead lamp. He drew on a cigarette as he paced a short distance away from the door and back again. His agitation was manifest in his movements, but David felt it on a much more profound level.

Gary was afraid. Jesse had said he had no real cause to fear *her*, but she hadn't reckoned on the terrible bonds of a cursed brotherhood.

Or on the powers of a ghost who had reason to hate. David drew that hatred into himself as a drowning man would suck in air, let it fill him completely. He'd gone countless years without the stimulus of basic human emotion. No passion could long survive the prison to which he'd been condemned. Even guilt had abandoned him in limbo, leaving him with an emptiness designed by expert torturers to punish for eternity.

Jesse had changed all that. She'd given him a taste of life, reawakened lust, anger, frustration, jealousy, joy—and other feelings he dared not examine too closely. Complicated feelings he no longer had the skill to control and employ to his advantage as he'd done in his former life.

This was different. This was clear and simple. Liberating. Right.

Avery had never been punished. David had come here for Jesse's sake: this man was her enemy. Gary had the power to hurt her. He had to be stopped. He deserved to pay for his crimes.

Pay in full.

David moved closer to Gary, close enough to touch. Gary hadn't seen him at the party, but David wasn't ready to risk appearing in solid form. He would take his time making himself known to his former brother, step by gradual step. And then he would test his power to act. . . .

"We meet again, Gary," he said. "Or should I call you Avery?"

Gary dropped the cigarette with a filthy curse, shaking his fingers. His head snapped toward David.

"You know I'm here, don't you?" David asked. He gave his body dim shape and leaned against the flimsy railing that ran the length of the inn. "How much are you aware of, brother? Is it your guilt that hones your senses?"

Gary cocked his head, staring intently just to the right of David's shoulder. He reached under his coat and drew out another cigarette. He lit it with a small metal device that produced a spurt of flame.

"Your hands are trembling, dear brother," David said. "Do you wonder what's happening to you?"

"Jesus," Gary whispered.

"Coming from you, that's no invocation. You made your pact with the devil long ago. Is that how you've escaped punishment?" He watched the fall of ash from Gary's cigarette and casually smeared the fine powder into the ground with his boot. "It's a bloody miracle that's brought us together. We never did get an opportunity to bid our farewells."

Gary closed his eyes and pinched the skin between his brows.

"I'm quite certain you can't understand everything I say," David said. "But the gist of it will surely make an impression. Tell me—" He pushed away from the railing and stood next to Gary, companionably close. "What did you do to Jesse's mother?"

Gary took a long drag on his cigarette. The outgoing smoke hissed through his teeth. "Joan," he muttered.

"Was that her name? Jesse seems quite convinced that you committed some evil, brother. That would scarcely be out of character for you, would it? But of course you weren't cursed to remember. Only to play it out all over again." He gripped the hilt of his saber. "The one thing that's different is that this time I'm here to stop you."

The overhead lamp flickered, and Gary looked up. The yellowish glow made his skin sallow, deepened the hollows under his cheekbones, and accented the lines of dissipation around his eyes. His throat worked above the collar of his shirt.

"And I will stop you," David said, "I shall make sure that you never get the chance to hurt Jesse again."

Gary's laugh was hoarse and incredulous. "Damn you," he swore.

"Do you address me, brother?" David made himself more substantial and plucked the dangling cigarette from

Gary's mouth. His grip was as lifelike as Gary's own; he *did* have the power to affect Gary, just as he could Jesse.

He had the power.

He dropped the cigarette and ground it under his boot as he'd done the ashes. Gary's mouth hung open as he stared at the pavement.

"Perhaps now you're fearful for your sanity," David said. "How does it feel?" He grabbed the lapel of Gary's coat in his fist. Still Gary didn't see, though he plainly felt the touch. His face went white.

"Condemning you to a madhouse would be a fit repayment for what you did," David said. "But that would take too long."

He dropped his hold on Gary and drew his saber. "Can ghosts kill, I wonder? More directly than by fear or madness?" Yellow light raced up and down the bared blade. "Will a haunted sword do as much damage as a real one? I should like to find out."

With exquisite care he positioned the tip of the blade against Gary's flat belly, just above his smooth leather belt. The fabric of his shirt dimpled. Gary made a low sound, like a moan, and slapped his hand down.

At the same instant David withdrew the sword, and Gary's hand hit his own belly. Slick beads of sweat had gathered on his forehead; he blinked rapidly to clear his eyes. All at once he spun around and strode for the nearest door. His hand slipped on the doorknob before he got it open.

David followed, stunned by the significance of what he'd done. The sword *had* been physical, because he'd willed it so. The blade had begun to make an impression. If Gary had touched it, would he have bled?

Could he be killed?

Could David kill him?

The dark and stuffy room provided Gary no deliverance, though he slammed and locked the door behind him. He sat down heavily on the wide bed. David stood over him, the saber in his hand.

Hatred. He still felt it in full measure, and now, for the

first time in two centuries, he had Avery at his mercy. He could even the score and protect Jesse at the same time. One quick thrust and it would be over. Surely *they* wouldn't have given him this power, this chance, if he weren't meant to take it.

He stepped closer to the bed and raised the sword. Now it was *his* hands that shook, and he couldn't seem to get a proper grip. . . .

"Lancelot," Gary said in a low, hoarse voice.

David lost his hold on the sword. It fell, vanishing into midair.

"Avery?" he whispered.

Gary's stare had gone blank and strange, as if he looked on more than darkness. David plunged headfirst into memory.

Lancelot. When they were boys, before they'd grown so far apart, they'd played at games of King Arthur's court. Avery had claimed Arthur from the first, younger though he was. And David had been pleased to take Lancelot, who was the warrior and hero and had all the grand adventures.

Children. They'd both been children once. Gary had invoked that childhood nickname as surely as if he knew what it meant. He raised his hand to his mouth and gnawed the tip of one finger. It was the habit Avery had when he was young, the one Mother had constantly scolded him for. He'd always done it when he was afraid. Or when David went off alone, leaving his most annoyingly tedious younger brother behind. . . .

David brushed at his hip for the wooden sword that swung from the simple rope belt he'd made. His fingers closed on metal. The saber was back in its sheath as if he'd never drawn it.

Now he knew he couldn't. Oh, the hatred wasn't gone. But when he looked at Gary it wasn't Avery the murderer he saw, but Avery the child. Avery the younger brother, who hadn't always been evil. Who'd wanted, once upon a time, to be like his elder brother.

David had made life-and-death decisions every day

during the war, yet now he could only stand and tremble, unmanned by utterly useless memories.

Avery would laugh. But he didn't yet have the victory.

With a low curse David unbuckled his sword belt and flung it across the room. It vanished before it hit the wall.

"Listen to me, Avery," he said. "I'll spare your life, but I won't be a fool. Leave this place. Tonight."

Gary raised his hand from his mouth and raked it through his hair, gaze unfocused. "I . . . don't—"

"Get out of town," David said. "Forget about Jesse Copeland. You can't touch her. You'll be destroyed if you don't put her out of your thoughts forever. Do you understand?"

He stared into Gary's eyes, stared until comprehension returned and Gary was shivering and sweating.

"If I see you here tomorrow," David said, "I'll haunt you. I'll haunt you to your death." He raised his fist. "Don't mistake me. I will do as I promise. I have a purpose now."

He forced himself to step away from Gary, to believe that his brother understood the warning. He didn't know whether to hope that Gary obeyed him—or drove him to take his revenge.

But when he imagined killing Gary, the image froze in his mind as he'd frozen a few moments ago with the saber in his hand.

Even if Gary left tonight, the pattern was yet to be broken. David lacked the courage to break it.

He left Gary still sitting on the bed, alone and vacant eyed with fear. But a grim foreboding pursued David long after the inn was far behind him.

It wasn't only the business with Gary that remained incomplete. There was something else that David, for all his otherwordly vision, couldn't see. Another unknown pitfall awaiting him just around the corner, a hidden trap on the narrow road to liberty.

On impulse he used the last of his nearly depleted energy to return to the party. It was full dark now, and the festive lanterns strung between the trees illuminated a scene of music and laughter.

Jesse was there, laughing with the others, her gestures animated as she talked with her friends. If her happiness was a little forced, her laughter a bit feverish, no one with her would know it. She played her part well.

They all played their parts, dancing to the steps fate laid out for them: Jesse, Gary, David himself.

Even now he watched Jesse and felt his heart clench, his loins tighten. Instinctive reactions he would have acted on in his old life, and inevitably suffered the consequences.

He'd been at the mercy of his gaolers for nigh on two hundred years, and he'd had his fill of it. His dangerous and ambiguous feelings for Jesse could only be deadly liabilities. Today he'd been distracted by protectiveness, desire, admiration; he'd been ready to go after Gary simply to protect Jesse, driven by emotion when cold logic would have served him far better.

As it should have served him when he'd held Gary's life in his hands. Jesse had made a crack in his heart that let weakness in. A crack he must mend. He would keep from walking right into the ambush.

His war was far from ended, and his greatest enemy was himself.

※ ※

GARY KICKED THE sweat-soaked sheets from his legs and sat up in the bed. His heart slammed inside his ribs and his breath came short, as if the dream had been real.

He glanced at the vacant space beside him. He'd had no desire for Marie's company tonight, not after the bizarre meeting with Jesse; now he was grateful for his impulse.

What would Marie have thought to see him now, shaking and dry mouthed and wondering if he was as crazy as Jesse Copeland?

He swung his legs over the bed and walked unsteadily

to the bathroom. The tap water was lukewarm, but he gulped it down and felt for the aspirin he'd left on the sink.

Not that it would do any good. Ever since the party something had been wrong. An illness, he'd thought at first; the shivers and cold sweat, the weakness in his knees and irrational fear. He'd made a fool of himself leaving the party, driven off by some notion that his life was in danger.

His life. *Jesus.* He couldn't put the nightmare out of his mind: the tall dark-haired man in some kind of uniform, plunging a curved sword into his chest. Gary staggering under the blow. The shock and terror of knowing he was about to die. Staring down at the gaping hole and wondering why there was so little blood.

And the voice that kept yammering in his ears, never quite audible enough to understand, maddening in its persistence. Mockery. Contempt. Warnings he couldn't quite hear.

Worst of all, the feeling that he should know the man, the voice—that he had cause to be afraid. And with the fear was the envy, the yearning, the hatred.

And guilt. God, the guilt—formless, sourceless, devastating.

It sickened him.

He had to get away from this place—this room, this town, these people. He was certain now that Jesse Copeland had nothing on him. At the party she'd been afraid, just as she'd always been. He'd slipped up when he'd grabbed her, but even if she suspected anything, she didn't *know.* He'd swear to that.

Gary stumbled back to the bed, thought better of it and fell into the armchair by the window. *Yes.* It made perfect sense. Jesse wasn't a threat. The man he'd hired to search Jesse's cabin would come back empty-handed, because there was nothing to find.

He had no reason to stay in Manzanita another second.

Gary lurched to his feet and staggered to the chest of

drawers against the wall. He yanked open the drawers and removed the neatly folded shirts, tore his suits from the closet. He didn't bother to do more than throw his things in the expensive leather suitcase and garment bag, heedless of wrinkles and creases in his equally expensive clothing.

By six A.M. he was in the motel office, paying his bill to the sleepy clerk. The man had the brains not to say a word. Gary left him with a generous tip and a facile comment about an early start for home.

There would be questions. He knew and didn't care. The devil snapped at his heels, and for the first time in his memory he could taste the fear of damnation.

But the devil wouldn't have him. He'd always stayed one step ahead, and he'd give the bastard the run of his life.

CHAPTER EIGHT

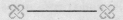

JESSE ALMOST EXPECTED to find David waiting for her. She walked into her cabin, into dimness painted with dawn light that filtered through the blinds. He wasn't there. In spite of her weariness after an unanticipated long night of talking, laughing, and forgetting, her senses were hyperalert.

And no wonder. She kept reliving the conversation in the woods: pouring out her heart to David, his quiet sympathy, his gallant protectiveness, his touch. Especially his touch. And the tension between them, a second kiss that didn't quite happen.

It seemed that he should be here, when so much was unfinished. But perhaps she should be glad of the respite. She kept resolving to hold him at a safe distance, and he found the chinks in her armor again and again.

She paused in the darkened entryway, her hand near the light switch. No, David wasn't here. But it took her a moment to realize that what she felt was something else entirely.

The small hairs prickled along the nape of her neck as she turned on the entryway light. Everything looked as it should. Shadows receded before the kitchen and living room lights, and nothing seemed wrong.

She walked into the bedroom. The bed was neatly made, unslept in. Her clothes still hung undisturbed in her closet. But her chest of drawers—

Her heart skipped a beat as she went to the simple pine chest she'd made eight months ago. The bottom drawer was slightly open. Only an inch—but she knew she hadn't left it that way.

She pulled the drawer all the way out and stared at the contents. Her travel journal lay where she'd left it, and the various envelopes and papers were tucked away in their color-coded folders. She didn't have a lot of paperwork, had no need for file cabinets full of records or mementos from the past. Her work with the Peace Corps and her deliberately frugal lifestyle had never allowed her to carry much from place to place.

Still . . . She set aside the journal and checked each of the folders. By the third one she was certain that the folders had been shifted. A subtle matter of papers out of order, dates rearranged. Most people wouldn't have noticed.

But Jesse had always been orderly. She liked to know everything was where she could find it at a moment's notice. Whoever had been in her bedroom hadn't known that about her, careful as he'd been.

She replaced the folders and sat back on her heels, numbed by a sudden wash of adrenaline that left her muscles shaking.

Someone had been in her cabin. Someone had gone through her things.

Slowly she got up and walked to the window. It hadn't been locked; that was one thing she wasn't paranoid about, though crimes were occasionally recorded in Manzanita. Petty thefts, shoplifting, drug possession—a transgression more serious every decade or so. It had never seemed necessary for her to keep her windows barred.

So she'd made it easy for the invader to enter her sanctuary. He hadn't even had to break the window. One of the slats of her window blind was bent back; that was the only evidence.

Dry mouthed, Jesse made a circuit of the cabin. Aside from her chest of drawers, the few boxes in her closet, and the smaller drawers in her bedside table, nothing else in her bedroom had been visibly handled, and the invader had done little rearranging. In her living room, only the junk drawers built into the bookshelves had been disturbed, though she found a few books slightly out of alignment. Her workshop seemed to have been ignored.

There was very little worth stealing, except for some spare cash she kept hidden in the kitchen. The assorted small bills hadn't been removed.

But in the kitchen she found the envelopes on top of the refrigerator, the letters from her late father's lawyer, scattered out of their usual pile. Every one was there, but the invader had obviously looked through them.

Why? Jesse sat down heavily in one of the kitchen chairs and gazed out the window, hardly aware of the cheerful morning sunlight on her face. What had he wanted, the person who'd so easily shattered her privacy? If he were a thief, he wouldn't have been so careful to leave things nearly as she'd kept them, or spent so much time going through her drawers and paperwork. Any local would know she didn't own any real valuables and kept her money in the local bank.

The intruder hadn't been after money or valuables, and he'd been systematic in his search.

For what? Why? And . . .

Who. Jesse sat up. Who in Manzanita had a grudge against her? Who seemed to want something from her— who'd taunted and mocked her in an effort to extract some unknown information? Who knew she hated him?

Who was her one enemy in the world?

Gary. The evening's confrontation came back to Jesse with crystal clarity. Toward the end, she'd accused him of bullying her mother, desperate to make him acknowledge the only crime she knew he'd committed. The fight she'd remembered in the dream.

And then he'd threatened her—grabbed her, eyes wild, as if he was almost afraid. *"What did she say about me?"* he'd said. *"What dirty little lies did she tell you?"* Even after he'd calmed down again, after David had frightened him off, he'd made it plain that it wasn't finished between them.

Because Gary *had* committed some crime, he was afraid it might be discovered . . . and he believed Jesse could expose him.

Jesse shot up from the table and paced the length of the kitchen, flexing her fists. She hadn't been wrong to sense his guilt. At the party she'd been too scared to think clearly or analyze the subtle implications of their conversation.

Gary believed she not only knew something that could hurt him, but that she might have tangible evidence. Why else go through her paperwork? Why demand what her mother might have told her?

Through this act of violation Gary had given himself away. Oh, he wouldn't have done the work himself. It wasn't his style. But he had influence and money. He could have hired someone to break in and do the looking for him.

Did he think Joan had left her daughter proof of his crime, whatever it might be? Proof that he'd had a part in Joan's death, regardless of his airtight alibi?

Jesse moved through the cabin like a whirlwind, driven by the turbulence of her thoughts. What could this mysterious evidence be? She had very little of Joan's, just a few knickknacks sent to her a year after her mother's death.

Yet if Gary believed she could hurt him, it meant there was a chance. A chance she could find that proof and use it against him. With any luck, the trespasser hadn't found whatever he was looking for.

That tide of hope carried her in a vigorous and thorough survey of the cabin, but her investigation turned up nothing. Exhausted, she went into her workshop to take comfort from the reliable solidity of her furniture and the knowledge that here, at least, the invader hadn't intruded.

She could ask the police to dust for fingerprints, though she doubted that Gary's flunky would have been that careless. Nevertheless, she'd pursue every avenue. And in the meantime, she'd keep searching her memory—and search as well for the proof she knew must exist. Somewhere.

She sank down on the cool and dusty floor. As her mind calmed, her thoughts took a new direction, as inevitable as the sunrise.

David. She closed her eyes and imagined him, imagined sharing her breakthrough with him. She'd told him about Gary; for the first time she'd been able to talk about her remembered past, and he'd listened with apparent sympathy and concern.

He'd also protected her. He'd gone at Gary with real anger, as if he were shielding something . . . some*one* precious to him. As if it had been intensely personal, not a convenient favor he could easily perform.

A strange and wonderful thing, to be protected, defended. Even by a ghost. Jesse smiled and touched her mouth. David had proved his friendship. He'd called her brave. He'd offered to haunt Gary, for her sake. At the time she hadn't fully appreciated the gesture.

He'd acted like . . . like a man defending the woman he loved. Like a knight with his shining sword facing down the dragon.

Her smile faded. But of course, *she* was supposed to be helping *him* win his salvation. She was of value to him, in theory—though so far she'd done little of any use.

Jesse leaned her head against a low, half-finished cabinet and breathed in the sweet smell of the pine. No reason to blow the episode out of proportion. She had no expectations of David Ventris. She'd made it clear enough that she wasn't that naive young girl named Sophie anymore, not the woman he'd once loved. Just as he'd made equally clear how badly he wanted freedom from his eternal punishment.

But her heart ached in spite of all her logical, rational protestations. She was beginning to trust him. Even . . . need him. After three short days.

There was the danger. She didn't want to need him. Her problems with Gary were none of his concern. The sooner she could dump her emotional baggage, the sooner she could help David move on to wherever it was he was supposed to go.

A wave of dizziness caught her unaware, and she closed her eyes. Thank God she had the day off; maybe she could get some sleep. Even Gary's intrusion couldn't eliminate that necessity. This time she'd be sure to lock the windows, and when she was rested she could think about the next step.

She got up to check the doors and windows, then went into the living room and collapsed on the sofa. There was someone else she had to think of—Megan, whom she was determined not to neglect in the midst of everything else.

Later today she'd visit again, check on the girl. Maybe she'd have better luck breaking through that tough shell. And Megan didn't have to know anything about Gary or Jesse's problems with him; Gary couldn't neglect his affairs and stay in Manzanita much longer. Especially if his search of Jesse's cabin had convinced him she had nothing on him.

Jesse's concentration dissolved as she drifted into sleep. Later she'd worry about it. Later . . .

She woke to find the sun angled for afternoon. Her first thoughts were not of Gary, but David; he hadn't come, and she wasn't about to call him as if she were incapable of handling the situation on her own.

She set water boiling in the kitchen and made tea and

oatmeal to quiet the rumbling in her stomach. Such ordinary activities made her feel oddly detached from this morning's unnerving discovery. It helped to focus on Megan as well, and she found herself anticipating a second meeting with the girl.

After breakfast—or, more accurately, a late lunch—she dressed and crossed the field to Al's house. She hadn't even had the chance to relate last night's and this morning's incidents to Al. He deserved to be told after his efforts to help her.

But he, like David, had advised her not to get more involved with Gary. There was no point in bringing either of them any deeper into this than they already were.

She walked to the front of the house and knocked on the door. Mrs. Plummer answered after a long delay, her eyes heavy with recent sleep, her gray curls kinked and flattened.

"Jesse?"

"Hello, Mrs. Plummer. Is Megan here?"

Mrs. Plummer's puckered mouth turned down. "She's either in her bedroom or the study. All she does all day is read and work on that computer. She never talks to me."

Her tone was that of a disgruntled adult who had suffered through more than one battle of wills with a recalcitrant child. She stepped back and let Jesse in. The house was cool and dark. The living room television buzzed with some inane game show.

Mrs. Plummer patted her hair. "I've been resting. Let me go look for Megan and tell her you're here."

Jesse would have preferred to go herself, but she waited at the end of the hall and worked on calming her nerves. Why did she feel that so much rode on getting through to Megan, making Megan trust her? It was more than empathy for Megan's plight and remembering how being orphaned and unwanted felt to a sensitive child.

There seemed to be layers upon layers in everything that was happening to Jesse, too complex to unravel. If only—

Mrs. Plummer reappeared, her gaze darting about the

room. "She's not in her bedroom or the study," she said. "I don't understand it. I've looked places she doesn't normally go into. I can't find her."

A purely irrational thrill of alarm punched Jesse in the stomach. "Could she be outside, playing in the yard?"

"She never goes outside. Mr. Aguilar said she was to go no farther than your cabin in the back. She hasn't shown any interest—"

"I just came that way. Megan wasn't there."

Mrs. Plummer clasped her hands over her ample belly. "Oh, she's such a difficult child. I can see her staring at me, always watching—and I had to rest. Well, she can't be far, can she?"

Of course not. "Why don't you look around the house again, and I'll check outside."

Seemingly grateful for direction, Mrs. Plummer nodded and waddled off. Jesse went for the front door. A rapid but methodical search of the front yard, the nearest lane, and the back acreage, including the patch of woods, turned up no sign of Megan.

Jesse paused to look up at the hills rising behind her cabin. Could Megan have taken the narrow trail up there? Or perhaps she'd simply gone into town. It wasn't much of a walk.

"I can take care of myself," Megan had insisted. She had something to prove. Had she finally felt driven to show just how well she could do that? How little she needed the guidance and protection of indifferent adults?

In all likelihood Megan was wandering down Main, poking into the tourist boutiques. Jesse strode back to Al's house to consult with a nervous Mrs. Plummer.

"I think she took some food and bottled water with her, and a little backpack she has," the older woman offered. "Where can she have got to?"

"How long do you think she's been gone?"

Mrs. Plummer blushed under her pale crepe skin. "I don't know. I hadn't talked to her since just before breakfast."

Hours, then. It was nearly four o'clock. "It's okay,"

Jesse said. "No one could have predicted that Megan would suddenly decide to—" Run away? It was premature to assume that. "Why don't you call Al and let him know—but don't make him worry. There's no sense in panic. I'm driving into town to look for her. I'm sure we'll have her back in no time. She might even be at the library already."

But Jesse doubted that. No closeness had developed between Al and his niece.

Jesse jogged to her cabin, gathered up some extra water, healthy snacks, and a few supplies from her search and rescue work. She started her truck and drove down the lane to Main Street.

Only the usual low-key activity marked the boutiques and stores, burger joints and garages along the strip. Jesse stopped to talk to several town residents she knew, asking about Megan. None had seen the girl; most were surprised that Al's niece was in town at all.

Jesse visited the tiny police office and briefly mentioned her search to the officer on duty, who promised to keep his ear to the ground. Jesse considered and discarded the idea of mentioning the morning break-in—that could come at another time.

She drove up the main drag a few more times, a little too slowly for some of the hot-rodders in town, and then parked to walk the strip of boutiques for a closer look. Further questioning turned up no reports of a little girl on her own.

Of one thing Jesse was certain: Megan was far too wary and savvy to walk off with or accept a ride from a stranger. Wherever she'd gone, she'd surely done it solo. Both a relief and a danger.

If she wasn't in town, she might have gone hiking—up the hills that rose into steep, challenging mountains. No inexperienced adult went up there alone, much less a child. If Megan knew these hills as well as Jesse at the same age, she'd have had less cause to worry. But Megan was a city girl who longed to prove herself independent. There was no predicting what she might attempt.

And it was getting later by the minute.

Jesse returned to Al's house, checked in with Mrs. Plummer—who was muttering and fanning her flushed face—and then used the phone to call Kim at Blue Rock. Kim was due back from a kayak lesson, and Jesse left a message for the other woman to call as soon as possible. Kim could mobilize search and rescue very quickly if need be.

Jesse prayed there'd be no need. She left the truck in her driveway, put together a more elaborate backpack of supplies, and started on foot up the hill behind her cabin. Here the trail, which she herself had made, was distinct and at an easy switchback grade. A good choice for a child, if she knew how to avoid rattlers and ticks.

Megan couldn't have made it very high up, inexperienced as she was. The day was warm, and she wasn't used to hiking. Surely she'd have stopped somewhere cool to rest. As long as she stayed in one place, Jesse could find her.

But Megan wasn't on the hill. Jesse took mental stock of every other easily accessible trail leading out of town and debated the next to try, pausing to call Kim again. Kim promised volunteers within the hour, and in the next few minutes she'd be arriving in the rescue truck with all the major equipment and supplies. But Jesse knew she couldn't wait.

There was someone else who might help, who had abilities no ordinary person possessed. She wasn't breaking her resolve not to rely on him. She called him only for Megan's sake.

"David," she whispered. "Come to me. I need you."

⚜ ⚜

HE WAS SITTING among the hills above town when he heard her. The boulder on which he perched gave him a broad view of the town and its denizens, shiny roofs like varicolored stones set along a black paved river winding among the mountains. Brighter flashes of light bounced off the hoods of the horseless carriages—cars—favored by the modern traveler.

Jesse was down there. She wanted him. The urge to go to her was powerful; only a night and most of a day had passed by human reckoning, but it felt like an eternity since he'd left her at the party.

He wanted to go, but he did not. In her call was a certain urgency, but he sensed it was not for herself. It didn't pertain to her safety, or the business with Gary Emerson. He would have known if she faced any danger. He'd made his decision last night to keep a greater distance, and somewhere the line must be drawn.

Soon David would have a handle on his weakness, and then he'd be able to pursue his goals with all the studied calculation he'd intended. . . .

A patter of falling rocks to his left alerted him from his thoughts. Someone was coming along the narrow, well-used trail that ran along the side of the hill, up from town and to the edge of the cliff overlooking the river twenty yards distant.

That someone moved clumsily but with little weight behind the uneven footfalls. Small, perhaps, and no wilderness expert, this unintended visitor. David stayed where he was and waited, secure in his invisibility.

But he didn't expect to see the sweaty, dusty, and plainly exhausted child who trudged around the bend and into his view.

A child. A little girl, in fact, though her short-cropped hair and spectacles and baggy clothes made the identification less than immediate. She was clutching a transparent, empty bottle in one hand, and perspiration plastered her bangs to her forehead.

David rose quickly and began to walk toward her. He had no idea what a young child might be doing alone and well away from town, but she looked in need of assistance. . . .

He stopped himself with a cynical inner laugh. How in bloody hell was he to assist her? She wouldn't even know he was there. He might be able to make her feel his presence, as he'd done with Gary—*if* such a technique would work on a total stranger unbound to him by the laws of Karma and fate. But he'd be more likely to frighten her beyond recovery.

The girl wiped the back of her hand across her mouth and sank into a crouch where she was, in the full sun, squeezing the empty bottle. After a moment she sighed and shrugged off her pathetic scrap of a pack and jammed the bottle under the top flap.

David flexed his hands, aware of his helplessness. Helpless to control his unwanted feelings for Jesse, helpless to put an end to Avery's threat once and for all, helpless to aid this child. He swore under his breath.

And the girl looked up—up, and straight at him. She pulled off her spectacles and set them on the ground, her movements unsteady. Then she squinted and rubbed her eyes before returning the spectacles to a precarious balance on her small snub nose.

"Who are you?" she asked.

David was stunned into temporary silence. *Good Lord.* There was no mistaking the direction of her gaze.

The girl could *see* him. And hear him, evidently. He remembered his foul curse and wondered how well the child understood it. He could only hope for her ignorance.

After his legs would move again, he crouched to her level at a reasonable distance, hands dangling over his knees.

"Good afternoon," he said.

Her posture was hunched and defensive, but she didn't run or ward him away. "Why are you dressed so funny?"

How was he to answer? Why should this child be able to see him as only Jesse could? He hadn't made himself solid or assumed deliberate visibility. Even when he'd threatened Gary most assiduously, the man hadn't been granted sight of him. David couldn't simply will that dubious privilege.

And he hadn't willed it now. But the girl regarded him

with a frown behind the smudged glass of her spectacles. He had to find some response, take care not to alarm her.

"Please forgive my attire," he said with a slight smile. "I am only recently come to this region, and . . ." He shrugged.

"Is it some kind of costume?" she asked. Her voice was thready and breathless but held a note of challenge nonetheless. "You're from England, aren't you?"

She was quick. "Indeed," he said. "I am pleased to make your acquaintance. David Ventris, at your service."

She didn't volunteer her name in exchange, but continued to stare at him as little runnels of perspiration trickled from the wet bangs at her forehead. She studied his sword and then examined his boots. "Aren't you hot?"

The child was obviously suffering from the heat herself, but David noticed such conditions only if he concentrated on them; one boon of ghosthood was that he could pick and choose the sensitivity of his assumed body. The warmth of this day was nothing to the heat of the Peninsula in summer, where David had seen his share of men collapse under their burdens, bound up in their uniforms like mummies in shrouds.

But this girl was no trained soldier. The first thing he must do was get her out of the sun. He reined in his impulse to offer his hand.

"It is warm," he agreed. "Will you join me in the shade of those trees? It should be a considerably more congenial place for conversation."

She glanced aside, never quite letting him out of her field of vision. "What are you doing up here?" she said.

Why should I trust you? rang behind the question. There was no mistaking the girl's wariness, and David sensed it had little to do with his odd appearance. Did she feel there was a wrongness about him? If she knew what he was, surely she wouldn't be so calm.

And why did he get the distinct impression that he should know something about the girl, something he was missing?

"I might ask the same of you," he said. "I've seen no

one else here in hours. Aren't you a bit young to be walking so far from town?"

She planted her hands on the ground to steady herself
and pushed awkwardly to her feet. "I'm not a child."

The statement sounded well rehearsed and a bit too
vehement. "I see," he said. "So you've come up here by
yourself, I gather?"

"I'm not afraid," she said. Another too-pointed declaration. "I'm about to go home."

"And where is home?"

She made a vague gesture toward the town below. But
she stood where she was, making no move to resume her
walk, and licked her lips. "Do you have any water?"

David felt for his canteen before he remembered that it
hadn't been deemed a necessary accoutrement for his
material presence on Earth. "None at present," he said.
"But I do think a rest out of the sun would be beneficial
for both of us."

The look in the girl's eye threatened an all-too-familiar
rebellion. Young or not, she didn't like being given suggestions that smacked of orders. David had little experience with children. A firm hand was what the girl
required, but if he were to move too decisively—

Suddenly he realized why he recognized her defiant
mien. It was like looking at a miniature version of Jesse.
Oh, not in feature or coloring, but in the stubborn cast of
her jaw and that touch of vulnerability she struggled so
fiercely to hide.

Was that the source of his impression that he ought to
know her? A simple enough explanation. But it didn't
satisfy him, and he was compelled by an even greater
urgency to protect her. As he'd wanted, needed, to protect Jesse.

The irony of it was that he'd come here to distance
himself, physically and symbolically, from unwanted
emotions. From the origin of them. From Jesse. But re-
minders of her were everywhere, inescapable.

Chains. Always the chains.

"There's a river nearby," he told the girl, deliberately hardening his tone. "Give me your bottle."

She blinked at him as if startled by his unexpected gravity. But the change of approach worked; she fumbled in her backpack and withdrew the bottle without further argument. He took it from her hand. "Go sit under those trees and I'll bring you water."

He waited to make sure she obeyed. A little of the starch had gone out of her spine; sheer fatigue, perhaps. Or she recognized the voice of command. She endeavored to keep her dignity as she marched for the stand of pines and plopped down in the shade.

God. She was so small, so . . . fragile. David nearly squeezed the soft bottle flat in his fist before he shook off his maudlin sentiment. He moved out of the girl's sight and half scrambled, half floated down a sheer cliff to a narrow bank alongside the water.

The river here was deep and foaming with turbulence, forced into a narrow gorge between high stony walls and punctuated with large boulders. It was a bit of a trick to keep his hand solid enough to grip the bottle and yet maintain enough ethereality to float above the surging water. He managed to fill the bottle halfway and returned to the top of the cliff, aware of the drain his efforts had made on his limited reserves of energy. He was better now at mastering his use of that energy, but limbo never released its hold on him. Even after a long "rest" in nothingness, he still felt the aftereffects of last night's confrontation with Avery.

The girl was where he'd left her, head drooping over her drawn-up knees. She pushed at her spectacles with a delicate finger and looked blankly at the bottle he offered.

"I don't think I'm supposed to drink water from the river," she said. "It can make you sick."

By Boney's dangling—David sighed and speared his fingers through his hair. The child wasn't thinking clearly, and neither was he. He set down the bottle and crouched in front of her.

"What is your name?" he asked.

Her lips trembled a little, but she held his gaze. "Megan."

"Then listen to me, Megan. It's a long way down that hill."

She tucked her hands under her arms. "I can go back by myself. In a minute."

"I suspect you are lost, and someone is no doubt looking for you as we speak."

She shook her head with a sharp toss of her bangs. "No. No one."

"That I don't believe. Would you like to try again? Who cares for you?"

Her gaze fixed on the dirt between the toes of his boots. "My uncle. Al Aguilar."

David almost laughed. "Your uncle?"

"I only came to stay with him on Monday. He doesn't care where I go."

Al Aguilar. Jesse's friend and confidant. And this girl was his niece?

David hesitated, oddly afraid to ask the next question. "Do you know Jesse Copeland?"

The girl's skin flushed with more than the heat, but she didn't answer. David stood up and paced the length of the little grove of trees. His agitation made no sense, but he knew he had to deliver this girl to her home as quickly as possible. Making and keeping himself physical long enough to carry her all the way down the mountainside was certainly not within his power. But if he stayed by her side . . .

He turned abruptly and extended his hand. "Come. I'll help you get home."

She paused, stared at his hand, reached for it. For a moment her fingers curled in his, and then they slipped through as if she had tried to grasp air. She gasped.

David realized the enormity of his carelessness. For an instant he hadn't concentrated, had allowed himself to relax and let go of his physical form, and that instant had been too long.

He had no time to berate himself further. Megan had scrambled to her feet and was running—away from him, as fast as her small feet would carry her and with no regard to direction. David set off in pursuit, wondering how in hell he was to stop her, quiet her terror. If he touched her again, would he make it worse?

It hardly signified, for Megan was headed directly for the river. For the high cliffs that overlooked the turbulent water. David abandoned physical form for a burst of speed. He'd almost reached her when she came to a sudden stop, flailed her arms, gave a heart-stopping cry, and slipped over the crumbling edge. Her glasses went flying into emptiness.

David took shape, flung himself belly-down on the earth and clawed for her hand. He caught her just before she was out of reach. This time the contact lasted more than a second, long enough for David to see the panic in her unshielded eyes.

Her eyes. Windows to the soul.

Even a ghost could be expected to stand only so many revelations in a matter of hours. He recognized her as completely as he'd recognized Gary at the party, and the effect was no less startling. Or devastating.

Elizabeth. Megan . . . was Elizabeth.

Perhaps it was those few seconds of inattention, or merely that his strength wasn't sufficient. Or maybe she felt the same shock he did, and let go. Her fingers slipped through his, and she fell.

But he'd slowed her just enough. She landed on a narrow stone ledge halfway to the river, her small body very still. David heard a cry between a moan and a roar and knew it came from his own throat. He went to her, perched on what little flat space remained beside her.

"Megan," he whispered hoarsely.

She stirred, rising on her arms, and gave a low whimper of pain. He took her arm and helped her to her knees. She was all right—not badly hurt, though her skin showed scrapes and would be bruised later on.

She was all right. She looked at him from those great

tear-washed eyes, only the immediate trauma of her fall numbing her fear of him. When she recovered, the fear would return and might drive her to fatal recklessness. There was nowhere for her to run but into the river itself.

David could feel his strength waning rapidly. Soon he'd be no more than a wraith even to eyes that could see him, incapable of aiding Megan. He could barely touch her now.

Later he could reflect on this new twist of fate. Now he had to find another who could help the girl, and he knew who that person must be.

But he couldn't leave Megan. He would have to try again what he'd done at the party, and use his thoughts to call for help. If urgency were enough, he could reach halfway across the world.

He had only to reach one woman.

While Megan shivered, eyes tightly closed against the sight of the river below, David threw his consciousness into one thought, one vivid image. He projected a part of himself across space, a fragment of his soul borne on a spectral wave of desperation.

He called Jesse as Jesse had called him. Within his mind he saw a moving picture of her standing beside the woman Kim, speaking without sound, looking up as if distracted.

And focusing. Seeing him. Her mouth formed an "Oh" of surprise. And then the shape of his name.

"Jesse," he called. He made another picture of himself where he watched over Megan, the lay of the land around them. He willed Jesse to see what had happened, to know how little time he had left on this plane.

There was nothing more he could do. He withdrew and crouched like a pale shadow beside a girl who wouldn't look at him, praying that Jesse had understood. And would come before he was forced to leave.

With any luck he was about to witness a miracle.

CHAPTER NINE

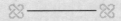

"THANK YOU, DAVID," Jesse whispered.

"What is it, Jesse?" Kim, who'd arrived at her cabin a few minutes ago, gave her a quizzical look. "You had this weird expression on your face."

Jesse started for the truck parked in the driveway. "I know where Megan is," she said.

"Did I miss something?" Kim said, jogging to keep up. "Or did you suddenly become psychic?"

"No time to explain." *And how in hell do I explain when there is time?* Jesse thought, tossing her backpack into her truck. How to explain that she'd asked her own personal ghost for help—and he'd responded? She'd almost given up on David before his image appeared, startlingly vivid, in her mind.

She knew he hadn't been with her in anything but thought. Some kind of telepathy, which was par for the course on top of the rest.

And she didn't give a damn how David had done it. Or how he'd found Megan. All she cared was that he'd been able to show her where Megan was.

That picture was indelibly etched in Jesse's memory. Megan wasn't badly hurt, thank God. And Jesse recognized the exact place where Megan had fallen.

The ledge. The ledge where Bobby Moran had died.

Jesse had no time to dwell on the past; she was too busy calculating the quickest route to Megan. A dirt road wound along the river, close to the spot in question.

"You know the ledge over the river where Bobby Moran fell?" she said as Kim came up beside her at the truck's door. "That's where we're going. Megan's fallen, but I don't think we'll need an ambulance."

Kim's open face reflected the concerns Jesse didn't put into words. The ledge was dangerous, but Megan, unlike Bobby, wouldn't be half gone on drugs and fighting her rescuers. A descent and rescue from the cliff to the ledge wasn't a complicated or lengthy maneuver. The greatest peril was that Megan would fall the much longer distance from the ledge to the rocky riverbank below.

Jesse slid into the driver's seat and closed the door. Kim leaned on the open window.

"How do you know, Jesse?" she asked.

"Trust me, Kim." Jesse started the engine and met Kim's gaze. "Please."

It was a blessing that Kim wasn't the kind to stand around debating a point when there was work to be done. She gave a quick nod. "All right. You go, and I'll be right behind you with the rescue truck. I'll radio the others to meet us there, and alert Doc Thielman that we may be bringing in a patient."

Jesse was already halfway down the lane toward the highway when Kim reached her own truck. She was only vaguely aware of the way her heart slammed in her throat, her tense grip on the steering wheel. Once she reached the dirt road, she concentrated on driving as fast as safety would allow. The tumult of the river seemed as loud as the roar of her truck.

The last span she had to cover was off-road, but she'd been this way before. She pulled up parallel to the cliff above the ledge and stopped the truck. She nearly dropped the keys as she yanked them from the ignition.

She hadn't expected to be here again. Not so soon. She got out of the truck and swallowed a surge of nausea. It was still daylight, not night, and there were no frightened teenaged boys watching a rescue that failed. The situation was totally different.

But the stakes were just as high.

With stubborn determination she ran to the edge of the cliff and looked over.

Megan was there, drawn up in a compact ball on the ledge. She must have heard Jesse or the truck, for she was looking up, her gray eyes large and vulnerable without the glasses to shield them. Her stare hinted of mild shock, but at least she was responsive. Her legs and arms were obviously working, and Jesse saw no signs of blood.

And David . . .

David was barely visible beside Megan, the river and rocks below filling the transparent outline of his body. He too was looking up, and she thought she saw him smile and lift one hand in a silent salute.

Then he vanished. Megan didn't seem to see him go. But of course not; she wouldn't be able to see him at all. Thank God the child hadn't had that to contend with as well.

"Megan," Jesse called. "Listen to me, honey. I'm going to get you back up here as quickly as I can. I just want you to sit very still and wait while I make up a special harness for you. Okay?"

Megan's chin twitched in the slightest of nods. She *was* responsive. She was okay. Jesse felt a flood of joy that went beyond relief, came from a source far deeper than the satisfaction of helping someone in trouble.

Self-doubt couldn't hope to stand against such joy. She was ready when Kim's rescue truck pulled up beside her own, and together they set about sorting and preparing the ropes and gear necessary for Megan's rescue.

"Bruce, Craig, Nance, and Manuel are on their way up," Kim said, "And Doc knows we'll be coming in. How is Megan?"

"She's okay, but I want to get down to her as soon as possible. It looks as if she'll only have a few minor cuts and bruises."

"Thank God," Kim murmured, passing Jesse a length of rope. Pulleys, carabiners, and harness were rechecked and assembled. Jesse inventoried her personal first-aid kit once more.

"You okay with this, Jesse?" Kim asked. "You're still the best one to go down to the ledge. But I'll assign someone else if you don't feel you can—"

"I'm doing it, Kim. Megan knows me, at least a little. If I can't handle it, I don't belong on this team."

Kim had no argument for that. Lives depended on each search and rescue team member acting as a professional. And Jesse knew she was a professional. When she went down over the cliff, she'd be challenging herself—but she'd also be saving something, someone, infinitely precious.

And not just because Megan was a child and a human life. The determination Jesse had felt earlier to help the girl had blossomed into an almost maternal attachment, though she and Megan had only spoken the one time in Al's study. Danger could do that sometimes, create such instant bonds. But she couldn't dismiss her feelings as mere instinct.

Maternal. Jesse returned to the cliff's edge, stunned by the direction of her thoughts. She had never planned on having children, of even being married. She'd never questioned that assumption or probed for the source of her conviction.

She was questioning now. First David, and then Megan . . .

She crouched and looked down at the girl. Megan remained pale and tight-lipped, but her eyes fixed on Jesse as on a lifeline.

"Only a few more minutes," Jesse said. "Hang in there, Megan. I won't let anything happen to you."

And she meant it. She meant it with her entire soul. She'd give her own life for this child's, gladly. Personally.

Within minutes the other team members arrived and went to work helping Kim put the evacuation system in place. Fortunately, the cliff area afforded several good anchor points in the form of sturdy trees and outcrops. The volunteers moved efficiently to secure the ropes and pulleys, complete with the harnesses that would allow Jesse to descend and bring Megan back up.

"We'll get a litter ready, in case you need it," Kim said.

Jesse nodded, secured her harness, and positioned herself for the descent, while Kim stayed above to act as belayer and the others stood ready to help. The river roared below them, a blue and white blur, but Jesse did not look down. She looked only at Megan's pleading, frightened eyes.

When her feet hit the ledge, she tested her balance and went immediately to Megan. The girl unfolded from her defensive huddle, and Jesse was engulfed in the sweaty, dirty, grateful warmth of a child's arms.

Jesse returned the hug and brushed dusty bangs from the girl's forehead. "You okay, Megan? Does anything hurt? Any part of you hard to move, or feel like it's broken?"

Megan's lower lip quivered, but she shook her head. Nevertheless, Jesse did a quick examination of Megan's body, making sure that she wouldn't need the litter or splints. All the blood was from minor surface scratches, and there were no telltale bumps on Megan's skull to suggest a concussion. Jesse cleaned and bandaged the worst cuts and gave Megan water and energy food from her pack.

"We're going to get you back up now, Megan," Jesse said. "I'll need you to help me. You're going to climb into this special harness, which will let you ride up on the rope. I'll be right behind you, so there's no way you can fall. Does that sound okay?"

Megan clung to Jesse for dear life, her fingers digging into the folds of Jesse's jacket. "Okay," she whispered.

Jesse gave Megan her brightest smile. "You've been very brave."

Megan squeezed her eyes shut, nodded, and let Jesse help her into the harness. Jesse gave Kim the signal to begin. Soon Megan was being lifted into Craig's arms, and two other volunteers helped Jesse over the lip of the cliff.

At first Jesse felt lucky to lie flat on the dirt and simply breathe. Everything was okay. Everything was *wonderful*. She felt Kim's touch on her shoulder and scrambled to her feet.

"Good job," Kim said. "And you were right about Megan. Nance says she's lucid and doing fine—only a little scratched and sunburned. Nothing that a few days and some rest won't heal, but we'll take her to Doc's just to be certain."

Absurdly giddy with happiness, Jesse joined Nance as she bandaged Megan's scraped palms. Megan was quietly cooperative until the last of the cleanup was done, and then she flung herself at Jesse again. Jesse held on tight and stroked her hair.

"We're going by Doc Thielman's just to give you another quick checkup," Jesse said, "and then home. Your uncle will be very glad to see you."

The accident had subdued Megan's rebelliousness. "I was so scared," she said. "I thought I was going to die."

"No. I'd never let anything happen to you. I promise."

Megan drew back and wiped her nose with the back of her bandaged hand. "You were right," she said with painful dignity. "I shouldn't have come up here alone. I wanted to show you that I—" Her face crumpled.

"Hush. It's over." Jesse gathered her close. "We'll talk more about it later, when you're feeling better. And I'm not going to yell at you."

Megan almost smiled, but she wouldn't quite meet Jesse's gaze. "Good." She yawned. "I'm really tired. I . . . don't know why."

"I do." Jesse scooped the girl up and half carried her back to the truck. "This kind of thing would wipe anyone out, and you've been walking all day."

She opened the passenger door and began to boost Megan into the seat. But Megan hesitated and looked back at her. "How did you know where to find me?" she asked.

Kim had asked the same question, and it was just as impossible to answer now. "I had a feeling," Jesse said. "A very strong feeling."

"Did you . . . see anyone else around when you found me?"

Anyone else? Jesse searched Megan's eyes. "Was someone here with you when the accident happened, Megan?"

Megan bit down on her lower lip. "No. I just wondered."

And that was not a satisfactory answer, either. But Jesse wouldn't press the girl now. Megan couldn't have seen David—he'd defined his "rules" pretty clearly. And David hadn't projected a sense that someone else had been with Megan.

Further explanations would have to wait. She settled Megan into the seat and tucked a light blanket around the girl while Kim and the others disassembled and packed the equipment. Jesse joined the team for a final conference.

"You take Megan to Doc's and home, get her into bed," Kim said. "We'll handle the rest. I've radioed town to let Megan's uncle know she's okay." She glanced toward the truck. "The way she was hanging on to you, I'd think you'd known her more than a few days."

"It is a bit unusual," Jesse admitted.

"Kind of like your intuition about her being up here."

"Speaking of intuition," Jesse said quickly, "I've been thinking that we ought to put some signs or a fence along the cliff. We might be able to ward off some of these accidents."

Kim took the abrupt change of subject in good stride.

"I've been thinking the same thing myself. I'm sure folks in town would be more than willing to contribute some money after what happened today and last week. In fact, that Emerson guy would have been good at drumming up support. Although—" She looked sideways at Jesse. "I got some pretty mixed vibes from him at the party. Heard that you and he had some kind of argument. . . ."

It took a mental wrench for Jesse to force her mind to the subject of Gary Emerson. Only this morning she'd discovered the break-in, but since Megan's disappearance she'd put Gary out of her thoughts.

Now she had to deal with what she'd left undone. Her confrontation with Gary hadn't gone unnoticed, even if no one had heard the words exchanged.

There wasn't any point in prevaricating with Kim. "We never liked each other. There are some . . . matters between us that haven't been resolved."

"Well, I guess that's none of my business. I was just sorry to hear that he'd caused you trouble at the party."

"Don't let it worry you, Kim. I can handle it."

Kim made a noncommittal sound and hooked her thumbs in her front pockets. "Marie's been in a bad mood since this morning when she found out he'd left town—"

"Left town?"

"Took off around dawn, apparently. Marie called to tell me. She couldn't understand why he left so suddenly." Kim shot Jesse a knowing look. "I'd stay away from her for a while, if I were you. For some reason she thinks you made him leave."

It sounded absurd, but there wasn't anything laughable about it. Jesse had caused Gary to take action, even before she'd determined how to get at him. He'd had someone break into her cabin. He'd tried to intimidate her with subtle taunts and direct threats. He thought she knew something, had something on him.

Now he was gone. Maybe David had spooked him at the party, but Jesse wasn't deceived. It wasn't over. Not by a long shot. Certainly not for her, however far Gary went.

Sooner or later she'd find out what Gary was afraid of, and then he'd have good cause to run.

"I'd better get Megan home and into bed," she told Kim. "Thank you. For trusting me."

"No problem. That's what we're here for. You did good, Jesse."

On impulse Jesse gave Kim a quick hug, a show of affection she'd seldom risked. Even Kim seemed a little surprised by it, for all her quick response.

Then they went to their separate trucks. Megan was already asleep in her seat, head lolling against the rolled-up window. Jesse buckled her in and drove down the hillside at a considerably slower pace than she'd set on the way up. Megan never stirred.

They dropped by Doc Thielman's, who confirmed Jesse's first diagnosis and gave the same advice of rest and quiet, as well as a sample tube of sunburn lotion. Megan was only half awake during the examination.

Al was waiting when Jesse's truck pulled into his driveway. He was silent as he picked up Megan's little body and carried her to her bed. But Jesse sensed that his stoic demeanor was, for once, a real mask and not cool discipline. He'd been worried.

After Megan was asleep in her own bed, she and Al went into the study. Al sat down behind his desk, his manner even more subdued than usual.

"Thanks for what you did, Jesse," he said. "I came home as soon as I could close the library, but you'd already left. Mrs. Plummer told me you'd gone looking for Megan, and then Kim Mayhew called. She told me to wait here—"

"You did the right thing, Al. We got to her quickly. She wasn't hurt."

"But she could have been. Because of my . . . neglect."

It was strange to realize that Al needed comfort and

reassurance. He'd always been the rock, the one so sure of his place in the world.

She touched his hand. "Megan learned something today," she said. "We all did. We can start over."

Al rested his head on his hand. "You will continue to see her, Jesse? She trusts you now."

"Wild horses couldn't keep me away. I'll be here every day, whenever I can. She won't be lonely."

"Thank you." He got up and moved for the door as quickly as his limp would permit. He paused with the door half open. "Can you stay with her for a while? I left some unfinished business at the library."

"Go ahead. I'd planned on staying the night, if that's okay."

Al nodded and left the room without another word. Jesse sank into the recliner and closed her eyes.

Hard to believe how complicated her life had become in only a few short days. First Gary's return, then David's appearance, now Megan. The weirdest part was that none of it felt like mere coincidence. It was a notion she wasn't ready to examine too closely.

David had been responsible for Megan's rescue, and she owed him a huge debt of gratitude for that. And for defending her at the party, whatever his motives.

But gratitude wasn't uppermost in her mind. That simple and limited emotion she would have been able to confine and control. Seeing David at Megan's side had given her a jolt she hadn't even recognized until she could think beyond Megan's safety. Her feelings where he was concerned were becoming increasingly urgent, linked to desires that were frightening in their intensity.

If she called him now, he probably couldn't come— not if her impression of his weakness by the river was correct. But she badly wanted to see him. To thank him. To tell him . . .

But her mind couldn't come up with the right words. It shut down at the mere attempt to find them.

She stood up, went to the kitchen for water, a snack of

grapes, and a chair, and returned to Megan's room for a long vigil.

Gary. David. Megan. She drifted into a light doze with those names spinning around and around like a juggler's balls.

Answers. There had to be answers. Meaning. Resolution. Somewhere . . .

She woke to the sense of someone watching. Megan's eyes were half open, peeping up over the edge of her blanket. The small clock by the bed said four A.M.

"Are you awake?" Jesse asked unnecessarily, pulling her chair closer to the bed. "It's still early. You should go back to sleep."

"Have you been there all the time?" Megan said, muffled under the blanket.

"Yes." Jesse smiled and reached over to smooth Megan's hair. "Making sure you're okay and getting your rest."

Megan's glance slid to the lamp on the nightstand and then back to Jesse's face. "I had bad dreams."

"I'm not surprised. It's only natural." She paused. "Are you feeling all right now?"

Megan twisted the blanket between her hands. "I'm afraid if I go back to sleep—"

"Come here, then," Jesse said, opening her arms. "Sit with me until you feel sleepy again."

Any evidence of stiffness or pain was gone from Megan's movements as she clambered out of bed and into Jesse's lap. The position was a little awkward, but Jesse didn't care. Having this child in her arms was the most natural thing in the world. The bond formed at the rescue hadn't lessened; it had only grown stronger.

She pulled Megan's head into the crook of her shoulder. "Do you want to tell me about the nightmare?"

Megan snuggled in with uninhibited trust and nodded. "It was about the cliff. I was there, but I wasn't alone. A boy was there with me. I watched him fall into the river, and I was going to fall too."

Jesse rocked her gently. "Who was the boy?"

"I heard them talking about him," Megan said. "The other people who came when you saved me. They said his name was Bobby."

Bobby. Jesse stopped rocking for a moment and then resumed, amazed at how unfettered her mind was of the guilt she'd carried ever since the teenager's death.

"Did he really fall off the same cliff and die?" Megan whispered.

Honesty was always better, and Megan deserved it. "Yes. It was very sad. He'd taken some drugs, and it made him dizzy and hurt his judgment. We . . . tried to save him."

"I'm sorry." Megan patted her back. "I know you wouldn't have let him die."

The innocent solace of a child was a remarkable gift. Jesse let out a long breath and hugged Megan, taking care not to put pressure on bruises and bandages. "It was different with you, Megan. You were very brave and did the right things."

"I wasn't brave." Megan pushed back to meet Jesse's eyes. "I did everything wrong, after you warned me. But I can learn to do it right."

"Do what?"

"Hike. The things you said you'd show me how to do." Megan's lower lip thrust out. "I want to go back to the same place. I want to look over the cliff and show I'm not afraid."

Jesse closed her eyes. A girl like Megan would want to confront her fears rather than let them fester. Maybe she didn't understand the psychology behind it, but her instincts were sound. Over and over she reminded Jesse of herself, and all the times she'd tried to face her own demons.

"You'll still take me, won't you?" Megan asked in a small voice. "You aren't too mad at me?"

"Mad?" Jesse kissed Megan's brow. "No. But you need to rest a little more before we tackle something like that."

Megan snorted. "I don't need a lot of rest. And I can

learn." She searched Jesse's eyes, her own wide and pleading. "Can we go tomorrow?"

"Whoa. You're moving too fast for me." She lifted Megan and steered her back to the bed. "You need a good night's sleep. A whole night, mind you. And a good breakfast and taking it easy for a day or so. Then we'll decide when and where to go."

Megan made no protest as Jesse tucked her under the blankets. "You promise we will go? You promise?"

"I promise." She plumped the pillow around Megan's head and touched the tip of her nose. "But only if you rest."

The girl's eyes were already growing heavy-lidded in spite of her efforts to stay awake.

"You won't go away, will you? You won't leave me?"

"I'll be here until morning."

"I mean after that. Tomorrow and after that. You'll be here, won't you?"

Jesse knelt beside the bed. "I live right across the yard, Megan. Except when I'm at work, I'm always here. I'm not going away."

Megan's hand shot out from under the blankets and felt for Jesse's. Her grip was surprisingly firm for such a small child's. "My parents died when I was just a baby," she said. "I don't even remember them much. But I . . . miss them."

"I know." Jesse leaned into the bed and gathered Megan's bundled body as close as she could. "I lost my mother when I was about your age. I was so lonely and scared. If you want to talk about that, we can. As much as you want."

"You were by yourself, too?"

"For a long time."

The touch of Megan's hand seemed to convey sympathy far beyond her years. "Grandma never talked about Mom and Dad. She didn't want me around, either. I could tell. But I could take care of myself." She sniffed. "Now she's gone. I don't want—" Residual pride stopped Megan from admitting more than she already had, but her feelings couldn't be dammed up. Tears welled in her eyes and trickled down her cheeks.

"You don't want to be alone," Jesse finished for her, stroking away the tears with her fingertips. "You won't be. I'll be your friend, Megan. For as long as you want."

Megan couldn't answer, and she was still uncomfortable enough with her tears to bury her face in the pillow. Jesse let her be, staying close in case Megan needed her.

But Megan's weariness did its inevitable work. Gradually her sobs quieted, and her little body went limp under the blankets. Jesse tucked Megan in again and returned to her chair.

The day's turmoil had taken its own toll on her, as well. After a few more minutes she stopped fighting the inevitable, and closed her eyes. A new and wonderful contentment, and a fresh purpose, carried her into sleep.

❊ ❊

THEY MADE A perfect pair.

David didn't need to see them together for more than a few minutes to know the miracle had happened. It was almost flawless. As nearly flawless as one short year in a troubled marriage, when a tiny girl had bound two people together as nothing else could have done.

The pattern played out—joyfully now, as it was meant to. David watched them both sleeping, Megan in her bed and Jesse in her chair, and knew a sharp bayonet-thrust of loneliness. Hadn't this been intended from the beginning? He'd sensed more pitfalls ahead, but instead he'd been given the opportunity to do a good deed to be weighed to his account.

Sophie and Elizabeth had been reunited.

And Jesse must know by now that Gary had left town, his immediate threat erased. Megan would surely be enough to distract her from that dangerous pursuit.

Every piece was falling into place. Then why did David feel so little triumph? Why did he want to be there with the woman and the child, a happy family that existed only in a fool's dreams?

He knew he should keep his distance. But he moved closer, crouched beside the child who had once been his daughter.

Elizabeth wouldn't have looked like this if she'd lived to Megan's age. She would have been fairy-bright and feminine in frills and lace. Sophie would have seen to that.

But Elizabeth hadn't lived. Fragile happiness had shattered. David had run from Sophie's grief—from his own. But the method of escape was the same as with any other unbearable situation. The strategy of forgetting was highly effective when one fought for one's life in war.

But losing one's life wasn't the solution he'd thought it would be. Now, at last, the scales were coming back into balance. The odds stacked higher and higher in David's favor. First Avery, and now this. Surely Jesse would find it easy to pardon him his sins.

He looked at Jesse's face, the lines of tension and care eased from her eyes and mouth in sleep. He'd seen that face suffused with love for the daughter she didn't remember. And he wondered what it would be like to feel that love directed toward him. Unjudging, unconditional, strong and true.

Fool, he told himself. Jesse's forgiveness would be more than sufficient. And as for Megan . . .

The girl need never know she'd had anything but a strange dream at a time of crisis. She wouldn't see him again, by accident or design. No child needed a ghost for a father. His absurd desire to embrace her, hold her like the babe she'd once been, would pass soon enough.

He was preparing to leave when Jesse stirred in her chair and opened her eyes.

"David?" she murmured sleepily. She blinked and sat up. "David!"

Her voice was low, pitched so as not to wake the sleeping child, but she looked at him with an open gladness that caught him like a rabbit in a snare. She rose swiftly and moved toward him, arms outstretched.

He wasn't quick enough to avoid her approach. She reached the place where he stood and began to walk through him, just as she'd done on the hillside. Her entire being jolted through him, blending and merging as if he'd failed in all his defenses. Desire, hunger, urges beyond his control clamored within him, driving out reason.

"Jesse," he breathed. "I can't—"

She stepped back, her arms wrapped around herself. "You're still too weak," she said with immediate comprehension. "You can't make yourself solid. I should have guessed."

Her calm acceptance made it possible for him to master his unexpected passion. "I came back to see that you and Megan were safe."

She smiled with a warmth that sent his phantom blood pumping hot all over again. "You saved Megan's life," she said softly. "I owe you more than I can ever repay."

It was what he'd wanted, this gratitude. But at the moment, he was busy cursing the limitations that deprived him of the form to properly accept her thanks.

"I'm glad that I could help," he said. "The child has pluck. Very much like her friend."

Jesse blushed, but she gazed at him in such a way that David thought he *could* guess what it must be like to be the recipient of her love. But then she looked away toward the bed, as if to reassure herself that Megan was too insensible to hear her conversation with a ghost.

"How did you find her?" she asked. "Did you hear me call?"

"Yes." No need to admit he'd first ignored her, and only luck had led him to Megan. Or her to him.

"You got through," Jesse said. "I saw you, even though you weren't really with me."

He floated back to the farthest wall. "Our connection, Jesse," he reminded her. "I trusted that it would be enough, and I didn't want to risk leaving the child."

"She didn't see you?"

He wondered at the question but had no intention of answering it honestly. "How could she?"

"It seemed as if—" She stopped, hesitated. "It doesn't matter. The important thing is that she's safe, and it's thanks to you."

"You're very fond of her."

She settled back into her chair. "Yes. I've only known her a few days, but—" She cast David a speaking glance. "We've developed an affinity very quickly."

Like you and me? he asked silently. "I can see that," he said. "You never told me of your rescue work, Jesse. I was able to watch a little of what you did to help Megan. I was greatly impressed."

She shook her head. "The credit belongs to the team." She was quiet for a long time, and then spoke as if she had held something inside too long and had finally found a means of release.

"That cliff where Megan fell . . ." she said slowly, "there was an accident last week. A boy named Bobby died." She swallowed and met his gaze. "I was the one who went down to get him. I felt responsible. But when I was able to help Megan, it made me realize how useless my guilt was. How little good it did anyone, including the people who suffered most."

Ah, yes. Guilt was such a useless sentiment. Who better to know than David Ventris? Jesse knew nothing of his own culpability, and yet she shared this with him, as she'd shared her childhood fears. He knew such admissions did not come easy for her.

"I'm telling you this," she said, "because there's something I need to do tomorrow after work, a visit I've been putting off too long. Megan should rest all day, and I can't stay with her. I thought . . . if it's possible . . . that you could keep an eye on her for me, for just a few hours. I know you don't know her, and she can't see you, but you were the one who saved her. It seems . . . right, somehow."

Right. Little did she know how appropriate it was, or how ironic. He should have excused himself with a story of his weakness, that he couldn't remain on the earthly plane, but he was weary of cowardice.

And he wanted this. Against all sense and reason, he wanted to please Jesse, to make her look on him again with those warm and welcoming eyes. To spend a few hours with the daughter he'd barely known and would never know beyond those hours. There could be no harm in that.

"Maybe I shouldn't have asked," Jesse said, looking away. "You must need to go back. I can't expect—"

"You trust me so much, Jesse?" he said.

Her voice dropped to a husky whisper. "Shouldn't I? After what you've done?"

He pushed away from the wall, crossed halfway to her, stopped. "Then I will watch her for as long as I can, and let you know if she needs you."

"Thank you," she said. "If there's any way—"

"Jesse?" Megan murmured. She stirred in her bed and pushed up under the blankets. David faded himself to invisibility, and Jesse moved to Megan's side.

"It's nearly dawn," she told the child. "How do you feel?"

"Tired. I thought I heard you talking."

"I'm sorry I disturbed you." She ruffled Megan's hair. "I have an early hike this morning, but you've got a lot more resting to do if we're going to take that camping trip. I promise to come back to see you as soon as I can. In the meantime, I want you to imagine there's a guardian angel here with you. You can't see him, but I've asked him to watch over you while I'm gone."

Megan's sleepy eyes surveyed the room. "I don't think I believe in guardian angels," she said.

"You don't have to believe. Just imagine. Imagine that he's whoever you want him to be."

Megan yawned and closed her eyes again. "Then I imagine that he has a blue coat and black boots. And a sword . . ."

Jesse paused as she tucked the blankets back around Megan's chin. Megan was already asleep. David rematerialized beside Jesse and waited for the inevitable question.

"Are you sure she didn't see you?" she asked.

"I'm sure of very little. But I will play guardian angel to the best of my ability."

"I know you will. I—" She gazed at him and seemed to lose her train of thought. "Can you come to the cabin this evening?"

David remembered how, only yesterday, he'd vowed to regain some emotional detachment from Jesse Copeland and her problems. But he'd been pulled into her life more deeply than before, and her invitation sounded dangerously sweet to his ears.

"I'll be there," he promised. He reached out to take her hand before he remembered his inability to do so. "When I see you again, I will not be so constrained by these limitations."

If she grasped his innuendo, she chose to ignore it. But her farewell was warmer than any he remembered.

When he was alone again, he set himself to floating beside Megan's bed and contemplated the snub-nosed, elfin face. She slept with a child's total absorption, lost in a world of dreams.

Pleasant dreams, he hoped. Dreams unburdened by the weight of past lives. There was little enough of her life with him that she could remember. One short year.

He wasn't tempted to call her by that other name. But his heart was in his throat, as if he were capable of the fatherly feelings a man ought to have for his only daughter.

Tenderness. Pride. Love. Hadn't he possessed such feelings, once upon a time? Or had they merely been illusion?

He rested a weightless hand on her forehead. If it were within his power, he would have given her everything a child could wish for: a world secure from all harm, a happy home, parents who loved her. One of those she had in Jesse. But a child deserved a father. When he was gone, Jesse would be free to find someone to fill that role.

The surge of hot denial David felt was unforeseen and indisputable. By God, the thought of Jesse with another man—in another man's arms, possessed by him, bearing his children, sharing his life . . .

Megan made a thin, fretful sound and moved her head on the pillow. David's withdrawal was not quite swift enough. She opened her eyes and stared at him from under heavy lids.

"You?" she whispered. "Are you . . . the angel?"

Oh, the innocence of children. "You're having a dream, Megan," he said. "Only a dream, about a friend who wishes you well. Who wants you to be happy. Go back to sleep, and dream of happy things."

She obeyed him as she might a beloved father, and soon was at rest again. But he knew better than to take further chances. He retreated across the room to wait out the time he had promised.

Let Megan dream. Let her dream of perfect fathers with tender hearts and angels who truly existed. He hoped she would never learn the truth.

CHAPTER TEN

FOR JESSE, THE new day came with a strengthening of resolve that a little more obsolete emotional baggage was about to be discarded once and for all.

She'd told David that she planned to make a visit she'd put off too long. Ever since Bobby Moran's funeral, she'd struggled with her own sense of responsibility for the boy's death, the harsh self-judgment that she hadn't been good enough. She'd been half afraid to face Mrs. Moran after their brief meeting at the funeral, and she'd let her own discomfort keep her from reaching out.

What had happened with Megan opened her eyes, and she recognized the futile self-indulgence of her guilt. She didn't know Bobby's mother well; like Joan Copeland, Mrs. Moran lived at the fringe of town life—husbandless, apparently unemployed, her son a minor lawbreaker and troublemaker. Perhaps she had friends enough to see her through her grief. But Jesse couldn't be complacent any longer, not when she'd been granted the miracle of being able to save someone she loved.

Now, with Megan safe at home and the afternoon's work behind her, Jesse turned her truck toward the edge of town and the small trailer park where Mrs. Moran lived.

The Moran trailer was set slightly apart from the others, flanked by a pair of well-rusted junker cars. The trailer itself was old and small but in relatively good condition. The tiny patch of lawn beside the trailer was surprisingly well cared for, graced with a scraggly row of sun-beaten flowers in a narrow bed.

Jesse parked and walked up to the door, wiping her damp palms on her jeans. Her knock went unanswered for several moments, and when Mrs. Moran came to the door she opened it only a crack.

She looked much as she had at the funeral: wan, face pinched, her petite figure bent with sorrow. When her son was buried, she'd worn dark glasses to cover her eyes; now Jesse could see the ravages of her grief, the swelling and redness of recent weeping, the blankness that came from the most terrible loss.

Mrs. Moran's eyes widened a little at the sight of her visitor, and Jesse almost expected the door to slam in her face. But it opened another few inches, enough for Jesse to see the little boy clutching his mother's hand. His name was Kirk, Jesse remembered—Bobby's younger brother. He was near Megan's age. And, like Megan, he'd learned suffering early.

"Mrs. Moran?" Jesse said. She'd rehearsed this visit any number of times in her mind, and she still didn't know how to say it. "My name is Jesse Copeland. I've come by . . . to offer my sympathy on the loss of your son."

The woman stared at her, unmoving. "I remember you. You're the woman who tried to save him."

"Yes. And I'm very sorry, Mrs. Moran. I wish I could have done more."

The words were so inadequate. Jesse wished for some

great eloquence, the skill to comfort this woman and reach out in a meaningful way. Maybe she was only adding to Mrs. Moran's pain.

But the woman blinked and stepped away from the door. "Come in," she said.

The trailer was cramped but immaculate, giving the lie to the old clichés about "trailer trash." Mrs. Moran sat down at a two-seat table in the kitchenette, Kirk at her side. Jesse sat opposite.

"I want to thank you for what you tried to do," Mrs. Moran said, her voice low and rough. "I know you did the best you could."

It was more than Jesse hoped for, this absolution. She wouldn't have blamed Mrs. Moran for raging at her, needing to hold someone accountable for her loss.

"I came to . . . see if there was anything I could do," Jesse said. "Any way that I could help."

"Thank you," Mrs. Moran said. "But you don't need to do anything. Bobby—" She closed her eyes. "He was already gone."

Already gone. Already lost to his mother, who couldn't control him anymore. Couldn't help him overcome his addiction. Could only stand by and watch him destroy himself.

Jesse didn't question her impulse. She reached across the table, covered Mrs. Moran's slack hand with her own and tried with all her heart to convey what she felt.

"Don't blame yourself," she said. "Please don't. It wasn't your fault."

Mrs. Moran let out a shuddering breath. Her hand trembled beneath Jesse's. "You don't know," she said. "You can't."

"You're right," Jesse said. "But I can listen. If you need someone to talk to. If you just . . . don't want to be alone. I know about being alone when it hurts."

A tear escaped the corner of Mrs. Moran's eye. She pulled her hand from under Jesse's and stroked Kirk's hair. "Did you come here because you blamed yourself?"

The question was piercing and direct and cut right to

the quick. Twenty-four hours ago it would have been a bitter blow. Jesse remembered finding Megan on the ledge, her joy when she'd known the girl was unharmed. Her sense that something had been released within her heart.

"I did blame myself, for a while," Jesse answered. "But that's not why I'm here. I don't have any . . . easy answers, Mrs. Moran."

"No. It wasn't easy for you to come here, was it?" She looked out the small, curtained window. "I heard about your mother. How she drowned in the river."

Jesse swallowed. "It's one reason why I joined search and rescue. Because I—" She broke off and shook her head, but Mrs. Moran didn't seem to require an explanation. She looked at Jesse with tears in her eyes.

"Maybe you do know what it's like," she whispered.

They gazed at each other, more communication in their silence than words could convey. Mrs. Moran was the first to break away. She rose and went to the kitchen counter, hiding her face.

"Thank you for coming," she said.

Jesse rose. "I meant what I said. If there's any way I can help . . ."

Mrs. Moran half turned, Kirk still her quiet shadow. "I'll remember."

There was nothing else Jesse could do but hope the other woman believed in her sincerity. She knew how difficult it was to break down barriers between people who had to learn how to trust.

But the barriers *could* be broken. It had happened with Megan.

And David. Hadn't he been the first to test her own defenses? Hadn't he begun the crack in her heart that was widening a little more with every passing day, with every person whose life touched hers?

She paused at the trailer door and pulled out the notepad she kept in her jeans pocket. "I've written down my number and address," she said, setting the paper on the table. "Please, call anytime."

She was almost to her truck when Mrs. Moran's voice stopped her.

"Thank you, Jesse. I never told you my name. It's Lisa." She smiled and watched Jesse from the door when she could have gone inside. Even Kirk raised a small hand in a tentative wave.

The fullness in Jesse's chest expanded in a rush of warmth that made her eyes prickle. Maybe she hadn't done much, but she felt good, damned good for having tried. Maybe Mrs. Moran—Lisa—would call. And maybe Megan would be willing to visit Kirk, who was probably just as isolated as his mother.

At least there was hope.

Megan was waiting for her at Al's, and proved how well recovered she was by barreling into Jesse the instant she walked in the door.

"I was waiting for you," Megan said. "You *did* come back."

She spoke with the grudging wonder of a skeptic forced to admit that miracles were possible. Now that the initial euphoria over Megan's rescue had passed, it was even more important that Jesse keep her promises to Megan and show the girl that she could rely on the care and consistency of another human being.

"I've been to see Bobby's mother," Jesse said. "Our talk last night made me decide to go. She has a son named Kirk, about your age."

Megan's expression grew grave. "They must be very sad."

"Yes." She put her arm around Megan. "I've been thinking—if you'd like, and if Mrs. Moran agrees—we could invite him over sometime. He and his mother don't have much. You could show him the computer. He probably really needs a friend right now."

Megan frowned, and Jesse wondered if she'd pushed things too fast. She'd barely begun to know Megan herself, though she felt as if their relationship were years rather than days old.

"Just think about it," Jesse said. "In the meantime,

you and I have a camping trip to plan, don't we? And we have to get you some new glasses."

"I'm only a little nearsighted," Megan protested.

"But you won't want to miss the beautiful things we'll see on our hike. I'll set up the appointment." She gave Megan another quick hug. "Have you been getting plenty of rest?"

"All day." Megan wrinkled her nose. "You know that angel you talked about last night? He was there this morning. But when I woke up later, he was gone."

Was it possible that Megan had seen David after all? If so, she didn't seem troubled by the vision. And somehow Jesse was not surprised. She'd felt not the slightest qualm in asking David to keep watch after she left. There'd been a rightness to it that couldn't be denied.

David might be waiting for her now, at the cabin. Her heart picked up speed, and she remembered vividly their meeting in Megan's room—her inability to touch him when she'd nearly flung herself into his arms, his promise that he wouldn't be so insubstantial when next they met.

She had *wanted* to touch him. She had felt such happiness at seeing him, as if his presence were the only thing lacking to make her world complete.

Could so much have changed in a handful of days? How could she justify the irrational feeling that David, like Megan, was becoming an essential part of her life?

"Are you going to have dinner with us, Jesse?" Megan said, tugging at her hand. "It's tacos."

Jesse squeezed Megan's fingers. "I'll stay for dinner— but then it's off to bed with you, young lady. Agreed?"

Megan rolled her eyes. "Okay. Let's go tell Mrs. Plummer we're ready to eat."

Jesse made the most of her time with Megan, but her thoughts turned again and again to David—and the other matter that remained far from settled.

Gary might be gone from Manzanita, but he was not forgotten. The events of the past twenty-four hours hadn't erased the impact of the confrontation at the party and the break-in, or weakened Jesse's resolution to track down the source of Gary's guilt. But at last she had come to recognize what she must do if she were to go any further in her quest for justice—what she'd been avoiding just as she'd put off visiting Mrs. Moran. The one thing she feared most.

She had to return to the old resort. She had to walk the grounds again and go into the cabin she and her mother had shared, relive it all once more. If answers existed, they had to be there.

She was just beginning to understand how much more than herself she had to fight for.

⚙ ⚙

THE SUN WAS sliding behind the mountains when Jesse walked into the cabin. She hesitated only a moment when she saw David, and then she went to him—with outstretched hands and a smile, as she'd done before. But this time he took her hands in his, and they looked at each other as if they were old and dear friends who had shared some great trial and come through safely.

David had thought their hours apart would give him all the distance he needed to master his inconvenient response to her newfound warmth and trust. But the feel of her slender fingers cradled in his own, the sincere gladness in her upturned face, had a devastating effect. He was already pulling her close before he realized the danger.

He released her hands and stepped back. "And how is our Megan?"

Jesse let her arms fall, suddenly self-conscious. "She's fine. Resting." She looked him up and down, a delicate flush to her cheeks. "You're solid again."

"As promised." He whisked an illusory bit of dust from his ragged jacket. "Though I seem to have a deucedly limited wardrobe."

She laughed, though the sound was tense with unspoken thoughts. By silent agreement they settled in the kitchen, where they'd held their first conversation—the table separating them as it had then, a quiet return to their original bargain. Whatever had happened between them since the party, Jesse remembered the risks of intimacy with her personal ghost.

"You asked me," Jesse said at last, "if I trusted you."

David clasped his hands on the table in a pose of mock relaxation. "And you," he said, "asked me why you shouldn't."

She looked at his hands. "Do you know . . . how difficult it is for me to trust? I'd lost the habit for a very long time, except with a handful of people. Like Al, and Kim."

"But now?"

"Now—" She met his gaze with heartbreaking directness. "After the party, and what you did for Megan . . . I believe you are my friend."

Such a simple word, "friend." So unsatisfying if one wanted more. But David heard in that word a wealth of meaning and significance that went far beyond its definition. Friendship was nothing simple or casual for Jesse. Nor was her trust.

Her trust was always what he'd wanted. Why, then, did he feel as if it were an unexpected gift—a gift he both desired and did not desire, an offering that weighed as much as a cannonball?

"You've already done so much for me," she said, "when I've given you nothing in return."

He dipped his head to hold her gaze when she would have looked away. "You'll get your chance. There are no debts between friends."

If only that were true. But hope was in her face—hope he'd put there, unworthy though he might be. "I told you about my past with Gary," she said. "He's left town, and I don't know why. But the situation with him isn't resolved. Not for me." She squared her shoulders. "I'm still looking for my answers, and my memory. And I know where I have to continue the search."

So she wasn't giving up. Unfortunate—but Avery wasn't here to harm her or stand in the way.

"How can I help?" he asked.

"I need to return to the place where I grew up, the resort my mother ran when I was a child. I haven't been there since I left Manzanita years ago."

And she was afraid. David got up and moved around the table. "You don't want to go alone."

The corner of her mouth twitched. "It's a . . . bit like walking into the dragon's lair. Does that sword of yours work?"

"I've yet to slay a dragon, but I'm willing to try." He lifted his hand, laid it gently along the curve of her neck under the silky wisps of loose hair. She went very still.

"You said you trusted me," he said. "I would slay a thousand dragons for you, Jesse."

A deep shudder ran through her body. Slowly she raised her own hand, reached behind to cover his.

"Thank you."

How was it that the lightest of caresses, the unaffected words of gratitude, could be so charged with erotic power? David sucked in a breath and tried to remember that they'd been discussing his saber, not the other weapon he'd be very happy to employ at this very moment, on the floor or on the sofa or the table or wherever Jesse would permit.

However often he told himself that wanting her did nothing to further his cause, he couldn't stop it. That desire was as much a part of this body he assumed as the feel of a heartbeat and the flow of air in his lungs. And it wasn't Sophie he thought of. Never Sophie.

Jesse's kiss had shown that she responded to him. Responded as *herself*. He'd come back to Earth to win forgiveness from his former wife. But Jesse was the one he wanted to win.

"Jesse," he whispered.

She dropped her hand from his and moved restlessly, cueing him to withdraw. "I want to get an early start in the morning. I haven't been sleeping much, so I'm going to bed early tonight. If you're coming with me, maybe you need to conserve your energy."

A dismissal if ever he'd heard one. And he knew why. She couldn't help but feel what passed between them with every touch. "You'd send me back so soon?"

She flushed. "I'm sorry. I keep forgetting . . . the place you come from. If you want to rest here . . ."

Yes. To stay with her as she made ready for sleep, to watch her lie down in her nightclothes in her solitary bed and imagine lying there with her, atop her, inside her—

"I'd offer you the couch," she said, "if you need it, since you're—"

"A ghost?" he said, forcing a smile. "I cannot maintain my physical form forever, but perhaps I can take my rest in a pleasanter place than limbo."

"Then you're welcome to stay." She turned away quickly. "I don't suppose you eat or drink? I never thought to ask."

David was deluged by visions of steak and kidney pie, fresh butter on new-baked bread, chunks of pungent cheese. But the mere act of eating would deplete his energies, and he preferred to spare them for other opportunities.

"Thank you, but no." He strolled into the living room and sat on the sofa. "Don't let me interfere with your routine. It gives me pleasure to observe the simple tasks of daily life."

She followed him to the doorway. "You . . . do remember what you promised."

"I'll not play Peeping Tom," he said, leaning back and crossing his legs. "Though you are a very beautiful woman, Jesse. The temptation is considerable."

She stared at him, color high, and folded her arms across her chest. "It's not that I'm beautiful, is it? Or even that we used to be lovers. You haven't had sex for nearly two centuries."

He choked on a startled laugh. By Boney's shrunken balls, she wasn't so demure as she liked to pretend. A modern woman. He thought he could come to like modern women very much indeed.

"Would you take pity on me, Jesse, and cure my deprivation?" he asked, leaning forward.

"Will it save your soul?"

If only it could. But if there was a way to bed Jesse and win his freedom at the same time . . . David groaned inwardly at the increasing pressure in his groin.

Jesse was backing away, disappearing into the kitchen. But she had almost—almost—made an offer. David censored his increasingly torturous thoughts and closed his eyes, drifting into a semiphysical state where he could still feel the sofa under him and smell the delicious scents that came from the kitchen. Bread, he guessed, and jam, and hot tea. His mouth watered.

Small things he'd never appreciated when he'd had them, like the sound of a baby's cry and the rhythm of hoofbeats on cobbles and the faintly off-key strains of a country dance. The fragrance of dew-splashed roses in the morning and the pungent odor of London's streets on a hot summer's day.

In Jesse's home he could begin to remember these things. The armor of years sloughed away, and he was a boy again. Lancelot, who still had hope and could find pleasure in so little.

He caught Jesse tiptoeing across the room as if not to wake him. He maintained the illusion of sleep until she'd gone into her bedroom and closed the door.

He could walk through any wall she chose to put between them. When there was silence in the cabin, he went to her door and paused.

Once before he'd found her sleeping. The sight had been arousing then—but now, with his desire heated to fever pitch, he wondered how he could keep his hands from her. From her hair, her skin, her body. Or his mouth from her lips and breasts and sweet feminine secrets.

Had he been a truly honorable man, he could have used that excuse for not intruding on her privacy and breaking his word. But he was not honorable. He retreated because he knew he would not be able to control himself, and a false step would destroy Jesse's trust in him.

He'd been wrong about being able to remain in this house with Jesse, bound as he was. He sought relief outside, under the hills and the stars and the sky. Living men and women could lose themselves in true sleep, but he could only choose his form of wakeful emptiness.

He set himself to wait out the lonely night.

❈ ❈

"Have you ever ridden in a car?"

Jesse stood beside the open door of her vehicle, smiling at David with a mischievous glint in her eye.

For a woman about to face a challenge she greatly feared, Jesse had greeted him quite cheerfully. She was armored in determination, and even the bright summer morning seemed to bolster her tenacious good humor.

David moved closer to the horseless carriage and touched the warm metal surface. "I know about them," he said. "News of the world did reach my corner of limbo from time to time. Your modern conveniences don't unduly shock me."

She slid into the seat behind the wheel and pushed open the opposite door. "You can ride with me—unless you'd rather meet me there."

No, indeed. David had a peculiarly keen desire to stay at Jesse's side. "I can hardly decline such a fascinating experience," he said.

"Then hop in."

He did so, gingerly, and in spite of his bravado he winced when the engine engaged. He felt a stab of longing for his faithful army mount, Cyril. If there was any justice, Cyril had survived the war and conferred his courage on many generations of colts and fillies.

Cyril wouldn't have had much use for this contraption. Jesse maneuvered the noisy vehicle down the paved roads while David observed with impunity the passing townsfolk who weren't aware of his existence. Within a quarter of an hour they'd left Manzanita's outskirts and reached Jesse's destination.

From outside the heavy wire fence that protected it, the resort appeared as a cluster of smallish buildings barely visible behind a thick screen of trees, a wide clearing, a miniature lake, and woods that bounded it on three sides. Jesse got out of the truck, released her breath in a long rush, and strode toward the locked gate.

"The place was sold after my mother died," she said, subdued as she wrapped her fingers around the wire. "I was told that someone else tried to run it for a while, but they couldn't make it profitable."

"And you grew up here," David said, joining her.

She didn't answer but knelt to examine the base of the fence. "Someone's already been in here. The fence is cut." She returned to the truck for a pack, then knelt to pry open the cut section of fence. The resulting opening was wide and tall enough for a man on hands and knees.

David melted through the fence and met Jesse on the other side, offering assistance. She brushed off her jeans, gaze sweeping the deserted compound.

"I don't . . . even know where to start," she said.

David kept a firm grip on her arm and felt her tremble. "What exactly do you hope to find?"

"I had a dream . . . about my mother and Gary fighting in the cabin where we lived. I'm convinced it had an important meaning, but that something was missing."

Her words didn't make complete sense, but David didn't blame her for her distraction. He remembered returning to the ruins of Parkmere Hall after Sophie's death, numb and empty, unable to bear the sight of the devastated rose garden she'd loved or the home he'd spent so much effort avoiding. The ghosts—real or illusory—of his indifferent father and autocratic mother walked what was left of the charred halls and blackened chambers, leaving no room for any shade Sophie might have left behind.

How he'd hated being there. He knew how Jesse must feel, and he wouldn't let her suffer alone.

"Were you ever happy here?" he asked. "Have you any good memories at all?"

She closed her eyes. "Yes. Sometimes my mother would be sober for a while—months at a time. Before Gary came—" She shook her head and burst into motion, striding toward the nearest buildings. David matched her frantic pace. At the last moment she veered away from the cabins and went to the lakeshore, to a crumbling pier that jutted out over the water. The skeleton of an old rowboat lay beached on the gravel.

"We used to row out on the lake, when no one else was staying here," Jesse said. "There were usually just enough guests during the year to keep us going, but I liked it when it was just me and Mom. Then she had time for me. It was our own little world."

"And your father?"

"He left when I was seven. He just disappeared. I think he sent money for a while, but . . ." Her fists clenched.

"Why did he leave you?"

"I think that he . . . expected more than my mother could give. He hated her drinking." She jerked her head in a silent gesture of denial. "He abandoned us. That's all there is to it."

"And you hate him for that."

She looked at him bleakly. "Shouldn't I? He never bothered to get in touch with me. Not even when Mom died. Not until he was dead. Then I found out he'd become very rich after he'd left us, and he willed his fortune to me."

David let go of her arm and moved away, staring at the fringe of woods along the opposite shore. *Not until he was dead.* Ironic that David should be in the same position. Had Jesse's father hoped to win her forgiveness postmortem? Had it been belated love or guilt that had motivated him at the end?

It didn't matter. Jesse hadn't forgiven.

"There's no point in putting it off," Jesse said. She threw David a look of appeal that reminded him how ignorant she was of his need for her absolution. "Will you come with me to the cabin?"

He rejoined her, and they walked across the open meadow to the buildings along the east shore of the lake. The twelve or so small cabins were strung along the lake, anchored at one end by a slightly larger cabin, a second structure Jesse identified as the lodge dining room, and several outbuildings.

Jesse headed for the larger cabin. Unlike a few of the smaller cottages, it hadn't been badly damaged by the ravages of time and weather. A battered, rustically carved "Welcome" sign hung askew on the door. Jesse hesitated at the threshold, biting her lower lip.

"I haven't been here since they took me to the hospital," she said. "I . . . don't know what I'm going to find."

David touched her shoulder. "I'm with you, Jesse."

She turned to him suddenly, grasped his hand, and stared into his eyes, as if testing his sincerity. Then she released him and gripped the doorknob.

It turned easily, unlocked. She let the door fall open. Over her shoulder David could see a small room and adjoining kitchen, a few pieces of worn furniture, a scattering of dried leaves and pine needles and other debris. Festoons of cobwebs hung from the walls and ceiling. The kitchen window was broken, another badly cracked.

Clouds of dirt and dust flew up under Jesse's feet as she walked in. That another person had been in the cabin before her was obvious from the track of footprints crisscrossing the room. Jesse hardly seemed to notice.

She didn't speak at all, and David could well imagine the reason for her muteness. She made a circuit of the room, touching the furniture and coughing behind her hand at the dust she raised.

"I remember . . . we used to play Scrabble, sitting right here on the couch with a TV tray," she murmured. "Just Mom and me. And in winter we'd read aloud in front of a blazing fire." She crouched before the cobwebbed fireplace. "I was always scared of getting too close to the flames. Mom never teased me about it, but Gary . . ."

Gary. Avery. Jesse might well be afraid of fire. David swallowed and watched her rise and walk to the nearest window.

"It's so dark in here," she said. She pulled at the curtains to open them, and the rotten fabric ripped in her hands.

She stumbled back into David's arms. He steadied her and listened to the rasp of her breathing, so charged with distress. He wanted to hold her close to his heart, ease a little of that familiar pain.

But she pulled free and walked into the kitchen.

"It . . . used to be filled with sunlight," she said. She turned her back to the dirty, broken window and opened a cupboard above the tile counter. "They didn't even bother to take out the dishes." She removed a chipped plate and pressed it to her breast. "No one would have wanted them, anyway."

Except Jesse. She continued to hug the plate as she gazed about the room. "My dream was set here. They argued, and then it filled up with water. . . ." She put the plate down and opened each of the cupboards in turn, then left the kitchen for a short hallway.

She seemed in control of herself, able to master the crippling emotions she had feared. But when she entered the first of two bedchambers, she went rigid and far too quiet.

The room had the look of one designed for a young child, with faded but cheerful wallpaper, plain furnishings, and the remnants of toys. Jesse picked up a three-legged model horse and set it carefully on a shelf. It toppled over again, and Jesse simply stared. Minutes passed, and still she didn't move.

"Jesse," David said. He gathered her in the curve of his arm, ignoring the baser feelings that arose in him when he touched her. "You've seen enough for now."

"No." But she remained where she was, neither fighting his embrace nor returning it. "Something's missing. Somewhere—"

"Then perhaps a bit of fresh air will help restore your memory." He turned her toward the door. "Come. Let me take you out of here."

She crumpled in his hold, her body admitting what her face would not disclose. She held on to him, and he felt strong—strong and wanted and needed, hating the people that had made her suffer as he'd hated little in his life.

He took her outside and found a seat for her on a tree stump, his hand at her back. She ducked her head between her knees and covered her eyes. He thought she might be weeping; he hoped she would grant herself that release.

But when she looked up her eyes were dry, and he knew she'd won another struggle against the weakness she saw in her own soul. To be so vulnerable before David would surrender too much of herself—more than even her newfound trust for him would permit.

So her pain stayed locked inside. David felt it nonetheless, and it pounded away at the walls he'd built within himself so long ago. Walls he hadn't known existed until he began to discover Jesse's.

He didn't want to look behind his own walls. He preferred the surface, the shiny facade, the protective veneer. Limbo had stripped that from him, but he hadn't learned. He was still—

"Tell me about your childhood," Jesse said, startling him. "I know you said you don't remember much of your life. But maybe now that we've been talking . . . maybe it's coming back to you. As mine is to me." She looked at him with earnest entreaty in her troubled eyes. "Did I . . . did Sophie know you as a boy?"

He wasn't tempted to laugh, though she might have read his very thoughts. Wasn't it a way he could offer consolation—by sharing his past, letting her know she wasn't alone? Wasn't it the right time to begin preparing her for what she had to be told, sooner or later?

He sank into a crouch beside her. "I am starting to

remember," he said. "Do you wish to know about my idyllic upbringing among the landed aristocracy?"

"Was it idyllic?" she asked. "Did you have a happy childhood?"

He closed his eyes, as if drawing on images that were only just returning. "I was privileged," he said. "I wanted for nothing. My father and mother came from long and distinguished bloodlines and considerable fortune. The viscounts of Ashthorpe were good *ton,* even if they seldom ventured from the country."

"And the place we . . . you grew up in was beautiful," Jesse said, her gaze distant. "Hills and lakes and streams."

"It was beautiful," he agreed. "Everything a child could wish for. Avery and I—"

"Avery?"

"My brother." His throat was tight and harsh around the word. "We played many a dashing game in the meadows and hills. As much time as we could away from the Hall."

Jesse was quiet for a moment, flexing her fingers between her knees. "That was what I did," she said, "after Gary came." She looked up. "What were you running from, David? What were your parents like?"

How much did she remember, and how much guess? "We were a wealthy, privileged family with little else to recommend us," he said lightly, making a jest of it. "My father was a silent and distant man who married as his parents willed, and lived his life among his books. He had no use for children. My mother—was a paragon of duty. She raised us to understand our destiny as breeders of future peers and upholders of the family honor. And I, as heir, was the one of whom she demanded obedience and unquestioning compliance with my carefully planned future."

"It was a different world then," Jesse said. "A different age. But some things had to be the same. Your mother . . ." She paused, staring at her clasped hands. "She must have loved you."

She spoke so hopefully, as if she wished he'd known such happiness. "Do you fancy that love was a necessary ingredient in the bearing and raising of the dynasty's next generation?" he asked. "My mother surely wouldn't have agreed with that policy. She had a better method. She trained us from earliest infancy to be self-reliant and not bother her with our juvenile needs and fears. We were not, after all, as ordinary children. We were aristocrats of an ancient and noble line, unbroken for centuries."

Jesse glanced at him, brows drawn. "You mean you weren't allowed to be children, you and . . . Avery."

As you were not, he thought. *Yet you had faith in your mother's love, however flawed it was.*

"Ah, but we had something better," he said aloud, "as my mother so often pointed out to us. Duty and honor." He rose and paced a few feet away. "What need for pleasure or maudlin sentiment? Duty and honor last forever."

"But you found ways to play. You said you were able to escape, have fun. You had a brother."

He didn't wish to speak of Avery. He didn't want to feel again what he'd felt confronting Gary in his hotel room, that gut-wrenching tangle of guilt and pity and hatred that had no part in his plans.

"I wanted a brother or sister when I was younger," Jesse said. "But after my father left—"

"You thought it was better that you didn't." David gazed at the lake, at the reflection of drifting clouds on the nearly still surface.

"Tell me about your brother," she said.

He couldn't avoid the subject. If she didn't flinch at Avery's name in spite of her hatred for Gary, there was little chance she'd react badly to David's censored tale. And it might lay the groundwork for his ultimate revelation.

"Avery was five years younger than I," he said. "When he was small, my mother doted on him. She'd not yet decided that I was . . . not all she expected in the heir, and didn't demand as much of him. But when I turned eleven, she began to mold him into the son she truly wanted."

"She . . . stopped loving him?"

"She taught him to rely on no one but himself. But it was a lesson he never learned. When our mother denied us pleasure, I made certain to grow up quickly and find my own. I was fortunate because I didn't care about my mother's lack of affection or my father's distance. They were of no importance to me. There was much more of the world to interest me than Parkmere Hall, and I discovered it soon enough."

"You rebelled."

"I simply felt no desire to obey my mother's dictates or take on responsibilities I never asked to bear." He laughed. "How sad for my mother that I became the ne'er-do-well she tried so hard to prevent."

He heard her get up and move about restlessly. "You must have been very unhappy."

"Unhappy? I found a way out once I reached the age of moderate independence. I was very good at earning my own income at the gaming tables, when my mother withheld my allowance."

"But you said that Avery was different," she said. "What happened to him?"

"He seemed to require the tender affections my mother couldn't give him. He was quite tedious in his efforts to please her. He set himself an impossible task, and suffered for it."

"But he had *you*," she said. "Someone to look up to."

Ah, yes. The bold elder brother. Lancelot. The knight who never feared to slay dragons. Avery had been timid away from the Hall until he'd realized only manly stoicism would win Mother's approval. Then he'd flung himself into their games with a full heart, playing Arthur but watching his "first knight" for any sign of brotherly approbation. Watching with something very like worship.

For a time they'd been close. David hadn't thought of

those days in centuries, and he took no satisfaction in it now.

When had it ended? Had Avery believed he could win the parental favor David had failed to earn? He was not the heir, but he could have had everything else. If he had been *good* enough. Dutiful enough. Was that when the first break between them had occurred?

Or was it when David realized his younger brother had become a dead bore, prosing on about proper behavior just like their mother? When David recognized that Avery was a burden, not a companion, too young to join him in his quests for sensual oblivion?

Was he to admit this to Jesse, that he'd abandoned his brother in the end, as he'd abandoned duty to his name and abandoned Sophie years later? He was painting himself a villain, not the hero he wished to appear in Jesse's eyes. He'd admitted to being a ne'er-do-well and a gamester. Why did he feel the need to purge himself of a past he had no reason to resurrect?

"Yes," he said after a long silence. "Avery had me."

"Then neither one of you was without love," Jesse said. She came up beside him, a softness in her eyes. "In a way, you lost your family, too. You never really had parents at all."

Could she find sympathy for him when she'd suffered so much? How much had *he* truly suffered? His childhood miseries were long behind him.

"That's why you joined the army," she said. "To escape. The same reason I worked for the Peace Corps after I got out of college. So I wouldn't have to come back here and face . . . all this."

Her voice was small and held a note of shame he couldn't bear. He turned to her and took her arms in a firm but gentle clasp.

"You give yourself far too little credit, Jesse," he said. "If you worked for peace, it was scarcely a selfish motive. Mine was not so noble. I wanted to leave the Hall, get as far away as possible, and the war presented the perfect opportunity."

"And you also left . . . because your father died," she said slowly. "You grieved for him, in spite of everything."

He stiffened and almost let her go. She could know that only from her memories as Sophie, and in that life he'd never seen any indication that Sophie perceived so much. But Jesse didn't elaborate, only searched his eyes too deeply.

In her steady gaze he saw reflected scenes of the day he'd ridden off to war. His mother ordering him not to go, never backing down an inch, never offering compromise. Sophie sobbing in his arms, not for the last or most terrible time, begging him not to leave her so soon after their one sweet loving.

And Avery, his lips suspiciously stiff, reminding David of his responsibilities, that he was viscount now, that if he left, the consequences must be on his own head. Avery's curse had rung in David's ears long after he'd ridden away. But he'd dismissed Avery as the jealous boy he appeared to be—jealous because Avery had chosen to bind himself to the Hall and his own misery, while David had chosen freedom.

But he hadn't hated Avery then. After he'd come home for a hasty marriage to Sophie, after Mother had died, after Elizabeth had gone as well and he'd returned to the Peninsula—he'd left the Hall and his wife in Avery's care.

Avery had been the first to hate.

"I think you did care what your mother thought of you," Jesse said. "I think you wanted her love, and your father's attention. But you didn't know how to get it. You could never be good enough to make them love you, so you went the opposite direction. And when that didn't work, you pretended it wasn't important." She disengaged herself from his weakened hold and stroked his arm in a gesture of consolation that he felt like fire searing him to the bone. "You . . . finally just gave up."

David was afraid that any sudden movement, any hasty response, would shatter something unexpectedly fragile within him. "Do I seem such a coward to you?" he asked, unable to keep the bitterness from his words.

"No. Oh, no. I think I . . . understand you better than before. We're more alike than I realized, even though it wasn't exactly the same for me. My mother . . . loved me." She massaged her throat, rubbing at the ache David knew would be there, as it was in his own. "But sometimes I couldn't deal with her drinking. The way she changed from day to day. The way I couldn't seem to help her."

She shook her head to forestall David's incipient protest. "Then Gary came, and I spent more and more time away . . . until she died, and I wasn't there to save . . ."

He didn't consciously plan to take her in his arms. He didn't even know she was crying until she was against him and he heard the catch of her breath and felt the moisture of her tears. She pressed her face into the collar of his uniform and clutched at his back, making no sound other than the soft gasps of her weeping.

Sophie had wept often. When they'd first married, he'd responded to her tears. But he'd become jaded and impatient, unwilling to cater to her seemingly bottomless need for comfort.

With Jesse he felt fiercely protective. And ashamed. Ashamed because Jesse had *been* Sophie, and he'd failed her. Because he hadn't been able to love Sophie, not as he should have.

Once, perhaps, he'd known what love was. But he'd chosen to let the ability die out of him. It was too much work, too confining, too demanding of what he was not strong or wise or good enough to give.

Jesse lifted her head. "I'm sorry," she said, scrubbing at her face with her knuckles. "I don't usually do this."

No. She wouldn't. An unbearable tenderness washed through David. "Do you think I begrudge you, Jesse?"

She sniffed. "It's . . . embarrassing."

He held her a little apart from him and smiled. "If I

had a handkerchief, I'd gladly lend it to you. As it is . . ."

He bent his head and kissed the high curve of her cheekbone, catching the salt of a tear on the tip of his tongue. He found another tear trapped in the lashes of her left eye, two at the edge of her jaw and one more nestled in the corner of her lips.

One by one he disposed of her tears, entranced by the velvet texture of her skin and the scent of her hair and the subtle alteration in her breathing from distress to excitement.

It wasn't seduction he'd had in mind. If she'd raised a hand to ward him off, he would have stopped. But she leaned into him, giving him his way, and his body began to hum with the desire he'd so long suppressed.

There was no good reason to do so any longer. This closeness was what they both wanted. Mutual solace, a forgetting of sadness and pain. Would it be so terrible to surrender? Would he be risking so much?

Be damned to the consequences.

He touched his mouth to hers. Her fingers dug into the back of his jacket, and her lips parted. Her breasts pushed against his ribs as she fitted her body to the hollows of his own.

The kiss intensified, David's tongue slipping inside her mouth to savor her warmth and the passion he'd sensed so close beneath the surface. Her forays were more hesitant, but their very innocence excited him all the more.

It hadn't been like this in Al's study. This time she was fully as eager as he. And he couldn't remember a single instance, in a life of countless amorous adventures, when he'd ever felt so astonished by his own response. So consumed with an urgent hunger to know and be known to the very core of his being.

Jesse moaned, a sound of erotic challenge that drove him to the brink. A fraction of his mind cast about for a place to lie with her, near enough that the mood would not be broken. To take her in the cabin, where the memories were so oppressive, would be cruelty. But a soft bed

of leaves under the trees, with his jacket as a cushion for
her bare skin. . . .

"I think we'd better go home."

After a stunned moment he realized she was pulling
away—releasing his jacket, stepping back, stealing the
heat and ardor they had created between them. Her skin
was flushed, but she was carefully averting her face.

Rejecting him.

His body raged while his mind tried to make sense of
her behavior. He couldn't have spoken if he'd wanted to.
She walked toward the fence, pausing once as if to make
certain he followed.

It no longer seemed an adequate explanation that she
was simply inexperienced, guarded, and afraid of what
might happen between them. She'd said she trusted him,
and proven her words. Whatever her reasons for ending
the kiss, she'd done it deliberately, coolly, almost without emotion. As if it meant nothing.

She must know what she did to him. By withholding
herself now, she punished him. But wouldn't be seeking
revenge. She still didn't know enough about their mutual
past.

Not yet.

"Are you coming?" she called, crouching beside the
fence.

He moved stiffly to join her, helped her through the
opening, sat beside her in her vehicle. They returned to
her cottage in silence. She unlocked the door, ushered
him in, and retreated into her bedchamber.

Leaving would have been the wisest course. If he'd felt
only anger and frustration, the decision would be easy.
Rebellion, running from what he could not have, came
naturally to him.

What he felt was hurt. He was appalled by it, by the
knowledge that after two centuries he could experience
the aching misery, the desolation he'd endured as a boy
and until today had put from his mind.

But his desires weren't those of a child. He could deal
with her rejection. He could confront it rather than re-

treat. She must still need him, or she'd have sent him away.

So he waited in the cottage with the stillness he'd learned in limbo, his thoughts blank, refusing to feel anything at all. He was thoroughly prepared when Jesse emerged from her room.

She paused in the doorway, and he saw that she'd changed her garments from sturdy trousers and blouse to the loose-fitting shirt he'd seen her wear to bed. Her slender legs and feet were bare beneath. Her hair was free about her shoulders.

She looked like a woman who wanted to be taken to bed.

His heart skipped a beat, and he didn't dare to move. She wet her lips and remained where she was.

"I—" She cleared her throat. "I didn't want . . . it to happen there. At the resort. There were just too many memories."

Could he understand her aright? "What would have happened?" he asked hoarsely.

Her cheeks reddened. "Maybe I . . . misunderstood," she said. "Can you . . . I mean . . . is it even possible—"

It would have been most ungentlemanly to leave her floundering. David transported himself across the space between them in the blink of an eye and made himself solid again.

"What are you offering, Jesse?"

She stared at the tarnished buttons of his jacket. "Do I have to explain?"

He lifted a tendril of her hair with his finger. "You know I want you."

"Yes," she whispered.

"Were you in any doubt of the reality of my kiss?"

"No."

He took a moment to look at her, to savor the sight of her womanly body and the sensation of his own inexpressible joy. "I'm here for *you*, Jesse. Do you want me?"

She lifted her gaze to his. "I didn't believe this could happen."

"That you could desire a ghost?" He stroked her cheek with his palm. "But it's not new between us. Anything is possible."

"I'm beginning . . . to think you're right."

"Then if you want me—if you want me, Jesse, I have the ability to be with you now. In every way."

He molded his hand to the shape of her breast, felt the hardness of her nipple, its readiness for his caresses. By God, he could lie with her, even if it sapped every ounce of his energy. He didn't give a damn.

Jesse closed her eyes and arched against the doorframe. "I do . . . want you," she said. "I want . . ."

But she didn't finish. David pulled her close, kissed the curve of her neck, and lifted her into his arms.

CHAPTER ELEVEN

So that was all it took, Jesse thought incoherently, for the walls to come tumbling down.

She wasn't quite sure when the fatal crack had appeared, or when she'd made the decision. Maybe it wasn't really a decision at all. It wouldn't have been if she'd followed her gut and let matters proceed at the resort. There'd been nothing reasoned about her response to David's kiss, or what her body was telling her to do.

But the resort had too many resident ghosts of its own. And what she'd felt in David's arms—knowing he was with her, truly *with* her, through the pain and sorrow of facing her past—was too wonderful to let go.

Wonderful. New. Overwhelming. And undeniable. She'd felt David's withdrawal, his anger when she'd pulled away. But explanations were beyond her. It took every bit of her courage to bring him home and follow

through, as if she were a practiced seductress and not a
near-virgin with laughably little experience. .

Here, in the home she'd built, she had a measure of
security. She wasn't giving up every vestige of control. So
she told herself.

She was mistaken. David lifted her in his arms and
carried her into her bedroom. Her mind raced with
bursts of their conversation, his revelation of his own
childhood and adolescence, and experiences that gave
them common ground she hadn't been aware of before.
That made her understand him, pity him, want to comfort him. And take comfort in turn.

Their shared sorrow would have been some excuse for
her surrender. His rescue of Megan was another. But this
had been building from the day they'd met—smoldering
since their first kiss in Al's study—and she didn't believe
it was merely the remnant of some previous life.

She'd fought it, refused to acknowledge it. But she was
tired of fighting. Her resistance was worn down and out.

This was for *her*. And for David, because he'd been
devoid of human contact for too long, bereft of love
longer still. And as for the consequences of just . . . giving in, for once in her life . . .

She couldn't think anymore, because David had laid
her on her bed—just wide enough for the two of them—
and he was standing over her, looking at her in a way
that sent fresh shivers tumbling along her nerves.

Raw desire burned in his blue eyes. What must it have
been like to not touch a woman for nearly two centuries?
She hadn't been with a man in years, but that was nothing compared to his deprivation. She hadn't realized how
much her body could want a man's touch.

David's touch, not any man's. She'd hardly been
tempted in the past, even at close quarters with men in
the Corps. Now it seemed she was dry tinder just waiting
to ignite. And David was the spark.

He sat beside her on the bed, his weight substantial.
He'd said he could do this, and if mere wanting were
enough she had no doubt of it. If *her* wanting were

enough, he wouldn't have to leave time and again. He could . . .

His hand came to rest on her breast, and she swallowed her gasp. His fingers molded her nightshirt to her aching nipple, drawing slow circles around the peak.

She was afraid to look at him, but she forced herself to meet his eyes. She'd always been aware of how handsome he was, but for the first time she studied him as a woman studies her lover, caught up in the miracle of intimacy. There was a web of sun-lines radiating out from his eyes, and tiny scars along his firm jaw. His hair was forever falling into his eyes. He always had a faint five-o'clock shadow, as if he'd needed a shave when he died.

God, no. No place for death in any of this. She pushed herself up on the bed and wrapped her arms around his shoulders, pulling him down for another kiss.

He obliged. But she refused to dwell on her inexperience and took command, boldly opening her mouth and meeting the thrust of his tongue. They'd gone well beyond preliminaries. She knew that if she demanded it, he would go slowly, taking cues from her hesitance.

Slow was dangerous, because slow meant thinking. Doubting. Dwelling on what couldn't be changed. She couldn't bear such intrusions.

So she invited him to devour her, to use his lips and tongue on hers in ways she'd never experienced. She pushed her fingers into his thick hair and arched her body to meet his. His snug trousers left no doubt of his desire for her, but she wanted to feel the corded muscles hidden under the uniform, his skin on hers.

"Jesse," he said in a husky whisper. He drew back and cupped her face with his hands. "You're a wonder."

She couldn't answer. She'd meant to begin unbuttoning his jacket, but her burst of daring was deserting her. His palms felt cool on her feverish cheeks.

"I've been wanting to see you," he said, "since the first moment I came. All of you."

Part of her wanted to jump up and peel off the nightshirt with utter nonchalance, as if that could protect her from her sudden self-consciousness.

Another part of her—a part she'd barely known existed—wanted something else entirely. She wanted to know the delicious sensation of David's hands unbuttoning the shirt, smoothing it open, pulling it down to her breasts, her waist, her hips . . .

She didn't need to say a word. David's fingers were already at the short row of buttons at the neck of her shirt, undoing them with teasing deliberation. The lowest button was at the level of her nipples, making it just possible for David to spread the neckline apart, pull her shirt beneath her breasts so that they were lifted and taut and exposed.

Exposed. She couldn't remember when she'd felt so naked. David murmured something—an oath, a prayer—and simply stared at her.

"I . . . hope you're not too disappointed," she managed in a lame effort at humor, her mouth gone dry.

His gaze flashed to hers. "Disappointed?" he rasped. He swooped down, kissed her with enthusiasm, and cupped her breasts between his hands on either side. Then his mouth was on her nipples, closing around them, dragging a gasp from her throat.

She thought dimly that he must have been a very accomplished lover. He did things to her breasts with his tongue that she hadn't imagined even in the rare sexual fantasies she'd allowed herself. He suckled, he licked, he kneaded and caressed until she was writhing on the bed like some clichéd storybook virgin.

And she didn't give a damn. She pressed up, begging him to continue. A keen, painful pleasure shot in a straight course from her breasts to her belly and below. She dared to imagine what it would be like to feel his tongue there, where she was growing wet and hot and swollen. . . .

But his fingers found her first. His mouth was still on her breast while he slid his hand between her slick thighs, stroked over skin that offered no resistance, parted her, discovered the place where all sensation gathered. She jerked, and he moved his thumb in a tiny circle, building the pressure higher and higher. When it was close, so close to exploding, he moved his hand and thrust his finger inside her.

"No," she protested. "I want—I want—"

He moved nearly on top of her, his weight on one arm. "Tell me what you want, Jesse," he said against her ear. "Tell me."

"I want—you. All of you."

Abruptly he withdrew, and she wanted to cry out loud. But he didn't make her wait long. He worked at the front of his trousers and pushed her nightshirt above her thighs, so there was only a narrow band of material covering her waist.

"Feel me, Jesse," he commanded.

She reached down blindly, felt his hand guiding hers. He was hard, big and very hot, so hot she thought she would scorch her fingers. But he shuddered when she closed around him, felt the smoothness and subtle ridges of him. He closed his eyes and reared back under her caresses, as helpless as she had been.

They were equal. Equally vulnerable, equally wanting, equally needing. There was no loss here, no surrender.

Only desire. Only completion. Jesse knew an emptiness that could only be filled with David inside her, parting and entering. His body shuddering with ecstasy in time with her own. His masculine power awakening all the womanliness she'd almost forgotten.

She became the guide, showing him the way. He poised above her for an endless moment, waiting until she met his gaze.

Then he thrust, long and deep. She'd thought she was ready, but the shock after so long was unexpected. And unbearably erotic. Her body stretched to hold him. She'd wanted to see him naked, but there was a forbidden excitement in his being clothed as he made love to her, as if he were about to ride off to battle straight from their bed.

He thrust again, impossibly deeper, and the force of his movements pushed Jesse into the mattress. She reveled in it, in the proof of his undoubted reality, even as she knew it couldn't last forever.

But the ending was the most remarkable of all. Jesse was the first to go flying over the edge, carried by a waterfall of pleasure that tumbled her into a place of pure light. David was quick to follow, his body stiffening and releasing with a final, urgent push. His light joined hers, and they floated in it together.

Jesse wondered if they'd found a piece of that heaven David had been denied. She didn't feel sad when the wild elation changed to something quieter, when the loving was over, because she was still in David's arms. He didn't fade or disappear as she'd half feared he would, drained of his energy by what they'd dared to attempt.

She didn't know who held whom, if her will alone was enough to keep him with her. She didn't care about her nudity, but David pulled the nightshirt over her, smoothing it to her skin with a caress.

He kissed her damp forehead. "Ah, Jesse," he said. "It was more than I imagined."

She smiled shyly. "Really? I admit that I . . . wasn't sure what to expect myself."

He propped himself up on one elbow. "But you did enjoy it."

Insecurity from David Ventris? Jesse's smile became a grin. "I just found it wonderful." She snuggled more tightly against him, not minding the little jabs where stiffened fabric and buttons pressed into her skin. "You're not . . . too tired?"

"I feel strong as a lion."

"Strong enough to stay for a while?"

His finger traced the contour of her nose and came to rest on her lips. "As long as I can, Jesse," he said. "I promise you."

As long as I can. Jesse closed her eyes and listened as his breathing slowed and her heart gave up its urgent drumming. *And how long is that, David? Can it ever be long enough?*

For it was getting more and more difficult to deceive herself. To dismiss David as only a temporary addition to her life, a spiritual aberration, a man who'd come to fulfill his own purpose and had simply offered to be her friend while they helped each other.

What they shared now wasn't friendship. Some men and woman could sleep together with no expectation of more, but that kind of casual relationship wasn't in Jesse's nature. Not where her heart was concerned. It was why she had almost no experience with sex—and why she knew, inexorably, that her and David's love-making had forged the very bond David insisted had always existed between them.

Until now she'd felt the bond in bursts and snatches: in fleeting memories of Sophie, in gratitude for David's help, in unpredictable emotion and a desire for his company. With their loving, that erratic beat had settled into a steady rhythm in her soul.

Her soul, which longed for a man who was fighting for his *own*. A man who wasn't a man. How many times had she reminded herself of that fact? How much difference did it make in the end?

With a deliberate effort Jesse stilled her desperate thoughts, turned them away from what she couldn't control. She concentrated on David's profoundly male scent, the feel of his body close to hers. She lost herself in the newly awakened sensations of her own sated body.

"You're very quiet," David said, coiling a lock of her hair around his finger. "What's wrong, Jesse?"

She opened her eyes and met his solemn blue gaze. Was it the bond that let him sense what she felt?

She shifted to face him. "I just realized," she said, grasping at the first subject that came into her mind, "that I jumped into this without even thinking about . . . protection."

Comprehension followed a brief, puzzled silence. "Ah. You wonder if I could have got you with child."

Put so bluntly, the idea stunned her. She sat up. "Could you do it?"

His face turned expressionless, and he let his hand fall from her hair. "No. Life can't come from death, Jesse. My potency is limited." He glanced at the far wall. "Does that disappoint you?"

"No." Amazing, how well she could discern his . . . shame? Sorrow? Enough that he hurt, and she had the power to do something about it. She stroked his rough cheek. "I never even hoped for what's already happened."

He captured her hand and pressed it to his face. "I told you that your wanting could make it so," he said.

If only that were true. If only she had that power. "Let's talk about something else. I still want to know more about your life. About—" She hesitated, asking herself how much she really *did* want to know. "About you and . . . Sophie."

In the past he'd always been ready, even eager to assert their relationship in a former life. She'd been the reluctant one, because she didn't want to be lost in memories and sensations so far outside her experience, so frightening. She hadn't wanted to acknowledge that she'd been another person very much in love with David Ventris.

But David looked almost uncomfortable with her question. He opened his mouth and closed it again, as if he were censoring his first response.

"Did you and she know each other as children?" Jesse persisted. "Were you friends?"

David turned her hand palm-up and rubbed his thumb across it, back and forth. "We met when I was sixteen. Sophie was a few years younger, the daughter of the local squire. I didn't have much use for her at first, but when she grew up—" He folded Jesse's hand and kissed her knuckles. "Ah, you were a beauty then, as well."

You. How could she be jealous of herself? But she couldn't completely claim that other incarnation. She wasn't sure she'd ever be ready. "When did you fall in love with her?"

"Who can say when such a thing happens? We both came from situations we wished to escape." He toyed with Jesse's fingers in apparent fascination. "She was impetuous and full of life, eager for all the things I could show her."

"Like making love," Jesse said. "You seduced her on the hillside the day before you left for the war."

He frowned at her, the expression more in his eyes than his mouth. "Do you remember that, Jesse?"

"She . . . begged you not to leave her."

He rolled away and moved to the edge of the bed. Jesse realized that she could quite literally see through him—he was starting to fade, and she didn't want him to go. Too many questions still crowded her thoughts.

"I couldn't stay," he said. "I'd made my decision and it was too late to change."

"And you knew that when you slept with her."

He tilted his head so that she could see his strong, taut profile. "Do you doubt that she wanted it as much as I did?"

The answer was clear in Jesse's mind. She'd lived through that day with Sophie, and she knew how much Sophie had desired David even without understanding the consequences of her act. Jesse had the benefit of modern sophistication; she *knew* what she'd gotten into when she'd offered herself.

Jesse sat up and laid her hand on David's back. "I'm not accusing you. You were both young. And you loved each other."

He fixed his gaze at some point on the floor. "I sold my commission and came home when I learned that Sophie was with child."

"Then you proved your responsibility. You didn't keep running."

"It was the only course I could take. I wouldn't have left her to face her family and society alone." He sighed and turned to meet her gaze. "We married within a month of my return from the Peninsula. My mother died shortly after that, and we settled in at Parkmere Hall.

"A place you hated."

"But Sophie was eager to make it into a new home for both of us." He smiled, a bit of the uncharacteristic grimness leaving his eyes. "She was constantly rearranging and decorating and planning balls, even when she had become quite . . . ponderous."

Jesse was torn between envy and curiosity and other feelings she couldn't begin to name. "Was Avery there with you? Did he and Sophie get along?"

"Avery was essentially running the Hall then. I saw no reason to take that from him after our parents were dead."

"He must have been glad to have you back."

David's body flickered like a candle in a breeze. "My remaining time is short, Jesse," he said. "I must leave soon."

She caught his hand and held it, willing him strength. "Try to stay a little longer. I want to know . . . about the child."

"The child." David closed his eyes for the briefest moment. His smile had a sad cast. "She was born in October. Her name was Elizabeth, and she was perfect."

A father's love was in David's voice, in his expression, and it warmed Jesse's heart in a way that only added to the wonder of their loving. "You and Sophie must have been very happy."

And that very first dream came back to her, fully formed and vivid—herself dressed in a pale gown, amid a garden filled with roses. A child was in her arms, and a handsome man came through the gate—a man she loved to the depths of her soul.

It *had* been real.

"How could we not be?" David said. "We had the Hall and a town house in London, and Sophie had her parties and balls and musicales. And we had Elizabeth."

Jesse could have left it at that, released David to recoup his energy. But she was beginning to recall flashes of other, cloudier scenes that had come to her during her sessions with Al—hypnotic visions that touched an unexplored realm of darkness within her. Terrible visions she could barely remember, except that they had been about unbearable loss, wanting, fear. . . .

"But you rejoined the army," she said, swallowing. "Something happened . . . to Elizabeth."

He looked so bleak that she wished she'd kept silent. She was *not* Sophie, but he remembered it all personally. He didn't have the distance of one life removed from the pain.

"Elizabeth became ill," he said. "She lived a little more than a year."

Because she'd been expecting his revelation, because she had anticipated his sorrow, Jesse pushed her own irrational grief aside and moved close to David, put her arms around him and hugged him with all her strength. Her body made contact, and then she felt him melt away, sliding from her grasp.

He vanished and rematerialized on his feet beside the bed, a dim specter of himself. Unable to touch him, Jesse could only reach out with words that were all too inadequate.

"I'm sorry," she said. "I know how much it hurt."

"It was difficult for both of us. I—" He glanced at her, faltered. "We needed to be apart . . . for a while."

Jesse understood. Nothing could be worse than the death of a child. Sophie's anguish—David's—was her own.

"You blamed yourself. But it wasn't your fault." She closed her eyes at a sudden certainty. "Sophie blamed you, didn't she?"

He flickered again, stared at her while his fists flexed at his sides.

"But you still loved each other," Jesse insisted. She stood and walked toward him, driven by a compelling need to hear his agreement. "You didn't lose that."

"I must go," David said. He held out his hand "Jesse—"

But whatever he'd meant to say was lost. He winked

out like a light switched off. A trace of his scent lingered in the air, the ghost of a ghost.

Jesse moved through the space where he'd been, trying to recapture what they'd shared and berating herself for wasting their precious time together. Instead of savoring his presence, she'd grilled him about things that had nothing to do with *now*. She'd worried about a life they'd both left behind.

When David had first come to her, he'd said that *his* answers were in the memories he'd lost. Yet helping him revive those memories had been for herself as much as for him. At the resort, she'd watched him recall his childhood with sadness and regret. He'd relived the loss of a beloved child, and separation from his wife.

She had yet to see evidence in David's words, his behavior, his very nature, of a single crime that would have condemned him as he said he was condemned. Somewhere a big mistake had been made, because David Ventris didn't deserve to be damned.

He was a good man. A man she could trust as she'd never trusted before.

And in understanding that, she recognized what was happening to her. What *had* happened. Fight it though she might, it wasn't going to disappear with a mere act of will. Jesse hugged herself, lost in a war between elation and fear.

Ever since her mother's death she'd worked to give her life structure. She'd learned to make her own certainties, and even when she'd taken on the most challenging jobs in the Corps or search and rescue, she'd always protected her innermost self from the far more dangerous hazards.

The kind that went straight for the heart.

She hadn't armored that organ quite well enough. Was it possible to fall in love with a ghost? She knew the answer to that question. Was she willing to take the ultimate risk of loving, and losing, a being who was fighting to escape the tragic fate decreed for him? A man who couldn't promise her even the simplest future two ordinary people could expect?

When had David Ventris promised her anything but to go when she asked him to go—and to be her friend? All she and David had was *now*. There were no certainties, no guarantees, no last-minute miracles.

Could she live with that? Could she take the final and irrevocable step?

The sound of a knock on her front door pulled her from her dilemma. She quickly tugged on her clothes and went to answer.

Al was there, holding a handful of envelopes and looking out of place on her doorstep. Jesse felt a blush heat her cheeks, knowing how tousled she must look and what Al might think. . . .

Except he'd never guess. Not in a million years.

"I . . . happened to go by the post office and picked up your mail," Al said. He looked at her intently. "Are you all right?"

She wanted to pour out the story to Al, confide in the one person who might not think she was crazy. But even Al couldn't be required to stretch belief that far. She wouldn't put a dear friend in that position.

"I'm fine," she said, patting at her hair. She tried to remember if she'd closed the bedroom door. "Want to come in for some coffee?"

He shook his head and handed her the envelopes. "I haven't seen much of you lately. Just wanted to check in." He turned to go. Jesse felt a rush of affection for him and touched his arm.

"I'm sorry I haven't come by the library. I've been a little preoccupied."

"I understand. I'm grateful for what you've done for Megan."

They stood and looked at each other, and Jesse wondered when things had become so awkward between them. Was it because she had to hide the truth from him? Because he wasn't the one she turned to as she'd done in the past?

Or was it that she no longer considered Al's detachment from the world an ideal to aspire to? Was it she who'd changed so much?

"I was about to go see Megan," she said. "If you'll wait a couple of minutes, I'll walk over with you."

She stepped back to let him through the door, and he went in after a moment's hesitation. She steered him to the kitchen.

"If you don't want coffee, there's juice in the fridge," she said.

He leaned on the kitchen table. "I heard about what happened with you and Gary at Kim's party."

She shouldn't have been surprised at his straightforwardness, or that the town gossip had circulated through the library just like one of Al's books. But she'd already made the decision not to let him get more involved in her problems.

"I guess that kind of thing would get around," she said lightly.

"It sounded like a serious confrontation," he said. "And now Gary's left town. What happened, Jesse?"

"I'm sorry I didn't have a chance to tell you about it at the time, but it really . . . didn't amount to much. Gary made a fool of himself and left. There's nothing more to worry about."

❧ ❧

SHE WAS LYING.

Al knew her too well. She'd never let Gary off scot-free if she believed he was responsible for her mother's death. She'd said as much to him at their second and last hypnotherapy session.

He'd heard enough of the gossip to know that Gary had virtually attacked Jesse at the party. That wasn't an incident to disregard, and for Jesse to act this way now was sure evidence that something significant had changed.

Jesse . . . had changed.

If it had been this one instance, Al might have

shrugged and let it pass. But he knew there was more here than Jesse pretending to dismiss the situation with Gary after she'd been so obsessed with him. More than the hypnotic visions for which he hadn't found an adequate explanation. More even than her uncanny bonding with Megan after an equally uncanny rescue.

He had only to look at her now, and he was reminded. He'd been shocked when he saw her at the door: lips swollen, skin flushed, hair tangled, eyes heavy-lidded in the telltale signs of satisfied desire.

He recognized the indications. There'd been a time when he'd known what it was to love a woman and see that look on her face. Jesse's uneasiness when she'd opened the door, her nervous glances over her shoulder, her misbuttoned blouse . . . all those little clues gave her away.

Al had made a life's work of observing people—observing only, never experiencing except vicariously and with the safety of analytical distance.

Jesse made that distance impossible. He'd been acutely aware of how seldom he'd spoken to her over the past several days, and how much he'd missed those conversations. Except where Megan was concerned, she hadn't come to him since their second session. Not to confess her fears, or admit her anger, or share her dreams and visions.

He'd known with that first session that an untapped part of Jesse was slowly awakening. He'd worried about it, though he seldom worried—speculated and wondered about things that had never concerned him before.

Now he understood how much had escaped him.

Jesse had been with a man. She'd been held and kissed and made love to, and it had been good for her. If Al had ever made an accurate assessment of another human being, he knew what Jesse had become.

A woman in love.

He realized that Jesse was still expecting a response to her evasion about Gary. "Go ahead and do whatever you have to do," he said. "I'll wait."

She hesitated, nodded and left the kitchen. Al sank onto a chair and stretched his feet under the table. This was one of those times when the damaged leg ached like hell, echoing the turmoil of his thoughts.

Who was it? He searched his memory for any man in town Jesse had shown interest in, and came up blank. She was too wary, too reserved to flirt or seek casual relationships, and the men she worked with at the Lodge or search and rescue were partners, not lovers.

It was incredible to Al that Jesse could have taken a lover in secret. No one in town knew about it. Al lived across the yard, and he hadn't guessed. No one had left Jesse's cabin in the past few minutes.

Who? He laid his good arm on the table and rested his forehead against his knuckles. Jesse would tell him if he asked. They were friends. He'd felt good when she'd come to him for help. Better than he'd been able to acknowledge.

Knowing she didn't need him anymore felt as if someone had mangled his other leg. And he couldn't tell her what it was like. He could barely accept the truth he'd hidden from himself since Jesse had returned to Manzanita.

A truth that made no difference. He'd created a life of ignoring emotion, devoting himself to intellect and detachment. It had seemed the sanest course in a demented world.

But there was something vital missing inside him. Jesse sensed that. Megan did as well. He'd left a part of himself buried in the jungles of 'Nam, and he hadn't even suspected it was gone.

He didn't know how to get it back.

"You look tired," Jesse said as she returned to the kitchen. She touched his shoulder with casual affection that sent icy shivers racing to the end of his raw nerves. "You need to get another assistant at the library."

He sat up and looked at her. Gone was the evidence of her recent tryst; her hair was neatly pinned back, her face

scrubbed, her clothes in place. She was once again the
Jesse he knew.

Except for her eyes. They were brilliant with warmth,
and the faint lines between her brows had been smoothed
away as if by a gentle touch.

He couldn't bring it up. He couldn't ask. But there was
another issue he could pursue.

"Jesse," he said, "I know you haven't dropped this
business with Emerson. You told me you were going to
keep searching your memories for answers."

She sighed and walked to the kitchen window. "Okay.
Gary did confront me at the party, and some of the
things he said convinced me I was on the right track. This
morning I went to the old resort."

That would have taken a great deal of courage. Al
knew how assiduously she'd avoided the resort since
she'd come back to town.

"And did it help?" he asked.

"I . . . don't know. But I'm closer all the time." She
turned around, arms across her chest. "I get little
snatches of memories, pieces that just need to come together. Like the first fragment, remembering the funeral
and accusing Gary—" She closed her eyes. "Screaming
that he killed my mother."

"Is that how you remember it?"

She shuddered. " 'You killed her.' That's what I said
when I attacked him."

Al positioned his cane and pushed to his feet. "But that
wasn't what you said, Jesse. I was there. Your exact
words were 'You killed *me*.' "

Her eyes snapped open. "What?"

"I've told you that memories can play tricks with the
mind. They have ways of—"

But she wasn't listening. She pressed her fingers to her
temples. "That makes no sense," she said. "No sense."

"Jesse?"

The strange light in her gaze died. "Did I say anything
else I don't remember?"

"Only that. Jesse, if you want to talk—"

"No." She shook off her fey mood and smiled. "I promised to see Megan today, and here it is already afternoon. Walk with me?"

Forcing the issue was beyond Al's capacity. He kept his silence while they crossed the yard and Jesse spoke of inconsequential things. Her arm was linked through his, but she was miles away. Hiding from him. Lost.

He watched Megan run to her and left the two of them with some excuse about work at the library, though it was his day off. He walked into town, passing over the same familiar ground without seeing any of it. He wasn't surprised when he ended up in front of the bar.

His hesitation was brief. The bar was dark, the ambience oddly soothing at midday. A few tables had occupants, but the overall emptiness suited Al's mood. He looked for a table in the corner of the room, far from the jukebox and the loudest table of drinkers.

A beer, maybe something more potent—that would numb the futile emotions he couldn't seem to discard. To hell with sobriety and self-discipline. They were highly overrated.

He was halfway to the bar when he overheard a snatch of conversation.

"Damned if he didn't just pick up and leave without a word to me. I can't believe he did it. I'm his buddy, fercrissake. He needs me in this town."

Al glanced down at the speaker. Wayne Albright sat with several other men at a pockmarked table, nursing a drink. Al recognized a number of Gary Emerson's cronies—men who'd been working to set up his "campaign office" in Manzanita and fawned all over him when he'd been in town.

"Well, shit," another man said in obvious disgruntlement. "He promised a lot of big things, but I heard what happened at the party. The way he attacked that girl—"

"He didn't attack nobody. That's some damned gossip." Wayne jerked his mug to his mouth and took a long swallow.

Al was aware of a knotting in his stomach, the way he

remembered feeling in the hours before a mission in 'Nam. Wayne had been Gary's drinking buddy back when Joan had died. His loyalty to a "friend" who hadn't bothered to keep in touch for seventeen years was nothing short of miraculous, the mark of a small man who looked for bigger coattails to ride on.

But even Wayne sounded angry now.

"Do you mind if I join you?" Al asked.

Wayne tipped back in his chair. "Well, if it ain't Al the librarian. Don't think I've seen you in here for about a century. Given up on teetotaling?"

Al shrugged and pulled out a vacant seat. No one protested. "I heard you talking about Gary leaving town," he said. "I heard about the party, too—that Gary threatened Jesse Copeland."

Wayne scowled but didn't answer. Al ordered a beer from the barmaid and glanced around the table.

"You know, I remember Gary from way back. Everyone liked him, but I always got the feeling that he was hiding something. Strange for him to make such a splash the past few days and then skip town so suddenly. No one saw him after that party."

The expressions of the drinkers ranged from mild curiosity to disgust. Someone shuffled his feet under the table. Wayne took another long drink and banged his mug down.

"He musta had his reasons," Wayne said. "He's an important man now. I know he'll call and let me know what's up."

Poor Wayne, with his delusions of indispensability. "Well, you knew him better than anyone else, Wayne—except Joan Copeland. He left pretty quickly after Joan's accident, come to think of it. He does have a habit of disappearing."

Men glanced at each other. The barmaid returned with Al's beer. He folded his hands around the frosted glass.

"I've always wondered about that relationship," he went on. "Joan never drank so much as when Gary went to live with her."

"She was a lush," someone said. "No good."

Al stared into his mug. "Who decides these things, I wonder? Who figures that Gary Emerson is the best thing that ever happened to our town and Joan Copeland was no good?"

"Everyone knew," Wayne muttered.

"The way everyone knew that Gary abused Joan?"

Wayne nearly dropped his mug. "What are you talking about?"

Al met his stare. "I'm trying to find some reason that Gary dislikes Jesse so much. Enough to threaten her in a public place. She was only a child when he knew her. Why should he be afraid of her?"

"Afraid?"

"He ran away, didn't he?"

"That's bullshit."

"Is it?"

Wayne's leathery skin had lost a little of its color. "I remember that funeral. I remember how crazy she was."

"So do I. But she was a little girl then. Seventeen years have passed. I know Jesse Copeland, and she's as sane as anyone in this town." He heard his voice rise, take on a harsh tone that startled even him. "She saved my niece and risked her life for the Moran boy. She may save one of you someday. That's the kind of person she is."

An old man in the corner—Fred, Al thought his name was—raised a timid hand. "She . . . seemed like a nice enough girl to me," he offered. "Didn't look crazy."

Wayne only shook his head. "What is this, Aguilar? You sweet on her or something?"

As if he'd become a different man, Al pushed back his chair and slammed his fist on the table. Wayne jumped.

"Jesse is my friend. She'd be yours if you'd let her, but she isn't full of flattery and oily ass-kissing like Gary Emerson." He snorted in disgust. "Why should you owe more loyalty to a drifter who didn't give a shit about any of you for seventeen years than to a woman who had the guts to return to the town that turned its back on her and her mother? Because Gary makes you feel big even when he uses you?"

"He'll make something of this town—"

"He'll take your votes and forget you ever existed. You don't matter to him. Jesse does. She scares the hell out of him. What is it about Jesse that *you're* afraid of?"

They stared at him, eyes wide and mouths gaping. Quiet, mild, uninvolved Al had changed before their eyes. And he felt liberated. Angry.

Alive.

"Maybe you all ought to give some thought about who you'd rather have holding your hand when you're about to fall off a cliff," he said. For once, as he got to his feet, his balance was perfect. He hardly needed the cane.

His anger carried him to the door of the bar without a single misstep. No one called after him. It wasn't until he was outside in the clean sunlight that he realized he hadn't taken a single sip of his beer.

He paused at the end of the block, breathing deeply. He'd given Jesse all the credit for changing, but something was happening to him as well. He didn't know where it had begun, and he was more than a little afraid that he wouldn't be able to control the process now that it had begun.

Of one thing he was certain: his chance with Jesse was over. He'd never really had one. But maybe it wasn't too late to make sure he didn't repeat the same mistakes.

Maybe it was time to start being human again.

CHAPTER TWELVE

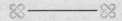

I DON'T KNOW," Megan said, pushing her new glasses
up her nose and studying her distorted reflection in the
smudged metal of the napkin dispenser. "Do you like
them, Kirk?"

Kirk Moran gave the question the concentration it deserved. He cocked his head, frowned, and nodded
slowly.

"I think they look good," he said.

Jesse looked from one child to the other, absently
blending the fudge topping of her sundae with the melting ice cream. Kirk hadn't said more than a few sentences
in the past hour and half, but what he *did* say was promising.

Mrs. Moran had been happy to let Kirk visit with
Megan on the trip to the optometrist and the Frosty
Freeze, though she'd declined to accompany them her-
self. And Kirk, after a temporary reluctance to leave his

mother alone, had accepted the invitation with stoic resignation. He hadn't acted like a child eager to make new friends. Not at first.

But he was beginning to open up a bit. A double ice cream cone was a great icebreaker. And Megan was helping tremendously. For a child who'd been locked in her own shell just a few days ago, she was expert at coaxing Kirk out of his. Perhaps it was the unspoken knowledge that both had suffered loss, that they had something vital in common.

Regardless of the reason, they were getting along, and Jesse could only be grateful.

She had so much to be grateful for. The taste of the ice cream on her tongue was better than she could remember; the sun felt warmer, the tangy scent of pine needles more memorable, the sound of children's laughter joyful enough to bring tears to her eyes.

There was a simple explanation for the way her senses had opened up, the way her appreciation for life itself had expanded to encompass so much more of the world she'd taken for granted.

Funny how clear it had become. Megan had new glasses, but Jesse had acquired her own set of rose-colored lenses without paying a dime.

And whatever she *did* have to pay, she'd give it gladly.

She smiled to herself and took a big bite of sundae. Megan giggled as she tried to catch a drip of syrup before it plopped from her chin onto the table. Even Kirk looked happy as he polished off his cone.

"Well, you two," Jesse said, gathering up the sticky napkins, "we still have another hour or so left. Why don't we go over to the park next door? They have some great swings there."

Megan glanced at Kirk. "Want to?"

He shrugged, but the sparkle in his eyes betrayed him. He wasn't yet ready to talk about his brother, but he was healing just the same.

"Come on, then," Jesse said. She led them out the door, nodding to another family as she passed, and headed for the park. In the midst of so much natural, rugged beauty, the groomed lawn and trees formed an oasis at the heart of town. Megan started toward the swing set, paused to wait for Kirk, and then challenged the boy to a race. They reached the swings at a dead heat.

Jesse sat down on one of the benches and sprawled lazily, watching the children through half-lidded eyes. Her mouth kept curling up into a foolish grin. Though she hadn't for one moment forgotten her commitment to exposing Gary for what he was, it was possible to let that obsession fall by the wayside for minutes at a time. Possible to think of other things and bless her good fortune.

Her thoughts wandered to the morning—and David. Hours later she could still feel his touch, the electric charge of pleasure shooting through her body as he kissed and caressed her. Her nipples tightened, and she almost blushed at having such fantasies in the middle of a public park.

She missed him. She missed more than the lovemaking, remarkable discovery though it was. Far more. She missed his wry smile, the cynicism that covered hurts he couldn't acknowledge. She missed the dusty male smell of him and the uniform with its holes and tarnished buttons. She missed his reluctant tenderness and his unexpected fierceness in protecting her. She missed his very presence.

But he'd be back. She let herself fill with that promise. A magnificent, powerful conviction told her that nothing could keep them apart, whatever the laws of heaven and earth. She was so close to finding her answers, and when they found his . . .

"Jesse."

She opened her eyes and sat up. The terse word wasn't much of a greeting, and when Jesse recognized the speaker she wasn't surprised.

Marie stood with hands on hips, looking as pugnacious as a bulldog—if considerably more attractive. In body, at least. Her makeup and clothing were, as usual, impeccable, but her eyes held a glitter that suggested her intentions were anything but civilized.

"I'm so glad I ran into you," she said in a rancid-honey voice. "You must be feeling pretty victorious about now, aren't you?"

Jesse glanced toward the children, who were lost in their own games. Megan lifted her arms in a grand gesture and laughed, while Kirk reacted with appropriate appreciation for the tale she was spinning.

"This isn't the time, Marie," Jesse said. "I know you don't like me, but we can find a more private place to talk things out, if that's what you want."

Marie tilted her head back and smiled unpleasantly. "Always the plain speaker. It so happens that what I have to say to you won't take very long." She took a step closer to the bench. "I know you have it in for Gary. You went after him from the moment he showed up in town. Well, you succeeded, didn't you?"

Success wasn't how Jesse would have defined it. "I know he left town, Marie," she said. "I'm sorry it was inconvenient for you. I don't want to fight about this, but if you—"

"You should have thought about that before you used your tricks on him!"

Jesse sighed. "He was the one who threatened me at the party—"

"Don't play games with me, little town girl. You drove him to it. You have some hold over him. Whatever it is, you won't get away with it. Unlike you, Gary's popular in this town. He brings class to the place, and that's exactly what people want."

Jesse stood up. "Look, Marie, you barely know Gary. No one in town does, not now—if they ever did. But he lived with my mother seventeen years ago. If anyone—"

Marie's pretty mouth formed a very ugly epithet. "I know enough about you, Jesse Copeland. You were never sane about Gary. Maybe you hate him because you can't have him. I don't care, but I'm warning you—"

Jesse felt her temper slipping its leash. "I don't need

the warning, but maybe you do. You've lost your head over him, and you're the one who's going to lose. He used my mother, and he'll use you—"

She knew it wasn't going to work as soon as she finished the first sentence. Marie was livid, playing Drama Queen to the hilt, and she obviously felt she had nothing to lose.

"What do you know about men?" she said contemptuously. "Who'd want you anyway, in your scrubby jeans? But you can't wait to ruin it for everyone else, can you? All you see is your own miserable little life!"

"Believe it or not, Marie, it's your life I'm thinking about." She threw caution to the winds. "Gary's no good. I don't know how I'm going to prove it, but I know. And you'll be the one who gets hurt—"

"You bitch. When I tell Gary what you've said—"

"That's enough, Marie," someone said behind them.

Jesse caught her breath and glanced at the woman who'd come up to stand at her shoulder. She did a double take.

Lisa Moran was staring at Marie with quiet composure, her gaze steady and stern. Marie's lush lips flapped like a fish's but couldn't produce any sound. It was quite an interesting sight.

Lisa turned to Jesse. "I thought I'd come to meet you here instead of waiting for you to bring Kirk home. It's such a beautiful day." She waved to Kirk across the lawn, effectively shutting Marie out of the picture. "They look like they're having fun."

"They are." Jesse took her cue from Lisa and didn't look at Marie. "I think they've really hit it off. Don't be surprised if they want to see a lot more of each other." She managed a smile. "They're not quite at the age where the boy-girl stuff takes over."

"Yes," Lisa said. "They still have a while to be children."

They watched in silence. Marie, behind them, couldn't bear to be ignored. "You just wait until Gary comes back, Jesse Copeland," she said. "You'll be the one who's sorry."

Lisa looked over her shoulder. Not a word was spoken, but Marie blushed, and Jesse thought she was actually ashamed of herself. She'd have to be without a heart to be unaffected by Lisa Moran's pain.

Apparently Marie had some scruples, because she spun on her high heels and strode toward the parking lot.

"Thanks," Jesse said.

Lisa didn't answer, but their silence remained companionable. After a few more minutes Kirk and Megan ran over to join them, and Kirk gave his mother a big hug. Megan did the same for Jesse.

Still warmed by Lisa's support and the children's affection, Jesse waved Mrs. Moran and son off in their car and took Megan home. Al was out, so Megan helped Jesse make a big pot of spaghetti for dinner.

The contentment that had come with the day and the anticipation of seeing David again stayed with Jesse through the evening. She went home and worked on her furniture, letting her thoughts wander where they would.

It was too bad about Marie; she had a fall coming when she found out what Gary really was. She wasn't going to listen to reason—certainly not from Jesse Copeland.

But that was the only dark spot in a world that suddenly seemed full of hope. The fact that David didn't show up by bedtime didn't unduly disturb her. Together they'd drained his energy pretty thoroughly, and she was willing to be patient.

She was ready to take the greatest risk of all.

❈ ❈

THE MUSIC FROM the expensive string quartet was exquisite, the caviar superior, the wine of the finest vintage. Gary knew to the dime the cost of every luxury Heather's parents had lavished on this happy gathering, where Sacramento's political elite hobnobbed with the friends and family of the rich and beautiful Heather Pfeiffer in celebration of the happy event to come.

Nearly everyone at the engagement party was a valuable contact or influential patron; Gary was under no illusion about just how important this day was. It was what he'd been striving for, the position that would make it possible for him to realize all his ambitions. Heather was the necessary burden he accepted along with her wealth and family connections.

He should have been enjoying his victory. He should have been on top of the world. He'd left Manzanita and driven back to Sacramento and his bride-to-be, vowing to put Jesse Copeland and her pathetic accusations from his mind.

It hadn't worked out that way. Even after the first irrational fear had subsided—after he'd shaken off the bizarre conviction that some invisible presence was dogging his every footstep—he hadn't been able to stop thinking about her. The way she'd stood up to him. The way she'd stared at him with those steady hazel eyes, as if she *knew*.

Memories he hadn't let into the light for seventeen years were suddenly resurrected and exhibited in glaring relief. Acts and decisions he'd never questioned replayed behind his eyes, so vivid that he was sure they were visible to any passing stranger.

Jesse had done this to him. Jesse Copeland.

He hated her.

Gary downed his fifth glass of champagne and grimaced at the feeble sting of the bubbles. He slammed the delicate glass down on the nearest server's tray and started toward the bar for something stronger. Heather wasn't here to nag him about that, since she was off preening for some bimbo friends from the exclusive private school she'd attended. That ought to keep her busy for hours.

Gary smiled and glad-handed a passing assemblyman on the way to the bar, his words and motions those of an automaton. He lost the thread of the inane small talk in mid-sentence, earning an odd glance from the politician. Gary covered his slip with a joke about the insanity of planning a wedding. The assemblyman rolled his eyes in sympathy, slapped Gary's back, and moved to the buffet table.

The bartender poured Gary a whiskey straight, politely ignoring the tremble in Gary's hands as he took the drink.

What in hell was happening to him? Little by little he was being eaten alive by fears he couldn't name, guilt he couldn't shake. He looked at himself in the mirror and found wrinkles he hadn't seen before, shadows under his eyes, a man he didn't recognize. Even airheaded Heather had noticed and offered her whining opinion that he ought to take better care of himself.

Gary downed the liquor and had the glass refilled, waiting for the welcome numbness to wash over him.

The trials that came by day were bad enough. The blunders were still minor, like the one with the assemblyman, but they were increasing. He'd nearly insulted Heather's mother last night, some remark about her hideous dress that he'd been thinking but never would have spoken if he'd been in his right mind. His real opinions about the fools and saps around him were slipping out of his control, as if he were the most inept political aide who'd ever set foot in the capital.

At night . . . at night it was far worse. He hadn't slept more than a handful of hours in the past two nights. Heather wouldn't let him screw her before their wedding, but even if he'd had the luscious and imaginative Marie in his bed it wouldn't have made any difference. He was all but impotent.

And there were the dreams.

Gary choked on his second whiskey and waved off the bartender's concern. He hid the glass behind a potted plant as an elderly—and affluent—society couple walked by. He hardly saw them, because he was reliving the dream that wouldn't go away.

It always started with Jesse. Jesse as a child, just the

way he remembered her from that day of the funeral. He felt the ineffectual pummeling of her hands and feet through his suit, the rake of her fingernails. But she couldn't hurt him, and he laughed at her rage.

Until she changed. The blond little girl was gone, and someone else stood in her place. A petite brown-haired beauty with a white, high-waisted dress and an old-fashioned hairstyle. She stared at him with Jesse's eyes—the wrong color, but he knew they were Jesse's. Hatred was a living thing between them. They hated each other.

But *she* also feared him. She feared and despised him, shrank from his touch. He realized with shock that what he felt for her wasn't so simple as hatred.

He wanted her. More than desire, more than lust. He wanted to possess her. In possessing her he would gain what had been taken from him. Have what was rightfully his. Show them all.

So he reached out to her. He offered himself. She would get nothing better, not from the one she waited for so hopelessly. Did she truly believe she'd ever see *him* again?

She stumbled back and looked at Gary with loathing, as if she had the right to judge. She laughed with that wild edge and threatened him with retribution, even as she shook with terror. She told him that he was not a man. She told him he was disgusting and dishonorable.

She told him he was evil, and kept on laughing.

Mad. She passed that madness on to him, driving him to his only way out. The only escape from that look in her eyes.

So he did what he couldn't do to the child. He killed her.

The process wasn't quick or painless. Gary felt righteous power fill him, surge to the end of his fingertips. He didn't have to touch her. Heat sprang from his hands, and flames caught the delicate folds of the woman's sheer gown.

She didn't even struggle when the fire took her, caressed and licked at her with such deceptive gentleness.

But when it seemed she should crumble to ashes, she rose like a phoenix. Her body cast off the flames and stood untouched.

And she laughed. She pointed at him and laughed, an ugly sound laced with hysteria.

"I'll always come back," she shrieked. So he killed her again. And she returned. Again, and again. Each time he grew more terrified, his strength leached from him by her accusing, triumphant eyes. Each time the guilt wrapped loop after loop of heavy chains about his feet, his knees, his thighs, his hips. Dragging him down into the grave that opened up beneath him, a gaping maw of earth waiting to swallow him alive . . .

"Señor Emerson?"

Gary nearly struck the maid before he remembered where he was. Consuela stared at him, her plump face wary, and took a step back.

"What is it?" he snapped.

She ducked her head. "A call for you, señor. The woman said it was urgent, from a place called Manzanita." She hesitated, poised to flee. "I am sorry if I did wrong, señor."

A woman. From Manzanita. Gary clasped his hands to keep them from shaking.

"You did the right thing, Consuela. *Gracias.*" He pulled a fiver from his pocket and pressed it into her hand. "Don't tell anyone else. Go back to your duties."

She nodded and slipped away. Gary glanced around the room. The party was going so well that no one was likely to notice his absence for a few minutes. He walked out of the Pfeiffers' ballroom, down the wide marble-floored hallway, and into Ross Pfeiffer's private office. He reached the phone and punched the hold button.

"Hello? Who is this?"

"Gary? Is that you?"

He recognized the voice immediately. "Marie? What in hell are you doing, calling me here? How did you get this number?"

Her voice held a definite pout. "Your secretary said you were with your fiancée. You talked enough about Heather. It wasn't a problem to track you down."

Gary almost let her have it. Taking his anxiety and frustration out on Marie would have been easy and relatively harmless. But he kept his temper. There was a possibility that Marie had something useful to say.

"You didn't call," Marie whined. "You just picked up and left without saying anything. I was worried—"

So she was becoming possessive after a single night together. Gary gripped the phone so hard that his fingers hurt.

"I had to leave on short notice. I'm busy right now, Marie—unless you have something important—"

"As a matter of fact, I do. You know that bitch Jesse Copeland? Well, she's been spreading all kinds of lies about you. She told me that I should stay away from you, that you're no good."

The satisfaction in Marie's words only fed into Gary's rage. "Did she?"

"Yes. I know she has it in for you, and I thought you ought to know what she's doing. People heard about that thing at the party, and since you left so quickly—"

"What are they saying about me?"

"Oh, they aren't going to believe *her*. But her friend Al Aguilar is spreading the same dirt. He was with Wayne and your other friends in the bar, and—"

Al Aguilar. Gary vaguely remembered him as a passive, bookish sort seventeen years ago. He hadn't even met the man on his recent visit, though he'd heard Aguilar was Jesse's friend.

"What did he tell them?"

"Stuff about Jesse's mother. Look, Gary, I think you should come back and set them straight. Put Copeland in her place once and for all. Don't let her get away with—"

But Gary had stopped listening. His hand had gone numb, and his stomach was knotted with unreasoning terror.

He'd been wrong. Dead wrong. He shouldn't have left Manzanita without being sure about Jesse. Sure that she didn't know. Sure she'd stay quiet and afraid and crazy.

He'd never listened to his dreams, but now he knew they'd been warning him. Telling him that it would never be over unless he took action.

Marie was right. He had to go back.

"Gary? Are you there?"

He licked his lips. "Keep an eye on Jesse, Marie. Remember that she's a lunatic. Nothing she claims is true. It's like you said—she hates me, and she'd do anything to ruin everything I've worked for."

"I knew it." Marie breathed heavily into the phone, as if she thought she could seduce him over the line. "I'll do whatever I can to help you, Gary. Are you coming back?"

"As soon as I can. But don't tell anyone, Marie. It's only going to make things worse if this gets more complicated than it already is."

"What are you going to do?"

He didn't answer for a long moment. What did Marie think he'd do? Sit down and have a heart-to-heart with Jesse, convince her of the error of her ways? Or perhaps Marie was not averse to his applying a few direct threats to silence her. Marie would have made an excellent politician's mistress.

"I'll deal with that when I get there. You just keep quiet about this, Marie. Do you understand?"

"Yes." She sounded a bit chastened; maybe she was just perceptive enough to hear the warning in his voice. "I can't wait to see you, baby. I'll give you something to look forward to."

At any other time Gary would have anticipated getting between Marie's legs again, but he couldn't even picture her face. Jesse's face was there instead—blond and hazel-eyed and tan, then wavering to pale and dark-haired as she was in the dream.

He was going insane, and there was only one cure.

He'd hung up before he realized that he hadn't bothered with a goodbye. To hell with that. Marie would have to live without it. She'd crawl after him no matter what he did, like all the women he'd ever known.

Except Jesse.

He left the office and strode farther down the hall to the residential section of the mansion where his guest room was kept ready for him. The area was deserted, just as he wanted it. He made a beeline to the briefcase he kept in a locked desk beside his bed.

He'd never had occasion to use the gun. It felt familiar in his hand, better than the ones he'd owned during his brief criminal career.

That had ended with Manzanita. So he'd told himself. But Jesse wouldn't let it end. She wouldn't let him go.

The gun slipped from his hand and clattered to the desktop. He raked his fingers through the hair at his temples and squeezed his eyes shut.

He kept seeing himself in the dream, killing her. Over and over. And each time the guilt and hatred and fear got worse. Each time the grave at his feet got deeper. It filled up with old sins, and the chains wound tighter and tighter.

Guilt ate at his heart like acid. Because he couldn't stop himself. He didn't know how.

It had to end. The guilt and terror had to end. He picked up the gun and gripped it in both hands until it was the only reality left in the world.

Gradually his frantic pulse slowed, and a measure of sanity returned to his thoughts. He replaced the gun in the briefcase, shoved the briefcase into the desk, and locked the drawer.

He had a party to wrap up. Heather would be looking for him. He'd come up with an excuse to go back to Manzanita tomorrow. Heather would believe him. She always did.

His most practiced smile was back in place by the time he reached the ballroom.

✖ ✖

"JESSE?"

She tossed on the bed, coming abruptly out of a dream about David. The room was utterly dark; no hint of moonlight filtered through the blinds.

The covers bunched around her waist as she sat up. "David?"

But she knew it wasn't David who'd called her name. For an instant she thought it might be Megan, because the voice was female.

"Jesse?"

No matter how much she tried, she couldn't make out the figure she felt standing beside her bed. But she knew. Dizzying shock lanced through her, and she could barely force her breath through her throat.

"Mom?"

Silence.

"Mom?" She flung the sheets away and scooted to the edge of the bed. The darkness was unnatural, eerie. She reached out into the empty space in the middle of the room.

Nothing. No one.

"You've been looking so hard, honey," her mother said. Her words were faintly slurred but distinct enough, as if she'd had just a little to drink, but not too much.

"Where are you, Mom?" Jesse whispered. "I can't see you."

"You're trying to remember," Joan Copeland said. She laughed, that husky chuckle Jesse had nearly forgotten. "It's not easy, I know. But you're so close."

Jesse's legs almost gave out when her feet hit the floor. "Let me see you, Mom," she begged. "I want to see you."

She could feel a draft of air swirl past, a current that might have been caused by someone shaking her head. "Remember the games we used to play? The messages we always left for one another? The special hiding place?"

It was difficult to concentrate on what her mother was

saying. She tried to stand up again, but an invisible force kept her pinned to the bed.

"Think, Jesse."

She focused on the words. *Games. Messages. Hiding place.*

And the image came back to her. She saw herself as a little girl, running into the kitchen.

The kitchen. The cupboard in the corner, with the linoleum-covered shelf inside. The linoleum was peeling from the wood, leaving a flat pocket just the right size for secret messages. Messages a mother and daughter could leave for each other where no one else could find them.

She'd been in that kitchen yesterday morning, opened the cupboards because she'd sensed they were important. Felt a strange frustration when she'd found only the dishes and a few old pots and pans.

She shuddered as another memory took her. It was the dream-picture of Mom and Gary fighting. Only now Jesse moved back in time, watched from the window as Gary first came into the kitchen to confront his lover.

Her mother was opening the corner cupboard. She had a folded piece of paper in her hand. She was pushing it under the linoleum on the shelf, looking up, slamming the door closed. Straightening to meet Gary's ominous contempt.

A message. Jesse swayed and braced herself with stiffened arms. Mom had left her a message she'd never read.

A message . . . with the answers.

"I remember, Mom," she said. "I know where to look."

The air current had stilled. A surge of panic gave Jesse the strength to break loose of the force that held her captive. She staggered to the middle of the room, spinning in a circle.

Her mother was gone. Somewhere outside the window an owl hooted. Moonlight found its way through the blinds again.

Sudden enervation overcame Jesse, and she felt her way back to the bed. She shivered as she lay down.

Heaviness weighted her eyelids. Her tears seemed to belong to someone else.

She woke before dawn. Her body was stiff and chilly; the sheets were pushed low around her ankles, and all at once she remembered what had happened in the middle of the night.

"Mom," she whispered.

Someone appeared beside her bed, a blur of blue and white and glints of metal. Jesse scrambled up and flung herself into David's arms.

He was solid as her mother hadn't been, and his embrace gave her all the comfort she could want. His palms stroked up and down her back as he rested his chin on the crown of her head.

"Jesse? What's wrong? I apologize for not returning earlier—"

She stepped back, keeping a firm grip on his hands. "I saw her, David."

"Who?"

"My mother. She came to me. Last night."

He cupped her face in his hands. "You saw your mother?"

"I didn't . . . actually see her. She told me what I've been trying so hard to remember. The clue I was looking for." She wiped at her eyes. "Did you send her?"

He sighed and pulled her close, into the warm circle of his arms. "I don't have that power, Jesse. I wish I did."

"But you said you've seen others passing through your limbo—"

"Soldiers. Men like myself. They all moved on."

Jesse broke away and turned to face the bed, arms across her chest. "She spoke to me."

"I don't deny that, Jesse." His voice was unusually soft and gentle. "Believe me, if I could have made such communication possible, I would have done it long since."

"But you don't think it really was my mother, do you?"

"How can I answer?" His hand came to rest on her

shoulder, and his fingers worked into the taut muscles just below her neck. "*I was able to come back.*"

Yes. He was able to come back—but how likely was it that Jesse would be haunted, however lovingly, by more than one ghost? And as much as she wanted to believe she'd spoken to Mom, the thought that her mother was—*trapped,* as David was trapped—was too grim and sad to contemplate.

Better to conclude that it had been a dream, a trick her mind had played to release needed information from her subconscious memories. Better to hope that her mother was beyond human suffering. Somewhere.

Jesse had begun to truly face her childhood loss when she'd remembered the funeral and her attack on Gary. Visiting the resort had been another phase in the process she'd so long deferred. This . . . visitation was one more step, and the message was clear.

It was time to say goodbye and let her mother go.

But it wouldn't be finished until Gary was brought to justice. Jesse lifted her chin and let the tears dry. Whatever the source of the information, she knew it was what she'd been waiting for.

A fresh sense of urgency propelled her across the room to her closet. She pulled a pair of jeans from her chest of drawers and tugged them on under her nightshirt.

"Isn't it a bit early to be dressing?" David asked. He was watching with interest and appreciation. Jesse struggled to set aside the distraction of his gaze and the effect it had on her.

"I've been known to get up earlier than this. But I have something I need to do. It can't wait."

"No?" David stepped up beside her and molded his hands to her waist, sliding the shirt up her ribs. "I'm sorry to hear that."

She almost lost her resolve. After an agonizing moment she trapped his hands in their upward progress just before they covered her breasts.

"I have to get to my mom's resort right away," she

said. She lifted his hands and kissed the tanned, roughened skin of his knuckles. "I'm sorry. But later—"

He gave her a crooked smile. "A pity. I'd saved up all my strength for you."

Even such a prosaic sentence hid a wealth of erotic promise. She hadn't known she had it in her to feel this way, to want to tumble right back into bed with him for an hour or two at the very least.

If her mother's message meant what she hoped, she'd be able to turn her full attention to David in the very near future. Put the rest behind her and think only of the present. Live to the fullest, free of the burdens of fear and anger. The past would truly become the past.

"I want you to come with me," she said. "I want you to be there when I find out the truth."

He frowned. "What truth?"

"About Gary. I know what to look for now. My mother left me a message before she died." Jesse moved away and skimmed off her nightshirt—she was still feeling modest enough to turn her back—and replaced it with a sturdy flannel shirt. "Will you come?"

The grim expression remained on his face, but he nodded. His playfulness had vanished, and it seemed to her, as she finished dressing, that he was deeply preoccupied.

"Only a little longer, David," she said seriously, catching his gaze. "Then Gary will be out of our lives."

Our lives. An odd choice of words, given that David didn't know the man. But it felt right. Hope was a wonderful thing.

She gathered up her flashlight and backpack and went to the garage for the truck, David at her side. There were few vehicles on the road in this predawn hour, and the mountains made a dark wall around the valley, the eerie guardians of a thousand untold secrets.

One of those secrets was about to see the light of day.

They went through the fence as they had before, and Jesse lit their way to the cabin she and her mother had shared. She opened the cupboard with the peeling linoleum. The layers had stuck together over the years; she pried at them until the edges came apart. She peeled the linoleum back and felt between.

Her fingers touched paper, brittle and stiffly folded. Her heart pounded as she pulled out the envelope. "Jesse" was written in her mother's hand on the outside.

"Oh God. She was right." She stared at the envelope, feeling layers of paper inside. David was suddenly behind her, just when she needed the support of his hard, strong body.

His presence enabled Jesse to steady her hands and open the envelope. She found another piece of folded paper and a second envelope, firmly sealed.

The folded paper was a letter. She propped the flashlight up on the counter and tilted the paper so that the light shone on it. She began to read aloud.

Dearest Jesse,

When you find this note, there is something I want you to do right away. I've put another envelope inside. I want you to take the envelope to your friend Al Aguilar in town. Make sure he reads the letter.

This is very important, Jesse. Please do exactly as I ask. And remember—no matter what happens, I love you. No matter what mistakes I've made, remember that, my darling. I love you and always will.

I'm not strong, Jesse. But you are. I know you'll make something wonderful of your life. Please never give up hope.

Jesse closed her eyes and held the note to her heart. David's fingers massaged her upper arms.

"Is this what you came to find?" he asked.

She shook her head, unable to speak, and pried open the flap of the second, smaller envelope.

The wording of this message was terse and factual and thoroughly sober, with few emotional flourishes. The very coldness of the events laid out chilled Jesse beyond any warming.

It started with a simple and terrible declaration: *I know Gary Emerson killed someone.*

Killed someone. The unexpectedness of it made Jesse lose her mental bearings. She'd thought to find proof of his part in her mother's death, but not an accusation that he'd been involved in others as well.

She was right. He was evil.

She didn't realize she'd dropped the note until David bent to retrieve it and smoothed the crushed papers between his fingers. "Shall I read it for you, Jesse?" he asked.

In her imagination, Jesse was strong enough to handle anything. Face anything. But she was ready to hand it over to David without a single protest.

"Please," she said hoarsely.

He cleared his throat, and she noticed that his hands were not quite steady.

"*This is my account,*" he read, "*of what happened between March 28th and April 5th. We were preparing the resort for the spring season. It was vacant except for myself, my daughter Jesse, and Gary Emerson. Gary has been living and working on my property for two years. Until recently I trusted him, though I have never known much about his background. But on March 28th, while he was out of town on business for the resort, a man came by to see him.*

"*This man was very insistent about seeing Gary and claimed that Gary owed him money. His manner was threatening, and I didn't want to let him in. But when Gary returned, the man was still in town, and Gary invited him to stay at the resort.*

"*They seemed to get along well, but I could tell there was something wrong. When they caught me listening to one of their discussions, about splitting money between them, it was obvious that they didn't want me to overhear. Gary told me to mind my own business. But I didn't think much of what was happening until I found* the stash of money in a briefcase, tens of thousands of dollars in large bills, hidden under one of the floorboards in Guest Cabin #5. The cabin was in need of repair and hadn't been occupied for years, and I was looking into renovating it when I found the money.

"I didn't know what to do, so I kept watching Gary and his friend. One day they had a terrible argument. Gary was very angry for the rest of the day. Later I saw him speaking to his friend, but something was different.

"By then I suspected that Gary and his friend had committed some crime and stole the money I'd found, but when I looked again it was gone.

"On the fourth day, Gary told me that his friend had to move on and had already left town the night before. That night, after we'd gone to bed, I saw light outside the cabin. I went to look and saw Gary with the body of his friend, digging a grave in the woods near the boundary of my property.

"While I was returning home, I found metal tags in the dirt. They had numbers and the name of Gary's friend on them, and I guessed they'd fallen off his body when Gary buried it in the woods. I saved the tags and hid them where Gary wouldn't find them. They are under the painted rock by the stream. Jesse can tell you where to look.

"I know now I've been wrong about Gary since the day he came to us. I saw what I wanted to see. I was blind to how he mistreated Jesse. He is a murderer and he wouldn't hesitate to kill me and Jesse to hide what he did.

"I don't know what to do. Gary suspects I saw something. I am afraid to go to the police. Gary is very popular in town and I know that no one will believe me. I have to make him leave—" David hesitated.

"What is it?" Jesse asked, staring out the cracked window at the brightening sky.

"The writing is different here, as if she'd been interrupted and continued at another time."

"The argument I remembered," Jesse said. "She must

have been writing this note just before Gary came in, and hid it. I didn't hear the whole conversation, but she must have said something to scare him. He threatened her." She leaned into David and sucked in a shaky breath. "Go on."

David clenched his jaw and continued. The tone of the letter changed, became rambling and disjointed and frantic, and somehow David conveyed that in the way he read.

"*I made a terrible mistake. Gary knows I know. He has made threats to hurt Jesse if I ever tell. Oh, forgive me, my darling.*

"*I'm trapped. I know I'm no good. I've failed as a mother. I let this happen and put my daughter in danger.*

"*I can't take care of Jesse anymore. She'd be better off without me. She doesn't know what happened. If I'm not here, Gary can't use her against me. He'll leave her alone. I can't live with this any longer.*

"*I beg whoever reads this to take care of Jesse after I'm gone.*"

David stopped reading and turned the paper over. "It just ends there," he said, his mouth a grim line.

Jesse covered her face with her hands. David set down the letter and held her close. "Do you believe he killed your mother?" he asked softly.

She knew what he was asking. Jesse had heard the desperation in her mother's letter. The hopelessness. The state of mind that convinced Joan Copeland that her absence might somehow save Jesse from the menace of Gary Emerson, even if it plunged her daughter into grief and loss and utter aloneness. She'd seen only one way out.

Gary'd had a perfect alibi. He hadn't even needed to make the effort to silence her.

Jesse gripped David's jacket convulsively, focusing on the physical sensation of cloth on skin. "If I'd found this earlier, I could have stopped her—"

"Shhhh." He stroked her hair. "You were a child. You were powerless."

"But Gary wasn't. I know he would have killed her if she hadn't . . . made it unnecessary. He's guilty, David. He's a murderer, and he has to pay."

David was quiet so long that she pulled back to look up at his face. "The evidence is here," she said. "I do know where those tags are buried. We can find the grave. It's enough to start an investigation, and that alone will destroy Gary's hopes for—"

"No, Jesse."

"No?" She pulled free. "What—"

His hands caught her, gripping her arms above the elbows. "Don't do this," he said flatly. "Don't . . . let this hatred poison you."

"Poison me?" She laughed. "I've finally found what I've been looking for, and you tell me to let it go? Never. I intend to see that justice is served."

But his expression remained closed, and he didn't loosen his grip. "Do you think you'll come out of this unscathed?" he demanded. "Do you believe Gary can't defend himself? You said he was a murderer. He's already threatened you. Do you think he'd hesitate to do it again?"

For a ghost he could be remarkably strong. She fought down her anger and stopped struggling. "All my life I've been waiting for this, even though I didn't know it. It's worth the risk—"

"Not if it means you'll be hurt," he said, almost shaking her. "I won't let that happen. Not while I'm here to stop you."

Her first reaction was to remind him that he had no right. But then she recognized what he meant, and remembered what she'd been so eager to tell him before the dream of her mother.

He was trying to protect her. His sincerity couldn't be doubted; he'd scared Gary away, and now she knew that his actions hadn't been either casual or random. His eyes burned with a passion different, but no less potent, than what he'd shown in her bed.

He was afraid for her. Desperately afraid.

He cared for her, far more than he'd ever admit.

"David," she whispered. She let herself sink against him. His arms locked around her as if he'd never let her go.

"Don't do it, Jesse," he said. "Let the past lie. Sooner or later Gary will suffer the consequences of his actions—"

"Don't you see?" She touched his cheek and his grim mouth, willing him to understand. "If I don't act now, he could go on hurting people. He could gain more power and use it for evil. If I'm the only one who knows what he is, I'm the only one who can stop him."

He turned his head. "Then revenge has nothing to do with it, Jesse?" he asked bitterly.

It was a question she couldn't answer. Her heart was too full of contradictory emotions, and as the triumph and sorrow and anger ebbed she was left with only one certainty.

"Your support has meant so much," she said. "More than I can ever explain. I can't completely make sense of what's happened to me in the last few days. I've fought it, denied it . . . . but ignoring it just won't work anymore. There *are* some risks worth taking."

He looked down at her again, very still and pale.

"What I'm trying to say is . . . no matter how it turns out with Gary, or what I do from now on, there's one thing I'm sure of. I don't even care what you did in your past life that condemned you to limbo. It wouldn't make any difference.

"Oh, hell." She grimaced and laughed weakly. "What I mean is . . . I love you, David Ventris. I think I always have."

CHAPTER THIRTEEN

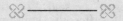

THE GROUND DROPPED out from beneath David's feet, and he felt himself lose his grip on the worldly plane. Jesse wavered in and out of his vision, but her touch kept him anchored.

She waited, gazing up at him with those candid hazel eyes, and he knew he'd won. The love that shone from her face was unmistakable, but he hadn't let himself assume that such a victory was possible. Now there could be no doubt.

She loved him. For Jesse Copeland to admit such an emotion was a marvel, and she could no more feign it than he could make himself live again. She presented him with this gift when he'd done virtually nothing to earn it.

She loved him. He should have been crowing with triumph. Wasn't it what he'd wanted—to influence her so well that she would willingly offer him whatever he asked? A few smooth words of love in return, and she'd be eating out of his hand. She was strong, his Jesse, but not invulnerable. And though she demanded nothing from him, he knew what she wanted to hear.

All he had to do was give it to her. He could take her to bed and then, when she was starry-eyed with passion, ask for the one further gift he required. Surely she wouldn't refuse it.

She'd said so herself. She didn't care what he'd done. She claimed she was not Sophie. What would a past life matter to her now?

For a few moments David saw only freedom. Freedom from limbo, from the chains of his wasted life, from guilt he couldn't bear. Freedom to live again, even in a new body. He would welcome that forgetfulness.

Then slowly, gradually, he came back down to earth. He was aware of the anxious pressure of Jesse's hold, though her eyes remained resolute and unwavering in their conviction. He remembered that he stood in Jesse's old home. He remembered what she had said about Gary. He relived his own alarm for her when she insisted on continuing with this mad quest for vengeance. . . .

And he felt a twisting tension in his gut, a bitter comprehension that shattered his brief conceit of freedom. Jesse spoke to him of love, but her obsession with Gary was every bit as powerful. She didn't begin to understand the forces at work behind her actions, but she'd convinced herself that it was some greater duty and not hatred that motivated her pursuit.

Just as she'd convinced herself that she loved David Ventris.

Didn't they all play games of self-deception? Jesse, Gary, himself . . . not one of them was spared.

He most of all. He was afraid for Jesse's safety, but he could no longer believe his concern was only for his success. He had lost that cold, cynical detachment. His shield had been taken from him, and he was as naked as a turtle laid on its back in the burning sun.

He'd thought he could affect Jesse without being affected, keep his emotions securely locked inside. The

early warning signs had been twinges he'd done his best
to ignore.

Ignorance was no longer an option. He looked into
Jesse's eyes and wanted more than forgiveness. He
wanted her love to be real, and it was illusion.

"David?" Her voice was hesitant, tinged with unease.
"Talk to me."

Love me, she meant. He wanted to shout at her, mock
her for her foolish, deadly vulnerability. He tried to summon up the indifference that would provide just the right
answer to keep her at a distance but not drive her away.

"I don't know what to say," he said, choking on the
truth. "Jesse . . . I'm not what you think—"

"I know you're not like other men," she said. Her fingers grazed his cheek. "I know your limitations. I'm willing to take whatever we can find, David. Whatever we
can make for ourselves as long as we can."

His own philosophy: live for the moment. Never think
ahead. Never consider the consequences. He'd taught
Jesse that.

His mind was as useless as wet powder in a jammed
musket. His heart was frozen. When he spoke, his voice
was that of a battle-hardened officer and not a lover.

"What would you do to keep me with you, Jesse?" he
asked. "Would you give up on Gary if it meant I could
stay?"

The softness left her eyes. "What are you saying?"

"Can you forgive for the sake of your love?"

"Forgive . . . Gary?" Her hands dropped to her
sides, and her fingers clenched. "I don't understand.
What does he have to do with us?"

His mouth flooded with the acrid taste of more lies.
More evasions to avoid what must be. He could keep on
manipulating her, but it merely delayed the inevitable
reckoning.

There was only one way out.

Tell her, he thought. *Tell her now.*

But his body was as ineffectual as his tongue and his
brain. He lost control of it, and without the act of will

that kept him substantial on the earthly plane, he began to fade. Jesse's lips moved, but he couldn't hear her. She reached for him, but she couldn't hold him.

He spun away, the room and the resort and the woods and the mountains dissolving into a colorless mist. It always seemed as if time and space ceased to exist when he made the transition. The place to which he returned was No Place.

It surrounded him again, familiar and hated. His own personal slice of hell without even the diversion of everlasting flames.

The body he possessed in limbo was identical to the one Jesse knew, but in limbo there was nothing to smell, to taste, to see, to feel. The form itself came only from his mind. Sometimes he could create a temporary solidity around him, built from memory—a misty battlefield, dirt under his feet, the cries of the wounded, the scent of gunpowder and sweat.

He'd never been able to re-create the hills and blue water of the Lakes, or any kind of beauty. Mostly he walked . . . another illusion . . . through an emptiness lacking shape or hue, endless and borderless.

Limbo had never seemed as empty as it did now. The mist—he hadn't found a better word to describe it—pressed in on him, and yet he was almost grateful for the blankness that entered his soul. No time, no connections, no emotions at all if he chose to forget them. *Here* that was possible.

Inevitable. Eternal.

He sat on a hummock of vapor and put his head in his hands. *Coward*, the silence whispered. He accepted the brand as his due. Jesse was his mirror, and he saw reflected, with perfect clarity, the irredeemably flawed man he'd refused to acknowledge.

Irredeemable. Damned.

"Self-pity is a prodigiously comforting thing, is it not?"

David jerked up his head. First he saw the polished boots, and then the snug breeches and the sword and neat coat. He observed the very large nose that graced the man's face below the equally beaky brim of his dark bicorne hat. David jumped to his feet.

"Your Grace," he said, and caught himself. The man who'd come to him here was not who he appeared to be. That was quite impossible. The chance that Wellington would turn up in David's limbo, so long after the commander and victor of the war against Napoleon had met his own death, was virtually nil.

Ancient habits were very difficult to break. David relaxed at Wellington's nod, but he knew this was illusion. The being who confronted him was not necessarily human. There was a certain radiance from the tanned and distinctive face, and David, who'd met the real Iron Duke but a few times in his career, couldn't quite swallow a reluctant awe.

"Cat got your tongue?" Wellington inquired, lifting a brow.

"No, Your Grace. But I wondered to what I owe the honor of this visit."

Wellington smiled and a chair materialized behind him. He sat down. "No need to stand on formality, Captain. I hear you've dug yourself a hole and are having a bit of trouble climbing out of it."

David stood rigidly in place. "I confess to being surprised that you would take an interest in my affairs, Your Grace."

"It seems someone must, since you persist in making things difficult for yourself." He sighed. "I know damned well you're no coward, Captain Lord Ashthorpe. Yet you cling to these addled beliefs."

David laughed with a marked lack of respect for a superior officer. "May I assume you know everything about me? Did my gaolers send you?"

Wellington shook his head. "Do you really suppose that someone is punishing you, Ventris? I would have thought you'd have reached the more obvious conclusion by now. You're not a stupid man, however much you wasted your intelligence when you were alive."

"If it's for my sake that you lecture me on my numerous flaws, you're wasting your time. Your Grace." David sat on the hummock again. "They are old friends."

Wellington leaned back and crossed his legs. "Indeed? Do you tell me that you've actually faced yourself at last?"

He couldn't meet his commander's gaze. "I can take no credit for that."

"Ah. You refer to the lovely Jesse." Wellington glanced over the arm of his chair, as if he were looking at some distant view. "I see she's waiting for you. Wondering why you vanished after her declaration of love." He tsked softly. "A damned discourteous thing for an officer and a gentleman to do, Captain."

Discourteous. David knew himself for the worst villain alive or dead. "Yes," he said. "How wonderful that I have made her love a man who doesn't exist."

"I believe her exact words were: 'I know your limitations. I'm willing to take whatever we can find. Whatever we can make for ourselves as long as we can.'"

David shot to his feet and paced out a savage measure, six steps one way and six the other. "But she doesn't know what I *am*," he said with glacial self-loathing. "I haven't had the courage to tell her. And now—"

"You're afraid of what she'll do when she learns the truth. That you're not entirely the heroic, sympathetic figure she's imagined. How you've failed again and again to give your life meaning. That your courage in battle was the only escape from the dark, untended corners of your own soul. That you betrayed her."

David ground to a stop and met Wellington's gaze. "Yes."

"Surely no love can stand in the face of so much imperfection." Wellington straightened in his chair, and the glint in his eye grew stern. "She will judge you as you deserve, send you back here forever."

David closed his eyes. "Isn't it what I deserve? Why should I be able to save myself when I can't anyone else? Jesse, Megan—"

"Don't you have it the wrong way 'round, Captain? How can you save anyone else until you've saved yourself?"

It was a question David could not answer. "I seem to lack the facility for it, Your Grace," he said bitterly.

"So you call yourself a coward," Wellington said. He slapped his hand on the arm of his chair, and the sound echoed like thunder. "You're afraid, Ashthorpe. The one part of your life where you couldn't take risks was with your heart. Not when it might be deeply touched, or threatened by loss. Better to stop it before it began, or run away. But that isn't possible now, is it? Because Jesse is already in you, and you'll never be free of her."

"But she can be free of *me*." David strode close to the chair, stared down at his supreme commander without flinching. "What favor have I done her? She has a full life ahead of her. She'd be willing to waste it on a man who can't be real for more than a few hours at a time. The longer I'm with her, the worse it will be for her when I must leave. It could . . . destroy her."

"How little faith you have in love, Captain. Even your own."

"Mine? I'm not capable of it."

"Of course not. Forgive my presumption." He looked up at David steadily. "After having prepared and schemed to win her forgiveness, and received her love instead, you want her to go on with her mortal life and forget you."

"Yes."

"Then it seems quite clear to me. If you tell her the truth, surely she'll hate you and forget you the more quickly. You will not have won your salvation, but you will at least have finished what you started. You may return to your punishment and she to her life, and all complications are ended. Isn't that what you wish?"

Of course. It *was* perfectly clear. It was what had to be, and David's wishes were of no consequence. Jesse had to be set free. Whether she forgave or repudiated him, *she* must break the bonds between them.

He would have to cajole or beg or trick her into abandoning her obsession with Gary; only that would keep her tied to the past, and she was in danger as long as she pursued it. He had to end that danger before he left her forever.

"Thank you, Your Grace," he said, coming to attention. "I shall take your advice."

Wellington rose. "Ah, but it wasn't my advice. You'd already made the decision before I arrived. I am merely the reflection of your thoughts. It does help to see them from a fresh perspective." He saluted. "Good luck, Captain. You died well. Perhaps you can learn to live with equal skill."

David watched the erect figure turn and walk away, receding until he melted into the horizonless distance. But David no longer felt paralyzed by self-disgust. He had a plan of action, and it was like that final battle at Waterloo when he'd flung himself head-on into certain death—it didn't matter what existed beyond the moment.

He didn't think beyond the next hour. His spirit was strong now, and he knew a mere thought would have him back at Jesse's side.

Enough time had passed on the earthly plane that Jesse was no longer at the resort. He should never have left her, but at least she hadn't taken any rash action against Gary. He found her at home, working in the shop where she built her sturdy, simple furniture.

She looked up as he came in. Her eyes widened and she went very still, her fingers locked around the smooth wooden handle of a hammer. Slowly she set it down.

"You came back," she said.

He couldn't bear the relief and gratitude in her gaze, the fragile happiness that made her words tremble. He strode to her and bent to lift her into his arms. She came willingly, tucking her head beneath his chin.

"David," she said. "If anything I said . . . I should never have—"

He silenced her with a finger across her lips. The gesture became a caress; he explored the seam of her lips until they parted, and then replaced his finger with his mouth.

There in her workshop, leaning on a sawdust-covered table, he kissed her. The previous time he'd felt an incredible urgency to respond to her innocent seduction, as if the opportunity might be stolen from him with the slightest hesitation. He'd wanted to bury himself in her body after decades of celibacy. He'd been thinking only of himself, no matter that he'd tried to pleasure her in the process.

This loving would be for Jesse. It was the last chance he had to communicate without words, without deception, while she could still look upon him with trust and love. He wanted her to remember him with something other than hatred when he was gone.

He wanted to be close to her in the truest way of all.

He lifted her to the tabletop, drew her against him and gave full tribute to her lips. Her fingers dipped into his hair and her eyes closed, pale brown lashes fanned over her flushed cheeks. Her tongue met his gentle feints, but he reined in his eagerness. He explored her mouth, outside and inside, with patience and tenderness.

But he couldn't master his body's yearning. Jesse's legs had locked around his hips, and his sex strained his breeches in a manner she couldn't mistake. She pushed into him, and he swallowed a groan.

No. There'd be no taking her quickly and thoughtlessly now. Not even if she thought she wanted it. He licked each corner of her mouth and mapped her face with his kisses: chin, cheeks, jaw, nose, eyelids, brow, temples, forehead. She made impatient little sounds as if she wished to return the favor, but he gently locked her hands at her sides and continued uninterrupted.

Her ear was a remarkably dainty shell. He took his time tracing its contours and suckled the delicate lobe. Jesse shivered and arched back her neck, giving him access to that slender column. He licked the length of her neck from the hollow at her throat to the pulse point

tucked under her jaw, then kissed the juncture of neck
and shoulder, using his teeth and tongue to increase the
sensual pressure.

Jesse was gasping now, her arms tense under his
hands. A part of her was still afraid of letting go, surren-
dering to him, receiving without giving in return.

He released her arms and kissed her lips again while
his fingers found the top button of her shirt. Her hands
grasped for his jacket, slid up to his shoulders. Her restless motions didn't interfere with his deliberate progress.

The first button slipped free, and he bent to kiss the
tanned vee just below her neck. The blood beat fast in
the hollow of her throat. The second button came undone, and the paler upper swell of her breasts waited to
be caressed. He took his time about it, and then unfas-
tened the third button.

Her breasts were beautiful and very white, only the
brown nipples a contrast to the smooth, erotic curves. He
stroked them with his fingertips, unhurried sweeps that
ended in the hardening tips.

If he'd followed his lust, he'd have those nipples in his
mouth, firm under his tongue, and her trousers already
down around her ankles. He ached to taste her fully. But
he cupped and weighed the soft globes, kneaded them
lightly, traced the circumference of her nipples until he
had memorized every tiny contour.

"David," she said hoarsely. "Please."

Her plea was enough. He bent his head and pressed his
lips to the swell of one breast above the nipple, kissed a
circle that just avoided the brown center. Only when she
laced her fingers in his hair and demanded more did he
take her nipple into his mouth.

She arched up. He filled his mouth with her, sliding up
and down, ending each pull with a deeper draw on her
nipple. He wrapped his tongue around it, flicked it, suckled it, teased it while her breath came in short, hot pants.
He pressed her breasts together and thrust his tongue
into the valley he created, thumbing her nipples in
rhythm.

Her eyes were glazed with passion when she looked up, but she was far from insensible from the pleasure. She'd found the buttons to his breeches and was already trying to work them free.

He pushed her hands away. "No, Jesse," he said. "It's not over yet."

He opened her shirt fully and slid it halfway from her shoulders, baring her belly. He shrugged out of his jacket and laid it on the table. She didn't protest when he eased her onto her back, leaving only her legs below the knees bent over the edge.

The fastening of her trousers was simple enough to manipulate once he saw how it worked. He unlocked the tiny metal teeth from her waist to the juncture of her thighs and tugged the trousers below her hips. She arched her back to help him. The trousers fell to the floor, and he pushed them aside with his boot.

She wore only a thin, narrow slip of silky cloth to pass as an undergarment. The sight of the sheer material, barely hiding what lay beneath, had the effect of hardening David more than he believed possible. He closed his eyes and began to trace the rim of banding that hugged the lower edge of her hips.

The white slickness of the cloth couldn't disguise Jesse's response to his caresses. He stroked down, over the mound of her sex, feeling the lush brown curls and the unmistakable wetness that had begun to dampen the delicate material.

He lingered there, pressing into the indentation where she was most sensitive. She shuddered as he ran his finger up and down the hidden cleft. Her scent was like a heady perfume. He bent and touched his tongue to the moistened cloth, inhaling her and taking his first taste.

Jesse moaned and opened her legs in invitation. David withdrew just long enough to dispose of the flimsy drawers and then returned to his explorations.

Now there was nothing between his mouth and her sex. She lay before him without embarrassment or coy modesty, and the victory was almost as sweet as the nec-

tar of her body. Her curls were no impediment. The soft
pink flesh was swollen and wet, slick to his touch, a deli-
cacy he badly wanted to sample.

The tip of his tongue touched the top of her cleft,
stroked down into the moist valley. Jesse cried out. He
licked her, drank from her, laved her again and again.
When he found the swollen bud hidden beneath, he drew
it into his mouth and suckled.

He felt her rising excitement in the sounds she made,
the little contractions of her muscles, the convulsive
clenching and unclenching of her hands in his hair. He
gave her joy, but he was himself lost in the wonder of her
body, in the pleasure he took in pleasing her.

He didn't stop wanting to be inside her. But that
wasn't necessary for her fulfillment. He continued his caresses until he sensed a new tension in her body. Her
fingers tightened in his hair. With no warning she shattered against him, and he rode with her through the
storm until she relaxed and tugged him down beside her.

"Thank you," she whispered. "I . . ."

"Don't speak, Jesse," he said. "Words will come
later."

Such words as would destroy what they had in this
moment. But he savored the present, the lingering taste
of Jesse on his lips, her hands stroking him, her flushed
and peaceful happiness.

"All right," she said. "No words." She sat up, un-
abashedly naked, and began to push off his jacket. The
determination in her eyes was indisputable. She wanted
him naked as she was; she wanted to see him. He
couldn't deny her.

He helped her with the buttons of his shirt and with
his belt. She laughed a bit nervously when she tried to
find a fastening for his trousers similar to her own and
discovered only more buttons. But then his clothing
joined hers on the wooden floor, and he pulled off his
boots and paused, oddly vulnerable and almost afraid.

This was nothing to what he must face when he bared
his soul to her. But he waited, watching her take in his

countless scars and the ugly gash on his thigh that had
healed improperly after the battle of Badajoz.

She opened her mouth as if to speak, then remembered
their agreement. Instead, she gave him her verdict with
her touch. She ran her hands the length of his arms,
cupped his shoulders and then his chest, slipping her fingers through the hair and following its downward path
to his belly.

He was afraid if she touched his aching sex he would
shame himself. He was afraid she wouldn't touch him at
all. But her hands closed gently but firmly around him,
and he gave himself up to her ministrations.

For a woman with little experience she knew exactly
what to do. He hadn't wanted her to be the one giving in
this exchange, but he didn't have the will to resist her.
She made him helpless. She stroked him, tormented him
as he'd done her, first with her fingers and then, astound-
ingly, with her mouth.

Somehow he kept command of his body. She drove
him to the peak of pleasure and at the last moment, when
he was losing the battle, she pulled away. Her fingers
laced through his and she led him from the workshop
and to her bed.

There she drew him down. They were two beings, and
then one—joined, flawless, whole. For David it was more
than physical gratification. As he moved within her he
caught a glimpse of something that had always eluded
him, which once he'd sought but given up on long, long
ago.

He reached out to grasp it, but then sensation took
him: the rocking, the rhythm, the all-consuming fire of
ecstasy. He spent himself in Jesse and felt her reach her
culmination a second time. They came down together,
locked in each other's arms.

❧ ❧

JESSE FLOATED IN a dream world, anchored by the length
of David's hard-muscled body beside her on the bed.

Even as her nerves hummed with the aftereffects of his lovemaking, another part of her was in a place where happiness was the only reality.

She snuggled closer into the curve of his arm and ran her hand lazily over the flat ridges of his belly, her eyes heavy-lidded with contentment. David's heart thumped under her ear, and his fingers curled around her arm in a satisfying gesture of possessiveness. She was aware of a purely female appreciation for the unencumbered beauty and power of his body, a certain awe that he was here with her now.

But the happiness was something more powerful. It was infinite. Fleetingly she could remember her initial despair when David had vanished—the yearning, the fear and then, finally, the acceptance. She'd come to realize that whatever he chose to do, her love would remain as unshakable as the Trinity Alps themselves.

The fact that he'd returned to make love to her eliminated the need for explanations, the words he couldn't say. Words would drag her down from this lofty height of supreme joy, where no darkness could reach.

Her eyes drifted shut. So relaxed; the only other time she'd felt like this was under hypnosis, when all the lines between fact and fantasy, past and present, had blurred and disappeared.

It seemed as if she and her lover lay on a grassy hillside, with a canopy of blue sky above and the trickle of a tiny creek nearby. It felt as though her elation had transformed her into someone else, someone who believed implicitly in happy endings.

Yet it didn't even matter who she was, or when, or where. She was with the man she loved.

She wanted to stay this way forever.

"Jesse."

Her hand felt weighted with lead as she tried to lift it, to quiet him and make the timeless bliss last a little longer.

"Jesse, there is something . . . I must tell you."

She ducked her head halfway under his arm like a

child dodging a scolding. He shifted under her, levering her up.

"I've waited too long," he went on stubbornly. "You must listen to me."

She opened her eyes halfway and looked at him through the screen of her lashes. His handsome face was deadly serious. It seemed alien, almost frightening. She bent down to plant a kiss on the firm swell of his chest, then moved an inch lower and kissed him again.

"No."

The word was all command, but she giggled and kept going. There was no room in her heart for such gravity. She felt possessed, as if another, giddier will guided her mouth and hands. Just as she reached the most potent part of him, his hand slapped down over hers.

"Damn it, Jesse." He closed his eyes and let out a harsh breath. "The deception has to end." He sat up and pulled her with him, setting her on her knees. She felt as limp and defenseless as a rag doll, but her mind was still floating, undisturbed by his vehemence.

"What is it, David?" she said. She thought she sounded drunk. Drunk on love. She giggled again.

He gripped her arms. "I came back to tell you the truth. The truth I've always known but pretended I'd forgotten."

The truth. What was truth? Too profound a question. But a little piece of her consciousness anchored itself to his declaration, and she focused on his face.

"I deceived you from the beginning, Jesse," he said. "When we first met, I told you I didn't know why I was damned, or how I was to win my salvation. I said I knew only that you could help me."

She smiled and touched his jaw, the slight roughness that didn't change each time she saw him. "You helped *me*," she said.

He seized her wrist. "I tricked you. I manipulated you. Because I knew all along that I could win salvation only if you were willing to give it to me. And that meant I'd eventually have to tell you—" He stopped, let go of her hand and looked away. "Oh, I was honest about some small facts. You and I were married in that other life. We had a child. While she was alive, our marriage . . . was as good as it could be."

"You loved . . . me," she said. She released her hold on her mind and turned inward, journeyed back. She could *remember*. "We had Elizabeth."

"But Elizabeth died," he said. "And when she died, so did any happiness we had together. You thought we comforted each other? Sophie—" He shook his head almost violently. "No. *You*. In your grief, you blamed me for Elizabeth's death. I had never wanted to give up my freedom. I had married you only because of the child, and now there was no reason to stay."

Jesse heard him, and as he spoke she felt herself shift from one reality to another. The familiar room and bed wavered around her, was overlaid by a second just as familiar but far more ornate. Two vastly different worlds existed in the same time and space.

And David was in the center of both. He was the link that made it possible. Suspended between past and present, Jesse could only listen in numb silence to his confession.

"I knew you were suffering," he said in a dull, flat monotone. "But I couldn't think of anyone but myself. It was my duty to protect you, but I chose to abandon you to your pain. So I left you at the Hall in Avery's care, and bought a new commission in the army. When you begged me to stay, I ignored you."

As if she were viewing separate movies showing side by side, Jesse saw herself as two people: at her mother's resort, feeling sympathy and sorrow as David related his loveless past of constant running—and in the chill foyer of a great sprawling mansion, her throat hoarse with weeping, half mad with grief and fear and anger.

She was Jesse—*and* Sophie. Two women who struggled for supremacy over the soul they shared.

"I expected Avery to handle your affairs as he ran the Hall," David continued inexorably. "He had always done it well, and I wanted none of that responsibility. I hardly read the letters you sent me in the Peninsula, entreating me to return. When you began to write that you feared Avery, that he despised you, that he was watching you with evil intent, I discounted it as more of your female vapors. It was only when you convinced me that you were very ill that I took leave to come home."

Jesse swayed and clutched at the headboard for support. Fear clawed at her chest—senseless, maddening terror. Sophie's terror.

Avery.

"I found you ill only in your own mind," David said. "I was enraged by your trick. I spoke with Avery, and he convinced me that you were imagining his dislike. I never thought to disbelieve him.

"The more you clung to me, the more certain I was that I'd be swallowed up in your need. You were a chain I couldn't break, but I could pretend you didn't exist."

Jesse's breath came in short gasps. She no longer knew where she was; her face felt alien under her groping fingers.

It was Sophie's face. Sophie's tears wet her cheeks. Sophie's dread and despair were her own.

"Once again I left you," David said. "Once again I ignored your letters, even when you told me that Avery was attempting to seduce you. *Avery*, seduce a woman." David grated a bitter laugh. "You said he threatened you openly when you refused him, and you had no protection against him. You said he hated me, but you were my wife and in his power."

Overcome by a chaos of memory, Jesse felt for the sheets and pulled them up over her shivering body. A faint whiff of smoke hung in the air.

"I knew it was your own mad fancy. Avery's passions had become dried up long ago. You'd tricked me before when you summoned me home, pretending to be ill—so I told myself. I didn't listen, even when you wrote that Avery was scheming to take your life."

Jesse's shaking stopped, stilled by a coldness that turned her blood to ice.

"Your last letter," David said in a harsh whisper, "came to me on the eve of battle. It was almost incomprehensible. Mad. I threw it in the fire that night and watched it burn.

"That was the night I killed you."

CHAPTER FOURTEEN

T HE LAST OF the color left her face, and David saw the transformation complete itself.

The change had come on gradually as he'd watched her memories return. It was to Jesse he'd begun telling the tale, Jesse's lithe body that crouched before him. But now it was Sophie's eyes that met his, Sophie's fear he was forced to witness, Sophie's unspent hatred that answered him.

"You . . . killed me," she repeated, her voice as hoarse and accented as his own.

"Yes." The confession seared his throat like vitriol. "I could have saved you. Months later I received word that you had died in a fire that had destroyed the Hall. A fire set by my brother."

"He burned me," she said. A savage battle went on behind her wide and stricken gaze, and she jerked like a puppet with cut strings. David imagined that he saw flames dancing in her hazel eyes. They focused on him with terrible intensity.

"I begged you to save me," she said, fingers curled into claws. "I told you, and you wouldn't believe me."

He didn't allow himself the brief respite of looking away. "Yes."

"He hated you," she hissed. "He couldn't bear to see me in his precious Hall. He was convinced that everything you possessed should have been his." She spoke faster and faster, the long-dammed rage driving the words from her mouth like musket balls. "He hoped you'd die in the war; he prayed for it daily. He found a thousand ways to make my life hell. He knew you'd never believe what I said of him, because you were blind."

David had no excuses to give her. He *had* been blind to what Avery had become, grown out of the bitter seeds planted in childhood. A stranger who could wish for his own brother's death.

A murderer.

"He wanted me because he thought it would hurt you," Jesse said. "But you wouldn't have cared. You never did." She laughed with a frantic edge. "You wanted to be rid of me, and you had your way. You both had your way."

True blindness would have been a blessing in this moment. There was no forgiveness in the woman who wore Jesse's face and body. She was the avenging angel bent on sending him back to perdition.

Where he belonged.

"You were everything to me," she said. "My world, my life." Her bent fingers raked at the sheets as if they were his flesh, and she laughed again. "That one time you came back to me—that last night we shared—you put another child in me."

David had been naive to think there were limits to shame and anguish. "It . . . was true," he said.

Her smile was grotesque and bitter. "You didn't believe anything I wrote to you. But Avery did. He feared I would give you an heir. He said he would kill me before I robbed him of what should be his."

The murder had been of two lives, not one. David bent his head, a cry of mourning trapped in his chest.

"I was ill," she went on mercilessly. "Too weak to move from my bed. Avery would not send for the doctor. He was drinking the night he—" She paused, visibly struggling for words. "I heard the flames. The smoke was coming in. I tried to call for help—"

The control that had allowed her to speak with such devastating precision melted out of her voice, her face, her gaze like ice in the heat of a Spanish sun. She coughed, arms wrapping around her belly.

"The red light . . ." She shook her head, whipping hair into her eyes. "So hot. I can't move. Can't breathe—"

"Jesse," he said urgently, "it's not real—"

"The door—it's open—" She thrust her hands out in front of her face. "The flames—*David!*"

Her shriek ripped through him, cutting out his heart. The plea choked off in a dry rattling wheeze, and she raked at her throat. "Help . . . me . . ."

He lunged toward her and she fell back, arched in a spasm of intolerable agony, her body convulsing and flailing among the sheets in the hopeless struggle of a woman reliving her own unspeakable death.

"*Jesse,*" David cried, pinning her with his body. She heaved under him in a parody of their lovemaking. Her eyes rolled up in her head, and he reared up to strike her white cheek with the flat of his palm.

She went rigid, frozen in an unnatural position like a woman turned to stone. David prepared to strike her again, frantic in his own dread of losing her.

She collapsed beneath him just as he raised his hand. The witless terror left her gaze, and she looked at him with total comprehension.

"You," she rasped. Without warning, a new convulsion seized her, one of her own making. She bucked beneath him, her arms and legs imbued with uncanny strength, until he rolled away. He made no attempt to retreat when she pursued him like a banshee, her fists and feet pummeling every part of his body she could reach.

Sophie's voice spat loathing at him, a litany of hatred that beat in time to her blows. All her fear had been transmuted in the crucible of fire, and the only purpose left to her was vengeance.

But gradually the energy drained from her, the mad force deserting the strike of her fists. Her hands flattened and hit his chest with hollow slaps. Her voice went hoarse and ragged on the hundredth "I hate you." Tears fell, bathing his skin.

The change came last to her eyes. They were bleached, almost colorless as emotion subsided, the pupils wide and vivid in darkness.

Jesse's eyes. Jesse's mind reclaiming itself, reclaiming her body, slowly realizing what she had done. The last blow fell and she snatched back her hand. She bent her arms behind her back, tears drying on her cheeks.

He had never seen her face so blank. Not even a trace of hatred remained, but there was nothing else to take its place. Her gaze swept his body and fixed on his eyes with that same emptiness.

"I'm sorry," she said.

He wanted to laugh. He would have gladly borne her punishment, and far worse, for days on end rather than witness the cold void left in the wake of Sophie's rage.

"No, Jesse," he croaked. "I'm sorry."

She didn't answer. He knew she still remembered everything he had told her, everything she'd experienced. Sophie's memories were hers.

She gathered up the tangled sheets and tugged them from the bed. Carefully she wrapped them around herself, chin to ankle, like a shroud. She sat at the very edge of the bed with her back to him, and her voice reached him muffled and flat and lifeless as a tomb.

"I understand now," she said. "The dreams. The things I was afraid of. And Gary—" Her breath shuddered out, the only movement in her body. "You knew who Gary was, didn't you?"

He'd prayed she wouldn't make that connection, as she hadn't recognized Megan in this life. Even that was not to be spared her. "I knew," he said bleakly. "I'd hoped to protect you—"

"Of course. It's as if it's happening again. The dreams and memories started when Gary returned to Manzanita—" Her head lifted a little. "Is that why you came to me? Because Avery was here?"

So simple to lie one last time, give her one good thing to remember about him. But he couldn't. "I didn't know Avery had been reborn until after I came," he said. "I knew more than I admitted, but not that."

"Then why did you come?"

"Haven't you guessed?"

"You said I held the key to your salvation."

"Yes." He smiled with self-contempt, though she couldn't see. "Your forgiveness was to be my deliverance."

"My . . . forgiveness?"

She had found some emotion—disbelief, irony, weary amusement. David forced himself to keep from touching her.

"Your forgiveness—for what I did to you. Only that will release me from limbo and allow me to . . . move on."

"That easy?" The sheets pulled snug against her body. "Why come to me now, if you didn't know about Gary?"

"It was your call that allowed me to return. You opened the way, Jesse."

"Maybe you should thank Gary for that. He triggered it all. My dreams. My memories."

He would have called it bitterness except for the indifference in her voice.

"I could have killed him the night of the party," he said softly.

She hardly reacted beyond tilting her head. "Did he know who haunted him? Is that why he ran?"

"I don't know," he said. And he didn't, save that Gary had, for a few moments in the room at the inn, shared his mind with Avery as Jesse did with Sophie. And that he'd sensed David's warning.

"I always felt there was a pattern in the things that happened," Jesse murmured. "I understand why you tried to make me love you the way Sophie did. Sophie would have given you anything you asked for if you'd only loved her—even forgiveness. But you never really did love her. You didn't know how."

It was chilling to hear Sophie's intolerable realization reduced to such simplicity by the even, distant cadence of Jesse's words. To hear her say what David had believed to be true.

Until he recognized what he was about to lose.

"Do you hate me, Jesse?" he asked, sick in his heart.

"Hate you? You didn't hurt *me*." She gave a broken laugh. "Are you worried I'll send you back to limbo forever?" She shook her head. "It would have been so much easier if you'd told me this from the beginning. No deception, no entanglements, nothing between—" She stopped and the muscles in her jaw contracted.

No. Of course he hadn't hurt her. Of course she was completely removed from Sophie's passion and suffering, didn't give a damn what he'd done in deceiving her. So she would try to make him believe, rather than give in to her own justified pain and anger.

Rather than let him continue to think she had ever truly loved him.

"Should I have expected you to accept so much at the beginning?" he said. "You weren't even convinced I was real. You were already remembering pieces of your past, and they frightened you. Should I have—" But he stopped himself, hearing the excuses he made, just as he always had. Another way of escaping. Another disavowal of responsibility.

"I think you were the one who was afraid," Jesse said

into his silence. "All this elaborate game . . . was for nothing."

David closed his eyes and raged inwardly—not at her for rejecting him, nor even at his gaolers who would chain him for eternity, but because he finally understood, to the very center of his soul, the only thing that mattered. The only thing worth living, or dying, for.

He understood too late.

"It doesn't really matter if you lied to me," she said with that same steady, uninflected dispassion. "You helped me. You saved Megan and tried to protect me from Gary. I owe you for that." She half turned, allowing him a glimpse of her profile. It was white and still as a mask. "Whatever you did in that last life, it's over. Long over. I don't want your damnation on my conscience."

He knew then she would give him what he hadn't earned, present him with the gift as dutifully as she might dispatch some minor debt to an indifferent acquaintance.

"I forgive you, David," she said in a whisper. "You're free."

At first he felt nothing. The cold hollow core in the middle of his chest had been expanding minute by minute, and it grew colder still as she released him. His celestial gaolers would require sincerity in her forgiveness; surely this wouldn't qualify under their stringent rules.

But all at once he sensed a peculiar buoyancy in his borrowed body, the familiar pull away from the earthly plane. Familiar and yet different, for he knew, with a more profound conviction than any he'd experienced in life or death, that Jesse's forgiveness had been accepted.

He *was* free. The force that drew him back came not from his limbo but from a far more wonderful place. It sang to him like a chorus of angels, promising the liberation he'd sought. Joy such as he'd never known. The severing of bonds he'd worn like chains.

Everything he'd wanted since the day he'd died.

For a moment he almost let it take him. And then he looked down at Jesse—Jesse, who stared at him with that blank, lovely shield of a face—and knew it was impossible.

He couldn't go. That certainty was absolute, silencing the celestial chorus to a faint hum. The peculiar triumph of a decision made inevitable washed through him, lending him an unanticipated reserve of strength.

He couldn't leave Jesse. She knew who Gary was, and had reason to hate her nemesis now more than ever. In her current state she would be capable of anything. . . .

And, by God, he loved her.

The words took shape in his mind for the first time, stunning him with their power.

He loved her. Not the casual, shallow love he'd given Sophie. Not the dutiful emotion he'd once owed his parents, or the camaraderie he'd shared with friends and fellow soldiers in the midst of battle.

He had no definition for this. It was a bolt of white lightning through his heart, setting afire everything it touched until his body was incandescent. In the emptiness at his core he found the other half of his soul.

Jesse was his salvation, and he was hers. Love made it possible. He was utterly unworthy of her; he'd betrayed and wounded her time after time, given her nothing but sorrow. But he would never abandon her again.

He concentrated on solidifying his body, summoning every scrap of energy to keep it in place. He held out his hand to Jesse, readying the argument that would make her believe.

But Jesse opened her mouth and cried out in deepest pain.

"Go," she shouted. "Please, go!"

Her command hit him like a gale of arctic wind, shredding the outlines of his form as if they were made of mist. The force of her will allied with the pull of the other plane battered him, and he lost what little control he still maintained.

He became a creature of air, torn from Jesse's presence and hurled skyward. Only his desperation allowed him to remain on Earth, a soul without shape, hovering over the cottage and the town like an invisible bird.

No amount of struggle could alter his condition. The best he could manage was this in-between, another kind of limbo, and he knew the state could not endure.

Jesse wanted him gone. His gaolers wanted him back and out of their guardianship.

No. He launched the refusal to whoever listened. *No. No!*

With senses far greater than earthly vision he looked down on Jesse's cottage and watched her run to her truck. In her movements was all the anguish she'd refused to let him see. She drove down the lane and onto the main road. David knew where she was going.

He tried to follow, but her denial of him worked like an unscalable rampart, a siege wall invulnerable to any attack. He searched for a way around it, under it, some chink in her defenses.

There was none. He retreated rather than exhaust his dwindling strength. The oblivious citizens of Manzanita were like scurrying ants far below, no part of his battles, and yet some prick of awareness caught his attention and set off warning bells in his mind.

He knew immediately what had summoned him. *Who.* At the edge of town, near the Manzanita Inn, two men were arguing. One of them was short and rotund and middle-aged, his face flushed with agitation.

The other was Gary. Gary, his suit rumpled and his motions angry, demanding something of the older man.

Gary was back. It had been inevitable, simply a matter of time before he and Jesse should meet again. David had known, and he'd passed up the chance to end the threat.

Now he could only observe as Gary's voice rose to a shout, as the other man backed away, wide-eyed and wary. "You're either with me or against me!" Gary snarled. "You'll regret this, Wayne. When I win the election, you'll still be nothing. Nobody, do you hear me?"

Wayne tripped over his own feet in his haste to retreat. "I told you I can't help you!" he insisted hoarsely. "I've got to go." He spun around and jogged for the car parked on the lane beside the inn. Gary pursued a few steps and stopped, fists clenching and unclenching, as Wayne set the vehicle in motion with a screech of tires and a wild swerve for the road.

Gary stood, eerily still, his gaze turned inward. In his handsome face David could see a kind of madness, and he knew what Gary would do even before the man strode to his own car.

It didn't matter what drove Gary, whether reawakened memories of another life or the compulsion to eliminate a persistent nuisance in the one he lived now. Only a lucky guess could have sent him down the road, following the same route Jesse had taken mere minutes ago.

A guess, or instinct born of a connection he could no more resist than could Jesse. David saw the final pieces falling into place, the twice-told tale drawing to its inexorable climax.

By dint of sheer will David followed Gary as far as the gates of the resort. But his otherworldly senses were fading, the colorless mist of limbo closing around him again. Through a fog he saw Gary snap the lock on the gate with a heavy clipper, push the gate open with a violent kick.

Then David's sight deserted him completely, and his hearing, every last connection to the earthly plane. He screamed denial in his mind, and knew he'd lost.

Where the idea came to him he didn't know. As he tumbled into a brilliant tunnel of white light, he shaped his shout of defiance into an invocation. A prayer. A bargain offered to those who guarded the way between life and death.

Let me go back to her, he pleaded, infusing the appeal with all the humility and sincerity and heartfelt emotion he had so lacked in life. *Listen to me. If you let me protect her, I'll return to limbo forever. I'll pay any price to be real and whole for a few more hours. Any price. Every life I would have lived, for eternity. My soul. Do you hear me?*

There was no answer. The radiant tunnel drew him deeper.

Don't you understand? he cried. *I love her. Nothing else matters. I love—*

The white light exploded into a thousand fragments.

CHAPTER FIFTEEN

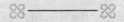

JESSE COULDN'T REMEMBER how she'd come to the resort.

She found herself kneeling in the dirt just outside her mother's cabin, her hands full of earth as if she'd been clawing the ground. Her face was stiff with dried tears, and as she felt her body again the sorrow came back, bending her double and drawing a moan from her raw throat.

David was gone.

That was the first, the unthinkable, the most unbearable certainty. David was gone, and she'd sent him away.

No. She'd set him *free*. For all the bitterness in her heart, the full knowledge of his deception and betrayal in this life and the last, she had given him what he wanted. Though she had raged at him, still something of her love for him had remained true, and now, in the numb aftershock of his revelations, in the wake of Sophie's memories relived, she understood.

She had hated him. She—Sophie—the soul they shared, had hated him. But more powerful than the hate was the love.

Here, in this place, she'd told David she loved him. She'd sworn to herself that nothing could weaken that love. She'd said that nothing David had done would change it.

She was right. How strange to realize that there was such a thing as unshakable love, that the stubborn core of it persisted even when the trappings had been burned away in a storm of fire and anguish.

Like the soul that went on, whatever outer shape it wore.

David was gone. He was free. She should be glad. She should rejoice for him. That he'd never loved her didn't make any difference. There was so much good in him, so much that deserved to go on and live and learn and find the love that eluded him.

And she had her own life, better than it had been before he came. That Sophie still existed somewhere within her was a matter she'd have to deal with. She *could* deal with it, now that she knew the truth.

She could live with the truth. She could learn to live without David. For Megan's sake. And because David had made her understand just how precious life was.

Jesse gathered her legs under her and stood, waiting until her knees stopped quivering, and glanced around the resort. It didn't frighten her anymore. She no longer feared the specter of childhood mental illness that hadn't been illness at all, but soul-deep memory triggered by her mother's death.

Her thoughts wandered at random, sorting themselves into logical patterns again. She could feel emotion waiting to erupt below the surface, a tempest ready for the right catalyst. But she forced it down under a layer of frigid calm, as she'd learned to do when feelings were too strong.

It wouldn't last, this numb self-possession. But there was a reason to hang on, now more than ever. One problem yet to be resolved, the final chapter of a book that must be read and put away. Then she, too, could begin to be free.

She felt under the collar of her shirt for her mother's letter, guarded against her heart. She was where she needed to be; she still had to find the tags Mom had hidden, and the grave in the woods.

Sophie stirred inside her: *He will pay.* Jesse didn't try to silence that vow. She wouldn't let Sophie's memories rule her, but in this they were united. Sophie would have her vengeance, and then be laid to rest forever.

Jesse started away from the cabin, moving her arms and legs as if they belonged to someone else. When she heard the crack of a twig behind her, she believed, for a miraculous instant, that David had come back.

But the smiling, handsome figure was dressed in a modern suit, and his brown eyes were narrowed in unholy satisfaction.

"I saw your truck out front," Gary said. "Lucky guess that you'd be here. But then I've always been lucky."

There was a frozen span of time in which Jesse was incapable of reacting. She was plunged back into childhood, remembering her attack on a younger Gary Emerson, screaming the same words over and over: *"You killed me. You killed me."*

And at the same time she was Sophie, choking on smoke but still alive to scream when the first flames touched sheets, nightrail, flesh. Carrying with her into death hatred for the two men who had betrayed her.

Sophie's eyes superimposed another shape on Gary's: shorter, less handsome, with a pinched and bitter face. He wore an antique suit, scrupulously neat and sober. His hair was darker, his eyes a muddy black and filled with malice.

"Avery," she whispered.

Gary's expression flickered and settled into its smug, familiar planes again. "I knew I'd find you sooner or later," he said. "But this is very convenient. No observers to interfere with our discussion."

Jesse snapped back to the present, and icy self-control returned to replace the momentary panic. It was all so clear; she knew that Gary would have been driven to face her eventually. She sensed the karmic connection between them as if it were a physical tie, and wondered how much he knew. If *he* remembered, or was compelled by impulses he would never understand.

If she were still the Jesse she'd been before David, before the memories, she might have taken the sensible path. She could have played ignorant, or simply afraid, and maybe he'd let her go. The police could handle the rest.

But this had been building for more than a single lifetime. She no longer cared about her own safety.

"I expected this," she said coldly. "I'm ready for you, Gary."

He barked a laugh. "You couldn't let it go, could you? I warned you, and you had to keep digging. Coming back here. Making trouble for me. I knew you wouldn't shut up."

Jesse held his gaze. "You're right. I always knew you had some part in my mother's death. Now I have the facts. And all the proof I need to expose you for what you are."

Gary's facade of confident menace began to slip. "Proof? Don't give me that shit."

"But you thought I might have something on you. You gave yourself away, Gary. You sent a flunky to search my house. You threatened me. You were the one who made me realize there was something to find, and I did."

"I never touched your mother—"

"Oh, you touched her. You treated her like dirt. It took me a while to remember that. I know you drove her to kill herself, even if you didn't push her in the water with your own hands."

If she'd believed it possible, she would have thought

she saw guilt in his eyes. "You're bluffing. She was a lush who jumped in the river—"

"Because of what she'd discovered. Your former 'business partner.' Remember him, Gary? There was a lot of money involved. He wasn't welcome, so you disposed of him. And my mother found out. She wrote it all down for me."

The color drained from Gary's face. "I don't know what the hell you're talking about."

"Seventeen years is a long time," Jesse said. "It must be convenient to be able to pretend it never happened." She took a step toward him, and his body jerked. "Where did you get that money, Gary? Robbery, or something subtler like extortion or blackmail? That would be just about your style. But maybe you would have gotten away with it if you hadn't resorted to murder."

She saw when it hit him: that she *knew*, that she wasn't bluffing, that she might truly be able to hurt him. "Your mother was a drunk," he spat. "No one would believe her, or you."

"They might believe when they find the body, or the dog tags my mother hid. They might start an investigation, and then where is your great political career?" Jesse felt righteous anger well up, a heady brew that made it impossible to be afraid. "It won't take much, Gary. Just a few doubts and questions and talk . . ."

"You bitch." He reached into his jacket. Jesse stiffened, but he only removed a dented cigarette pack. He produced a gold-plated lighter and lit a cigarette.

"You know, they do this in movies," he said in an oddly conversational tone. "The idiot who threatens the villain that she's going to expose him, when they're alone in some dark alley." He expelled a plume of smoke on a laugh. "Thought you were crazy, but not stupid."

"I have copies of my mother's letter," she lied. "And I've left instructions about finding the other proof if anything happens to me."

Gary took another drag and let out the smoke slowly.

He flipped the burning cigarette into the pine needles mounded near the cabin wall. "I always get what I want, Jesse. No one stops me."

She recognized in his very serenity something abnormal, as if he'd lost any judgment of the consequences of his actions. Things had come full circle. Now he was the one who'd gone crazy. He couldn't kill her and get away with it—and she knew nothing less would satisfy him. Just like before.

"I finally have everything I worked for," he said, turning to watch the first delicate fingers of smoke curl up from the clump of bone-dry needles. "I won't let you take it from me."

Jesse heard in his voice the echoes of that other life, words spoken by another man who shared Gary's soul. A man who'd feared that she—the child she carried—would steal his one chance at the power and status that should have been his save for an accident of birth.

"When does it end, Gary?" she asked. "When do you stop killing to get what you think you want?"

He only stared at the growing column of smoke, the tiny licks of fire igniting the desiccated pile.

Fire. The acrid smell filled Jesse's nostrils as if it were already a raging inferno. Fire that burned and killed. Within her, Sophie wailed and screamed.

Jesse could have stamped out the flame with one foot. She couldn't move. The flame grew larger, split into two tongues that moved with surprising speed toward the cabin wall. In such hot and arid conditions, a fire could spread stunningly fast.

Her training was stronger than Sophie's terror. She made a move toward the mound, foot positioned to scatter and bury the flames. In an instant Gary had a gun pointed at her chest.

"This place isn't much good to anyone," he said. "No one would miss it if it burned to the ground."

"You can't hide the evidence that way," Jesse said, keeping her voice level. "You can't hide from your own evil."

"Oh. Very dramatic." He smiled. "You should have been writing speeches."

Fire sent exploratory fingers up the side of the wall, finding it dry and ripe for conquest.

"Who was the first person you murdered?" she asked. "Or do you even remember?"

His face lost all expression. "Only that bastard—" He caught himself. "No more tricks." He gestured with his gun. "Go on. Into the cabin."

Jesse understood then. "You think that this will solve your problems. But it keeps repeating itself, Gary . . . there is no escape."

He stepped toward her. "Go."

"Did you think it was just my mother, Gary? There's more between us than what you did to her. You set another fire, in another life. You killed me before. But I'm back to face you. You didn't succeed. You never will."

Confusion warped his mouth into an ugly grimace. "You're still insane." But the strangeness in his eyes told her that he was disturbed by her words. The gun shook in his hand. Jesse gauged the distance, how quickly she could reach him and knock the weapon from his hand.

But he wasn't confused enough. His jaw hardened and he pushed the muzzle of the gun into her stomach.

"Funny," he said. "I'm actually sorry I have to do this. If only you'd kept quiet—"

Sophie's will surged to the fore, her bitterness and hatred joined with Jesse's own. "You'll pay, Gary," she said. "You'll never be free of me—"

With a grunt of fury he shoved her back, pinned her to the wall with the gun while he fumbled for the cabin door. The fire had caught on the wall now, inching toward the nearest cracked window, and it was only a matter of time until it reached the highly flammable curtains and furniture.

Jesse tried to dodge as he herded her into the cabin. He snatched her arm and nearly wrenched it from its socket.

·"I'm sorry," he repeated, as if he meant it. He struck her a glancing blow across the temple with the butt of the pistol, and she fell, red darkness dimming her sight. Then even that was gone.

⊗ ⊗

SHE WOKE TO find herself prone on the dusty floorboards, half blind, smelling the growing pall of smoke as it drove the clean air from her lungs.

The fire had spread rapidly in the time she'd been out. It had found its way inside and caught on the window drapes and furniture and the other walls. In minutes it would engulf the cabin. The door was shut between her and freedom.

Gary had trapped her. He would let her burn to death—

The part of her that was Sophie screamed in hopeless terror. Sophie had died in her bed, unable—*unwilling* to fight for her life. She'd died in hatred, succumbed to the despair that had become her whole existence.

She'd *wanted* to die, to punish the men who'd failed and tormented her. She would let the same thing happen now.

But Jesse didn't know how to give up. She stretched flat on the floor and reached out with her hands, feeling ahead through a maze of drifting smoke. Every inch of progress was a victory. Her consciousness wavered, and she formed an image in her mind: David, opening the door, arms outstretched to enfold her.

The vision was incredibly real, so real that she imagined David bursting into the room, sweeping her up like a swashbuckler hero, carrying her into sunlight and air she could breathe.

She coughed the smoke from her lungs and saw blue sky through a film of haze, the cabin wall a solid sheet of flame. And David was still there, his hands cupping her cheeks.

"Jesse," he said. Only that, but she knew then that he wasn't a figment of her desperate imagination. He had come back to save her. *He had come back.*

She lifted her hand to touch his anxious face, smooth the deeply etched lines that bracketed his mouth and furrowed his brow. "I'm all right," she whispered. "Gary—"

"Can you walk? Can you get to safety?"

Jesse didn't have to guess what he intended. She strained to look past him, at Gary who was on his knees on the dirt, dangerously close to the burning cabin. His gun was just out of reach, as if he'd fallen. Or been knocked to the ground.

Even as she stared, Gary looked up, and his eyes focused directly on David.

Gary *saw* him.

"No," Jesse said, struggling to rise. "David—"

But Gary had scrambled sideways for his gun, and there was no more point in protesting. David was already on his feet and charging Gary with deadly purpose.

❧ ❧

DAVID HAD EXPECTED the hatred to come back.

When his bargain had been accepted and he'd found himself at the resort, he'd felt only the reckless urgency of his mission. When he'd first knocked Gary out of the way, he hadn't had time to think of anything but saving the woman he loved. His heart still drummed from the closeness of that rescue, and he'd believed that finding her so near death was enough to justify any action he took against Gary, even the most lethal.

Hatred and vengeance would make his course clear, the decision easy. He'd tried to stop Gary before, and lost his resolve. This was his last chance. His only chance.

At the inn Gary hadn't been able to see or recognize the nature of his tormentor. But Gary saw David now, and they were on equal ground at last, acting out the final meeting David had been denied in that other life. It should have been a moment of triumph.

But as David raced across the clearing and met his

enemy's terrified gaze, he knew that everything was different.

He skidded to a halt in front of Gary as if an invisible hand had cut the smoky air between them, and realization seized his bartered soul.

What he'd expected to find within himself wasn't there. He felt no bitterness, no need for vengeance. The face staring at him in mingled panic and defiance wasn't Gary's. David could see beneath the mask, layer upon layer, and what he discovered he could no longer hate.

Where rage should have been was sorrow; pity instead of contempt. And the most profound insight David had ever experienced except in his love for Jesse.

Jesse's love had lifted the veil from his sight. He had looked into the very depths of his own flawed soul, and he could not pass judgment on the man who'd been his brother. The failure, the defect, the transgression was his *own*.

Slow acceptance left him defenseless as Gary leveled his pistol at David's chest. He glanced down at the weapon's dull muzzle and raised his eyes to Gary's.

There was only one way to prevent the inevitable tragedy from recurring. Only one hope.

"Avery," he said. "I know you can hear me."

The pistol twitched in Gary's grip. He stared at David, mouth working. "You," he said. "You aren't real."

"You know me," David said. "You remember."

Gary dragged his free hand across his face. Beside them the flames spread, catching the roof of the cabin and threatening the overhanging branches of the nearest pine. Gary's eyes twitched to the blaze and back to David. "They were dreams," he croaked. "Not . . . real . . ."

It wasn't working. David could see the strength of Gary's resistance, the madness that made that strength possible. A shock was necessary, one that would smash every barrier between them.

Abruptly he struck out, catching Gary's upper arm in a

painful grip. "I can't let you hurt her, Avery," he said. "It was always me you wanted to kill."

Gary's reaction was immediate. The gun went off with a shattering roar.

❋ ❋

SOMEWHERE A WOMAN screamed.

Gary heard the sound above the echo of the gun's report, staring at the man who should have been falling with a bloody hole in his chest.

The man, the ghost out of nowhere, the demon from hell hadn't fallen. He hadn't even flinched.

This was the presence Gary had sensed in the motel the last time he'd been here, the figure that rose again and again from the darkest corner of his brain.

Gary's nerveless fingers lost their hold on the gun, and it slid from his hand. His head was full of buzzing, white noise that blotted out every coherent thought. He could barely feel the man's grip on his arms, but he knew it was unbreakable. Not even death could make his tormentor go away.

The buzzing grew to a shriek that pierced his remaining defenses and whistled through his skull as if it were a barren cage of bone. He looked beyond the man's merciless face to the woman who stumbled to a halt behind him.

He knew her. She should be dead. Her accusing gaze locked on him as in the nightmare, damning him utterly.

He closed his eyes. The man said something, spoke the name again. The name he recognized inside the howling bedlam of his mind.

Avery.

The storm swept him up, ripped at his body, tore him apart with giant's hands and crushed the pieces. His soul was left naked and mewling in the center, the eye of the storm where there was no past or present.

And he remembered.

The silence was profound. Within its sheltering arms

he gathered up the fragments of himself and put them back together. He opened his eyes and met David's stare.

David, who knew what he had done. Who had found him at last.

Around them lay the blackened ruins of Parkmere Hall, still tainted with the miasma of fiery destruction. Even the tall and ancient ash trees had been scorched, stretching skeletal fingers toward the sky. There were no servants to pick among the stones and crumbled beams, no birds singing in the park. Only the eerie quiet.

Avery hadn't meant to return. He'd fled after the fire, snatching up whatever came to hand in his terror. He'd drunk himself into oblivion and kept on running.

But he was here, and David had found him. And for once in his life David saw him, *looked* at him as if he existed. As if he mattered.

Because now he had David's attention. He'd taken something from the brother who had everything. David would hate him, but hatred was better than indifference. Avery braced himself for the rage that would strike him down, ready to exchange hate for hate.

But David wasn't doing what he should have done. He wasn't raging or swearing vengeance. His eyes held an unfathomable depth of sadness.

And of pity.

"You despised me, Avery," he said. "And I couldn't see. Perhaps I didn't want to."

Avery blinked. His heart plunged into his belly, quivering with impossible emotions. He had feared this discovery, but now that it had come it was . . . wrong. There should have been a battle between life and death. Avery would have laughed, taunted David with those years of hidden contempt for his elder brother. No matter what David did to him, this time Avery would have been the master, and the pain in David's eyes would have been the sweetest victory.

David had stolen his thunder, disarmed him with a

simple acknowledgment that robbed Avery of the scathing revelation he'd anticipated for so many years. He was reduced to a little boy again, empty and alone.

He hated it.

He balled his fists. "Yes," he said. "I despised you. I despised the mockery you made of our family name. The way you gambled and whored and caroused your way across the countryside, leaving all the work to me. The way you broke Mother's heart, killing her with your neglect of duty and by marrying that lowborn slut. You deserved nothing, and you were given everything—" He broke off, feeling himself lose control. He swept his arm to the side, taking in the burned ruins. "What have you now, elder brother?"

David should have broken then, lashed out at the only man who'd ever dared to tell him the truth. But David didn't so much as glance away.

"All you say of me is true," he said. "I gave you the burden of my title, and none of the glory. But those were excuses for your hatred, Avery. Like the excuses I made for myself, so that I wouldn't have to feel." His handsome face closed up, as if he were feeling far too much. "I failed you. When we were boys. When I abandoned you for my own pleasures, and never looked back."

Avery froze. The devastated landscape shifted around them, was reborn to a green and sun-golden lushness that could come only of an idealized past. The Hall stood larger than it could ever have been, like some mythic castle. Arthur's Camelot.

In the space of moments Avery felt himself live through entire years—summers of play with wooden swords and imaginary chargers, winters telling tales by the fire. Admiration and worship for a brother who was everything he longed to be. His one true friend, bestower of a rough and careless affection, who kept the ice from closing around his heart.

Until the day David was no longer a boy, and Avery

ceased to exist in his brother's eyes. The betrayal was casual, without malice, and left Avery with nothing.

"You were my knight," Avery said, his voice that of the child he'd been, cracking and undisciplined. "You swore to defend the castle. You were supposed to be loyal."

David flinched. The green and golden Hall burst into flame, and the child in Avery burned with it, unmourned.

"If I'd stayed—if I'd been a true brother to you, it could have been different," David said hoarsely. "You wouldn't have—"

"I'd never let you take the Hall from me," Avery snarled. He wrenched his arm from David's hold. "I wouldn't have any brat of yours inherit what *I* made, what I held with my own hands. Never."

David's face finally hardened, his eyes chips of blue ice. "So you killed Sophie," he said. "You punished her for my misdeeds. Did it give you pleasure to hear her screams as she died?"

Why Avery faltered then he didn't know. He had thought himself beyond the guilt that had tortured him in the beginning, numbed by time and the fugitive's life he'd led since the burning of the Hall.

But the guilt wasn't dead. One sentence from David and it all came flooding back, a sick taste of bile on his tongue.

Sophie, screaming. He hadn't been too drunk to call the servants, move Sophie from her room. He'd known what he let happen when he overturned the candle in the hallway and did nothing to stop the inevitable consequences.

Screaming. Begging. Dying . . .

It was an accident, the coward in him cried. "You weren't here to save her," he spat. "Fine soldier, protecting the nation while your wife died alone."

"Yes," David said. "I failed her. I was as guilty as you—"

"No."

The voice was soft and feminine, but there was an edge of steel behind it. Sophie moved up beside David, resting her hand on his arm. She was dressed, not in one of the expensive gowns she'd insisted on wearing even when she spent most of each day in her bed, but in a simple white garment without ornamentation. She was beautiful.

Sophie, who was dead. Sophie, whose eyes held Avery's with a steadiness he'd never seen.

"You've more than paid for anything you've done, David," she said, and her gaze went to his face. Lovingly, with forgiveness, with a serenity alien to Sophie's temperament. "All the guilt in the world doesn't rest on your shoulders."

David looked at her, saying nothing. He didn't need to. His expression spoke for him. Tenderness, sadness, awe—love. Love that David Ventris was incapable of feeling.

But did.

Avery squeezed his eyes shut. A pressure was building within him, a terrible knowledge that left him nowhere to hide.

David had changed. Sophie was alive. They confronted him, glowing with an internal light that beat at him in waves of searing incandescence.

"It has to stop," David said, as if a silent conversation had concluded just out of Avery's hearing. "You're sick, Avery. You haven't escaped what happened to you, to Sophie, to all of us." He reached out again, snatched Avery's unresisting hand. "You can't bear to face her, so you keep trying to destroy her. Destroy your own guilt. But you can only end it by recognizing it. By owning up to what you've done—"

Avery moaned. "No. She—you deserved it—"

"You made your own trap." David's voice took on a sudden urgency. "You can set yourself free. Set Sophie free. Look into your heart—"

"The fire," Sophie said. "David—"

A blast of furnace heat pressed down on them like God's judgment. Avery opened his eyes.

A lick of flame caressed the hem of Sophie's white gown. It sent lecherous fingers groping upward with appalling speed.

She wasn't screaming. She continued to gaze at Avery as if the fire could not hurt her.

Because she was dead. She had been sent to haunt him forever.

Avery tried to back away. He staggered, nearly fell in his panic; hands grabbed at him, held, imprisoned.

David's hands. And Sophie's. By now the fire was wreathing Sophie's neck, and still she kept looking at him, her eyes shifting color from brown to hazel, her face melting and re-forming into contours both alien and familiar.

His throat locked on a scream. Through Sophie's touch he was carried back to the hallway, to the moment when he had decided to let her die.

Vengeance. *Make David hurt. Make him know what it is to be utterly alone. . . .*

And then he was in Sophie's room, lying in her bed, the flames racing among the bedclothes and curtains, too weak to fight.

He *was* Sophie. He felt the new life in his belly, dying before it had a chance to live. He felt the hatred, the terror, the despair.

Crying. Screaming. Suffering. Dying.

"*It has to end,*" David's voice said. "*Only you can stop it—*"

In the very core of the inferno, Avery found a single spark of pure, cool radiance. He reached for it, clung to it, absorbed it like fresh, healing air.

And the knowledge burst open inside him, no dreadful explosion but a desired release. Two halves of him came together, each aware of the other. Each in perfect agreement. Each unafraid.

He looked away from Sophie, from David, toward the blazing building that was beginning to collapse in on itself. The flames had spread to the nearest cabin. He could reach the heart of the fire in seconds.

He hurled himself to one side, breaking loose from the hands that held him, and sprinted toward the open maw of the collapsing cabin.

The fire accepted him into its loving embrace.

CHAPTER SIXTEEN

JESSE DIDN'T STOP to think. There was no time to explain to David, even if she'd been able to find the words.

She sucked in a deep breath of air and dashed toward the open door of the burning cabin. Gary had vanished inside, as if a flaming mouth had swallowed him whole.

"Jesse!" She heard David come after her as she dodged through the blackening door frame, and then all she could hear was the spit and hiss and roar of the firestorm.

She should have been paralyzed with terror. Sophie should have been a wailing and mindless presence within her, reliving her own death.

But a strange peace had settled in around Jesse's heart, and it felt as though the flames couldn't touch her. They had no power to hurt or destroy. Even as the heat singed the hair on her arms and flames barred her passage, she didn't question why she was here.

She covered her mouth with her hands and searched through the smothering billows of smoke. She found Gary crouched at the center of the blaze, protected by some fluke of architecture or air flow from the worst of the fire. It was only a matter of seconds before he lost that fragile reprieve. In the roiling light she could barely make out his face, but what she saw of it held that same unfamiliar peace.

He had known what he was doing. He wasn't insane.

"Gary!" she shouted, and held out her hand. "Let me help you!"

He saw her clearly. She knew that he heard. But he shrank back, shaking his head as the flames finally reached him.

Jesse coughed and began to fight her way forward. Something grabbed her from behind, pulled her back just as a blazing beam crashed down from the ceiling where she'd stood. The roof collapsed with a shriek and groan, sealing Gary into his self-made tomb.

Jesse didn't struggle as David carried her out of harm's way once again. She gasped in lungfuls of air and clung to him until he set her down a safe distance from the fire. Then she closed her eyes and let the tears come.

"David," she whispered. "Why—"

"Jesse!"

The warmth of David's body deserted her. She opened her eyes. He was gone, and the voice she heard was someone else's. The voice of a very dear friend.

"My God, Jesse," Al said, breathless as he dropped to his knees beside her. His forehead was beaded with sweat, and his eyes widened as they swept the fire and returned to her face. "Are you all right?"

She worked her way to her knees and managed a nod. Her mind was numb with shock and loss, but she'd had too much experience in crisis situations to lose her ability to think. "How did you find me?"

"Wayne Albright called me, said that Gary was back in town and was talking crazy about you. Making threats that Wayne thought were real. Gary said he was coming here. I came to look for him, to make him—" He caught his breath and gave a sharp shake of his head. "I saw Gary run into the fire. Saw you go after him. And—"

She balanced herself and grasped his hand. "He's dead. The cabin—" She didn't need to complete the sentence. The cabin was little more than a skeleton now, and the fire had moved on to fresh prey. It had spread to the second cabin, and only the clearing and the windless day had confined it to the buildings and the nearest trees.

No one in the mountains underestimated the danger of a fire in summer. "We've got to get help, Al. Can you go back to town and send the alert?"

"I could see the smoke as soon as I reached the road," he said. "Everyone in town will know by now—"

"Go back and make sure, Al. I'll be okay."

"I won't leave you alone here." He made a move to help her to her feet. "Come on. I'll get you to a doctor—"

"I can't. Not yet." She gripped his hand tightly. "I can take care of myself. Go."

He wet his lips. "Jesse—the other man who was with you, the one who brought you out—" He broke off, flushed under his dark beard.

He meant David. He'd seen David, just as Gary had seen him. But Al and David had no previous relationship that might have made it possible.

Jesse hadn't the will to summon up a single logical excuse. "Explanations later, Al." She held onto his hand as if the pressure alone could convince him of her sincerity. "I will be all right, but I have to stay."

"At least come outside the fence."

She nodded, and he helped her through the open gate and out onto the lane. She knelt on the pavement and gestured him away. "Go."

"I'll be back as soon as I can," he said. "Don't—" He met her gaze and scrambled to his feet. "Be careful, Jesse."

And then he was running toward his car. Jesse watched him until he'd pulled out of sight, and then she

etreated within herself and called to David with every-
hing she was worth.

He reappeared as suddenly as he'd gone, his expres-
ion carved in lines of grief and unutterable weariness.
His eyes when he looked at her were filled with relief and
pride and love.

Love.

But he waited, searched her face for permission to approach, as if he doubted his welcome.

She didn't wait for him to discover the truth. She took
ive shaky steps and wrapped her arms around him.

His return embrace nearly lifted her from her feet. He
buried his face in the hollow of her neck, breathing her in
s if the taint of smoke that clung to her hair and cloth-
ng were the finest perfume. His heart pounded under his
acket, and his hands worked ceaselessly over her back,
ntent on assuring himself that she was whole.

"David," she murmured into the solid strength of his
houlder. "You came back."

He held her close a moment longer and then pushed
her away gently. His eyes were very bright as he caught
her face between his hands. "I couldn't leave you to
Gary—to Avery. I knew what he was."

"Even though I told you to go?"

"You set me free. After all I revealed, you still forgave
me, even if you could no longer—" He stopped. "I
wanted no part of salvation without . . . knowing
you'd be safe."

"You saved me." She turned his hand and kissed his
rough palm. "In more ways than you'll ever know."

He went very still. "I intended to kill him when I came
back. I thought that was the only way to protect you. I
thought I could hate him enough. But I couldn't do it."

She leaned her forehead against his chest. "I wouldn't
have wanted that, David. Not ever. He was your
brother."

"He was your murderer. And the man who drove your
mother to her death. Did he—did Gary ever admit what
he'd done?"

"No."

"Yet you forgave him. Forgave them both."

She wondered how he recognized it before she did, how he felt the source of that peace within herself. She wondered when it had happened, when old hurts and old anger surrendered to something even more powerful.

Forgiveness.

"I didn't know it," she said. "Not until he ran into the fire, and I—" She looked up. "Why did he kill himself?"

Sorrow washed across his face, and she remembered what he'd said to Avery, how he'd admitted his own role in the tragic dance of three tangled lives.

"Perhaps the guilt was finally too much," he said. "Avery confronted his own evil. He felt Sophie's death—"

She shook her head. It had been more than that, though she knew Avery had relived Sophie's suffering just as Jesse had. "I saw his eyes, in the cabin," she said. "Gary knew what he was doing. He wasn't fighting any longer. He didn't hate me. He wasn't even afraid."

"But you risked your own life trying to save him, knowing what he was." He stroked her hair. "You humble me, Jesse."

She gave a ragged laugh. "I'm not that noble. I wasn't even thinking when I went in. It was instinct." She clutched the lapels of his jacket to stop his protest. "You still blame yourself, don't you? Even for what Avery became. You don't think two hundred years of limbo was enough punishment for mistakes you made in one lifetime." She closed her eyes. "God knows I've made plenty. I hated Gary without realizing how much of that hatred came from another life, just as he couldn't know . . . how much Avery was a part of him. And Sophie—"

Sophie hadn't been perfect. She had suffered, but she wasn't exempt of responsibility for her own life, her own happiness. She had forgotten how to communicate in any way but by manipulation, tricks, and outbursts of rage and weeping. She had lost herself.

"Sophie had so much anger left inside her when she

died," Jesse said. "We . . . had to work it out, she and I. She thought she wanted revenge, against you and Avery. For a while she . . . had to have her say." Jesse laced her fingers into the hair beneath David's high collar. "But I never completely lost who I was, David. I didn't stop loving you."

He looked skyward, and his throat worked. "Ah, Jesse," he whispered.

He still didn't believe. "I can feel that Sophie is at rest," she said. "She'll always be part of me, because we share a soul. But she's let go. The past won't control me anymore." She smiled sadly. "I've spent my entire life trying to avoid what Sophie was. Jesse, the self-reliant. Trying not to need anyone or put myself in a position where others could leave me. I made my own kind of isolation and thought I was safe. I didn't even know I was trying to break the old pattern. But I couldn't have done it on my own, David. Not without you, and Al, and Megan—" She swallowed. "Even Gary—"

"You are free, Jesse," David said. "The madness is over."

She pulled his head down to hers. "Maybe we all had lessons to learn. About forgiveness. Forgiving each other and letting go. Don't you think it's time we started forgiving ourselves?" Her mouth brushed his. "I love you, David."

David felt the warmth of her breath on his face and knew what she was offering. More than her lips, or her body, or her heart; she was offering her life, her hope, her future. Unconditionally. Eternally.

All the things they could never share.

Gently he set her back, though he was desperate to taste her lips one last time. It would be cruelty to deceive her now, after she'd borne so much. He'd lied to her again and again; he wouldn't leave her with more false hope.

"I can't stay, Jesse," he said. He forced himself to hold her gaze, to endure the bewilderment and rebellion that awakened in her eyes. "I could come back . . . only for a short time. Now my task is finished."

He sounded cold to his own ears, almost indifferent. He might as well have struck her; she went very pale, and then the angry color rushed back into her cheeks.

"No!" She balled up one small fist, as if she'd as soon plant him a facer as kiss him. "I won't accept that. When you've done so much, there must be a way—" She slammed her fist into his chest. "I won't let you go. I'll fight this every step of the way."

He caught her hand between his. "You can't, Jesse. I have no choice." He wanted to weep, but he kept his voice harsh with command. "You have a life to live. You have Megan. She needs you."

"*No*. She needs both of us—" A strange expression crossed her face. "Both of us, David. The way it was meant to be." She grabbed the hilt of his sword and half pulled it from its sheath. "You're as real as you've ever been—more. Al saw you. It must mean—"

"I was given these last moments," David said, "only at a price."

She froze, and her gaze fixed on his.

"I made a bargain," he said. "You'd set me free, and I was being called back to the other place. The only way I could return even for a few hours was to . . . give something in exchange."

"You mean . . . you could never come back to me," she said. "Not to this life."

She'd answered her own unspoken question, and it was best to let her believe that fiction. "Your life meant too much to me, Jesse. More than the chance to see you again."

"Oh God." She offered it up as a prayer—for courage, for strength, for an answer. Then, as if that answer had been given, she seemed to gather all the light around her and draw it inward, so that she burned as bright and hot as the fire beyond them.

"Do you think I won't wait for you?" she asked, her

love a deathless flame in her eyes. "This life. The next. It
doesn't matter. We will be together."

David wanted to shout and curse at the tragic injustice
of the pain she must suffer, of hope lost forever. But
there was no one to blame. Not even himself. He had
made the choice, and he couldn't regret it.

"No," he said thickly. "Don't wait for me. I beg you.
Live as you were meant to. Love, Jesse. For both of us."

"You're a part of me," she said with a radiant, unshakable conviction, the kind that only came of the purest
faith. "No matter how long it takes—"

"The bargain I made was in exchange for my soul," he
said in anguish. "My *soul*, Jesse. I won't be reborn.
There will be no more lives."

He hadn't wanted to tell her, make a sacrifice of what
he had done gladly for her sake. He didn't wait for her
shock, the cries of denial that he knew would come. He
pulled her into his arms.

"Your life is everything to me," he said. "I love you,
Jesse. Love can't be destroyed. Not while you live."

She was utterly limp in his embrace, passive for a
dozen heartbeats. And then she exploded, tearing free of
him, spinning away to confront the sky with arms wide
and face uplifted.

"Is this your idea of justice?" she cried to the heavens,
tears wet on her cheeks. "Is this what you want—sacrifice? Then I'm ready." She turned in a close circle, hands
raised in supplication. "I love him. Do you hear me? I
give my own life for his. My soul for his. Let him move
on. Let him live again, and be happy." She dropped to
her knees. "*Please*—"

David had almost reached her when the quality of the
air changed, an electric ambience that raced through
David's body and lifted the hairs on his head. He gathered Jesse into his arms. She was too quiet, too still—

"No need to worry about the fair Miss Copeland," a
voice said from the crackling air. "You were right, Captain. We could have used her like on the Peninsula."

Wellington floated comfortably in the boundless soft

luminescence that the world had become, an approving smile on his lean face. David saw that the road was gone, and the fence, and the woods; every edge and shape and form that defined the earthly plane. Jesse's eyelids fluttered and opened.

"Is this a dream?" she said groggily.

David cradled her in the protective curve of his own body. "Leave her alone," he said, glaring at his spectral commander. "She didn't mean what she said—"

"Oh, but she did," Wellington said. He floated lower and studied her intently. "She'd give up her life for you, out of love. There's hope for the human race yet."

"No," David said. "I won't let you take her. I'm ready to return with you. Let her go—"

"Ah, David." He shook his head. "You have nothing to fear. You chose the path of love. Don't you know by now that love makes anything possible? Your willingness to sacrifice even your soul to save her, and her willingness to do the same for you, without selfishness or regret—the ability to forgive even those who've done you great harm—such qualities have the power to make miracles."

David's heart stopped beating. Jesse stirred, her lips parted as she gazed at Wellington.

"I see I shall have to be more explicit," Wellington said. "You believed that you were being punished for your sins, Captain. But the punishment was of your own making—as is your salvation. There are always choices, but they can require time to become clear. Love is the choice that leads to freedom."

David rose, carrying Jesse with him. "Then Jesse is free to live her life?"

Wellington smiled at Jesse, almost tenderly. "Do you wish to share your life with this scoundrel, Jesse?"

She laced her fingers through David's and stared Wellington straight in the eye. "With all my soul."

"And is that also what you wish, David Ventris?"

His heart surged painfully back into motion. "If it is possible—if there's any hope—"

"Hope, like love, is everlasting," Wellington said. His face became suddenly stern. "There will always be battles, children. But how you face them is your decision."

Disbelief became joy as David felt Wellington's meaning, in his mind and then with his body, until acceptance seeped into his very soul. "Thank you," he whispered.

Wellington lifted his hands as if in benediction. "Love each other. Share your love. I ask no more." He turned to Jesse. "Do not weep for your mother, Jesse. She will find her own peace."

"And Avery?" David asked softly.

"He, too, is on his road. And now I must return to mine." He nodded to Jesse, saluted David, and began to fade into the omnipresent light.

"Wait!" Jesse said. "Who are you?"

"A friend. A messenger. Remember that you're never alone, Jesse Copeland."

Then he was gone, and the world closed around them again, sunshine and firm ground and the smell of pine and smoke. Jesse swayed in the curve of David's arm, blinking.

"What happened?" she asked. "Was I dreaming?"

He tilted her face to his. "A wonderful dream," he said, "that came true."

Understanding filled her eyes, overflowed as tears of joy and gratitude. "You can stay," she said, laughing aloud. "You can stay with me."

In answer he kissed her chin, the corners of her mouth, the curves and contours of her precious and beloved face. She grabbed him in a hug worthy of a bear and returned his kisses with unbridled enthusiasm. David was intent on making up for lost time, and Jesse would have pulled him to the ground where they stood if not for the piercing wail that invaded their private paradise.

Jesse broke away. "Sirens." She gave her head a little jerk of disbelief. "The fire. They're coming to put it out." Her practical rescuer's demeanor snapped back into place, and she gazed intently toward the broad plume of smoke that hung above the resort. The scarlet of flame was visible through the fence and screen of trees. "It hasn't been too long. I hope they can save—"

A dark blue automobile emerged around the bend of the lane and pulled to a stop behind them. Jesse tightened her grip on David's arm.

"Al," she said. "He's already seen you. Everyone else will be able to see you now—" She caught her breath and grinned, as if she'd realized all over again that she and David had a future to share. "I think that maybe we'd better hide you until we can figure out a good way to introduce you to Manzanita. You know how small towns love gossip. And there's going to be plenty after this." She gestured toward the fire and grew sober. "Al deserves to know what really happened—"

And Al, David thought, was likely to insist. He was already striding toward them, heavy brows drawn.

"The fire department's right behind me," he said. "I told them what happened to Gary, and the police are on their way. Now, would you mind explaining . . ."

Jesse grabbed David's hand and drew him forward. "Al, I'd like you to meet the man who saved my life, David Ventris. David, this is my closest friend, Al Aguilar."

Al's gaze raked David from boots to crown, restrained amazement in the lift of his brow. David offered his hand. If Al took it, that would be the final proof. . . .

"So, you're Jesse's David," Al said. Jesse threw him a startled glance, and he half smiled. "You did mention him once or twice during our sessions," he said. "I just never realized he existed."

"Jesse has spoken of you often," David said. "Thank you for being her friend, for standing by her."

After a moment's hesitation, Al gripped David's hand and shook it firmly. "Forgive my surprise, but you seem to have popped out of the woodwork."

They looked at each other, a silent acknowledgment that couldn't have been put into words. Al had loved Jesse. Still did, perhaps. His unflinching gaze held full recognition of what David and Jesse shared. But there was no jealousy in his face or in the clasp of his blunt fingers. Only infinite sadness.

He deserved to be told the truth. To know that Jesse would be well and deeply loved, in this life and beyond.

"I wasn't hiding him—not in the way you think," Jesse said. "There is an explanation, and you're probably the one man in the world who'll get the unexpurgated version." She chuckled dryly. "I hope you still have an open mind."

Al released David's hand. "After what I saw today, I could believe anything," he said. "I've come to understand . . . how much I still have to learn."

"Don't we all," Jesse said. "Don't we all."

The first fire truck arrived with a roar and shriek of sirens, followed by the police. Al gave David a brief nod, acceptance in his dark eyes, and went to join the uniformed men who rushed to ready their equipment.

Jesse started after him and cast David an apologetic glance. "I have to go talk to the police," she said. "Just a few more minutes, and then we can—"

David didn't argue. He swept Jesse behind the nearest tree and resolutely finished their interrupted kiss. Only after a rapturously oblivious interlude did he let her go.

"I won't be long," she said breathlessly, backing away step by reluctant step. "Wait for me . . ."

He caught up with her and cradled her face between his hands. "We have forever, my love. I'm yours, body and soul."

CHAPTER SEVENTEEN

❧ ———— ❧

MEGAN'S BIRTHDAY PARTY was a rip-roaring success. Nearly everyone Jesse invited had shown up at Al's for the occasion—a celebration as much for new beginnings as Megan's special day. Kirk Moran and his mother were the guests of honor. Kim was there, and several of the staff members from Blue Rock, but others had come as well—townsfolk Jesse'd never gotten a chance to know, people who would have called her crazy only a few weeks past.

Since Gary's death and unmasking a month ago, Jesse had become the celebrity of the day. And she didn't occupy that dubious pedestal alone.

She looked across the dining room during a brief lull to the table spread with colorfully wrapped gifts and a half-devoured birthday cake. A man sat on one of the chairs, laughing as Megan scrambled into his lap.

David looked almost ordinary now. As ordinary as an

incredibly handsome aristocrat could look, dressed in jeans that did as much for him as his previous snug trousers, and a T-shirt just close fitting enough to draw the admiring glances of every woman in the room.

His "formal" appearance in town had come on the heels of Gary's death, carefully orchestrated to seem as normal as possible in the midst of so much drama and commotion. No one saw any reason to question Jesse's story that David was an old Peace Corps colleague, traveling in California, whom she'd invited to stay with her. By the time the brouhaha over Gary had died down, Jesse's obvious relationship with her handsome guest was already starting to seem like old news.

David, however, was anything but old news. People were fascinated by his accent and sometimes quaint speech, which struck them as pleasantly exotic. He charmed everyone without trying, and the fact that Jesse had landed such a catch was another mark in her favor.

All too recently Gary had been the magnet who drew that kind of attention and admiration. Now even his memory was persona non grata. The police had found Gary's discharged gun at the resort after the fire was extinguished, and Al had given his account of Gary's self-immolation and Jesse's attempt to rescue him. Al had left out David's part in the drama, but with the addition of Wayne's testimony about Gary's explicit threats against Jesse in their final conversation, and Joan Copeland's letter and evidence, it was suddenly clear to even Gary's most ardent supporters that he'd been a fraud, a cad, and a murderer.

Poor Jesse, they said; a pity that she'd been at his mercy, but she'd stood up to him in the end. Everyone agreed that they'd never *quite* trusted Gary Emerson. Wayne had even come to Jesse, hat in hand, to apologize for his support of Gary and his misjudgment of her. It had been his warning phone call that sent Al to the resort in time to witness Gary's death.

Good old Al; he'd been prepared to confront Gary head-on to defend his friend. He had accepted David and his otherworldly origins with hardly a blink, and in spite of their differences the two men seemed well on their way to a strong friendship. Jesse had overheard Al mentioning Vietnam to David, one soldier to another, in a way he never would have done in the past.

Al had left behind his philosophy of noninvolvement, and Jesse had a feeling that he, like so many others in Manzanita, was about to make some changes in his life.

This party was a symbol of those changes. A kind of healing, Jesse thought—starting over, as she and David and Megan had begun to do. A fresh start for Kirk and his mother as well.

Jesse grinned as she watched Kirk run up to join Megan and David. All at once David was swinging Kirk up on his shoulders while Megan hung on to his leg and laughingly tried to pin him to the spot. David was good with kids—he seemed to share their uncomplicated joy in simple things. Merely being alive, and with those he loved, was for him a daily miracle.

As it was for Jesse.

She glanced around the room, basking in the pleasure of happy conversation and goodwill. The one person she was just as glad not to see was Marie. The woman had closed up her restaurant and left town shortly after Gary's death was declared official. Jesse doubted she'd show her face in rustic, déclassée Manzanita again.

"Great party, Jesse," Kim said, coming to join her in the corner of the room. "Too bad Eric couldn't be here."

Jesse turned to her friend. "Don't worry. There's still your wedding—if you don't mind my bringing a guest."

Kim grinned in David's direction. "Mind? I just hope he doesn't hog the limelight from the bride. Me, that is." She rolled her eyes to emphasize the joke. "Speaking of which, when are you two going to . . ." She arched a meaningful brow.

Jesse reddened. She had a tendency to do that lately. Sometimes it felt as if all the emotions she'd suppressed for most of her adult life were overflowing in blushes and tears and laughter.

"Come on," Kim said, leaning closer. "When's it going to be? Give."

"Did you talk to Eric about the things we discussed?" Jesse said quickly.

Kim chuckled. "Okay. Yes, I did, and he said he'd be more than happy to be your legal advisor. He's going to ask around down in San Francisco this week. It might take a while to set up, but . . . we both think it's a great idea, Jess."

"What's a great idea?"

Al loomed over them, a quiet smile on his face. Though he hadn't exactly been the life of the party, he'd offered his home willingly and done more talking with more different people than Jesse could remember. He acknowledged Kim with a tilt of his punch glass. "I didn't intend to interrupt . . ."

"It's a plan I've been putting together," Jesse said. "I haven't had a chance to discuss it with you, but now that Kim has Eric working on the legal end of things—" She felt a renewed flood of excitement. "You know my father left me a large inheritance when he died. I've been getting checks every month, but until recently I had no desire to touch that money."

She didn't need to elaborate. During the awkward hours when she and David had explained his origins to a dumbfounded Al, she'd admitted a lot more of her deepest feelings about her family and childhood than she'd ever shared, even with her closest friend. She didn't need to hug that anger and sorrow to herself anymore; she'd come to terms with all of it, including her father's desertion.

Now she could use her father's guilt money for a good cause. "I've already started paperwork to buy the old resort. After the fire it'll need a lot of fixing up, but—"

"You're reopening the old resort?" Al said. "But with Blue Rock—"

"I don't intend to go into competition with Blue Rock," she said. "What I had in mind was a kind of special summer camp, a retreat for kids from disadvantaged homes or in fosterage, the kind who don't get opportunities to come up to the woods. I remember what it was like going from foster home to foster home. No frills, no vacations, no one to listen when I was hurting." She glanced toward Kirk, who was swallowing a large mouthful of cake with Megan's encouragement. "Maybe even a place for kids like Bobby Moran, so they have a chance to try something besides drugs and alcohol. I thought of setting up a kind of survival training course, teaching kids some of the basics of search and rescue."

Al nodded slowly. "That's an ambitious plan, Jesse. And a worthy one."

"I know it's not going to be simple, but we have the money and the time. We're already researching the steps involved in setting it up. Eric's going to find us the legal help we need. We're starting to look at financing, insurance, staffing. I'm hoping to hire Lisa Moran as a part of the team." She met Al's gaze. "And we're going to need counselors, Al. For the kids."

He swirled the pink liquid in his glass. "I've been doing some thinking myself," he said. "I'm pretty rusty as a psychologist, Jesse. I left practice years ago because . . . I wasn't prepared to get involved with other people's problems. I thought they would drag me into a place I didn't want to go. But now . . ." He looked up, and his eyes were dark with emotion. "I've learned that the world isn't the way I thought it was. The rational isn't everything. I've spent too much of my life cut off from possibilities."

Jesse remembered when she'd admired that very detachment, wanted to emulate Al's safe and sane distance from pain and passion. "But you helped me, Al," she said softly.

"I could have done more harm than good. That's why I've been considering taking some refresher courses—catching up on the developments I've missed in the last decade or so." He glanced at Megan. "I know that Megan will be in good hands if I leave her with you and David. She already thinks of you two as her parents."

Jesse swallowed. "That doesn't mean she won't miss you. But I think she'll understand."

Since Al had loosened up around his niece, Megan had relaxed in turn. They were finally becoming friends. But if Al followed his plans to return to school, Megan wouldn't feel abandoned. Megan had taken to David as if he were the father she'd barely known. It was almost uncanny. She didn't question the fact that she'd seen him in dreams and visions of her own, or that her "angel" had become real.

And three days ago Megan had called Jesse "Mom" for the first time. It might have been an unconscious slip, but it meant the world to Jesse.

"I hope you'll consider helping us with the camp some-day," Jesse said. "But whatever you do—" She offered her hand, and Al engulfed it in his own. "We'll always love you."

The handshake became a hug—reminding Jesse how much strength lay behind that mild exterior—and then Al released her and walked quickly away. Jesse rubbed at her eyes, chagrined at her newfound tendency to go all weepy at the slightest provocation.

As if someone had called her name, she looked up and across the room. David stood alone, his gaze locked on hers, and the noise and bustle of the party disappeared.

He came to her now on ordinary mortal feet, as natu-rally as he'd once winked in and out of existence. She reached for his hand and he took it, wordless, his eyes promising the kisses that would have to wait for a more private moment.

Jesse thought she could watch him forever. She trea-sured his quiet companionship as much as his passion—for her, and for his newfound life. She'd discussed her plans for the old resort with him first, after he'd wryly wondered what use he, a soldier and ne'er-do-well, could be in this modern world.

She'd reminded him that he was nothing if not adapt-able, and they'd both have a lot to learn if they were to implement her dream. She didn't think it would take him long to learn carpentry, and she looked forward to the hours they'd spend together rebuilding the cabins and furniture for the resort.

They were going to be very busy, but never too busy for each other. Or the little girl they'd both come to love.

David cleared his throat. "I think this would be the right time for the announcement," he said, squeezing her hand.

"What announcement?"

He only smiled mysteriously and held up his hands until every eye in the room was focused on him and the buzz of noise died.

"Friends," he said, "thank you for coming to Megan's party." Megan abandoned the new model horse she'd been putting through its paces and ran to David, who grabbed her playfully and propped her against his hip.

"I wish to make you all witnesses to my request," he said, a certain solemnity in his manner in spite of the squirming, laughing child beside him. Gently he set Megan down and tweaked her nose with the tip of his finger. Then he turned, dropped to one knee before Jesse, and placed his hand over his heart.

"Jesse Copeland," he said, straight-faced, "I most humbly beg your hand in marriage."

She stared at him, blushing furiously.

His voice dropped to a whisper as he searched her face. "Will you be my wife, Jesse?"

"Say yes!" someone shouted. A chorus of voices joined the first, urging her swift agreement.

"Say yes," Megan said, grabbing Jesse's hand with an urgent tug. "Don't make him wait."

Jesse grinned and shook her head. "Of course I'll marry you," she said. David moved in a ghostlike blur and took her in his arms, and she didn't even care if people were watching.

And when Megan wrapped her arms around them both, Jesse knew they wouldn't have to wait for heaven.

About the Author

Susan Krinard graduated from the California College of Arts and Crafts with a BFA, and worked as an artist and freelance illustrator before turning to writing. An admirer of both Romance and Fantasy, Susan enjoys combining these elements in her books. She also loves to get out into nature as frequently as possible. A native Californian, Susan lives in the San Francisco Bay Area with her French-Canadian husband, Serge, a dog, and a cat.

Susan loves to hear from her readers. She can be reached at:

P.O. Box 272545
Concord, CA 94527

Please send a self-addressed stamped envelope for a personal reply. Susan's e-mail address is:
Skrinard@aol.com
and her web page is located at:
http://members.aol.com/skrinard/

COMING SOON . . .

Watch for Susan Krinard's next romantic fantasy, the first of a spectacular werewolf trilogy, due to be published in the summer of 1999.

Read on for a preview . . .

PROLOGUE

Braden stood in the broad shadow of his grandfather,
Barnabas Forster, Earl of Greyburn, and gazed about the
Great Hall into thirty pairs of eyes. Eyes that, like his,
seemed human but were not. Watchful eyes: fierce, ever
alert, weighing every other man and woman who waited
in silence for the Earl to speak. Even now, at this ninth
great meeting of the families, the delegates never forgot
what they were.

Loups-Garous. Werewolves. A breed apart from man-
kind, but living among humanity. A race that would have
faced extinction if not for the Earl of Greyburn's great
Cause.

Braden had been told the story so many times that he
knew it by heart. Barnabas had spent his youth searching
for his scattered people—in Europe, Russia, Asia, America. His special gifts let him sense them wherever they
survived—among the aristocracy and elite of their home-
lands, more like than not; more rarely among the common folk, hiding what they were.

The hiding was always necessary. It was a world of
humans, and humans far outnumbered the wolf-kind.
Yet the *loups-garous* had intermarried with humans, had
ceased to breed true.

Barnabas knew that their people would die out, fade to
nothing in a matter of years or decades—inevitably—
unless the blood bred true again. Unless those purest of
lineage and power were joined to others equally pure.

There was only one way it could be done. Boundaries
must be set aside; old national rivalries, old hatreds forgotten. The *loups-garous* must come together, must

make a great pact to preserve their race. Barnabas had cajoled, threatened, pleaded, argued, and used his considerable power to bend others to his will.

And they had come, to this stronghold in the inner heart of Northumberland, where the Forsters had held their land for hundreds of years—Forsters who shared a name with humans but were so much more. That first meeting in 1819 had been fraught with peril and suspicion, but in the end the *loups-garous* had chosen their salvation. The first marriage contracts had been negotiated, bloodlines traced for the new records.

So it had been now for forty years, twice each decade. But this was Braden's first meeting; at fourteen he had passed his trial, had learned to Change, and was at last worthy of taking part in the Cause.

He stared under drawn brows at the Russian delegate, the father of the girl who had been promised to Braden at this very meeting. A great landowner, this prince, who ruled a virtual kingdom of serfs in his distant country. The Russian blood was fierce and strong yet, and when joined to the ancient British strain—

Braden shook his head. It was too much to consider here, in this forbidding place with its banners and cold stone. He looked instead at the other delegates, memorizing faces: dour Scots from Highland and Lowland; French aristocrats, who with their powers had survived the purging of the nobility in their land; the Prussians who kept much to themselves; the small conclaves of proud Spanish and Italians from warmer climes, where their people clung to the mountains; Norsemen who'd crossed the sea to land again on shores where once their ancestors had raided and conquered.

There was a handful of guests from more exotic lands, who'd come reluctantly: an Indian prince, a Sheikh from the deserts, the last survivor of an ancient clan in Nippon. Only their nonhuman blood bound them to the others.

And then there were the Americans. They fiercely guarded their independence and looked askance at the British nobleman who claimed leadership of all who ran as wolves and men. But they, too, recognized Grandfather's warning, and so they had arrived at Greyburn—to talk, debate, hammer-out compromise.

Today, the ninth gathering of the families was at an end. The delegates would scatter for five more years, but new contracts were set in place, and there would be another generation of children born to carry on the revived bloodlines. Just as the first contract had bound Braden's late father to Angelique Gevaudan of the old French blood. Angelique had dutifully borne the Greyburn heir three children: Braden, Quentin, and Rowena. Each would, in turn, marry as the great Cause dictated, and their children as well, on into the distant future when the *loups-garous* would become the powerful, fearless people they were meant to be. . . .

"Boy."

Braden jerked out of this thoughts and stared up at his Grandfather. A glance from Barnabas could freeze any man, human or werewolf, and it had always reduced Braden's knees to jelly.

But Braden had learned to Change, and fear had turned to respect. "Sir?"

Barnabus cuffed him lightly and pushed him toward the massive wooden doors. "Go. I have final words with the others, but I will speak to you later." He dismissed Braden with a jerk of his shoulder, and Braden saw that all the strangers' eyes were on him this time, cool and assessing. The delegates knew Braden was to inherit the Earldom and his grandfather's great purpose. They watched him for any sign of weakness.

I'll be strong, like Grandfather, Braden thought. *One day they will all respect me.* He stood tall and marched from the room, closing the heavy carved doors behind him.

"Well?" hissed a voice as he passed into the entrance hall. "Was it as exciting as you thought it would be? Did you get to talk, or did they even notice you were there? What did you think about the one with the funny—"

Braden snatched at Quentin's arm. "Not here," he whispered. He glanced at Rowena who stood, as always, at her twin's elbow, and herded them both down the hall to the front doors. A footman hurried forward to open the doors, and then they were out in the fading sunlight. Once they were alone and beyond the high shield of the rhododendrons across the lawn, Braden fixed his sternest gaze on his younger brother and used his deeper voice to his best advantage.

"You were spying," he accused. "You had no right to be there. If Grandfather caught you—"

Quentin laughed. Nothing ever frightened him—no threat of punishment, no prospect of dire consequences. He was, as *Maman* had said before her death, impossible.

"Do you think it's just a game?" Braden said. "What Grandfather's done to save our people—"

"I know, I know." Quentin rolled his eyes. "So deadly serious. What's the use of being able to Change if you don't use it to have fun? When I make the passage, I'm going to enjoy it."

Rowena curled her small fingers around her twin brother's arm. "I don't like it," she whispered. "I wish I never had to Change at all."

"You don't have any choice," Braden said, more harshly than he'd intended. "We all have to do as we're told, or there won't be any of us left." His voice softened. "Anyway, when you can Change, you'll find out, Ro. It's amazing . . ." He closed his eyes and shuddered. "Poor humans. I almost feel sorry for them."

"Not me," Rowena began. "If I could, I'd—"

But her words were quickly drowned out by Quentin's. "I know you can't wait to take over when Grandfather dies," he said to Braden, his grin belying his words. "But he's going to be around for a long time, so you might as well relax."

Braden stiffened. "When I am leader, you'll have to do what I say."

Quentin snapped into a mock-salute. "Yes, my lord. But not quite yet." He gave a yelp as Braden grabbed for him, and suddenly there was a chase in progress, half serious and half in play. They tumbled onto the lawn, Quentin almost holding his own in spite of his lesser years. Rowena hopped a little, as if she'd join in, but she was far too proud of her new frock to dirty it, or to compromise her fragile twelve-year-old's dignity.

At last Braden had Quentin pinned. "Promise me," he said breathlessly, "promise me that you'll obey me when I am leader."

There was no surrender in Quentin's eyes, and his smile never wavered. "Are you afraid I'll do what Grandfather's brother and sister did, and mess up your Cause?"

Braden knew that story by heart as well. "They were both traitors. Great Aunt Grace married a human instead of the mate chosen for her. And Great Uncle William broke his word. He went to live in America, but he never sent his children back to England. Now he's dead, and we've lost his bloodline—"

"Bloodlines. You talk just like Barnabas."

"And you talk like a child, because you don't understand."

"Just because the families who come here are *loups-garous* doesn't mean they're any good. Like that Russian girl—"

"What about her?" Braden bent lower, showing his teeth.

"You like her, don't you? I saw the way you looked at her. Just because Grandfather's arranged it so you have to marry her in a few years. But she and her father have something wrong about them. I saw him hit a stableboy and call him a serf, and that girl said Ro was an ugly stick. She's nasty and conceited. She said when she came to live here, everyone will have to do what *she* says."

Braden tried to picture that delicate, exotic face framing such an insult to his sister. Surely not. Milena had smiled at him, made him think she liked him, too . . .

"I don't believe you," Braden said.

"Maybe not now. But I don't think she'll like it here with us."

The tone of his voice put Braden immediately on alert. Quentin's exaggerated, too-innocent expression was one Braden had seen many times—just before his younger brother pulled a prank on some hapless and unsuspecting victim. They were never dangerous, his little tricks, and never mean-spirited, except on those very rare occasions when he didn't like the recipient. . . .

"What did you do?" Braden demanded, grabbing Quentin's collar.

Quentin only grinned more broadly, but Braden hadn't long to wait for an answer. There was a shriek from somewhere inside the house, loud enough for nonhuman ears to hear even through the thick walls. Braden let Quentin up and gave him a shake.

"If you hurt her—"

"Remember those flowers in the garden that made her sneeze? I just made sure she had plenty to decorate her room." He cocked his head. "She won't look very pretty with a runny nose."

Braden closed his eyes. "Why, Quentin? Do you know what Grandfather will do to you when he finds out?"

Quentin knew. He'd been punished before. But he'd never played a trick on one of the family delegates.

"You'd better get out of here," Braden said, shoving Quentin away. "Ro, go with him."

Rowena, at least, had the wits to be frightened. She tugged at Quentin's arm. "Come on, Quentin!"

Quentin stood his ground. "You'll peach on me anyway, so what's the use—"

Braden snarled and charged at Quentin. "Get out of here!"

Under any other circumstances Braden might have been pleased at how quickly Quentin obeyed. The power of Braden's will was growing, and he could feel it coursing through his veins like the magic of the Change itself.

But he was nothing against the Earl. He swallowed and walked back to the house, reaching the broad steps just as Grandfather came charging out. His white hair was nearly on end, his eyes blazing, and such was his fury that Braden expected to be knocked from his feet.

But Barnabas stopped short, fists balled at his sides.

"Quentin," he growled. "Where is he?"

"I don't know," Braden said. "He was—"

"Do you know what he's done? The Count's daughter is insulted, and the Count himself—" Grandfather's will bore down on Braden like a stifling weight of water, making it nearly impossible for him to breathe. "The Russians have threatened to break the marriage contract. Because of that boy, the alliance itself is at risk. Tell me where he is."

For a moment Braden wavered. Quentin had to learn. But Grandfather's way of teaching was harsh at the best of times; in his current temper he might do far worse than administer a beating.

"I'm sorry, sir," Braden said. "I don't know."

There was something far more frightening about Grandfather's sudden stillness than in his short-lived open rage. "Do you think to betray me as well?" he said quietly. "No, I'd kill you first."

Braden shivered in spite of himself. He'd been raised from leading strings to believe that nothing mattered more than the Cause, that all else must be sacrificed to it. He had seen that principle at work in his Grandfather's marriage to the woman he had chosen for her "pure" blood, and again with *Maman* and Father.

But Barnabas would not kill the carrier of the very blood he was fighting to preserve. At least not the body. But there were other things to lose . . .

Abruptly Grandfather took Braden's arm in a savage grip and dragged him into the house. The Russian Count stood waiting at the foot of the grand staircase, his eyes silvery slits. Grandfather stopped before him, and some silent communication passed between lord and lord, the kind that Braden was only beginning to understand. Wills clashed, and it was the Count who broke away first.

"Go to my rooms," Barnabas ordered his grandson, and Braden didn't hesitate to obey. He could buy Quentin more time, and Grandfather would lose the first edge of his anger. He started up the stairs that led to the landing, which in turn ran the length of the first floor through the family and guest wings. A small group of the delegates and their mates stood watching with wary curiosity from the guest wing, but they melted away as Grandfather reached the landing. Human servants retreated with equal discretion.

Grandfather's suite was a place for which Braden had

never borne much affection. Here punishments were meted out, lectures given. And here the weight of the Cause was overwhelming.

Ancient armor stood against the wall, shields and weapons surviving from a more savage time. The Forster blood went much farther back than this house had existed, though the names Braden's ancestors carried had changed with the centuries. There was nothing of gentleness in the room. It was icy, for Barnabas denied anything that hinted of a human weakness. The *loups-garous* did not suffer from mere cold.

Grandfather sat down in his hard-backed chair. "Stand where you are, and listen," he said. "I had believed you were old enough to understand. I was mistaken. I shall make it clear to you again. Quentin is only worth to me whatever children he can sire. Rowena is the same. But you—you I expect far more."

Braden lifted his chin. "I understand my duty."

"No." Barnabas pounded his fist on the carved arm of the chair. "But you will, before I am done with you. Your father was worse than useless, but your blood is strong. You will not betray me in the end." He stood up and walked to the old mullioned window that looked over the park. His voice dropped to a rasping whisper. "I've been betrayed twice before. My dear sister eloped with a human before her marriage to the man I had chosen for her could take place. She rejected the ways of our people. And William's daughter ran off with some American peasant. He and Fenella have been dead these five years, and their daughter and her mate and whatever children they've produced are lost to the Cause."

"But if we could find them—" Braden said.

"In time they will be brought back. You will do it if I . . ." But it was impossible for Grandfather to speak of failure, or death. "There will be no more betrayals."

The passion and anguish in Barnabas's voice was very real and utterly unexpected, and it struck at Braden's heart as nothing else might have done. Grandfather had spent his life trying to save a race, and his own siblings had turned their backs on him. Only his innate power had kept the other werewolves cooperative when they had cause to doubt his strength and authority, even over his own family.

The *loups-garous* respected strength. But loyalty to family was burned into their very souls, and so a brother's and a sister's rebellions were wounds that would not heal. Braden could not imagine Quentin and Rowena doing that to him. Never.

He crept across the worn carpet to his grandfather's side. "I won't do what they did," he promised. "I won't let the Cause die."

Grandfather looked at him, and it was as if he'd never slipped to reveal a single moment of vulnerability. "By the time I'm finished with you, you will have no other purpose. You will live for the Cause, as I have. Nothing else will matter to you. Do you understand?"

Braden could say nothing. Grandfather's stare held him like the man-traps set in the woods to catch human poachers, and his tongue was leaden.

"You will never lie to me again. Today you will track down your brother and bring him to me. Then you shall administer the punishment the Count himself selects. Go."

Behind those words lay no room for negotiation, no latitude for compassion or mercy. The lesson was meant not for Quentin, but for Braden himself. It would be fashioned so as never to be forgotten.

Braden turned and left the room, his mind a blank. He followed the landing to a door that led into several twisting, narrow corridors, hidden stairs, and a back entrance used by the servants. There he paused, scenting the evening; autumn was coming, and he could smell hay and heather and sheep and the smooth-flowing waters of the river below the great sloping park.

He discarded his clothes behind the shrubbery along the wall and Changed with a single thought. On four legs he ran through the gardens, past the open park and into the woods an ancient ancestor had begun and Barnabas had nurtured, until now it was far greater than any private wood in northern England.

As he ran, leaping the burn and dodging pine and oak and ash, he ignored the spoor of rabbit and fox and all the other small creatures that shared the wood. There was only one he hunted. And soon enough he found the familiar scent. But it was Rowena who met him, her eyes wide and her face pale. Her skirt was muddied, her hair snarled with twigs and leaves.

"What will they do to him?" she whispered.

Braden Changed, and Rowena quickly looked away. Her modesty had always been exaggerated, but Braden had no time for her almost-human sensibilities.

"Where is he?" he asked.

"Did you come to get him?"

"I came to tell him to stay away." Braden wrapped his arms around his chest, though he hardly felt the chill in the air. "Grandfather told me to bring him back. The Count is to decide his punishment. But if Quentin stays away until the Russians leave, maybe it won't be so bad."

Rowena bit her lip. "You'll get into trouble if you don't bring him back."

Braden shrugged. "I know Quentin can find somewhere to hide for a few days. When you see Quentin, tell him—"

"You can tell me yourself." Quentin emerged from behind a thick stand of trees, his habitual smile nowhere in evidence. "I'm no coward. It's my fault. I'll come back with you."

"No." Braden glared at his younger brother, working his will. "You're not as strong as I am, and Grandfather has never liked you. But you owe me for this, Quentin. Never forget that you owe me."

Quentin clenched and unclenched his fists. "I won't forget."

Braden glanced at Rowena. "You'd better come back. Just stay away from Grandfather for a while. The delegates will be leaving soon, and things will be back to normal."

Normal. As normal as they ever were at Greyburn.

"I'll come to check on you, if I can," Braden said to Quentin. "But stay out of trouble, for once."

They stared at each other. Rowena wept without making a sound. After a moment Quentin took a step backward, and then another, until he had vanished behind the trees again.

Later Braden would talk to Rowena, try to comfort her if she'd let him. But she'd always been closer to Quentin, and the separation would be hard for her. He repeated his command that she return to the house, and then Changed once more.

His run home was not so swift nor certain. He knew what would come when he admitted his failure to Barnabas. The pain he could bear, but the humiliation and his grandfather's scorn would cut far more keenly than the whip.

But he would bear it without flinching, to prove his strength. To show he could not be broken. He would be worthy to carry on the work of the Cause.

I will, Grandfather, he promised. *I will make our people strong again. Nothing will stop me, ever.*

Within half a mile of the house he angled away and ran to the top of Rook Knowe. From here he could look down into the valley, across the small fields and isolated cottages and beyond to row upon row of heather-clad, treeless hills marching into the distance. This was his country; he loved it as he loved Greyburn, its hardy human tenants, the bleakness of a landscape that had been disputed and fought over and conquered time and again, but never been wholly tamed.

Yes, he would devote himself to the Cause. But he, unlike Barnabas, would find room in his life for other things. For family affection. For the beauty of moor and wood and burn. For the possibility of love in an arranged marriage. For an ideal not driven by anger and bitterness.

I'll do my duty, Lord Greyburn. But I'll do it my way, not yours.

Braden believed with all his heart that it was a promise he could keep forever.

Bestselling Historical Women's Fiction

✄ AMANDA QUICK ✄

____28354-5 SEDUCTION . . .$6.50/$8.99 Canada
____28932-2 SCANDAL . . . .$6.50/$8.99
____28594-7 SURRENDER . . . .$6.50/$8.99
____29325-7 RENDEZVOUS . . . .$6.50/$8.99
____29315-X RECKLESS . . . .$6.50/$8.99
____29316-8 RAVISHED . . . .$6.50/$8.99
____29317-6 DANGEROUS . . . .$6.50/$8.99
____56506-0 DECEPTION . . . .$6.50/$8.99
____56153-7 DESIRE . . . .$6.50/$8.99
____56940-6 MISTRESS . . . .$6.50/$8.99
____57159-1 MYSTIQUE . . . .$6.50/$7.99
____57190-7 MISCHIEF . . . .$6.50/$8.99
____57407-8 AFFAIR . . . .$6.99/$8.99

✄ IRIS JOHANSEN ✄

____29871-2 LAST BRIDGE HOME . . .$5.50/$7.50
____29604-3 THE GOLDEN
                BARBARIAN . . . .$6.99/$8.99
____29244-7 REAP THE WIND . . . . .$5.99/$7.50
____29032-0 STORM WINDS . . . .$6.99/$8.99

Ask for these books at your local bookstore or use this page to order.

Please send me the books I have checked above. I am enclosing $____ (add $2.50 to cover postage and handling). Send check or money order, no cash or C.O.D.'s, please.

Name _____

Address _____

City/State/Zip _____

Send order to: Bantam Books, Dept. FN 16, 2451 S. Wolf Rd., Des Plaines, IL 60018
Allow four to six weeks for delivery.
Prices and availability subject to change without notice.   FN 16 6/98

Bestselling Historical Women's Fiction

⚜ IRIS JOHANSEN ⚜

____28855-5 THE WIND DANCER . . . $5.99/$6.99

____29968-9 THE TIGER PRINCE . . . $6.99/$8.99

____29944-1 THE MAGNIFICENT
              ROGUE . . . . $6.99/$8.99

____29945-X BELOVED SCOUNDREL $6.99/$8.99

____29946-8 MIDNIGHT WARRIOR . . $6.99/$8.99

____29947-6 DARK RIDER . . . . $6.99/$8.99

____56990-2 LION'S BRIDE . . . . $6.99/$8.99

____56991-0 THE UGLY DUCKLING. . . $6.99/$8.99

____57181-8 LONG AFTER MIDNIGHT. $6.99/$8.99

____10616-3 AND THEN YOU DIE.... $22.95/$29.95

⚜ TERESA MEDEIROS ⚜

____29407-5 HEATHER AND VELVET . $5.99/$7.50

____29409-1 ONCE AN ANGEL . . . . . . $5.99/$7.99

____29408-3 A WHISPER OF ROSES . . $5.99/$7.99

____56332-7 THIEF OF HEARTS . . . . . $5.50/$6.99

____56333-5 FAIREST OF THEM ALL . . $5.99/$7.50

____56334-3 BREATH OF MAGIC . . . . . $5.99/$7.99

____57623-2 SHADOWS AND LACE . . . $5.99/$7.99

____57500-7 TOUCH OF ENCHANTMENT. $5.99/$7.99

____57501-5 NOBODY'S DARLING . . . $5.99/$7.99

- -

Ask for these books at your local bookstore or use this page to order.

Please send me the books I have checked above. I am enclosing $_____ (add $2.50 to cover postage and handling). Send check or money order, no cash or C.O.D.'s, please.

Name _____

Address _____

City/State/Zip _____

Send order to: Bantam Books, Dept. FN 16, 2451 S. Wolf Rd., Des Plaines, IL 60018
Allow four to six weeks for delivery.

Prices and availability subject to change without notice.   FN 16 6/98